# Praise for the Novels of ROBIN COOK

## ACCEPTABLE RISK

His most shocking thriller—a timely and terrifying glimpse into the dangers of antidepressant drugs . . .

"STERN AND BRACING . . . [A] SUSPENSEFUL THRILLER." —*San Francisco Chronicle*

"A STRONG WARNING . . . LIKE THE DRIP, DRIP, DRIP OF AN IV, THIS BOOK BUILDS THE SUSPENSE UNTIL IT EXPLODES." —*Culture Corner News* (Encino, CA)

"THE LATEST HIGH TECHNOLOGY." —*Dayton Daily News*

## FATAL CURE

One of the most controversial books Robin Cook has ever written—a terrifying look at the darker implications of managed health care in America . . .

"A RIVETING PLOT, FILLED WITH ACTION." —*San Diego Union-Tribune*

"A HAIR-RAISING, CAUTIONARY TALE ABOUT THE POSSIBLE PITFALLS OF IMPENDING HEALTH-CARE REFORM IN AMERICA." —*Detroit News*

"COOK RAISES TROUBLING QUESTIONS." —*Publishers Weekly*

Continued . . .

## TERMINAL

**Brain cancer patients are miraculously "cured"—when the rising cost of research sparks a medical conspiracy that lowers the price on human life . . .**

"A SPELLBINDER . . . UNBEARABLE TENSION."
—*Houston Chronicle*

"STRAIGHT OUT OF TODAY'S HEADLINES."
—UPI

## BLINDSIGHT

**How far will people go to obtain donors for eye operations? Murder is beyond comprehension. But seeing is believing . . .**

"GRABS THE READER . . . MAINTAINS SUSPENSE WITH SURPRISING STORY TWISTS."
—*Pittsburgh Press*

"RIVETING." —*Nashville Banner*

## VITAL SIGNS

**Dr. Cook explores the frightening possibilities of experimental fertilization—the passion to create life and the power to destroy it . . .**

"CONSTANT SUSPENSE . . . BELIEVABLE AND CHILLING." —*Houston Chronicle*

"VINTAGE COOK . . . NONSTOP ACTION."
—*Kirkus Reviews*

## HARMFUL INTENT

**The explosive story of a doctor accused of malpractice— a fugitive on the run who pierces the heart of a shocking medical conspiracy . . .**

"A REAL GRABBER!" —*Los Angeles Times*

"TRULY EXCITING." —Associated Press

## MUTATION

On the forefront of genetic research, a brilliant doctor tries to create the son of his dreams—and invents a living nightmare . . .

"HOLDS YOU PAGE AFTER PAGE."
—Larry King, *USA Today*

"*REALLY* FRIGHTENING." —*Booklist*

## MORTAL FEAR

A major scientific breakthrough becomes the ultimate experiment in terror when middle-aged patients begin to die—of old age . . .

"A CHILLING ODYSSEY INTO THE ORIGINS OF LIFE—AND DEATH." —*USA Weekend*

"COOK'S BEST BOOK SINCE *COMA*." —*People*

## OUTBREAK

Murder and mystery reach epidemic proportions when a devastating plague sweeps the country . . .

"HIS MOST HARROWING MEDICAL HORROR STORY." —*New York Times*

"THE ULTIMATE NIGHTMARE . . . SPINE-TINGLING INTRIGUE AND FEVER-PITCHED ACTION."
—Associated Press

## CONTAGION

His newest thriller based on medical fact—a battle for survival waged in the hot zone of a deadly new virus . . .

"EACH OF HIS THRILLERS HAS DEALT WITH A DIFFERENT ISSUE OR CONTROVERSY IN MEDICINE." —*Milwaukee Journal*

# ROBIN COOK

# ACCEPTABLE RISK

BERKLEY BOOKS, NEW YORK

ACCEPTABLE RISK

A Berkley Book / published by arrangement with
the author

PRINTING HISTORY
G. P. Putnam's Sons edition / January 1995
Berkley edition / February 1996

All rights reserved.
Copyright © 1994 by Robin Cook.
This book may not be reproduced in whole or in part,
by mimeograph or any other means, without permission.
For information address: The Berkley Publishing Group,
200 Madison Avenue, New York, New York 10016.

The Putnam Berkley World Wide Web site address is
http://www.berkley.com

ISBN: 0-425-15186-7

BERKLEY®
Berkley Books are published by The Berkley Publishing Group,
200 Madison Avenue, New York, New York 10016.
BERKLEY and the "B" design
are trademarks belonging to Berkley Publishing Corporation.

PRINTED IN THE UNITED STATES OF AMERICA

10  9  8  7  6  5  4  3  2  1

*For Jean*
*"the guiding light"*

The Devil hath power
to assume a pleasing shape

—*Hamlet*
  William Shakespeare

# PROLOGUE

## Saturday,
## February 6, 1692

Spurred on by the penetrating cold, Mercy Griggs snapped her riding crop above the back of her mare. The horse picked up the pace, drawing the sleigh effortlessly over the hard-packed snow. Mercy snuggled deeper into the high collar of her sealskin coat and clasped her hands together within her muff in a vain attempt to shield herself from the arctic air.

It was a windless, clear day of pallid sunshine. Seasonally banished to its southern trajectory, the sun had to struggle to illuminate the snowy landscape locked in the grip of a cruel New England winter. Even at midday long violet shadows extended northward from the trunks of the leafless trees. Congealed masses of smoke hung motionlessly above the chimneys of the widely dispersed farmhouses as if frozen against the ice blue polar sky.

Mercy had been traveling for almost a half hour. She'd come southwest along the Ipswich Road from her home at the base of Leach's Hill on the Royal Side. She'd crossed bridges spanning the Frost Fish River, the Crane River, and the Cow House River and now entered into the Northfields section of Salem Town. From that point it was only a mile and a half to the town center.

But Mercy wasn't going to town. As she passed the Jacobs' farmhouse, she could see her destination. It was the home of Ronald Stewart, a successful merchant and shipowner. What had drawn Mercy away from her own warm hearth on such a frigid day was neighborly concern mixed with a dose of curiosity. At the moment the Stewart household was the source of the most interesting gossip.

Pulling her mare to a stop in front of the house, Mercy eyed the structure. It certainly bespoke of Mr. Stewart's acumen as a merchant. It was an imposing, multi-gabled building, sheathed in brown clapboard and roofed with the highest-grade slate. Its many windows were glazed with imported, diamond-shaped panes of glass. Most impressive of all were the elaborately turned pendants suspended from the corners of the second-floor overhang. All in all the house appeared more suited to the center of town than to the countryside.

Confident that the sound of the sleigh bells on her horse's harness had announced her arrival, Mercy waited. To the right of the front door was another horse and sleigh, suggesting that company had already arrived. The horse was under a blanket. From its nostrils issued intermittent billows of vapor that vanished instantly into the bone-dry air.

Mercy didn't have long to wait. Almost immediately the door opened and within the doorframe stood a twenty-seven-year-old, raven-haired, green-eyed woman whom Mercy knew to be Elizabeth Stewart. In her arms she comfortably cradled a musket. From around her sides issued a multitude of children's curious faces; unexpected social visits in isolated homes were not common in such weather.

"Mercy Griggs," called the visitor. "Wife of Dr. William Griggs. I've come to bid you good day."

" 'Tis a pleasure, indeed," called Elizabeth in return. "Come in for some hot cider to chase the chill from your bones." Elizabeth leaned the musket against the inside doorframe and directed her oldest boy, Jonathan, age nine, to go out to cover and tether Mrs. Griggs' horse.

With great pleasure Mercy entered the house, and, following Elizabeth's direction, turned right into the common room. As she passed the musket, she eyed it. Elizabeth, catching her line of sight, explained: " 'Tis from having grown up in the wilderness of Andover. We had to be on the lookout for Indians all hours of the day."

"I see," Mercy said, although a woman wielding a musket was apart from her normal experience. Mercy hesitated for a moment on the threshold of the kitchen and surveyed the domestic scene, which appeared more like a schoolhouse than a home. There were more than a half dozen children.

On the hearth was a large, crackling fire that radiated a welcome warmth. Enveloping the room was a mixture of savory aromas: some of them were coming from the kettle of pork stew simmering on its lug pole over the fire; others were rising from a large bowl of cooling corn pudding; but most were coming from the beehive oven built into the back of the fireplace. Inside, multiple loaves of bread were turning a dark, golden brown.

"I hope in God's name I am not a bother," Mercy said.

"Heavens, no," Elizabeth replied as she took Mercy's coat and directed her to a ladder-back chair near the fire. "You're a welcome reprieve from the likes of these unruly children. But you have caught me baking, and I must remove my bread." Quickly she hefted a long-handled peel, and with short, deft thrusts picked up the eight loaves one by one and deposited them to cool on the long trestle table that dominated the center of the room.

Mercy watched Elizabeth as she worked, remarking to herself that she was a fine-looking woman with her high cheekbones, porcelain complexion, and lithesome figure. It was also apparent she was accomplished in the kitchen by the way she handled the bread-making and with the skill she evinced stoking the fire and adjusting the trammel holding the kettle. At the same time Mercy sensed there was something disturbing about Elizabeth's persona. There wasn't the requisite Christian meekness and humbleness. In fact Elizabeth seemed to project an alacrity and boldness that was unbecoming of a Puritan woman whose husband was away in Europe. Mercy began to sense that there was more to the gossip that she'd heard than idle hearsay.

"The aroma of your bread has an unfamiliar piquancy," Mercy said as she leaned over the cooling loaves.

" 'Tis rye bread," Elizabeth explained as she began to slip eight more loaves into the oven.

"Rye bread?" Mercy questioned. Only the poorest farmers with marshy land ate rye bread.

"I grew up on rye bread," Elizabeth explained. "I do indeed like its spicy taste. But you may wonder why I am baking so many loaves. The reason is I have in mind to encourage the whole village to utilize rye to conserve the wheat supplies. As you know, the cool wet weather through spring and summer and now this terrible winter has hurt the crop.''

"It is a noble thought," Mercy said. "But perhaps it is an issue for the men to discuss at the town meeting."

Elizabeth then shocked Mercy with a hearty laugh. When Elizabeth noticed Mercy's expression, she explained herself: "The men don't think in such practical terms. They are more concerned with the polemic between the village and the town. Besides, there is more than a poor harvest. We women must think of the refugees from the Indian raids since it is already the fourth year of King William's War and there's no end in sight."

"A woman's role is in the home . . ." Mercy began, but she trailed off, taken aback by Elizabeth's pertness.

"I've also been encouraging people to take the refugees into their homes," Elizabeth said as she dusted the flour from her hands on her smocked apron. "We've taken in two children after the raid on Casco, Maine, a year ago last May." Elizabeth called out sharply to the children and interrupted their play by insisting they come to meet the doctor's wife.

Elizabeth first introduced Mercy to Rebecca Sheaff, age twelve, and Mary Roots, age nine. Both had been cruelly orphaned during the Casco raid, but now both appeared hale and happy. Next Elizabeth introduced Joanna, age thirteen, Ronald's daughter from a previous marriage. Then came her own children: Sarah, age ten; Jonathan, age nine; and Daniel, age three. Finally Elizabeth introduced Ann Putnam, age twelve; Abigail Williams, age eleven; and Betty Parris, age nine, who were visiting from Salem Village.

After the children dutifully acknowledged Mercy, they were allowed to return to their play, which Mercy noticed involved several glasses of water and fresh eggs.

"I'm surprised to see the village children here," Mercy said.

"I asked my children to invite them," Elizabeth said.

"They are friends from attending the Royal Side School. I felt it best that my children not school in Salem Town with all the riffraff and ruffians."

"I understand," Mercy said.

"I will be sending the children home with loaves of rye bread," Elizabeth said. She smiled friskily. "It will be more effective than giving their families a mere suggestion."

Mercy nodded but didn't comment. Elizabeth was mildly overwhelming.

"Would you care for a loaf?" Elizabeth asked.

"Oh, no, thank you," Mercy said. "My husband, the doctor, would never eat rye bread. It's much too coarse."

As Elizabeth turned her attention back to her second batch of bread, Mercy's eyes roamed the kitchen. She noticed a fresh wheel of cheese having come directly from the cheese press. She saw a pitcher of cider on the corner of the hearth. Then she noticed something more striking. Arrayed along the windowsill was a row of dolls made from painted wood and carefully sewn fabric. Each was dressed in the costume of a particular livelihood. There was a merchant, a blacksmith, a goodwife, a cartwright, and even a doctor. The doctor was dressed in black with a starched lace collar.

Mercy stood up and walked to the window. She picked up the doll dressed as a doctor. A large needle was thrust into its chest.

"What are these figures?" Mercy asked with barely concealed concern.

"Dolls that I make for the orphan children," Elizabeth said without looking up from her labor with her bread. She was removing each loaf, buttering its top, and then replacing it in the oven. "My deceased mother, God rest her soul, taught me how to make them."

"Why does this poor creature have a needle rending its heart?" Mercy asked.

"The costume is unfinished," Elizabeth said. "I am forever misplacing the needle and they are so dear."

Mercy replaced the doll and unconsciously wiped her hands. Anything that suggested magic and the occult made her uncomfortable. Leaving the dolls, she turned to the children, and after watching them for a moment asked Elizabeth what they were doing.

"It's a trick my mother taught me," Elizabeth said. She slipped the last loaf of bread back into the oven. "It's a way of divining the future by interpreting the shapes of egg white dropped into the water."

"Bid them to stop immediately," Mercy said with alarm.

Elizabeth looked up from her work and eyed her visitor. "But why?" she asked.

"It is white magic," Mercy admonished.

"It is harmless fun," Elizabeth said. "It is merely something for the children to do while they are confined by such a winter. My sister and I did it many times to try to learn the trade of our future husbands." Elizabeth laughed. "Of course it never told me I'd marry a shipowner and move to Salem. I thought I was to be a poor farmer's wife."

"White magic breeds black magic," Mercy said. "And black magic is abhorrent to God. It is the devil's work."

"It never hurt my sister or myself," Elizabeth said. "Nor my mother, for that matter."

"Your mother's dead," Mercy said sternly.

"Yes, but—"

"It is sorcery," Mercy continued. Blood rose to her cheeks. "No sorcery is harmless. And remember the bad times we are experiencing with the war and with the pox in Boston only last year. Just last sabbath Reverend Parris' sermon told us that these horrid problems are occurring because people have not been keeping the covenant with God by allowing laxity in religious observance."

"I hardly think this childish game disturbs the covenant," Elizabeth said. "And we have not been lax in our religious obligations."

"But indulging in magic most certainly is," Mercy said. "Just like tolerance of the Quakers."

Elizabeth waved her hand in dismissal. "Such problems are beyond my purview. I surely don't see anything wrong with the Quakers since they are such a peaceful, hard-working people."

"You must not voice such opinions," Mercy chided.

"Reverend Increase Mather has said that the Quakers are under a strong delusion of the devil. Perhaps you should read Reverend Cotton Mather's book *Memorable Providences: Relating to Witchcraft and Possessions.* I can loan it to you since my husband purchased it in Boston. Reverend Mather says the bad times we are experiencing stem from the devil's wish to return our New England Israel to his children, the red men."

Directing her attention to the children, Elizabeth called out to them to quiet down. Their shrieking had reached a crescendo. Still, she quieted them more to interrupt Mercy's sermonizing than to subdue their excited talk. Looking back at Mercy, Elizabeth said she'd be most thankful for the opportunity to read the book.

"Speaking of church matters," Mercy said. "Has your husband considered joining the village church? Since he's a landowner in the village he'd be welcome."

"I don't know," Elizabeth said. "We've never spoken of it."

"We need support," Mercy said. "The Porter family and their friends are refusing to pay their share of the Reverend Parris' expenses. When will your husband return?"

"In the spring," Elizabeth said.

"Why did he go to Europe?" Mercy asked.

"He's having a new class of ship built," Elizabeth said. "It is called a frigate. He says it will be fast and able to defend itself against French privateers and Caribbean pirates."

After touching the tops of the cooling loaves with the palms of her hands, Elizabeth called out to the children to tell them it was time to eat. As they drifted over to the table, she asked them if they wanted some of the fresh, warm bread. Although her own children turned up their noses at the offer, Ann Putnam, Abigail Williams, and Betty Parris were eager. Elizabeth opened a trapdoor in the corner of the kitchen and sent Sarah down to fetch some butter from the dairy storage.

Mercy was intrigued by the trapdoor.

"It was Ronald's idea," Elizabeth explained. "It func

tions like a ship's hatch and affords access to the cellar without having to go outside.''

Once the children were set with plates of pork stew and thick slices of bread if they wanted it, Elizabeth poured herself and Mercy mugs of hot cider. To escape the children's chatter, they carried the cider into the parlor.

"My word!" Mercy exclaimed. Her eyes had immediately gone to a sizable portrait of Elizabeth hanging over the mantel. Its shocking realism awed her, especially the radiant green eyes. For a moment she stood rooted in the center of the room while Elizabeth deftly kindled the fire that had reduced itself to glowing coals.

"Your dress is so revealing," Mercy said. "And your head is unadorned."

"The painting disturbed me at first," Elizabeth admitted. She stood up from the hearth and positioned two chairs in front of the now blazing fire. "It was Ronald's idea. It pleases him. Now I hardly notice it."

"It's so popish," Mercy said with a sneer. She angled her chair to exclude the painting from her line of sight. She took a sip from the warm cider and tried to organize her thoughts. The visit had not gone as she'd imagined. Elizabeth's character was disconcerting. Mercy had yet to even broach the subject of why she'd come. She cleared her throat.

"I'd heard a rumor," Mercy began. "I'm certain there can be no verity to it. I'd heard that you had the fancy to buy the Northfields' property."

" 'Tis no rumor," Elizabeth said brightly. "It will be done. We shall own land on both sides of the Wooleston River. The tract even extends into Salem Village where it abuts Ronald's village lots."

"But the Putnams had the intention to buy the land," Mercy said indignantly. "It is important for them. They need access to the water for their endeavors, particularly their iron works. Their only problem is the proper funds, for which they must wait for the next harvest. They shall be very angry if you persevere, and they will try to stop the sale."

Elizabeth shrugged. "I have the money now," she said.

"I want the land because we intend to build a new house to enable us to take in more orphans." Elizabeth's face brightened with excitement and her eyes sparkled. "Daniel Andrew has agreed to design and build the house. It's to be a grand house of brick like those of London town."

Mercy could not believe what she was hearing. Elizabeth's pride and covetousness knew no bounds. Mercy swallowed another mouthful of cider with difficulty. "Do you know that Daniel Andrew is married to Sarah Porter?" she asked.

"Indeed," Elizabeth said. "Before Ronald left we entertained them both."

"How, may I ask, do you have access to such vast sums of money?"

"With the demands of the war, Ronald's firm has been doing exceptionally well."

"Profiteering from the misfortune of others," Mercy stated sententiously.

"Ronald prefers to say that he is providing sorely needed matériel."

Mercy stared for a moment into Elizabeth's bright green eyes. She was doubly appalled that Elizabeth seemed to have no conception of her transgression. In fact, Elizabeth brazenly smiled and returned Mercy's gaze, sipping her cider contentedly.

"I'd heard the rumor," Mercy said finally. "I couldn't believe it. Such business is so unnatural with your husband away. It is not in God's plan, and I must warn you: people in the village are talking. They are saying that you are overstepping your station as a farmer's daughter."

"I shall always be my father's daughter," Elizabeth said. "But now I am also a merchant's wife."

Before Mercy could respond, a tremendous crash and a multitude of screams burst forth from the kitchen. The sudden noise brought both Mercy and Elizabeth to their feet in terror. With Mercy directly behind her, Elizabeth rushed from the parlor into the kitchen, snapping up the musket en route.

The trestle table had been tipped on its side. Wooden bowls empty of their stew were strewn across the floor. Ann

Putnam was lurching fitfully about the room as she tore at her clothes and collided with furniture while screaming she was being bitten. The other children had shrunk back against the wall in shocked horror.

Dispensing with the musket, Elizabeth rushed to Ann and grasped her shoulders. "What is it, girl?" Elizabeth demanded. "What is biting you?"

For a moment Ann remained still. Her eyes had assumed a glazed, faraway appearance.

"Ann!" Elizabeth called. "What is wrong with you?"

Ann's mouth opened and her tongue slowly protruded to its very limit while her body began chorea-like movements. Elizabeth tried to restrain her, but Ann fought with surprising strength. Then Ann clutched at her throat.

"I can't breathe," Ann rasped. "Help me! I'm being choked."

"Let us get her upstairs," Elizabeth shouted at Mercy. Together they half-carried and half-dragged the writhing girl up to the second floor. No sooner had they got her onto the bed than she began to convulse.

"She's having a horrid fit," Mercy said. "I think it best I fetch my husband, the doctor."

"Please!" Elizabeth said. "Hurry!"

Mercy shook her head in dismay as she descended the stairs. Having recovered from her initial shock, the calamity didn't surprise her, and she knew its cause. It was the sorcery. Elizabeth had invited the devil into her house.

## Tuesday, July 12, 1692

Ronald Stewart opened the cabin door and stepped out onto the deck and into the cool morning air, dressed in his best knee breeches, his scarlet waistcoat with starched ruffles, and even his powdered peruke. He was beside himself with excitement. They had just rounded Naugus Point, off Marblehead, and had set a course directly for Salem Town. Already over the bow he could see Turner's Wharf.

"Let us not furl the sails until the last moment," Ronald called to Captain Allen standing behind the helm. "I want the town folk to see the speed of this vessel."

"Aye, aye, sir," Captain Allen shouted back.

Ronald leaned his sizable and muscled frame on the gunwale as the sea breeze caressed his tanned broad face and tousled his sandy blond hair peeking from beneath his wig. Happily he gazed at the familiar landmarks. It was good to be coming home, although it was not without a degree of anxiety. He'd been gone for almost six months, two months longer than anticipated, and he'd not received a single letter. Sweden had seemed to be the end of the earth. He wondered if Elizabeth had received any of the letters he'd sent. There'd been no guarantee of their delivery since he'd not found any vessel going directly to the Colony, or even to London for that matter.

" 'Tis time," Captain Allen shouted as they approached land. "Otherwise this craft will mount the pier and not stop till Essex Street."

"Give the orders," Ronald shouted.

The men surged aloft at the captain's command and within minutes the vast stretches of canvas were pulled in and lashed to the spars. The ship slowed. At a point a hundred yards from the wharf, Ronald noticed a small boat being launched and quickly oared in their direction. As it approached Ronald recognized his clerk, Chester Procter, standing in the bow. Ronald waved merrily, but Chester did not return the gesture.

"Greetings," Ronald shouted when the boat was within earshot. Chester remained silent. As the small boat drew alongside, Ronald could see his clerk's thin face was drawn and his mouth set. Ronald's excitement was tempered by concern. Something was wrong.

"I think it best you come ashore immediately," Chester called up to Ronald once the skiff was made secure against the larger craft.

A ladder was extended into the small boat, and after a quick consultation with the captain, Ronald climbed down. Once he was sitting in the stern, they shoved off. Chester sat next to him. The two seamen amidships lent their backs to their oars.

"What is wrong?" Ronald asked, afraid to hear the answer. His worst fear was an Indian raid on his home. When he'd left he knew they'd been as close as Andover.

"There have been terrible happenings in Salem," Chester said. He was overwrought and plainly nervous. "Providence has brought you home barely in time. We have been much disquieted and distressed that you would arrive too late."

"It is my children?" Ronald asked with alarm.

"Nay, it is not your children," Chester said. "They are safe and hale. It is your goodwife, Elizabeth. She has been in prison for many months."

"On what charge?" Ronald demanded.

"Witchcraft," Chester said. "I beg your pardon for being the bearer of such ill tidings. She has been convicted by a special court and there is a warrant for her execution the Tuesday next."

"This is absurd," Ronald growled. "My wife is no witch!"

"That I know," Chester said. "But there has been a witchcraft frenzy in the town since February, with almost one hundred people accused. There has already been one execution. Bridget Bishop on June tenth."

"I knew her," Ronald admitted. "She was a woman of a fiery temperament. She ran the unlicensed tavern out on Ipswich Road. But a witch? It seems most improbable. What has happened to cause such fear of malefic will?"

"It is because of 'fits,' " Chester said. "Certain women, mostly young women, have been afflicted in a most pitiful way."

"Have you witnessed these fits?" Ronald asked.

"Oh, yes," Chester said. "The whole town has seen them at the hearings in front of the magistrates. They are terrible to behold. The afflicted scream of torment and are not in their right minds. They go alternately blind, deaf, and dumb, and sometimes all at once. They shake worse than the Quakers and shriek they are being bitten by invisible beings. Their tongues come out and then are as if swallowed. But the worst is that their joints do bend as if to break."

Ronald's mind was a whirlwind of thought. This was a

most unexpected turn of events. Sweat broke forth on his forehead as the morning sun beat down upon him. Angrily he tore his wig from his head and threw it to the floor of the boat. He tried to think what he should do.

"I have a carriage waiting," Chester said, breaking the heavy silence as they neared the pier. "I thought you'd care to go directly to the prison."

"Aye," Ronald said tersely. They disembarked and walked quickly to the street. They climbed aboard the vehicle, and Chester picked up the reins. With a snap the horse started. The wagon bumped along the cobblestone quay. Neither man spoke.

"How was it decided these fits were caused by witchcraft?" Ronald asked when they reached Essex Street.

"It was Dr. Griggs who said so," Chester said. "Then Reverend Parris from the village, then everyone, even the magistrates."

"What made them so confident?" Ronald asked.

"It was apparent at the hearings," Chester said. "All the people could see how the accused tormented the afflicted, and how the afflicted were instantly relieved from their suffering when touched by the accused."

"Yet they didn't touch them to torment them?"

"It was the specters of the accused who did the mischief," Chester explained. "And the specters could only be seen by the afflicted. It was thus that the accused were called out upon by the afflicted."

"And my wife was called out upon in this fashion?" Ronald asked.

" 'Tis so," Chester said. "By Ann Putnam, daughter of Thomas Putnam of Salem Village."

"I know Thomas Putnam," Ronald said. "A small, angry man."

"Ann Putnam was the first to be afflicted," Chester said hesitantly. "In your house. Her first fit was in your common room in the beginning of February. And to this day she is still afflicted, as is her mother, Ann senior."

"What about my children?" Ronald asked. "Are they afflicted as well?"

"Your children have been spared," Chester said.

"Thank the Lord," Ronald said.

They turned onto Prison Lane. Neither man spoke. Chester pulled to a stop in front of the jail. Ronald told him to wait and alighted from the carriage.

With brittle emotions Ronald sought out the jailer, William Dounton. Ronald found him in his untidy office eating fresh corn bread from the bakery. He was an obese man with a shock of unwashed hair and a red, nodular nose. Ronald despised him, a known sadist who delighted in tormenting his charges.

William was obviously not pleased to see Ronald. Leaping to his feet, he cowered behind his chair.

"No visitors to see the condemned," he croaked through a mouthful of bread. "By order of Magistrate Hathorne."

Barely in control of himself, Ronald reached out and grasped a fistful of William's woolen shirt and drew his face within an inch of his own. "If you have mistreated my wife you'll answer to me," Ronald snarled.

"It's not my fault," William said. "It is the authorities. I must respect their orders."

"Take me to her," Ronald snapped.

"But . . ." William managed before Ronald tightened his grip and constricted his throat. William gurgled. Ronald relaxed his fist. William coughed but produced his keys. Ronald let go of him and followed him. As he unlocked a stout oak door he said, "I will report this."

"There is no need," Ronald said. "As soon as I leave here I will go directly to the magistrate and tell him myself."

Beyond the oak door they passed several cells. All were full. The inmates stared back at Ronald with glazed eyes. Some he recognized, but he didn't address them. The prison was enveloped with a heavy silence. Ronald had to pull out a handkerchief to cover his nose from the smell.

At the top of a stone staircase, William stopped to light a shielded candle. After opening another stout oak door, they descended into the worst area of the prison. The stench was overwhelming. The basement consisted of two large rooms. The walls were damp granite. The many prisoners were all manacled to the walls or the floor with either wrist or leg irons or both. Ronald had to step over people to follow William. There was hardly room for another person.

"Just a moment," Ronald said.

William stopped and turned around.

Ronald squatted down. He'd recognized someone he knew to be a pious woman. "Rebecca Nurse?" Ronald questioned. "What in God's name are you doing here?"

Rebecca shook her head slowly. "Only God knows," she managed to say.

Ronald stood up feeling weak. It was as if the town had gone crazy.

"Over here," William said, pointing toward the far corner of the basement. "Let us finish this."

Ronald followed. His anger had been overwhelmed by pity. William stopped and Ronald looked down. In the candlelight he could barely recognize his wife. Elizabeth was covered with filth. She was manacled in oversized chains and barely had the energy to scatter the vermin which freely roamed the semidarkness.

Ronald took the candle from William and bent down next to his wife. Despite her condition she smiled at him.

"I'm glad you are back," she said weakly. "Now I don't have to worry about the children. Are they all right?"

Ronald swallowed with difficulty. His mouth had gone dry. "I have come directly from the ship to the prison," he said. "I have yet to see the children."

"Please do. They will be happy to see you. I fear they are disquieted."

"I shall attend to them," Ronald promised. "But first I must see to getting you free."

"Perhaps," Elizabeth said. "Why are you so late in returning?"

"The outfitting of the ship took longer than planned," Ronald said. "The newness of the design caused us much difficulty."

"I sent letters," Elizabeth said.

"I never got any," Ronald replied.

"Well, at least you are home now," Elizabeth said.

"I shall be back," Ronald said as he stood up. He was shaking with panic and beside himself with concern. He motioned to William for them to leave and followed him back to the office.

"I'm just doing my duty," William said meekly. He was unsure of Ronald's state of mind.

"Show me the papers," Ronald demanded.

William shrugged, and after searching through the debris on the top of his desk, handed Ronald Elizabeth's mittimus and her execution warrant. Ronald read them and handed them back. Reaching into his purse, he pulled out a few coins. "I want Elizabeth moved and her situation improved."

William happily took the money. "I thank you, kind sir," he said. The coins disappeared into the pocket of his breeches. "But I cannot move her. Capital cases are always housed on the lower level. I also cannot remove the irons since they are specified in the mittimus to keep her specter from leaving her body. But I can improve her condition in response to your kind consideration."

"Do what you can," Ronald said.

Outside, it took Ronald a moment to climb into the carriage. His legs felt unsteady and weak. "To Magistrate Corwin's house," he said.

Chester urged the horse forward. He wanted to ask about Elizabeth but he dared not. Ronald's distress was much too apparent.

They rode in silence. When they reached the corner of Essex and Washington streets, Ronald climbed down from the carriage. "Wait," he said laconically.

Ronald rapped on the front door, and when it was opened he was relieved to see the tall, gaunt frame of his old friend Jonathan Corwin standing in the doorway. As soon as Jonathan recognized Ronald, his petulant expression changed to one of sympathetic concern. Immediately he ushered Ronald into his parlor, where he requested his wife give them leave to have a private conversation. His wife had been working at her flax wheel in the corner.

"I am sorry," Jonathan said once they were alone. " 'Tis a sorry welcome for a weary traveler."

"Pray tell me what to do," Ronald said weakly.

"I am afraid I know not what to say," Jonathan began.

"It is an unruly time. There is a spirit in the town full of contention and animosities and perhaps a strong and general delusion. I am no longer certain of my thoughts, for recently my own mother-in-law, Margaret Thatcher, has been cried out against. She is no witch, which makes me question the veracity of the afflicted girls' allegations and their motivations."

"At the moment the motives of the girls are not my concern," Ronald said. "What I need to know is what can I do for my beloved wife, who is being treated with the utmost brutality."

Jonathan sighed deeply. "I am afraid there is little to be done. Your wife has already been convicted by a jury serving the special court of Oyer and Terminer hearing the backlog of witchcraft cases."

"But you have just said you question the accusers' veracity," Ronald said.

"Yes," Jonathan agreed. "But your wife's conviction did not depend on the girls' testimony nor spectral demonstration in court. Your wife's trial was shorter than the others, even shorter than Bridget Bishop's. Your wife's guilt was apparent to all because the evidence against her was real and conclusive. There was no doubt."

"You believe my wife to be a witch?" Ronald asked with disbelief.

"I do indeed," Jonathan said. "I am sorry. 'Tis a harsh truth for a man to bear."

For a moment Ronald stared into the face of his friend while his mind tried to deal with this new and disturbing information. Ronald had always valued and respected Jonathan's opinion.

"But there must be something that can be done," Ronald said finally. "Even if only to delay the execution so I have time to learn the facts."

Jonathan reached out and placed a hand on his friend's shoulder. "As a local magistrate there is nothing I can do. Perhaps you should go home and attend to your children."

"I shan't give up so easily," Ronald said.

"Then all I can suggest is you go to Boston and discourse with Samuel Sewall," Jonathan said. "I know you are friends and classmates from Harvard College. Perhaps he may make a suggestion with his connections with the Colonial Government. He will not be disinterested; he is one of the justices of the Court of Oyer and Terminer, and he has voiced to me some misgivings about the whole affair, as did Nathaniel Saltonstall, who even resigned his appointment to the bench.''

Ronald thanked Jonathan and hurried outside. He told Chester his intentions and was soon outfitted with a saddled horse. Within an hour he set out on the seventeen-mile journey. He traveled via Cambridge, crossing the Charles River at the Great Bridge, and approached Boston from the southwest on the highway to Roxberre.

As Ronald rode the length of the Shawmut peninsula's narrow neck, he became progressively anxious. His mind tortured him with the question of what he'd do if Samuel was either unwilling or unable to help. Ronald had no other ideas. Samuel was to be his last chance.

Passing through the town gate with its brick fortifications, Ronald's eyes involuntarily wandered to the gallows from which a fresh corpse dangled. The sight was a rude reminder, and a shiver of fear passed down his spine. In response he urged his horse to quicken its pace.

The midday bustle of Boston with its more than six thousand inhabitants and more than eight hundred dwellings slowed Ronald's progress. It was almost one by the time Ronald arrived at Samuel's south end house. Ronald dismounted and tethered his horse to the picket fence.

He found Samuel smoking tobacco from a long-stemmed pipe in his parlor following his noonday meal. Ronald noted that he'd become significantly portly over the last few years and was certainly a far cry from the rakish fellow who used to skate with Ronald on the Charles River during their college years.

Samuel was happy to see Ronald, but his greeting was restrained. He anticipated the nature of Ronald's visit before Ronald even broached the subject of Elizabeth's ordeal. In response to Ronald's questions, he confirmed Jonathan Corwin's story. He said that Elizabeth's guilt was

unquestioned due to the real evidence that Sheriff Corwin
had seized from Ronald's house.

Ronald's shoulders slumped. He sighed and fought off
tears. He was at a loss. He asked his host for a mug of
beer. When Samuel returned with the brew, Ronald had
recovered his composure. After a long draft he asked Samuel the nature of the evidence used against his wife.

"I am loath to say," Samuel said.

"But why?" Ronald asked. He studied his friend and
could see his discomfiture. Ronald's curiosity mounted. He
hadn't thought to ask Jonathan about the evidence. "Surely
I have a right to know."

"Indeed," Samuel said, but still he hesitated.

"Please," Ronald said. "I trust it will help me understand this wretched affair."

"Perhaps it is best if we visit my good friend Reverend
Cotton Mather," Samuel said. He stood up. "He has more
experience in the affairs of the invisible world. He will
know how to advise you."

"I bow to your discretion," Ronald said as he got to his
feet.

They took Samuel's carriage and went directly to the Old
North Church. An inquiry with a charwoman told them that
Reverend Mather was at his home on the corner of Middle
Street and Prince Street. Since the destination was close,
they walked. It was also convenient to leave the horse and
carriage in Charles Square in front of the church.

Samuel's knock was answered by a youthful maidservant
who showed them into the parlor. Reverend Mather appeared posthaste and greeted them effusively. Samuel explained the nature of their visit.

"I see," Reverend Mather said. He motioned to chairs
and they all sat down.

Ronald eyed the cleric. He'd met him before. He was
younger than Ronald and Samuel, having graduated from
Harvard in 1678, seven years after they had. Age notwithstanding, he was already evidencing some of the physical
changes Ronald saw in Samuel and for the same reasons.
He'd put on weight. His nose was red and slightly enlarged,

and his face had a doughy consistency. Yet his eyes sparkled with intelligence and fiery resolve.

"You have my loving solicitude for your tribulations," Reverend Mather said to Ronald. "God's ways are often inscrutable for us mortals. Beyond your personal torment I am deeply troubled about the events in Salem Town and Salem Village. The populace has been overcome by an unruly and turbulent spirit, and I fear that events are spinning out of control."

"At the moment my concern is for my wife," Ronald said. He'd not come for a sermon.

"As it should be," Reverend Mather said. "But I think it is important for you to understand that we—the clergy and the civil authorities—must think of the congregation as a whole. I have expected the devil to appear in our midst, and the only consolation about this demonic affair is now, thanks to your wife, we know where."

"I want to know the evidence used against my wife," Ronald said.

"And I shall show it to you," Reverend Mather said. "Provided that you will keep its nature a secret, since we fear its general revelation would surely inflame the distress and disquietude in Salem even more than it currently is."

"But what if I choose to appeal the conviction?" Ronald demanded.

"Once you see the evidence you will not choose to do so," Reverend Mather said. "Trust me in this. Do I have your word?"

"You have my word," Ronald said. "Provided my right to appeal is not forsaken."

They stood up in unison. Reverend Mather led the way to a flight of stone steps. After he lit a taper, they began the descent into the cellar.

"I have discussed this evidence at length with my father, Increase Mather," Reverend Mather said over his shoulder. "We concur that it has inordinate importance for future generations as material proof of the existence of the invisible world. Accordingly, we believe its rightful place should be Harvard College. As you know he is currently the acting president of the institution."

Ronald didn't respond. At the moment his mind was incapable of dealing with such academic issues.

"Both myself and my father also agree that there has been too much reliance in the Salem witch trials on spectral evidence alone," Reverend Mather continued. They reached the bottom of the stairs, and while Samuel and Ronald waited, he proceeded to light wall sconces. He spoke as he moved about the cellar: "We are much concerned that this reliance could very well draw innocent people into the maelstrom."

Ronald started to protest. For the moment he didn't have the patience to listen to these larger concerns, but Samuel restrained him by laying a hand on his shoulder.

"Elizabeth's evidence is the kind of real evidence we'd like to see in every case," Reverend Mather said as he waved Ronald and Samuel to follow him to a large, locked cupboard. "But it is also terribly inflammatory. It was at my discretion that it was removed from Salem and brought here after her trial. I have never witnessed a stronger evidence of the devil's power and ability to do mischief."

"Please, Reverend," Ronald said at last. "I should like to return to Salem forthwith. If you will just show me what it is, I can be on my way."

"Patience, my good man," Reverend Mather said as he drew a key from his waistcoat. "The nature of this evidence is such that you must be prepared. It is shocking indeed. For that reason it had been my suggestion that your wife's trial be held behind closed doors and the jury be sworn to secrecy on their honor. It was a precaution not to deny her due process but to prevent public hysteria which would only have played into the devil's hand."

"I am prepared," Ronald said with a touch of exasperation.

"Christ the Redeemer be with you," Reverend Mather said as he slipped the key into the lock. "Brace yourself."

Reverend Mather unlocked the cabinet. Then, with both hands he swung open the doors and stepped back for Ronald to see.

Ronald's breath escaped in a gasp and his eyes momentarily bulged. His hand involuntarily covered his mouth in horror and dismay. He swallowed hard. He tried to speak, but his voice momentarily failed him. He cleared his throat.

"Enough!" he managed and averted his eyes.

Reverend Mather closed the cabinet doors and locked them.

"Is it certain that this is Elizabeth's handiwork?" Ronald asked weakly.

"Beyond any doubt," Samuel said. "Not only was it seized by Sheriff George Corwin from your property, but Elizabeth freely admitted responsibility."

"Good Lord," Ronald said. "Surely this is the work of the devil. Yet I knoweth in my heart that Elizabeth is no witch."

"It is hard for a man to believe his wife to be in covenant with the devil," Samuel said. "But this evidence, combined with the testimony of several of the afflicted girls who stated that Elizabeth's specter tormented them, is compelling proof. I am sorry, dear friend, but Elizabeth is a witch."

"I am sorely distressed," Ronald said.

Samuel and Cotton Mather exchanged knowing, sympathetic glances. Samuel motioned toward the stairs.

"Perhaps we should repair to the parlor," Reverend Mather said. "I believe we all could use a mug of ale."

After they were seated and had a chance to take some refreshment, Reverend Mather spoke: "It is trying times for us all. But we must all participate. Now that we knoweth the devil has chosen Salem, we must with God's help seek and banish the devil's servants and their familiars from our midst, yet in like purpose protect the innocent and pious, whom surely the devil doth despise."

"I am sorry," Ronald said. "I can be of no help. I am distracted and weary. I still cannot believe Elizabeth to be a witch. I need time. Surely there is some way to secure a reprieve for her even if it lasts but a month."

"Only Governor Phips can grant a reprieve," Samuel said. "But a petition would be in vain. He would only grant a reprieve if there were a compelling reason."

A silence descended over the three men. Sounds of the city drifted in through the open window.

"Perhaps I could make a case for a reprieve," Reverend Mather said suddenly.

Ronald's face brightened with a ray of hope. Samuel appeared confused.

"I believe I could justify a reprieve to the Governor," Reverend Mather said. "But it would rest on one condition: Elizabeth's full cooperation. She'd have to agree to turn her back on her Prince of Darkness."

"I can assure her cooperation," Ronald said. "What would you have her do?"

"First she must confess in front of the congregation in the Salem meeting house," Reverend Mather said. "In her confession she must forswear her relations with the devil. Secondly she must reveal the identities of those persons in the community who have signed similar diabolic covenants. This would be a great service. The fact that the torment of the afflicted women continues unabated is proof that the devil's servants are still at large in Salem."

Ronald leaped to his feet. "I will get her to agree this very afternoon," he said excitedly. "I beg you to see Governor Phips immediately."

"I will wait on word from Elizabeth," Reverend Mather said. "I should not like to trouble his excellency without confirmation of the conditions."

"And you shall have her word," Ronald said. "By the morn at the very latest."

"Godspeed," Reverend Mather said.

Samuel had difficulty keeping pace with Ronald as they hurried back to Samuel's carriage in front of the Old North Church.

"You can save nearly an hour on your journey by taking the ferry to Noddle Island," Samuel said as they drove across town to fetch Ronald's horse.

"Then I shall go by ferry," Ronald said.

True to Samuel's word Ronald's trip back to Salem was far quicker than the trip to Boston. It was just after midafternoon when he turned onto Prison Lane and reined in his horse in front of the Salem jail. He'd pushed the animal mercilessly. Foam bubbled from the exhausted animal's nostrils.

Ronald was equally as wearied and caked with dust. Vertical lines from rivulets of perspiration crossed his brow. He was also emotionally drained, famished, and thirsty. But he was oblivious to his own needs. The ray of hope Cotton Mather had provided for Elizabeth drove him on.

Dashing into the jailer's office, he was frustrated to find it empty. He pounded on the oak door leading to the cells. Presently the door was opened a crack, and William Dounton's puffy face peered out at him.

"I'm to see my wife," Ronald said breathlessly.

" 'Tis feeding time," William said. "Come back in an hour."

Using his foot, Ronald crashed the door open against its hinges, sending William staggering back. Some of the thin gruel he was carrying sloshed out of its bucket.

"I'm to see her now!" Ronald growled.

"The magistrates will hear of this," William complained. But he put down his bucket and led Ronald back to the door to the cellar.

A few minutes later Ronald sat down next to Elizabeth. Gently he shook her shoulder. Her eyes blinked open, and she immediately asked after the children.

"I have yet to see them," Ronald said. "But I have good news. I've been to see Samuel Sewall and Reverend Cotton Mather. They think we can get a reprieve."

"God be thanked," Elizabeth said. Her eyes sparkled in the candlelight.

"But you must confess," Ronald said. "And you must name others you know to be in covenant with the devil."

"Confess to what?" Elizabeth asked.

"To witchcraft," Ronald said with exasperation. Exhaustion and stress challenged the veneer of control he had over his emotions.

"I cannot confess," Elizabeth said.

"And why not?" Ronald demanded shrilly.

"Because I am no witch," Elizabeth said.

For a moment Ronald merely stared at his wife while he clenched his fists in frustration.

"I cannot belie myself," Elizabeth said, breaking the strained silence. "I will not confess to witchcraft."

In his overwrought, exhausted state, Ronald's anger flared. He slammed his fist into the palm of his hand. He shoved his face within inches of hers. "You will confess," he snarled. "I order you to confess."

"Dear husband," Elizabeth said, unintimidated by Ronald's antics. "Have you been told of the evidence used against me?"

Ronald straightened up and gave a rapid, embarrassed glance at William, who was listening to this exchange. Ronald ordered William to back off. William left to fetch his bucket and make his rounds in the basement.

"I saw the evidence," Ronald said once William was out of earshot. "Reverend Mather has it in his home."

"I must be guilty of some transgression of God's will," Elizabeth said. "To that I could confess if I knew its nature. But I am no witch and surely I have not tormented any of the young women who have testified against me."

"Confess for now just for the reprieve," Ronald pleaded. "I want to save your life."

"I cannot save my life to lose my soul," Elizabeth said. "If I belie myself I will play into the hands of the devil. And surely I know no other witches, and I shan't call out against an innocent person to save myself."

"You must confess," Ronald shouted. "If you don't confess then I shall forsake thee."

"You will do as your conscience dictates," Elizabeth said. "I shan't confess to witchcraft."

"Please," Ronald pleaded, changing tactics. "For the children."

"We must trust in the Lord," Elizabeth said.

"He hath abandoned us," Ronald moaned as tears washed from his eyes and streaked down his dust-encrusted face.

With difficulty Elizabeth raised her manacled hand and laid it on his shoulder. "Have courage, my dear husband. The Lord functions in inscrutable ways."

Losing all semblance of control, Ronald leaped to his feet and rushed from the prison.

# Tuesday, July 19, 1692

Ronald shifted his weight nervously from one foot to the other. He was standing at the side of Prison Lane a short distance away from the jail. Sweat stood out on his forehead beneath the wide brim of his hat. It was a hot, hazy, muggy day whose oppressiveness was augmented by a preternatural stillness that hovered over the town despite the crowds of expectant people. Even the sea gulls were silent. Everyone waited for the wagon to appear.

An emotional brittleness shrouded Ronald's thoughts which were paralyzed by equal amounts of fear, sorrow, and panic. He could not fathom what he or Elizabeth had done to warrant this catastrophe. By order of the magistrates he'd been refused entry into the prison since the previous day when he'd tried for the last time to convince Elizabeth to cooperate. But no amount of pleading, cajoling, or threatening could break her resolve. She would not confess.

From within the shielded courtyard Ronald heard the metallic clatter of iron-rimmed wheels against the granite cobblestones. Almost immediately a wagon appeared. Standing in the back of the wagon were five women, tightly pressed together. They were still in chains. Behind the wagon walked William Dounton, sporting a wide smile in anticipation of turning his charges over to the hangman.

A sudden whoop and cheer rose from the spectators, inaugurating a carnival-like atmosphere. In a burst of energy children began their usual games while the adults laughed and thumped each other on the back. It was to be a holiday and a day of revelry like most days with a hanging. For Ronald as well as for the families and friends of the other victims it was the opposite.

Warned by Reverend Mather, Ronald was neither surprised nor hopeful when he did not see Elizabeth among the first group. The minister had advised him that Elizabeth would be executed last, after the crowd had been satiated on the blood of the first five prisoners. The idea was to lessen the potential impact on the populace, especially those who had either seen or heard of the evidence used against her.

As the wagon drew abreast of Ronald and passed, he gazed up at the faces of the condemned. They all appeared broken and despondent from their brutal treatment and the reality of their imminent fates. He recognized only two people: Rebecca Nurse and Sarah Good. Both were from Salem Village. The others were from neighboring towns. Seeing Rebecca Nurse on the way to her execution and knowing her pious character, Ronald was reminded of Reverend Mather's grim warning that the Salem witchcraft affair could spiral out of control.

When the wagon reached Essex Street and turned to the west, the crowd surged after it. Standing out in the throng was Reverend Cotton Mather as the only person on horseback.

Almost a half hour later Ronald again heard the telltale sound of metal clanking against the cobblestones of the prison courtyard. Presently a second wagon appeared. In the back sat Elizabeth with her head bowed. Due to the weight of her iron manacles she'd not been able to stand. As the wagon lumbered past Ronald, Elizabeth did not raise her eyes nor did Ronald call out to her. Neither knew what to say.

Ronald followed at a distance, thinking it was like living in a nightmare. He felt great ambivalence about his presence. He wanted to flee and hide from the world, but at the same time he wanted to be with Elizabeth until the end.

Just west of Salem Town, after crossing the Town Bridge, the wagon turned off the main road and began to climb Gallows Hill. The road ascended through a scrub of thornbushes until it opened out onto an inhospitable rocky ridge dotted with a few oaks and locust trees. Elizabeth's wagon pulled next to the empty first wagon and stopped.

Wiping the sweat from his brow, Ronald stepped from behind the wagons. Ahead he could see the noisy throng of townspeople gathered around one of the larger oak trees. Cotton Mather was behind the crowd and still mounted. At the base of the tree stood the condemned. A black-hooded hangman who'd been brought from Boston had looped a rope over a stout branch. One end he'd tied to the base of the tree while the other he'd fashioned into a noose and fitted over the head of Sarah Good. Sarah Good at that moment was precariously poised on a rung of a ladder leaning against the tree.

Ronald could see Reverend Noyes of the Salem Town Church approach the prisoner. In his hand he clutched a Bible. "Confess, witch!" Reverend Noyes yelled.

"I am no more a witch than you are a wizard," Sarah yelled back at him. She then cursed the minister, but Ronald could not hear her words for a jeer rose up from the crowd followed by someone yelling for the hangman to get on with it. Obligingly the hangman gave Sarah Good a push, and she swung clear of the ladder.

The crowd cheered and chanted "Die, witch," as Sarah Good struggled against the strangulating rope. Her face empurpled then blackened. As soon as Sarah's writhing ended, the hangman proceeded with the others, each in her turn.

With each successive victim, the crowd's cheering mellowed. By the time the last woman had been pushed from the ladder and the first victims were being cut down, the crowd had lost interest. Although some people had drifted over to see the bodies tossed into a shallow, rocky, common grave, most had already started back toward town, where the revelry would continue.

It was then that Elizabeth was commended to the hangman. He had to help her walk to the ladder due to the excessive weight of her chains.

Ronald swallowed. His legs felt weak. He wanted to cry out in anger. He wanted to beg for mercy. But he did nothing. He could not move.

Reverend Mather, who caught sight of him, rode over. "It is God's will," he said. He struggled with his horse, which sensed Ronald's torment.

Ronald did not take his eyes off Elizabeth. He wanted to rush forward and kill the hangman.

"You must remember what Elizabeth did and what she made," Reverend Mather said. "You should thank the Lord death hath intervened to save our Zion. Remember you have seen the evidence with your own eyes."

Ronald managed to nod as he vainly fought to hold back his tears. He'd seen the evidence. Clearly it was the devil's work. "But why?" Ronald shouted suddenly. "Why Elizabeth?"

For a brief second Ronald saw Elizabeth's eyes rise to meet his. Her mouth began to move as if she was about to speak, but before she could, the hangman gave her a decisive shove. In contrast to his technique with the others, the hangman had left slack in the rope around Elizabeth's neck. As she left the ladder, her body fell for several feet before being jerked to a sudden, deathly stop. Unlike the others she did not struggle nor did her face turn black.

Ronald's head sank into his hands and he wept.

# 1

## Tuesday,
## July 12, 1994

KIMBERLY STEWART GLANCED AT HER WATCH AS SHE
went through the turnstile and exited the MBTA subway at
Harvard Square in Cambridge, Massachusetts. It was a few
minutes before seven P.M. She knew she would be on time
or only minutes late, but still she hurried. Pushing through
the crowd milling about the news kiosk in the middle of
the square, she half ran and half walked the short distance
on Massachusetts Avenue before turning right on Holyoke
Street.

Pausing to catch her breath in front of the Hasty Pudding
Club building, Kimberly glanced up at the structure. She
knew about the Harvard social club only in reference to the
annual award it gave to an actor and an actress. The building was brick with white trim like most buildings at Harvard. She'd never been inside although it housed a public
restaurant called Upstairs at the Pudding. This was to be
her first visit.

With her breathing restored to near normal, Kim opened
the door and entered only to be confronted by several sizable flights of stairs. By the time she got to the maître d's
podium she was again mildly winded. She asked for the
ladies' room.

While Kim wrestled with her thick, raven hair which
refused to do what she wanted it to do, she told herself
there was no need to be nervous. After all, Stanton Lewis
was family. The problem was that he had never before
called at the last minute to say that he "needed" her to
come to dinner and that it was an "emergency."

Giving up on her hair and feeling totally thrown together, Kim again presented herself at the maître d's podium. This time she announced she was to meet Mr. and Mrs. Stanton Lewis.

"Most of your party is here," the hostess said.

As Kim followed the hostess through the main part of the restaurant, her anxiety went up a notch. She didn't like the sound of "party." She wondered who else would be at the dinner.

The hostess led Kim out onto a trellised terrace that was crowded with diners. Stanton and his wife, Candice, were sitting at a four-top in the corner.

"I'm sorry I'm late," Kim said as she arrived at the table.

"You're not late in the slightest," Stanton said.

He leaped to his feet and enveloped Kim in an extended and demonstrative hug that bent her backwards. It also turned her face a bright red. She had the uncomfortable feeling that everyone on the crowded terrace was watching. Once she was able to break free from Stanton's bear hug she retreated to the chair held out by the hostess and tried to melt into her seat.

Kim always felt uncomfortably obvious around Stanton. Although they were cousins, Kim thought they were the social antithesis of each other. While she considered herself moderately shy, occasionally even awkward, he was a paragon of confidence: an urbane and aggressively assertive sophisticate. He was built like a ski racer and stood straight and tall, overpowering people as the consummate entrepreneur. Even his wife, Candice, despite her demure smile, made Kim feel socially inept.

Kim hazarded a quick glance around her, and as she did so she inadvertently bumped the hostess, who was attempting to lay Kim's napkin across her lap. Both apologized simultaneously.

"Relax, cousin," Stanton said after the hostess had departed. He reached across the table and poured Kim a glass of white wine. "As usual you're wound up like a banjo wire."

"Telling me to relax only makes me more nervous," Kim said. She took a drink of the wine.

"You are a strange one," Stanton said playfully. "I can never understand why you're so damn self-conscious, especially sitting here with family in a room full of people you'll never see again. Let your hair down."

"I have no control over what my hair chooses to do," Kim joked. In spite of herself she was beginning to calm down. "As for your inability to understand my unease, it's entirely understandable. You're so totally self-assured that it's impossible for you to imagine what it's like not to be so."

"Why not give me a chance to understand?" Stanton said. "I challenge you to explain to me why you are feeling uncomfortable right at this moment. My God, woman, your hand is shaking."

Kim put down her glass and put her hands in her lap. "I'm nervous mainly because I feel thrown together," she said. "After your call this evening, I barely had time to take a shower, much less find something to wear. And, if you must know, my bangs are driving me crazy." Kim blindly tried to adjust the hair over her forehead.

"I think your dress is smashing," Candice said.

"No doubt about it," Stanton said. "Kimberly, you look gorgeous."

Kim laughed. "I'm smart enough to know that provoked compliments are invariably false."

"Balderdash," Stanton said. "The irony of this discussion is that you are a sexy, beautiful woman even though you always act as if you haven't a clue, which, I suppose, is somewhat endearing. How old are you now, twenty-five?"

"Twenty-seven," Kim said. She tried more of her wine.

"Twenty-seven and improving with each year," Stanton said. He smiled impishly. "You've got cheekbones other women would die for, skin like a baby's bottom, and a ballerina's figure, not to mention those emerald eyes that could mesmerize a Greek statue."

"The truth of the matter is somewhat different," Kim said. "My facial-bone structure is certainly not exceptional although okay. My skin barely tans if at all, and 'ballerina's figure' sounds like a nice way of saying I'm not stacked.''

"You're being unfair to yourself," Candice said.

"I think we should change the subject," Kim said. "This conversation is not going to get me to relax. In fact it just makes me more uncomfortable."

"My apologies for being so truthfully complimentary," Stanton said, his impish smile returning. "What would you prefer we discuss?"

"How about explaining why my presence here at dinner was such an emergency," Kim said.

"I need your help." Stanton leaned toward her.

"Me?" Kim questioned. She had to laugh. "The great financier needs my help? Is this a joke?"

"Quite the contrary," Stanton said. "In a few months I'll be launching an initial public offering for one of my biotech companies called Genetrix."

"I'm not investing," Kim said. "You've got the wrong relative."

It was Stanton's turn to laugh. "I'm not looking for money," he said. "No, it's something quite different. I happened to be talking with Aunt Joyce today and—"

"Oh, no!" Kim interrupted nervously. "What did my mother say now?"

"She just happened to mention that you'd recently broken up with your boyfriend," Stanton said.

Kim blanched. The unease she'd felt when she'd arrived at the restaurant returned in a rush. "I wish my mother wouldn't open her big mouth," she said irritably.

"Joyce didn't give any gory details," Stanton said.

"That doesn't matter," Kim said. "She's been giving out personal information about Brian and me since we were teenagers."

"All she said was that Kinnard wasn't right for you," Stanton said. "Which I happen to agree with if he's forever traipsing off with his friends for ski trips and fishing forays."

"That sounds like details to me," Kim moaned. "It's also an exaggeration. The fishing is something new. The skiing is once a year."

"To tell you the truth I was hardly listening," Stanton said. "At least until she asked me if I could find someone more appropriate for you."

"Good Lord!" Kim said with mounting irritation. "I can't believe this. She actually asked you to fix me up with someone?"

"It's not my usual forte," Stanton said. A self-satisfied smile spread across his face. "But I had a brainstorm. Right after I hung up with Joyce I knew to whom I'd introduce you."

"Don't tell me that's why you got me here tonight," Kim said with alarm. She felt her pulse quicken. "I never would have come if I'd had any idea—"

"Calm down," Stanton said. "Don't get yourself in a dither. It's going to work out just fine. Trust me."

"It's too soon," Kim said.

"It's never too soon," Stanton said. "My motto is, Today is yesterday's tomorrow."

"Stanton, you are impossible," Kim said. "I'm not ready to meet someone. Besides I'm a mess."

"I already told you that you look terrific," Stanton said. "Trust me, Edward Armstrong is going to fall for you like a ton of bricks. One look into those emerald eyes and his legs will turn to rubber."

"This is ridiculous," Kim complained.

"One thing I should admit right up front is that I have an ulterior motive," Stanton said. "I've been trying to get Edward involved in one of my biotech companies ever since I became a venture capitalist. With Genetrix about to go public, there's no time like the present. The idea is to get him beholden by introducing him to you, Kim. Then maybe I'll be able to twist his arm to get him on the Genetrix scientific advisory board. If I get his name on the prospectus it will be worth a good four or five mil on the initial offering. In the process I can make him a millionaire."

For a moment Kim didn't say anything as she concentrated on her wine. On top of her anxiety, she was feeling used as well as embarrassed, but she didn't voice her irritation. She'd always had trouble expressing herself in confrontational situations. Stanton had amazed her as he always had, being so manipulative and self-serving yet so open about it.

"Maybe Edward Armstrong doesn't want to be a millionaire," Kim said at length.

"Nonsense," Stanton said. "Everyone wants to be a millionaire."

"I know it's difficult for you to understand," Kim said. "But not everyone thinks the same way you do."

"Edward is a nice gentleman," Candice said.

"That sounds suspiciously like the equivalent of a female blind date being described as having a nice personality."

Stanton chuckled. "You know, cousin, you might be a mental case but you do have a sense of humor."

"What I meant to say," Candice said. "Edward is a considerate person. And I think that's important. I was initially against the idea of Stanton fixing you up, but then I thought how nice it would be for you to have a relationship with someone civil. After all, the relationship you've had with Kinnard has been pretty stormy. I think you deserve better."

Kim could not believe Candice. She obviously knew nothing about Kinnard, but Kim did not contradict her. Instead Kim said, "The problems between me and Kinnard are as much my fault as his."

Kim eyed the door. Her pulse was racing. She wished she could just stand up and leave. But she couldn't. It wasn't her nature, although at the moment she sincerely wished it were.

"Edward is a lot more than considerate," Stanton said. "He's a genius."

"Oh that's just great!" Kim said sarcastically. "Not only will Mr. Armstrong find me unattractive, but he'll also find me boring. I'm not at my scintillating best when it comes to making conversation with geniuses."

"Trust me," Stanton said. "You guys will hit it off. You have common backgrounds. Edward's an M.D. He was a classmate of mine at Harvard Med. As students we teamed up for a lot of experiments and lab stuff until he took his third year off and got a Ph.D. in biochemistry."

"Is he a practicing doctor?" Kim asked.

"Nope, research," Stanton said. "His expertise is the chemistry of the brain, which is a particularly fertile area at present. Right now Edward's the rising star of the field: a scientific celebrity whom Harvard was able to steal back from Stanford. And speaking of the devil, here he comes now."

Kim swung around in her seat to see a tall and squarely built yet boyish-appearing man heading for their table. Hearing that he'd been Stanton's classmate, Kim knew he'd have to be about forty, yet he appeared considerably younger, with straight, sandy blond hair and a broad, unlined, tanned face. There was none of the pallor Kim associated with academics. He was slightly stooped, as if he were afraid he was about to bump his head on an overhead beam.

Stanton was instantly on his feet, clasping Edward in a bear hug with as much enthusiasm as he'd shown Kim. He even pounded Edward's shoulder several times as some men seem impelled to do.

For a fleeting moment Kim felt sympathy for Edward. She could tell that he was as uncomfortable as she had been with Stanton's overly demonstrative greeting.

Stanton made brief introductions, and Edward shook hands with Candice and Kim before sitting down. Kim noticed his skin was moist and his grip tentative, just like her own. She also noticed he had a slight stutter as well as a nervous habit of pushing his hair from his forehead.

"I'm terribly sorry for being late," Edward said. He had a little trouble vocalizing his *t*'s.

"Two birds of a feather," Stanton said. "My gorgeous, talented, sexy cousin here said the same thing when she arrived five seconds ago."

Kim felt her face suffuse with color. It was going to be a long evening. Stanton could not help being himself.

"Relax, Ed," Stanton continued as he poured him some wine. "You're not late. I said around seven. You're perfect."

"I just meant that you were all here waiting," Edward

said. He smiled self-consciously and lifted his glass as if in toast.

"Good idea," Stanton said, taking the hint and snatching up his glass. "Let me propose a toast. First I'd like to toast my darling cousin, Kimberly Stewart. She's the best surgical intensive-care nurse at the MGH bar none." Stanton then looked directly at Edward while everyone held their glasses in abeyance. "If you have to have your prostate plumbing patched up, just pray that Kimberly is available. She's legendary with a catheter!"

"Stanton, please!" Kim protested.

"OK, OK," Stanton said, extending his left hand as if to quiet an audience. "Let me get back to my toast of Kimberly Stewart. I would be derelict in my duty if I didn't bring it to the group's attention that her sterling genealogy extends back just shy of the *Mayflower*. That's paternally, of course. Maternally she only goes back to the Revolutionary War, which, I might add, is my, inferior, side of the family."

"Stanton, this is hardly necessary," Kim said. She was already mortified.

"But there's more," Stanton said with the relish of a practiced after-dinner speaker. "Kimberly's first relative to graduate from dear old Harvard did so in 1671. That was Sir Ronald Stewart, founder of Maritime, Ltd., as well as the current Stewart dynasty. And perhaps most interesting of all, Kimberly's great-grandmother times eight was hanged for witchcraft in Salem. Now if that is not Americana I don't know what is."

"Stanton, you can be such a pain," Kim said, her anger overcoming her embarrassment for the moment. "That's not information meant for public disclosure."

"And why the hell not?" Stanton questioned with a laugh. Looking back at Edward he said, "The Stewarts have this ridiculous hangup that such ancient history is a blight on the family name."

"Whether you think it is ridiculous or not, people have a right to their feelings," Kim said hotly. "Besides, my mother is the one who is most concerned about the issue, and she's your aunt and a former Lewis. My father has never said one thing about it to me.''

''Whatever,'' Stanton said with a wave. ''Personally I find the story fascinating. I should be so lucky; it's like having had a relative on the *Mayflower* or in the boat when Washington crossed the Delaware.''

''I think we should change the subject,'' Kim said.

''Agreed,'' Stanton said equably. He was the only one still holding up his glass of wine. It was a long toast. ''That brings me to Edward Armstrong. Here's to the most exciting, productive, creative, and intelligent neurochemist in the world, no, in the universe! Here's to a man who has come from the streets of Brooklyn, put himself through school, and is now at the pinnacle of his chosen career. Here's to a man who should be already booking a flight to Stockholm for his Nobel Prize, which he is a shoo-in to win for his work with neurotransmitters, memory, and quantum mechanics.''

Stanton extended his wineglass and everybody followed suit. They clinked glasses and drank. As Kim set her glass back on the table she glanced furtively at Edward. It was apparent to her that he was equally as abashed and self-conscious as she.

Stanton thumped his now empty glass on the table and proceeded to refill it. He glanced around at the other glasses, then jammed the wine bottle into its ice bucket. ''Now that you two have met,'' he said, ''I expect you to fall in love, get married, and have plenty of darling kids. All I ask for my part in bringing you together in this fruitful union is that Edward agrees to serve on the scientific advisory board of Genetrix.''

Stanton laughed heartily even though he was the only one to do so. When he recovered he said, ''Okay, where the hell is the waiter? Let's eat!''

Outside the restaurant the group paused.

''We could walk around the corner and get ice cream at Herrell's,'' Stanton suggested.

''I couldn't eat another thing,'' Kim said.

''Me neither,'' Edward said.

"I never eat dessert," Candice said.

"Then who wants a lift home?" Stanton asked. "I've got my car right here in the Holyoke Center garage."

"I'm happy with MTA," Kim said.

"My apartment is just a short walk," Edward said.

"Then you two are on your own," Stanton said. After promising Edward he'd be in touch, Stanton took Candice's arm and headed for the garage.

"Can I walk you to the subway?" Edward asked.

"I'd appreciate that," Kim said.

They headed off together. As they walked, Kim could sense that Edward wanted to say something. Just before they got to the corner he spoke. "It's such a pleasant evening," he said, struggling a bit with the *p*. His mild stutter had returned. "How about a little walk in Harvard Square before you head home?"

"That would be great," Kim said. "I'd enjoy it."

Arm in arm they walked to that complicated collision of Massachusetts Avenue, the JFK Drive portion of Harvard Street, Mt. Auburn Street, and Brattle Street. Despite its name it was hardly a square but rather a series of curved façades and curiously shaped open areas. On summer nights the area metamorphoses into a spontaneous, medieval-like sidewalk circus of jugglers, musicians, poetry readers, magicians, and acrobats.

It was a warm, silky, summer night with a few nighthawks chirping high in the dark sky. There were even a few stars despite the glow from the city lights. Kim and Edward strolled around the entire square, pausing briefly at the periphery of each performer's audience. Despite their mutual misgivings about the evening, ultimately they were enjoying themselves.

"I'm glad I came out tonight," Kim said.

"So am I," Edward said.

Finally they sat down on a low concrete wall. To their left was a woman singing a plaintive ballad. To their right was a group of energetic Peruvian Indians playing indigenous panpipes.

"Stanton is truly a character," Kim said.

"I didn't know who to be more embarrassed for," Edward said. "Me or you with the way he was carrying on."

Kim laughed in agreement. She'd felt just as uncomfortable when Stanton was toasting Edward as when he'd toasted her.

"What I find amazing about Stanton is that he can be so manipulative and charming at the same time," Kim said.

"It is curious what he can get away with," Edward agreed. "I could never do it in a million years. In fact I've always felt I've been a foil for Stanton. I've envied him, wishing I could be half as assertive. I've always been socially self-conscious, even a little nerdy."

"My feelings exactly," Kim admitted. "I've always wanted to be more confident socially. But it just has never worked. I've been timid since I've been a little girl. When I'm in social situations, I never can think of the appropriate thing to say on the spur of the moment. Five minutes later I can, but then it's always too late."

"Two birds of a feather, just as Stanton described us," Edward said. "The trouble is Stanton is aware of our weaknesses, and he sure knows how to make us squirm. I die a slow death every time he brings up that nonsense about my being a shoo-in for the Nobel Prize."

"I apologize on behalf of my family," Kim said. "At least he isn't mean-spirited."

"How are you related?" Edward asked.

"We're true cousins," Kim said. "My mother is Stanton's father's sister."

"I should apologize as well," Edward said. "I shouldn't speak ill of Stanton. He and I were classmates in medical school. I helped him in the lab, and he helped me at parties. We made a pretty good team. We've been friends ever since."

"How come you haven't teamed up with him in one of his entrepreneurial ventures?" Kim asked.

"I've just never been interested," Edward said. "I like academia, where the quest is for knowledge for knowledge's sake. Not that I'm against applied science. It's just not as engaging. In some respects academia and industry are at odds with each other, especially in regard to industry's imperative of secrecy. Free communication is the life-blood of science; secrecy is its bane.''

"Stanton says he could make you a millionaire," Kim said.

Edward laughed. "And how would that change my life? I'm already doing what I want to do: a combination of research and teaching. Injecting a million dollars into my life would just complicate things and create bias. I'm happy the way I am.''

"I tried to suggest as much to Stanton," Kim said. "But he wouldn't listen. He's so headstrong.''

"But still charming and entertaining," Edward said. "He was certainly exaggerating about me when he was giving that interminable toast. But how about you? Can your family truly be traced back to seventeenth-century America?''

"That much was true," Kim said.

"That's fascinating," Edward said. "It's also impressive. I'd be lucky to trace my family back two generations, and then it would probably be embarrassing.''

"It's even more impressive to put oneself through school and become eminently successful in a challenging career," Kim said. "That's on your own initiative. I was merely born a Stewart. It took no effort on my behalf.''

"What about the Salem witchcraft story?" Edward asked. "Is that true as well?''

"It is," Kim admitted. "But it's not something I'm comfortable talking about.''

"I'm terribly sorry," Edward said. His stutter reappeared. "Please forgive me. I don't understand why it would make any difference, but I shouldn't have brought it up.''

Kim shook her head. "Now I'm sorry for making you feel uncomfortable," she said. "I suppose my response to the Salem witchcraft episode is silly, and to tell you the truth, I don't even know why I feel uncomfortable about it. It's probably because of my mother. She drummed it into me that it was something I wasn't supposed to talk about. I know she thinks of it as a family disgrace.''

"But it was more than three hundred years ago," Edward said.

"You're right," Kim said with a shrug. "It doesn't make much sense."

"Are you familiar with the episode?" Edward asked.

"I know the basics, I suppose," Kim said. "Like everyone else in America."

"Curiously enough, I know a little more than most people," Edward said. "Harvard University Press published a book on the subject which was written by two gifted historians. It's called *Salem Possessed*. One of my graduate students insisted I read it since it won some kind of history award. So I read it, and I was intrigued. Why don't I loan it to you?"

"That would be nice," Kim said just to be polite.

"I'm serious," Edward said. "You'll like it, and maybe it will change the way you think about the affair. The social/political/religious aspects are truly fascinating. I learned a lot more than I expected. For instance, did you know that within a few years of the trials some of the jurors and even some of the judges publicly recanted and asked for pardon because they realized innocent people had been executed?"

"Really," Kim said, still trying to be polite.

"But the fact that innocent people got hanged wasn't what really grabbed me," Edward said. "You know how one book leads to another. Well, I read another book called *Poisons of the Past* that had the most interesting theory, especially for a neuroscientist like myself. It suggested that at least some of the young women of Salem who were suffering strange 'fits' and who were responsible for accusing people of witchcraft were actually poisoned. The suggested culprit was ergot, which comes from a mold called *Claviceps purpurea. Claviceps* is a fungus that tends to grow on grain, particularly rye."

Despite Kim's conditioned disinterest in the subject, Edward had caught her attention. "Poisoned by ergot?" she questioned. "What would that do?"

"Ooo-wee!" Edward rolled his eyes. "Remember that Beatles song, 'Lucy in the Sky with Diamonds'? Well, it would have been something like that because ergot contains lysergic acid amide, which is the prime ingredient of LSD.''

"You mean they would have experienced hallucinations and delusions?" Kim asked.

"That's the idea," Edward said. "Ergotism either causes a gangrenous reaction, which can be rapidly fatal, or a convulsive, hallucinogenic reaction. In Salem it would have been the convulsive, hallucinogenic one, tending more on the hallucinogenic side.''

"What an interesting theory," Kim said. "It might even interest my mother. Maybe she'd feel differently about our ancestor if she knew of such an explanation. It would be hard to blame the individual under those circumstances.''

"That was my thought," Edward said. "But at the same time it can't be the whole story. Ergot might have been the tinder that ignited the fire, but once it started it turned into a firestorm on its own accord. From the reading I've done I think people exploited the situation for economic and social reasons, although not necessarily on a conscious level.''

"You've certainly piqued my curiosity," Kim said. "Now I feel embarrassed I've never been curious enough to read anything about the Salem witch trials other than the little I did in high school. I should be particularly ashamed since my executed ancestor's property is still in the family's possession. In fact, due to a minor feud between my father and my late grandfather, my brother and I inherited it just this year.''

"Good grief!" Edward said. "You mean to tell me your family has kept that land for three hundred years?''

"Well, not the entire tract," Kim said. "The original tract included land in what is now Beverly, Danvers, and Peabody, as well as Salem. Even the Salem part of the property is only a portion of what it had been. Yet it is still a sizable tract. I'm not sure how many acres, but quite a few.''

"That's still extraordinary," Edward said. "The only thing I inherited was my father's dentures and a few of his masonry tools. To think that you can walk on land where your seventeenth-century relatives trod blows my mind. I thought that kind of experience was reserved for European royalty.''

''I can even do better than just walking on the land,'' Kim said. ''I can even go into the house. The old house still stands.''

''Now you're pulling my leg,'' Edward said. ''I'm not *that* gullible.''

''I'm not fooling,'' Kim said. ''It's not that unusual. There are a lot of seventeenth-century houses in the Salem area, including ones that belonged to other executed witches like Rebecca Nurse.''

''I had no idea,'' Edward said.

''You ought to visit the Salem area sometime,'' Kim said.

''What shape is the house in?'' Edward asked.

''Pretty good, I guess,'' Kim said. ''I haven't been in it for ages, not since I was a child. But it looks okay for a house built in 1670. It was bought by Ronald Stewart. It was his wife, Elizabeth, who was executed.''

''I remember Ronald's name from Stanton's toast,'' Edward said. ''He was the first Harvard man in the Stewart clan.''

''I wasn't aware of that,'' Kim said.

''What are you and your brother going to do with the property?''

''Nothing for the time being,'' Kim said. ''At least not until Brian gets back from England where he's currently running the family shipping business. He's supposed to be home in a year or so, and we'll decide then. Unfortunately the property is a white elephant considering the taxes and upkeep.''

''Did your grandfather live in the old house?'' Edward asked.

''Oh, goodness no,'' Kim said. ''The old house hasn't been lived in for years. Ronald Stewart bought a huge tract of land that abutted the original property and built a larger house, keeping the original house for tenants or servants. Over the years the larger house has been torn down and rebuilt many times. The last time was around the turn of the century. That was the house my grandfather lived in.

Well, rattled around in would be a better term. It's a huge, drafty old place.''

"I bet that old house has historical value," Edward said.

"The Peabody-Essex Institute in Salem as well as the Society for the Preservation of New England Antiquities in Boston have both expressed interest in purchasing it," Kim said. "But my mother is against the idea. I think she's afraid of dredging up the witchcraft issue."

"That's too bad," Edward said. Once again his slight stutter returned.

Kim looked at him. He seemed to be fidgeting while pretending to watch the Peruvians.

"Is something wrong?" Kim asked. She could sense his unease.

"No," Edward said a little too forcefully. He pondered for a minute and then said, "I'm sorry, and I know I shouldn't ask this, and you should just say no if it's not convenient. I mean, I'd understand."

"What is it?" Kim asked. She was mildly apprehensive.

"It's just that I read those books I told you about," Edward said. "What I mean to say is that I'd really like to see that old house. I know it is presumptuous of me to ask."

"I'd be happy to show it to you," Kim said with relief. "I have Saturday off this week. We could drive up there then if it's convenient for you. I can get the keys from the lawyers."

"It wouldn't be too much of a bother?" Edward asked.

"Not at all," Kim said.

"Saturday would be perfect," Edward said. "In exchange perhaps you'd like to go to dinner Friday night?"

Kim smiled. "I accept. But now I think I'd better be getting home. The seven-thirty shift at the hospital starts awfully early."

They slid off the concrete wall and strolled toward the subway entrance.

"Where do you live?" Edward asked.

"Beacon Hill," Kim said.

"I hear that's a great neighborhood," Edward said.

"It's convenient to the hospital," Kim said. "And I have

a great apartment. Unfortunately I have to move come September because my roommate is getting married and she has the lease.''

"I've got a similar problem," Edward said. "I live in a charming apartment on the third floor of a private house, but the owners have a baby coming and need the space. So I have to be out September first as well."

"I'm sorry to hear that," Kim said.

"It's not so bad," Edward said. "I've been meaning to move for years, but I've just been putting it off."

"Where's the apartment?" Kim asked.

"Close by," Edward said. "Within walking distance." Then he added hesitantly: "Would you care to come over for a visit?"

"Maybe another night," Kim said. "Like I said, morning comes early for me."

They reached the entrance to the subway. Kim turned and looked up into Edward's pale blue eyes. She liked what she saw; there was sensitivity.

"I want to congratulate you on asking to see the old house," Kim said. "I know it wasn't easy for you, and the reason I know is because it would have been equally difficult for me. In fact I probably couldn't have done it at all."

Edward blushed. Then he chuckled. "I'm certainly no Stanton Lewis," he said. "The truth of the matter is that I can be kind of a klutz."

"I think we have some similarities in that area," Kim said. "I also think you are a lot more socially adept than you give yourself credit for."

"You get the credit," Edward said. "You make me feel relaxed, and since we've only just met, that's saying something."

"The feeling is mutual," Kim said.

They gripped hands for a moment. Then Kim turned and hurried down into the subway.

# 2

## Saturday,
## July 16, 1994

Edward double-parked on Beacon Street across from the Boston Common and ran into the foyer of Kim's building. After ringing her bell, he kept his eye out for a Boston meter maid. He knew of their reputation from sore experience.

"Sorry to have kept you waiting," Kim said when she appeared. She was dressed in khaki shorts and a simple white T-shirt. Her dark, voluminous hair was pulled back in a ponytail.

"I'm sorry for being late," Edward said. By mutual consent Edward was dressed in a similar, casual fashion. "I had to run by the lab."

They both stared at each other for a beat, then burst out laughing.

"We're too much," Kim admitted.

"I can't help it." Edward chuckled. "I'm always apologizing. Even when it isn't warranted. It's ridiculous, but you know something? I wasn't even aware of it until you pointed it out at dinner last night."

"I only noticed it because I do it too," Kim said. "After you dropped me off last night, I thought about it. I think it comes from feeling overly responsible."

"You're probably right," Edward said. "When I was growing up I always thought it was my fault when something went wrong or someone was upset."

"The similarities are frightening," Kim mused with a smile.

They climbed into Edward's Saab and headed north out

of town. It was a bright, clear day, and even though it was early morning, the sun already gave adequate hint of its summer strength.

Kim lowered the passenger-side window and jauntily stuck her arm out. "This feels like a mini-vacation," she said.

"Particularly for me," Edward said. "I'm ashamed to admit it, but I usually spend just about every day in the lab."

"Weekends too?" Kim questioned.

"Seven days a week," Edward admitted. "The usual way I can tell it is a Sunday is when there are fewer people around. I guess I'm just a boring guy!"

"I'd say dedicated," Kim said. "I'd also say you're very considerate. The flowers you've been sending me daily are glorious, but I'm hardly accustomed to such gallantry. I certainly don't deserve it."

"Oh, it's nothing," Edward said.

Kim could sense his unease. He pushed his hair off his forehead several times in a row.

"It's certainly not 'nothing' to me," Kim said. "I want to thank you again."

"Did you have any trouble getting the keys to the old house?" Edward asked, changing the subject.

Kim shook her head. "Not in the slightest. I went over to the lawyers right after work yesterday."

They drove north on route 93, then turned east on 128. The traffic was light.

"I certainly enjoyed our dinner last night," Edward said.

"Me too," Kim said. "Thank you. But when I thought about it this morning I wanted to apologize for dominating the conversation. I think I talked too much about myself and my family."

"There you go apologizing again," Edward said.

Kim struck her thigh in mock punishment. "I'm afraid I'm a hopeless case." She laughed.

"Besides"—Edward chuckled—"I should be the one apologizing. It was my fault because I bombarded you mercilessly with questions that I'm afraid might have been borderline too personal."

"I wasn't offended in the slightest," Kim said. "I just hope I didn't scare you when I mentioned those anxiety attacks I used to get when I first went to college."

"Oh, please!" Edward laughed. "I think we all get them, especially those of us who tend to be compulsive, like doctors. I used to get anxiety attacks in college before every test even though I never had any problems with grades."

"I think mine were a little worse than run-of-the-mill," Kim said. "For a short time I even had trouble riding in the car, thinking I might get one while I was cooped up."

"Did you ever take anything for them?" Edward asked.

"Xanax for a short time," Kim said.

"Did you ever try Prozac?" Edward asked.

Kim turned to look at Edward. "Never!" she said. "Why would I take Prozac?"

"Just that you mentioned you had both anxiety and shyness," Edward said. "Prozac could have helped both."

"Prozac has never been suggested," Kim said. "Plus even if it had been I wouldn't have taken it. I'm not in favor of using drugs for minor personality flaws like shyness. I think drugs should be reserved for serious problems, not mere everyday difficulties."

"Sorry," Edward said. "I didn't mean to offend you."

"I'm not offended," Kim said. "But I do feel strongly about it. As a nurse I see too many people taking too many drugs. Drug companies have got us to think there is a pill for every problem."

"I basically agree with you," Edward said. "But as a neuroscientist I now see behavior and mood as biochemical, and I've reevaluated my attitude toward clean psychotropic drugs."

"What do you mean, 'clean' drugs?" Kim asked.

"Drugs that have little or no side effects."

"All drugs have side effects," Kim said.

"I suppose that's true," Edward said. "But some side effects are quite minor and certainly an acceptable risk in relation to the potential benefits."

"I guess that's the crux of the philosophical argument," Kim said.

"Oh, that reminds me," Edward said. "I remembered

those two books I'd promised to loan you." He reached in the backseat, grabbed the books, and slipped them into Kim's lap. Kim leafed through them, jokingly complaining that there weren't any pictures. Edward laughed.

"I tried to look up your ancestor in the one on the Salem witch trials," Edward said. "But there is no Elizabeth Stewart in the index. Are you sure she was executed? Those authors did extensive research."

"As far as I know," Kim said. She glanced in the index of *Salem Possessed*. It went from "spectral testimony" to "Stoughton, William." There was no Stewart at all.

After a half-hour drive they entered Salem. Their route took them past the Witch House. Edward's interest was immediately aroused, and he pulled to the side of the road.

"What's that place?" he asked.

"It's called the Witch House," Kim said. "It's one of the prime tourist attractions in the area."

"Is it truly seventeenth century?" Edward asked as he stared at the old building. "Or is it Disneyland-like re-creation?"

"It's authentic," Kim said. "It's also on its original site. There is another seventeenth-century house nearby at the Peabody-Essex Institute, but it had been moved from another location."

"Cool," Edward said. The building had a storybook appeal. He was enthralled by the way the second story protruded from the first, and by the diamond-shaped panes of glass.

"Calling it cool dates you." Kim laughed. "Call it 'awesome.' "

"OK," Edward said agreeably. "It's awesome."

"It's also surprisingly similar to the old house I'm going to show you on the Stewart family compound," Kim said. "But it's technically not a witch house since no witch lived in it. It was the home of Jonathan Corwin. He was one of the magistrates who conducted some of the preliminary hearings."

"I remember the name from *Salem Possessed*," Edward said. "It certainly brings history to life when you see an actual site." Then he turned to Kim. "How far is the Stewart compound from here?"

"Not far," Kim said. "Maybe ten minutes tops."

"Did you have breakfast this morning?"

"Just some juice and fruit," Kim said.

"How about stopping for coffee and a donut?" Edward asked.

"Sounds good," Kim said.

Since it was still early and the bulk of the tourists had yet to arrive, they had no trouble finding parking near the Salem Commons. Just across the street was a coffee shop. They got coffee-to-go and strolled around the center of town, peeking into the Witch Museum and a few of the other tourist attractions. As they walked down the pedestrian mall on Essex Street, they noticed how many shops and pushcarts were selling witch-related souvenirs.

"The witch trials spawned an entire cottage industry," Edward commented. "I'm afraid it's a little tacky."

"It does trivialize the ordeal," Kim said. "But it also stands as testament to the affair's appeal. Everybody finds it so fascinating."

Wandering into the National Park Service Visitor Center, Kim found herself confronted by a virtual library of books and pamphlets on the trials. "I had no idea there was so much literature available," she said. After a few moments of browsing, she purchased several books. She explained to Edward that once she got interested in something she usually went overboard.

Returning to the car, they drove out North Street, passing the Witch House again, and turned right on Orne Road. As they passed the Greenlawn Cemetery Kim mentioned that it had once been part of the Stewarts' land.

Kim directed Edward to turn right onto a dirt road. As they bumped along, Edward had to fight with the steering wheel. It was impossible to miss all the potholes.

"Are you sure we're on the right road?" Edward asked.

"Absolutely," Kim assured him.

After a few twists and turns they approached an impressive wrought-iron gate. The gate was suspended from massive stanchions constructed of rough-hewn granite blocks.

A high iron fence topped with sharpened spikes disappeared into the dense forest on either side of the road.

"Is this it?" Edward questioned.

"This is it," Kim answered as she alighted from the car.

"Rather imposing," Edward called as Kim struggled to open the heavy padlock securing the gate. "And not that inviting."

"It was an affectation of the age," Kim yelled back. "People with means wanted to project a baronial image." After removing the padlock, she pushed the gate open. Its hinges creaked loudly.

Kim returned to the car and they drove through the gate. After a few more twists and turns the road opened up to a large grassy field. Edward stopped again.

"Good Lord," Edward said. "Now I understand why you said baronial."

Dominating the enormous field was a huge, multistoried stone house complete with turrets, crenellations, and machicolations. The roof was slate and pockmarked with fanciful decorations and finial-topped dormers. Chimneys sprouted like weeds from all parts of the structure.

"An interesting mélange of styles," Edward said. "It's part medieval castle, part Tudor manor, part French château. It's amazing."

"The family has always called it the castle," Kim explained.

"I can see why," Edward said. "When you described it as a huge, drafty old place, I had no idea it was going to look like this. This belongs down in Newport with the Breakers."

"The North Shore of Boston still has quite a few of these huge old houses," Kim said. "Of course some of them have been torn down. Others have been recycled into condos, but that market is flat at the moment. You can understand why it's a white elephant for me and my brother."

"Where's the old house?" Edward asked.

Kim pointed to the right. In the distance Edward could just make out a dark-brown building nestled in a stand of birch trees.

"What's that stone building to the left?" Edward asked.

"That was once a mill," Kim said. "But it was turned into stables a couple of hundred years ago."

Edward laughed. "It's amazing you can take all this in stride," he said. "In my mind anything over fifty years old is a relic."

Edward started driving again but quickly stopped. He'd come abreast of a fieldstone wall that was mostly overgrown with weeds.

"What's this?" he asked, pointing at the wall.

"That's the old family burial ground," Kim said.

"No fooling," Edward said. "Can we look?"

"Of course," Kim said.

They got out of the car and climbed over the wall. They couldn't use the entrance since it was blocked by a dense thicket of blackberry bushes.

"Looks like a lot of the headstones are broken," Edward said. "And fairly recently." He picked up a broken piece of marble.

"Vandalism," Kim said. "There's not much we can do about it since the place is vacant."

"It's a shame," Edward said. He looked at the date. It was 1843. The name was Nathaniel Stewart.

"The family used this plot until the middle of the last century," Kim explained.

Slowly they walked back through the overgrown graveyard. The farther they went the more simple the headstones became and the older they got.

"Is Ronald Stewart in here?" Edward asked.

"He is," Kim said. She led him over to a simple round headstone with a skull and crossed bones done in low relief. On it was written: *Here lyes buried y body of Ronald Stewart y son of John and Lydia Stewart, aged 81 years Dec'd. oct. y 1, 1734.*

"Eighty-one," Edward remarked. "Healthy guy. To reach such a ripe old age he must have been smart enough to stay away from doctors. In those days with all the reliance on bloodletting and a primitive pharmacopoeia, doctors were as lethal as most of the illnesses."

Next to Ronald's grave was Rebecca Stewart's. Her stone described her as Ronald's wife.

"I guess he got remarried," Kim said.

"Is Elizabeth buried in here?" Edward asked.

"I don't know," Kim said. "No one ever pointed out her grave to me."

"Are you sure this Elizabeth even existed?" Edward asked.

"I think so," Kim said. "But I can't swear to it."

"Let's see if we can find her," Edward suggested. "She'd have to be in this general area."

For a few minutes they searched in silence, Kim going one way, Edward another.

"Edward!" Kim called.

"Did you find her?" Edward asked.

"Well, sort of," Kim said.

Edward joined her. She was looking at a headstone similar in design to Ronald's. It belonged to Jonathan Stewart, who was described as the son of Ronald and Elizabeth Stewart.

"At least we know she existed," Kim said.

They searched for another half hour but didn't find Elizabeth's grave. Finally they gave up and went back to the car. A few minutes later they pulled up in front of the old house. They both got out.

"You weren't kidding when you said it looked like the Witch House," Edward said. "It's got the same massive central chimney, the same steeply pitched gable roof, the same clapboard siding, and the same diamond-shaped panes of glass. And most curious, there is the same protrusion of the second story over the first. I wonder why they did that."

"I don't think anyone knows for certain," Kim said. "The Ward House at the Peabody-Essex Institute has the same feature."

"The pendants under the overhang are much more decorative than those at the Witch House," Edward said.

"Whoever turned those had quite a flair," Kim agreed.

"It's a charming house," Edward said. "It has so much more class than the castle."

Slowly they strolled around the aged building, pointing out its details. In the back Edward noticed a freestanding, smaller structure. He asked if it were equally as old.

"I believe so," Kim said. "I was told it was for the animals."

"A mini-barn," Edward said.

Returning to the front door, Kim had to try multiple keys before she found one that unlocked the door. As she pushed it open it creaked just like the outer gate to the compound.

"Sounds like a haunted house," Edward said.

"Don't say that," Kim protested.

"Don't tell me you believe in ghosts?" Edward said.

"Let's just say I respect them," Kim said with a laugh. "So you go first."

Edward stepped through the door into a small front hall. Directly ahead was a flight of stairs that twisted up out of sight. On either side were doors. The door on the right led into the kitchen, the one on the left to the parlor.

"Where to first?" Edward asked.

"You're the guest," Kim said.

"Let's check out the parlor," Edward said.

The room was dominated by a huge fireplace six feet wide. Sprinkled about the room was some colonial furniture as well as lawn tools and other paraphernalia. The most interesting piece of furniture was a canopied bed. It still had some of its original crewelwork bed hangings.

Edward walked over to the fireplace and glanced up the flue. "Still in working order," he said. Then he looked at the wall above the mantel. Stepping back, he looked at it again.

"Can you see that faint rectangle?" he said.

Kim joined him in the middle of the room and peered at the wall. "I see it," she said. "Looks like a painting used to hang there."

"My thought exactly," Edward said. Wetting the tip of his finger, he tried to smudge the outline. He couldn't. "It must have hung there a good many years for the smoke to outline it like that."

Leaving the parlor, they mounted the stairs. At the head of the stairs was a small study built over the front hall. Above the parlor and the kitchen were bedrooms, each with its own fireplace. The only furniture was a few more beds and a spinning wheel.

Returning to the kitchen on the first floor, Kim and Edward were both struck with the size of the fireplace. Edward guessed it was almost ten feet across. To the left was a lug pole, to the right a beehive oven. There were even some old pots, fry pans, and kettles.

"Can you imagine cooking here?" Edward asked.

"Not in a million years," Kim said. "I have enough trouble in a modern kitchen."

"The colonial women must have been experts at tending a fire," Edward said. He peered into the oven. "I wonder how they estimated the temperature. It's fairly critical in bread making."

They passed through a door into the lean-to part of the house. Edward was surprised to find a second kitchen.

"I think they used this during the summer," Kim said. "It would have been too hot to fire up that massive fireplace for cooking during warm weather."

"Good point," Edward said.

Returning to the main part of the house, Edward stood in the center of the kitchen, chewing on his lower lip. Kim eyed him. She could tell he was thinking about something.

"What's going through your mind?" she asked.

"Have you ever thought about living here?" he questioned.

"No, I can't say I have," Kim said. "It would be like camping out."

"I don't mean to live here the way it is," Edward said. "But it wouldn't take much to change it."

"You mean renovate it?" Kim questioned. "It would be a shame to destroy its historical value."

"I couldn't agree more," Edward said. "But you wouldn't have to. You could make a modern kitchen and bath in the lean-to portion of the house, which was an add-on anyway. You wouldn't have to disturb the integrity of the main part."

"You really think so?" Kim said. She looked around. There was no doubt it was a charming building, and it would be a fun challenge to decorate it.

"Besides," Edward said, "you've got to move out of your present apartment. It's a shame to leave this whole place vacant. Sooner or later the vandals will get in here and possibly do some real damage.''

Kim and Edward made another walk through the building with the idea in mind of making it habitable. Edward was progressively enthusiastic, and Kim found herself warming to the idea.

''What an opportunity to connect with your heritage,'' Edward said. ''I'd do it in a flash.''

''I'll sleep on it,'' Kim said finally. ''It is an intriguing idea, but I'd have to run it by my brother. After all, we are co-owners.''

''There's one thing about this place that confuses me,'' Edward said as he glanced around the kitchen for the third time. ''I wonder where they stored their food.''

''I imagine in the cellar,'' Kim said.

''I didn't think there was one,'' Edward said. ''I specifically looked for an entrance when we walked around the house when we first arrived, but there wasn't any. Nor are there any stairs leading down.''

Kim stepped around the long trestle table and pulled aside a heavily worn sisal mat. ''There's access through this trapdoor,'' she said. She bent down and put her finger through a hole in the floor and pulled the trapdoor open. She laid it back on the floor. A ladder led down into the darkness.

''I remember this all too well,'' Kim said. ''Once, when we were kids, my brother threatened to close me in the cellar. He'd been enchanted with the trapdoor.''

''Nice brother,'' Edward said. ''No wonder you had a fear of being cooped up. That would have terrified anyone.''

Edward bent down and tried to look around the cellar, but he could only see a small area.

''He had no intention of actually doing it,'' Kim said. ''He was just teasing. We weren't supposed to be in here at the time, and he knew I was already scared. You know how kids like to scare each other.''

''I've got a flashlight in the car,'' Edward said. ''I'll run out and get it.''

Returning with the light, Edward descended the ladder.

Gaining the floor, he looked up at Kim and asked her if she was coming down.

"Do I have to?" she questioned half in jest. She came down the ladder and stood next to him.

"Cold, damp, and musty," Edward said.

"Well said," Kim remarked. "So what are we doing here?"

The cellar was small. It only comprised the area beneath the kitchen. The walls were flat fieldstone with little mortar. The floor was dirt. Against the back wall was a series of bins made with stone or wood sides. Edward walked over and shined the light in several of them. Kim stayed close at his side.

"You were right," Edward said. "Here's where the food was kept."

"What kind of food, do you suppose?" Kim asked.

"Stuff like apples, corn, wheat, and rye," Edward said. "Maybe dairy products as well. The flitches of bacon were hung up, most likely in the lean-to."

"Interesting," Kim said without enthusiasm. "Have you seen enough?"

Edward leaned into one of the bins and scratched up some of the hard-packed dirt. He felt it between his fingers. "The dirt is damp," he said. "I'm certainly no botanist, but I'd wager it would be great for growing *Claviceps purpurea.*"

Intrigued, Kim asked if it could be proven.

Edward shrugged. "Possibly," he said. "I suppose it would depend on whether *Claviceps* spores could be found. If we could take some samples I could have a botanist friend take a look at it."

"I imagine we could find some containers in the castle," Kim suggested.

"Let's do it," Edward said.

Leaving the old house, they headed for the castle. Since it was such a beautiful day they walked. The grass was knee-high. Grasshoppers and other harmless insects flitted about them.

"Every so often I can see water through the trees," Edward commented.

"That's the Danvers River," Kim said. "There was a time when the field went all the way to the water's edge."

The closer they got to the castle the more awed Edward became with the building. "This place is even bigger than I had originally thought," he said. "My word, it even has a fake moat."

"I was told it was inspired by Chambord in France," Kim said. "It's shaped like the letter $U$, with guest quarters in one wing and servants' in the other."

They crossed a bridge over the dry moat. While Edward admired the gothic details of the doorway, Kim struggled with the keys just as she'd done at the old house. There were a dozen keys on the ring. Finally one opened the door.

They passed through an oak-paneled entry hall and then through an arch leading into the great room. It was a room of monumental size with a two-story ceiling and gothic fireplaces at either end. Between cathedral-sized windows on the far wall rose a grand staircase. A stained-glass rose window at the head of the stairs filled the room with a peculiar pale yellow light.

Edward let out a half-groan half-laugh. "This is incredible," he said in awe. "I had no idea it was still furnished."

"Nothing has been touched," Kim said.

"When did your grandfather die?" Edward asked. "This decor looks as if someone left on extended vacation in the nineteen twenties."

"He died just this past spring," Kim said. "But he was an eccentric man, especially after his wife died almost forty years ago. I doubt if he changed anything in the house from when his parents occupied it. It was his father who built it."

Edward wandered into the room while his eyes played over the profusion of furniture, gilt-framed paintings, and decorative objects. There was even a suit of medieval armor. Pointing to it, he asked if it were a real antique.

Kim shrugged. "I haven't the slightest idea," she said.

Edward walked to a window and fingered the curtain fabric. "I've never seen so much drapery in all my life," he said. "There must be a mile of this stuff."

"It's very old," Kim said. "It's silk damask."

"Can I see more of the house?" Edward asked.

"Be my guest," Kim said with a wave.

From the great room, Edward wandered into the darkly paneled library. It had a mezzanine accessed by a wrought-iron circular stair. The high shelves were served by a ladder that moved on a track. The books were all leather bound. "This is my idea of a library," Edward said. "I could do some serious reading here."

From the library Edward walked into the formal dining room. Like the great room, it had a two-story ceiling with matching fireplaces at either end. But unlike the great room, it had a profusion of heraldic flags on flagpoles jutting out from the walls.

"This place could have almost as much historical interest as the old house," Edward said. "It's like a museum."

"The historical interest is in the wine cellar and the attic," Kim said. "Both are completely full of papers."

"Newspapers?" Edward asked.

"Some newspapers," Kim said. "But mostly correspondence and documents."

"Let's take a look," Edward said.

They mounted the main stairs to the equivalent of the third floor since most of the first-floor rooms had two-story ceilings. From there they climbed another staircase two additional floors before reaching the attic. Kim had to struggle to get the door open. It hadn't been pried in years.

The attic space was enormous since it occupied all of the U-shaped floor plan of the house except for the area of the turrets. Each turret was a story taller than the rest of the building and had its own conical-shaped attic. The main attic had a cathedral ceiling in accordance with the roofline. It was reasonably well lighted from its many dormers.

Kim and Edward strolled down a central aisle. On both sides were innumerable file cabinets, bureaus, trunks, and boxes. Kim stopped randomly and showed Edward that all of them were filled with ledgers, scrapbooks, folders, documents, correspondence, photos, books, newspapers, and old magazines. It was a virtual treasure trove of documentary memorabilia.

"There must be enough stuff in here to fill several railroad cars," Edward said. "How far back in time does it all go?"

"Right back to Ronald Stewart's time," Kim said. "He's the one who started the company. Most of it is business-related material, but not all of it. There's some personal correspondence as well. My brother and I used to sneak up here a few times when we were kids to see who could find the oldest dates. The problem was that we weren't really allowed, and when my grandfather caught us he was furious."

"Is there as much down in the wine cellar?" Edward asked.

"As much or more," Kim said. "Come, I'll show you. The wine cellar is worth seeing anyway. Its decor is consistent with the house."

They retraced their steps down the main stairways and returned to the formal dining room. Opening a heavy oak door with huge wrought-iron hinges, they descended a granite stairway into the wine cellar. Edward understood immediately what Kim meant about its decor being consistent with the house. It was designed as if it were a medieval dungeon. The walls were all stone, the sconce lighting resembled torches, and the wine racks were built around the walls of individual rooms that could have functioned as cells. They had iron doors and bars over the openings into the hall.

"Somebody had a sense of humor," Edward said as they walked down the long central hall. "The only thing this place lacks is torture devices."

"My brother and I didn't see it as funny in the slightest," Kim said. "My grandfather didn't have to tell us to stay out of here. We didn't want any part of it. It terrified us."

"And all these trunks and things are filled with papers?" Edward asked. "Just like the attic?"

"Every last one of them," Kim said.

Edward stopped and pushed open the door to one of the cell-like rooms. He stepped inside. The wine racks were mostly empty. The bureaus, file cabinets, and trunks were pushed against them. He picked up one of the few bottles.

"Good Lord," he said. "This is an 1896 vintage! It could be valuable."

Kim blew derisively through pursed lips. "I sincerely doubt it," she said. "The cork is probably disintegrated. No one has been taking care of them for half a century."

Edward replaced the dusty bottle and opened a bureau drawer. Randomly he picked up a sheet of paper. It was a customs document from the nineteenth century. He tried another. It was a bill of lading from the eighteenth century.

"I get the impression there isn't much order here," he said.

"Unfortunately that's the case," Kim said. "In fact there is no order whatsoever to any of it. Every time a new house was built, which had been fairly frequent up until this monstrosity, all this paperwork was relocated and then returned. Over the centuries it got completely mixed up."

In order to make her point, Kim opened a file cabinet and pulled out a document. It was another bill of lading. She handed it over to Edward and told him to look at the date.

"Well, I'll be damned," he said. "Sixteen hundred and eighty-nine. That was just three years before all the witchcraft nonsense."

"It proves my point," Kim said. "We just looked at three documents and covered several centuries."

"I think this signature is Ronald's," Edward said. He showed it to Kim and she agreed.

"I just got an idea," Kim said. "You've got me interested in this witchcraft phenomenon and particularly in my ancestor Elizabeth. Maybe I could learn something about her with the help of all these papers."

"You mean like why she's not buried in the family burial plot?" Edward asked.

"That and more," Kim said. "I'm getting more and more curious about all the secrecy about her over the years. And even whether she truly was executed. As you pointed out, she's not mentioned in the book you gave me. It's pretty mysterious."

Edward gazed around the cell they were in. "It wouldn't be an easy task considering the amount of material," he said. "And ultimately it might be a waste of time since most of this is business related."

"It will be a challenge," Kim said as she warmed to the idea. She looked back in the file drawer where she'd found the seventeenth-century bill of lading to see if there were any more contemporary material. "I think I might even enjoy it. It will be an exercise in self-discovery, or, as you said in relation to the old house, an opportunity to connect with my heritage."

While Kim was rummaging in the file cabinet, Edward wandered out of the cell and deeper into the extensive wine cellar. He was still carrying the flashlight, and as he neared the back of the wine cellar he switched it on. Some of the bulbs in the sconces had blown out. Poking his head into the last cell, Edward shined the flashlight around. Its beam played across the usual complement of bureaus, trunks, and boxes until it stopped on an oil painting leaning backwards against the wall.

Remembering all the paintings he'd seen upstairs, Edward was curious as to why this one deserved such ill treatment. With some difficulty he managed to work his way over to the painting. He leaned it away from the wall and shined the light on its dusty surface. It appeared to be a painting of a young woman.

Lifting the painting from its ignominious location, Edward held it over his head and carried it out of the cell. Once in the hallway, he leaned it against the wall. It was indeed a young woman. The décolletage it displayed belied its age. It was done in a stiff, primitive style.

With the tip of his finger he wiped the dust from a small pewter plaque at the base of the painting and shined the light on it. Then he grabbed the painting and brought it to the cell where Kim was still occupied.

"Take a look at this," Edward said. He propped it against a bureau and illuminated the plaque with the flashlight.

Kim turned and looked at the painting. Sensing Edward's excitement, she followed the beam of the flashlight and read the name.

"Good heavens!" she exclaimed. "It's Elizabeth!"

Enjoying the thrill of discovery, Kim and Edward carried the painting up the stairs and into the great room, where there was adequate light. They leaned it up against the wall and stepped away to look at it.

"What's so damn striking about it," Edward said, "is that it looks a lot like you, especially with those green eyes."

"Maybe eye color is the same," Kim said, "but Elizabeth was far more beautiful, and certainly more endowed than I."

"Beauty is in the eye of the beholder," Edward said. "Personally I think it is the other way around."

Kim was transfixed by the visage of her infamous ancestor. "There are some similarities," she said. "Our hair looks similar and even the shape of our faces."

"You could be sisters," Edward agreed. "It certainly is an attractive painting. Why the devil was it hidden away in the very back of the wine cellar? It's far more pleasing than most of the paintings hanging in this house."

"It's weird," Kim said. "My grandfather must have known about it, so it's not as if it were an oversight. As eccentric as he was, it couldn't have been that he was concerned with other people's feelings, especially not my mother's. He and my mother never got along."

"The size looks pretty close to that shadow we noticed above the mantel in the old house," Edward said. "Just for fun, why don't we carry it down there and see."

Edward lifted the painting, but before he could take a step, Kim reminded him about the containers they'd come to the castle to find. Edward thanked her and put the painting back down. Together they went into the kitchen. Kim found three plastic containers with lids in the butler's pantry.

Retrieving the painting from the great room, they started for the old house. Kim insisted on carrying the art work. With its narrow black frame, it wasn't heavy.

"I have a strange but good feeling about finding this painting," Kim said as they walked. "It's like finding a long-lost relative."

"I have to admit it is quite a coincidence," Edward said.

"Especially since she's the reason why we happen to be here."

Suddenly Kim stopped. She was holding the painting in front of her, staring at Elizabeth's face.

"What's the matter?" Edward asked.

"While I've been thinking she and I look alike, I just remembered what supposedly happened to her," Kim said. "Today it's inconceivable to imagine someone being accused of witchcraft, tried, and then executed."

In her mind's eye Kim could see herself facing a noose hanging from a tree. She was about to die. She shuddered. Then she jumped when she felt the rope touch her.

"Are you all right?" Edward asked. He'd put his hand on her shoulder.

Kim shook her head and took a deep breath. "I just had an awful thought," she admitted. "I just imagined what it would be like if I were sentenced to be hanged."

"You carry the containers," Edward said. "Let me carry the painting."

They exchanged their loads and started walking again.

"It must be the heat," Edward said to lighten the atmosphere. "Or maybe you're getting hungry. Your imagination is working overtime."

"Finding this painting has really affected me," Kim admitted. "It's as if Elizabeth were trying to speak to me over the centuries, perhaps to restore her reputation."

Edward eyed Kim as they trudged through the tall grass. "Are you joking?" he asked.

"No," Kim said. "You said it was quite a coincidence we found this painting. I think it was more than a coincidence. I mean, when you think about it, it is astonishing. It can't be purely by chance. It has to mean something."

"Is this a sudden rush of superstition or are you always like this?" Edward asked.

"I don't know," Kim said. "I'm just trying to understand."

"Do you believe in ESP or channeling?" Edward asked.

"I've never thought much about it," Kim admitted. "Do you?"

Edward laughed. "You sound like a psychiatrist, turning

the question back to me. Well, I don't believe in the supernatural. I'm a scientist. I believe in what can be rationally proved and reproduced experimentally. I'm not a religious person. Nor am I superstitious, and you'll probably think I'm being cynical if I say the two are related.''

"I'm not terribly religious either," Kim said. "But I do have some vague beliefs regarding supernatural forces."

They reached the old house. Kim held the door open for Edward. He carried the painting into the parlor. When he held it up to the shadow over the mantel, it fit perfectly.

"At least we were right about where this painting used to hang," Edward said. He left the painting on the mantel.

"And I'll see to it that it hangs there again," Kim said. "Elizabeth deserves to be returned to her house."

"Does that mean you've decided to fix this place up?"

"Maybe so," Kim said. "But first I'll have to talk with my family, particularly my brother."

"Personally, I think it's a great idea," Edward said. He took the plastic containers from Kim and told her he was going to the cellar to get some dirt samples. At the parlor door he stopped.

"If I find *Claviceps purpurea* down there," he said with a wry smile, "I know one thing that information will do: it will rob a bit of the supernatural out of the story of the Salem witchcraft trials."

Kim didn't respond. She was mesmerized by Elizabeth's portrait and lost in thought. Edward shrugged. Then he went into the kitchen and climbed down into the cool, damp darkness of the cellar.

# 3

## Monday,
## July 18, 1994

As usual Edward Armstrong's lab at the Harvard Medical Complex on Longfellow Avenue was the scene of frenzied activity. There was the appearance of bedlam with white-coated people scurrying every which way among a futuristic array of high-technology equipment. But the sense of disorder was only for the uninitiated. For the informed it was a known fact that high science was in continual progress.

Ultimately it all depended on Edward, although he was not the only scientist who was working in the string of rooms affectionately referred to as Armstrong's Fiefdom. Because of his notoriety as a genius, his celebrity as a synthetic chemist, and his prominence as a neuroscientist, applications for staff, doctorate, and postdoctorate positions greatly outnumbered the positions that Edward had been able to carve out of his chronically limited space, budget, and schedule. Consequently, Edward got the best and the brightest staff and students.

Other professors called Edward a glutton for punishment. Not only did he have the largest cadre of graduate students: he insisted on teaching an undergraduate basic chemistry course, even during the summer. He was the only full professor who did so. As he explained it, he felt an obligation to stimulate the young minds of the day at the earliest time possible.

Striding back from having delivered one of his famous undergraduate lectures, Edward entered his domain through one of the lab's side doors. Like an animal feeder at a zoo he was immediately mobbed by his graduate students. They were all working on separate aspects of Edward's overall goal of elucidating the mechanisms of short- and long-term memory. Each had a problem or a question that Edward answered in staccato fashion, sending them back to their benches to continue their research efforts.

With the last question answered, Edward strode over to his desk. He didn't have a private office, a concept he disdained as a frivolous waste of needed space. He was content with a corner containing a work surface, a few chairs, a computer terminal, and a file cabinet. He was accompanied by his closest assistant, Eleanor Youngman, a postdoc who'd been with him for four years.

"You have a visitor," Eleanor said as they arrived at Edward's desk. "He's waiting at the departmental secretary's desk."

Edward dumped his class materials and exchanged his tweed jacket for a white lab coat. "I don't have time for visitors," he said.

"I'm afraid this one you have to see," Eleanor said.

Edward glanced at his assistant. She was sporting one of those smiles that suggested she was about to burst out laughing. Eleanor was a spirited, bright blonde from Oxnard, California, who looked like she belonged with the surfing set. Instead she had earned her Ph.D. in biochemistry from Berkeley by the tender age of twenty-three. Edward found her invaluable, not only because of her intelligence, but also because of her commitment. She worshiped Edward, convinced he would make the next quantum leap in understanding neurotransmitters and their role in emotion and memory.

"Who in heaven's name is it?" Edward asked.

"It's Stanton Lewis," Eleanor said. "He cracks me up every time he comes in here. This time he told me he wants me to invest in a new chemistry magazine to be called *Bonding* with a foldout Molecule of the Month. I never know when he's serious."

"He's not serious," Edward said. "He's flirting with you."

Edward quickly glanced through his mail. There was

nothing earth-shattering. "Any problems in the lab?" he asked Eleanor.

"I'm afraid so," she said. "The new capillary electrophoresis system which we've been using for micellar electrokinetic capillary chromatography is being temperamental again. Should I call the rep from Bio-rad?"

"I'll take a look at it," he said. "Send Stanton over. I'll take care of both problems at the same time."

Edward attached his radiation dosimeter to the lapel of his coat and wound his way over to the chromatography unit. He began fiddling with the computer that ran the machine. Something definitely wasn't right. The machine kept defaulting to its original setup menu.

Absorbed in what he was doing, Edward didn't hear Stanton approach. He was unaware of his presence until Stanton slapped him on the back.

"Hey, sport!" Stanton said, "I've got a surprise for you that's going to make your day." He handed Edward a slick, plastic-covered brochure.

"What's this?" Edward asked as he took the booklet.

"It's what you've been waiting for: the Genetrix prospectus," Stanton said.

Edward let out a chuckle and shook his head. "You're too much," he said. He put the prospectus aside and redirected his attention to the chromatography unit computer.

"How'd your date with nurse Kim go?" Stanton asked.

"I enjoyed meeting your cousin," Edward said. "She's a terrific woman."

"Did you guys sleep together?" Stanton asked.

Edward spun around. "That's hardly an appropriate question."

"My goodness," Stanton said with a big smile. "Rather touchy I'd say. Translated that means you guys hit it off, otherwise you wouldn't be so sensitive."

"I think you are jumping to conclusions," Edward said with a stutter.

"Oh, come off it," Stanton said. "I know you too well. It's the same way you were in medical school. Anything to do with the lab or science, you're like Napoleon. When it comes to women you're like wet spaghetti. I don't understand it. But anyway, come clean. You guys hit it off, didn't you?''

"We enjoyed each other's company," Edward admitted. "In fact, we had dinner Friday night.''

"Perfect," Stanton said. "As far as I'm concerned that's as good as sleeping together.''

"Don't be so crass.''

"Truly," Stanton said cheerfully. "The idea was to get you beholden to me and now you are. The price, my dear friend, is that you have to read this prospectus." Stanton lifted the brochure from where Edward had irreverently tossed it. He handed it back to Edward.

Edward groaned. He realized he'd given himself away. "All right," he said. "I'll read the blasted thing.''

"Good," Stanton said. "You should know something about the company because I'm also in a position to offer you seventy-five thousand dollars a year plus stock options to be on the scientific advisory board.''

"I don't have time to go to any damn meetings," Edward said.

"Who's asking you to come to any meetings," Stanton said. "I just want your name on the IPO offering.''

"But why?" Edward asked. "Molecular biology and biotech are not my bailiwick.''

"Chrissake!" Stanton said. "How can you be so innocent? You're a scientific celebrity. It doesn't matter you know dit about molecular biology. It's your name that counts.''

"I wouldn't say I know dit about molecular biology," Edward said irritably.

"Now don't get touchy with me," Stanton said. Then he pointed to the machine Edward was working on. "What the hell is that?''

"It's a capillary electrophoresis unit," Edward said.

"What the hell does it do?''

"It's a relatively new separation technology," Edward said. "It's used to separate and identify compounds.''

Stanton fingered the molded plastic of the central unit. "What makes it new?''

"It's not entirely new," Edward said. "The principles

are basically the same as conventional electrophoresis, but the narrow diameter of the capillaries precludes the necessity of an anticonvection agent because heat dissipation is so efficient.''

Stanton raised his hand in mock self-defense. "Enough," he said. "I give up. You've overwhelmed me. Just tell me if it works.''

"It works great," Edward said. He looked back at the machine. "At least it usually works great. At the moment something is wrong.''

"Is it plugged in?" Stanton asked.

Edward shot him an exasperated look.

"Just trying to be helpful," Stanton joked.

Edward raised the top of the machine and peered in at the carousels. Immediately he saw that one of the capped sample vials was blocking the carousel's movement. "Well, isn't this pleasant," he said. "The thrill of the positive diagnosis of a remedial problem." He adjusted the vial. The carousel immediately advanced. Edward closed the lid.

"So I can count on you to read the prospectus," Stanton said. "And think about the offer.''

"The idea of getting money for nothing bothers me," Edward said.

"But why?" Stanton said. "If star athletes can sign on with sneaker companies, why can't scientists do the equivalent?''

"I'll think about it," Edward said.

"That's all I can ask," Stanton said. "Give me a call after you read the prospectus. I'm telling you, I can make you some money.''

"Did you drive over here?" Edward asked.

"No, I walked from Concord," Stanton said. "Of course I drove. What a feeble attempt at changing the subject.''

"How about giving me a lift over to the main Harvard campus," Edward said.

Five minutes later Edward slid into the passenger seat of Stanton's 500 SEL Mercedes. Stanton started the engine and made a quick U turn. He'd parked on Huntington Avenue near the Countway Medical Library. They traveled around the Fenway and then along Storrow Drive.

"Let me ask you something," Edward said after a period of silence. "The other night at dinner you made reference to Kim's ancestor, Elizabeth Stewart. Do you know for a fact that she'd been hanged as a witch, or is the story a family rumor that has been around so long that people have come to believe it?"

"I can't swear to it," Stanton said. "I've just accepted what I'd heard."

"I can't find her name in any of the standard treatises on the subject," Edward said. "And there is no dearth of them."

"I heard the story from my aunt," Stanton said. "According to her the Stewarts have been keeping it a secret since time immemorial. So it's not as if it's something they've dreamed up to enhance their reputation."

"All right, let's assume it happened," Edward said. "Why the devil would it matter now? It's so long ago. I mean I could understand for a generation or so, but not three hundred years."

Stanton shrugged. "Beats me," he said. "But I probably shouldn't have mentioned it. My aunt will have my head if she hears I've been bantering it about."

"Even Kim was reluctant to talk about it at first," Edward said.

"That's probably because of her mother, my aunt," Stanton said. "She's always been a stickler for reputation and all that social garbage. She's a very proper lady."

"Kim took me out and showed me the family compound," Edward said. "We even went inside the house where Elizabeth was supposed to have lived."

Stanton glanced at Edward. He shook his head in admiration. "Wow!" he said. "You work fast, you tiger."

"It was all very innocent," Edward said. "Don't let your gutter imagination carry you away. I found it fascinating, and it has awakened Kim's interest in Elizabeth."

"I'm not sure her mother is going to like that," Stanton said.

"I might be able to help the family's response to the

affair," Edward said. He opened a bag he had on his lap and lifted out one of the plastic containers he and Kim had brought back from Salem. He explained to Stanton what it contained.

"You must really be in love," Stanton said. "Otherwise you wouldn't be taking all this time and trouble."

"My idea is that if I can prove that ergotism was at the heart of the Salem witch craze," Edward said, "it would remove any possible remaining stigma people felt who were associated with the ordeal, particularly the Stewarts."

"I still contend you must be in love," Stanton said. "That's too theoretical a justification for all this effort. I can't get you to do squat for me even with the promise of lucre."

Edward sighed. "All right," he said. "I suppose I have to admit that as a neuroscientist I'm intrigued by the possibility of a hallucinogen causing the Salem affair."

"Now I can understand," Stanton said. "The Salem witchcraft story has a universal appeal. You don't have to be a neuroscientist."

"The entrepreneur as a philosopher," Edward remarked with a laugh. "Five minutes ago I would have considered that an oxymoron. Explain to me the universal appeal."

"The affair is ghoulishly seductive," Stanton said. "People like that sort of stuff. It's like the pyramids of Egypt. There has to be more to them than mere piles of stone. They are a window on the supernatural."

"I'm not sure I agree," Edward said as he put away his dirt sample. "As a scientist I'm merely searching for a scientific explanation."

"Oh, bull," Stanton said.

Stanton dropped Edward off on Divinity Avenue in Cambridge. Just before Edward closed the door he reminded him once more about the Genetrix prospectus.

Edward skirted Divinity Hall and entered the Harvard biological labs. From a departmental secretary he got directions to Kevin Scranton's lab. He found his thin, bearded friend busy in his office. Kevin and Edward had gone to Wesleyan together but hadn't seen each other since Edward had returned to Harvard to teach.

They spent the first ten minutes rehashing old times before Edward got down to the reason for his visit. He put the three containers on the corner of Kevin's desk.

"I want you to see if you can find *Claviceps purpurea*," Edward said.

Kevin picked up one of the containers and opened the lid. "Can you tell me why?" he asked. He fingered a small amount of the dirt.

"You'd never guess," Edward said. He then told Kevin how he'd obtained the samples and the background concerning the Salem witch trials. He didn't mention the Stewart family name, thinking he owed as much to Kim.

"Sounds intriguing," Kevin said when Edward finished his story. Kevin stood up and proceeded to make a wet mount of a small sample of the dirt.

"I thought it could make a cute little paper for *Science* or *Nature*," Edward said. "Provided we find spores from *Claviceps*."

Kevin slipped the wet mount under his office microscope and began scanning the sample. "Well, there are plenty of spores in here, but of course that's not unusual."

"How's the best way to see if they're *Claviceps* or not?" Edward asked.

"There are several ways," Kevin said. "How soon do you want an answer?"

"As soon as possible," Edward said.

"DNA would take some time," Kevin said. "There are probably three to five thousand different fungal species in each sample. Besides, the most definitive method would be if we can grow some *Claviceps*. The problem is, it's not that easy. But I'll give it a shot."

Edward stood up. "I'd appreciate whatever you can do."

Taking a minute to collect herself, Kim raised her gloved hand so that her bare forearm could push her hair off her forehead. It had been a typically busy day in the surgical intensive-care unit, rewarding yet intense. She was exhausted and looking forward to getting off in another twenty minutes. Unfortunately her moment of relaxation was interrupted. Kinnard Monihan came into the unit with a sick patient.

Kim as well as the other nurses who were momentarily free lent a hand getting the new admission settled. Kinnard helped as did an anesthesiologist who'd come in with him. While they worked, Kim and Kinnard avoided eye contact. But Kim was acutely aware of his presence, especially when their efforts on the patient's behalf brought them side by side. Kinnard was a tall, wiry man of twenty-eight with sharply angular features. He was light on his feet and agile, more like a boxer in training than a doctor in the middle of a surgical residency.

With the patient settled, Kim headed for the central desk. She felt a hand on her arm, and she turned to look up into Kinnard's dark, intense eyes.

"You're not still angry?" Kinnard asked. He had no trouble bringing up sensitive issues right in the middle of the intensive-care unit.

Feeling a wave of anxiety, Kim looked away. Her mind was a muddle of conflicted emotion.

"Don't tell me you're not even going to talk to me," Kinnard said. "Aren't you carrying your hurt feelings a bit too far?"

"I warned you," Kim began when she found her voice. "I told you that things would be different if you insisted on going on your fly-fishing trip when we'd planned to go to Martha's Vineyard."

"We never made definite plans for the Vineyard," Kinnard said. "And I hadn't anticipated Dr. Markey offering to include me on the camping trip."

"If we hadn't made plans," Kim said, "how come I had arranged to have the time off? And how come I'd called my family's friends and arranged to stay in their bungalow?"

"We'd only mentioned it once," Kinnard said.

"Twice," Kim said. "And the second time I told you about the bungalow."

"Listen," Kinnard said. "It was important for me to go on the camping trip. Dr. Markey is the number-two man in the department. Maybe you and I had a little miscommunication, but it shouldn't cause all this angst.''

"What makes it even worse is that you don't feel contrite in the slightest," Kim said. Her face reddened.

"I'm not going to apologize when I don't think I did anything wrong," Kinnard said.

"Fine," Kim said. She started for the central desk again. Kinnard again restrained her.

"I'm sorry you are upset," Kinnard said. "I really thought you'd have calmed down by now. Let's talk about it more on Saturday night. I'm not on call. Maybe we could have dinner and see a show."

"I'm sorry, but I already have plans," Kim said. It was untrue, and she felt her stomach tighten. She hated confrontations and knew she wasn't good at them. Any type of discord affected her viscerally.

Kinnard's mouth dropped open. "Oh, I see," he said. His eyes narrowed.

Kim swallowed. She could tell he was angry.

"This is a game that two can play," he said. "There's someone I've been thinking about dating. This is my opportunity."

"Who?" Kim asked. The second the question came out of her mouth she regretted it.

Kinnard gave her a malicious smile and walked off.

Concerned about losing her composure, Kim retreated to the privacy of the storeroom. She was shaking. After a few deep breaths she felt more in control and ready to get back to work. She was about to return to the unit when the door opened and Marsha Kingsley, her roommate, walked in.

"I happened to overhear that encounter," Marsha said. She was a petite, spirited woman with a mane of auburn hair which she wore in a bun while working in the surgical intensive-care unit. Not only were Kim and Marsha roommates, they were also SICU colleagues.

"He's an ass," Marsha said. She knew the history of Kim's relationship with Kinnard better than anyone. "Don't let that egotist get your goat."

Marsha's sudden appearance disarmed Kim's control over her tears. "I hate confrontations," Kim said.

"I think you handled yourself exemplarily," Marsha said. She handed Kim a tissue.

"He wouldn't even apologize," Kim said. She wiped her eyes.

"He's an insensitive bum," Marsha said supportively.

"I don't know what I did wrong," Kim said. "Up until recently I thought we'd had a good relationship."

"You didn't do anything wrong," Marsha said. "It's his problem. He's too selfish. Look at the comparison between his behavior and Edward's. Edward's been sending you flowers every day."

"I don't need flowers every day," Kim said.

"Of course not," Marsha said. "It's the thought that counts. Kinnard doesn't think of your feelings. You deserve better."

"Well, I don't know about that," Kim said. She blew her nose. "Yet one thing is for sure. I have to make some changes in my life. What I'm thinking of doing is to move up to Salem. I've got the idea to fix up an old house on the family compound I inherited with my brother."

"That's a great idea," Marsha said. "It will be good for you to have a change of scene, especially with Kinnard living on Beacon Hill."

"That was my thought," Kim said. "I'm heading up there right after work. How about coming along? I'd love the company, and maybe you'd have some good ideas about what to do with the place."

"Give me a rain check," Marsha said. "I've got to meet some people at the apartment."

After finishing work and giving a report, Kim left the hospital. She climbed into her car and drove out of town. There was a little traffic, but it moved quickly, particularly after she passed over the Tobin Bridge. Her first stop was her childhood home on Marblehead Neck.

"Anybody here?" Kim called out as she entered the foyer of the French château–style home. It was beautifully sited directly on the ocean. There were some superficial similarities between it and the castle, although it was far smaller and more tasteful.

"I'm in the sunroom, dear," Joyce answered from afar.

Skirting the main stairs, Kim walked down the long central corridor and out into the room in which her mother spent most of her time. It was indeed a sunroom with glass on three sides. It faced south overlooking the terraced lawn, but to the east it had a breathtaking vista over the ocean.

"You're still in your uniform," Joyce said. Her tone was deprecatory, as only a daughter could sense.

"I came directly from work," Kim said. "I wanted to avoid the traffic."

"Well, I hope you haven't brought any hospital germs with you," Joyce said. "That's all I need right now is to get sick again."

"I don't work in infectious disease," Kim said. "Where I work in the unit there's probably less bacteria than here."

"Don't say that," Joyce snapped.

The two women didn't look anything alike. Kim favored her father in terms of facial structure and hair. Joyce's face was narrow, her eyes deeply set, and her nose slightly aquiline. Her hair had once been brunette but was now mostly gray. She'd never colored it. Her skin was as pale as white marble despite the fact that it was almost midsummer.

"I notice you are still in your dressing gown," Kim said. She sat on a couch across from her mother's chaise.

"There was no reason for me to dress," Joyce said. "Besides, I haven't been feeling well."

"I suppose that means that Dad is not here," Kim said. Over the years she'd learned the pattern.

"Your father left last evening on a short business trip to London," Joyce said.

"I'm sorry," Kim said.

"It doesn't matter," Joyce said. "When he's here, he ignores me anyway. Did you want to see him?"

"I'd hoped to," Kim said.

"He'll be back Thursday," Joyce said. "If it suits him."

Kim recognized her mother's martyred tone of voice. "Did Grace Traters go along with him?" Kim asked. Grace Traters was Kim's father's personal assistant in a long line of personal assistants.

"Of course Grace went along," Joyce said angrily. "John can't tie his shoes without Grace."

"If it bothers you, why do you put up with it, Mother?" Kim asked.

"I have no choice in the matter," Joyce said.

Kim bit her tongue. She could feel herself getting upset. She felt sorry for her mother on the one hand for what she had to deal with and angry with her on the other for her playing the victim. Her father had always had affairs, some more open than others. It had been going on for as long as Kim could remember.

Changing the subject, Kim asked about Elizabeth Stewart.

Joyce's reading glasses dropped off the end of her nose where they had been precariously perched. They dangled against her bosom from a chain around her neck.

"What a strange question," Joyce said. "Why on earth are you inquiring about her?"

"I happened to stumble across her portrait in Granddad's wine cellar," Kim said. "It rather startled me, especially since I seem to have the same color eyes. Then I realized I knew very little about her. Was she really hanged for witchcraft?"

"I'd rather not talk about it," Joyce said.

"Oh, Mother, why on earth not?" Kim asked.

"It's simply a taboo subject," Joyce said.

"You should remind your nephew Stanton," Kim said. "He brought it up at a recent dinner party."

"I will indeed remind him," Joyce said. "That's inexcusable. He knows better."

"How can it be a taboo subject after so many years?" Kim asked.

"It's not something to be proud of," Joyce said. "It was a sordid affair."

"I did some reading about the Salem witch trials yesterday," Kim said. "There's a lot of material available. But Elizabeth Stewart is never mentioned. I'm beginning to wonder if she was involved."

"It's my understanding she was involved," Joyce said. "But let's leave it at that. How did you happen to come across her portrait?"

"I was in the castle," Kim said. "I went to the compound on Saturday. I have it in mind to fix up the old house and live in it.''

''Why in heaven's name would you want to do that?'' Joyce asked. ''It's so small.''

''It could be charming,'' Kim said. ''And it's larger than my current apartment. Besides, I want to get out of Boston.''

''I'd think it would be an enormous job to make it habitable,'' Joyce said.

''That's part of the reason I wanted to talk to Father,'' Kim said. ''Of course he's not around. I have to say, he has never been around when I needed him.''

''He wouldn't have any idea about such a project,'' Joyce said. ''You should talk to George Harris and Mark Stevens. They are the contractor and the architect who just finished the renovation in this house, and the project couldn't have gone any better. They work as a team, and their office is conveniently located in Salem.

''The other person you should talk to is your brother, Brian.''

''That goes without saying,'' Kim said.

''You call your brother from here,'' Joyce said. ''While you're doing that, I'll get the phone number of the contractor and the architect.''

Joyce climbed out of her chaise and disappeared. Kim smiled as she lifted the phone onto her lap. Her mother never ceased to amaze her. One minute she could be the epitome of self-absorbed immobility, the next a whirlwind of activity, totally involved in someone else's project. Intuitively Kim knew what the problem was: her mother didn't have enough to do. Unlike her friends she'd never gotten involved in volunteer activities.

Kim glanced at her watch as the call went through and tried to guess the time in London. Not that it mattered. Her brother was an insomniac who worked at night and slept in snatches during the day like a nocturnal creature.

Brian answered on the first ring. After they had exchanged hellos, Kim described her idea. Brian's response was overwhelmingly positive, and he encouraged her to go ahead with the plan. He thought it would be much better to have someone on the property. Brian's only question was about the castle and all its furnishings.

"I'm not going to touch that place," Kim said. "We'll attack that when you come back."

"Fair enough," Brian said.

"Where's Father?" Kim asked.

"John's at the Ritz," Brian said.

"And Grace?"

"Don't ask," Brian said. "They'll be back Thursday."

While Kim was saying goodbye to Brian, Joyce reappeared and wordlessly handed her a scrap of paper with a local phone number. As soon as Kim hung up from Brian, Joyce told her to dial the number.

Kim dialed. "Who should I ask for?" she said.

"Mark Stevens," Joyce said. "He's expecting your call. I phoned him on the other line while you were speaking with Brian."

Kim felt a mild resentment toward her mother's interference, but she didn't say anything. She knew Joyce was only trying to be helpful. Yet Kim could remember times when she was in middle school and had to fight to keep her mother from writing her school papers.

The conversation with Mark Stevens was short. Having learned from Joyce that Kim was in the area, he suggested they meet at the compound in half an hour. He said he'd have to see the property in order to advise her intelligently. Kim agreed to meet with him.

"If you decide to renovate that old house, at least you'll be in good hands," Joyce said after Kim had hung up.

Kim got to her feet. "I'd better be going," she said. Despite a conscious attempt to suppress it, Kim felt irritation returning toward her mother. It was the interference and lack of privacy that bothered her. She recalled her mother asking Stanton to fix her up after telling him Kim had broken off her relationship with Kinnard.

"I'll walk you out," Joyce said.

"There's no need, Mother," Kim said.

"I want to," Joyce said.

They started down the long hall.

"When you speak with your father about the old house,"

Joyce said, "I advise you not to bring up the issue about Elizabeth Stewart. It will only irritate him."

"Why would it irritate him?" Kim demanded.

"Don't get upset," Joyce said. "I'm just trying to keep peace in the family."

"But it is ridiculous," Kim snapped. "I don't understand."

"I only know that Elizabeth came from a poor farming family from Andover," Joyce said. "She wasn't even an official member of the church."

"As if that matters today," Kim said. "The irony is that within months of the affair there were public apologies from some of the jury members and justices because they realized innocent people had been executed. And here we are three hundred years later refusing to even talk about our ancestor. It doesn't make any sense. And why isn't her name in any of the books?"

"Obviously it's because the family didn't want it to be," Joyce said. "I don't think the family thought she was innocent. That's why it's an affair that should be left in the closet."

"I think it's a bunch of rubbish," Kim said.

Kim got into her car and drove off Marblehead Neck. When she got into Marblehead proper she had to force herself to slow down. Thanks to a vague sense of unease and vexation, she'd been driving much too fast. As she passed the Witch House in Salem, she put words to her thoughts, and admitted to herself that her curiosity about Elizabeth and the witch trials had gone up a notch despite her mother's warnings, or perhaps because of them.

When Kim pulled up to the family compound gate, a Ford Bronco was parked at the side of the road. As she got out of her car with the keys to the gate's padlock, two men climbed from the Bronco. One was stocky and muscular as if he worked out with weights on a daily basis. The other was borderline obese and seemed to be out of breath merely from the effort of getting out of the car.

The heavyset man introduced himself as Mark Stevens and the muscular man as George Harris. Kim shook hands with both of them.

Kim unlocked the gate and got back into her car. With her in the lead, they drove to the old house. They all climbed out of their vehicles in unison.

"This is fabulous," Mark said. He was mesmerized by the building.

"Do you like it?" Kim asked. She was pleased by his response.

"I love it," Mark said.

The first thing they did was walk around the house to examine the exterior. Kim explained the idea of putting a new kitchen and bathroom in the lean-to portion and leaving the main part of the building essentially unchanged.

"You'll need heat and air conditioning," Mark said. "But that should be no problem."

After touring the exterior they all went inside. Kim showed them the whole house, even the cellar. The men were particularly impressed with the way the main beams and joists were joined.

"It's a solid, well-built structure," Mark said.

"What kind of job would it be renovating it?" Kim asked.

"There wouldn't be any problem," Mark said. He looked at George, who nodded in agreement.

"I think it will be a fantastic little house," George said. "I'm psyched."

"Can it be done without damaging the historical aspect of the building?" Kim asked.

"Absolutely," Mark said. "We can hide all the duct-work, piping, and electric in the lean-to and in the cellar. You won't see it."

"We'll dig a deep trench to bring in utilities," George said. "They'll come in beneath the existing foundation so we will not have to disturb it. The only thing I'd recommend is pouring a concrete basement floor."

"Can the job be done by September first?" Kim asked.

Mark looked at George. George nodded and said it wouldn't be a problem as long as they used custom cabinetry.

"I have one suggestion," Mark said. "The main bathroom is best situated in the lean-to as you have suggested.

But we could also put a small half-bath on the second floor between the two bedrooms without causing any damage. I think it would be convenient.''

"Sounds good," Kim said. "When could you start?''

"Immediately," George said. "In fact, to get it done by the first of September we'll have to start tomorrow.''

"We've done a lot of work for your father," Mark said. "We could run this job just like we've done the others. We'll bill you for time and materials plus profit.''

"I want to do it," Kim said with newfound resolve. "Your enthusiasm has overcome any of my reservations. What do we have to do to get started?''

"We'll start right away on a verbal agreement," Mark said. "We'll draw up contracts that can be signed later.''

"Fine," Kim said. She stuck out her hand and shook hands with both men.

"We'll have to stay for a while to get measurements," Mark said.

"Be my guest," Kim said. "As for the contents of the house, they can be stored up at the garage of the main house. The garage is open.''

"What about the gate?" George asked.

"If you are starting right away, let's leave it unlocked," Kim said.

While the men were busy with their tape measures, Kim wandered outside. From fifty feet away she looked at the house and acknowledged that it was indeed darling. Immediately she began to think about the fun of decorating it and debated with herself what colors to paint the bedrooms. Such details excited her about the project, but the excitement immediately conjured up Elizabeth's name. All at once Kim found herself wondering how Elizabeth had felt when she first saw the house and when she first moved into it. She wondered if Elizabeth had been equally as excited.

Returning back inside, Kim told Mark and George that she would be up in the main house if they needed her.

"We have plenty to keep us busy for the moment," Mark said. "But I'll have to talk with you tomorrow. Could you give me your phone number?''

Kim gave both her apartment and work numbers. Then

she left the old house, climbed in her car, and drove up to the castle. Thinking about Elizabeth had stimulated her to spend a little time looking through the old papers.

Kim opened the front door and left it slightly ajar in case Mark or George came looking for her. Inside she debated between the attic and the wine cellar. Remembering the seventeenth-century bill of lading she'd found on Saturday in the wine cellar, she decided to return there.

Striding through the great room and traversing the dining room, Kim pulled open the heavy oak door. As she started down the granite steps she became aware that the door had closed with a dull thud behind her.

Kim stopped. She had the sudden realization that it was far different being alone in the huge old house than it had been with Edward. She heard distant creaks and groans as the house adjusted to the heat of the day. Turning around, Kim looked up at the door with the irrational fear that it had somehow locked, trapping her in the basement.

"You're being ridiculous," Kim said out loud. Yet she couldn't shake the concern about the door. Finally she mounted the stairs. She leaned against the door, and as she expected, it opened. She let it close again.

Chiding herself for her overly active imagination, Kim descended and strode into the depths of the wine cellar. She hummed a favorite tune, but her equanimity was a façade. Despite efforts to the contrary, she was still spooked by the surroundings. The massive house seemed to make the air heavy and breathing difficult. And as she'd already noticed, it was far from silent.

Kim forced herself to ignore her discomfiture. Still humming the same song, she entered the cell where she'd found the seventeenth-century bill of lading. On Saturday she'd searched through the drawer where she'd found the document, but now she began to search through the rest of the file cabinet.

It didn't take her long to grasp how difficult searching through the Stewart papers was to be. She was dealing with one file cabinet out of literally scores. Each drawer was completely full, and she painstakingly had to go through document by document. Many of the papers were entirely written by hand and some were difficult to decipher. On others it was impossible to find a date. To make things worse, the light from the torchlike sconces was far from adequate. Kim resolved that on future forays to the wine cellar she'd bring additional lighting.

After only going through a single drawer, Kim gave up. Most of the documents where she could find a date were from the late eighteenth century. Hoping there might be some order to the mess, she began randomly opening drawers and sampling, looking for something significantly older. It was in the top drawer of a bureau near the door to the hall that she made her first find.

What got her attention initially were scattered bills of lading from the seventeenth century: each a little older than the one she'd shown to Edward on Saturday. Then she found a whole packet of them tied with a string. Although they were handwritten, the script was graceful and clear, and all of them had dates. They dealt mostly with furs, timber, fish, rum, sugar, and grain. In the middle of the packet was an envelope. It was addressed to Ronald Stewart. The handwriting was different; it was stiff and erratic.

Kim carried the envelope out into the hall where the light was better. She slid the letter out and unfolded it. It was dated *y 21st June 1679*. It was difficult to read.

Sir:
   There hath been several days synce your letter hath arrived. I hath had much discourse with y family over your fancy for our beloved daughter Elizabeth who is a high spirited gyrl. If it be God's will ye shall have her hand in marriage provided ye shall give me work and move y family to Salem Town. Y threat of Indian raids hath made it a hazard to our lyves here in Andover and caused us much Disquietude. Ye humble servant,

James Flanagan.

Kim slowly slipped the letter back into the envelope. She was dismayed, even shocked. She didn't think of herself as a feminist, yet this letter offended her and made her feel like one. Elizabeth had been chattel to be bargained away. Kim's sympathy for her forebear, which had been on the rise, now soared.

Returning to the cell, Kim put the letter on top of the bureau where she'd found it and began looking more carefully through the drawer. Oblivious to the time and her surroundings, she went through every slip of paper. Although she found a few more contemporary bills of lading, she found no more letters. Undaunted, she started on the second drawer. It was then that she heard the unmistakable sound of footsteps above her.

Kim froze. The vague fear she'd experienced when she'd first descended into the wine cellar came back with a vengeance. Only now it was fueled by more than just the spookiness of the huge, empty house. Now it was compounded by the guilt of trespassing into a forbidden and troubled past.

Consequently, her imagination ran wild, and as the footsteps passed directly overhead, her mental image was of some fearful ghost. She thought it might even be her dead grandfather, coming to exact revenge for her insolent and presumptuous attempt to uncover guarded secrets.

The sound of the footsteps receded then merged with the house's creaks and groans. Kim was beset by two conflicting impulses: one was to flee blindly from the wine cellar; the other was to hide among the file cabinets and bureaus. Unable to decide, she did neither. Instead she stepped silently to the door of the cell and peeked around the jamb, looking down the long corridor toward the granite steps. At that moment she heard the door to the wine cellar creak open. She couldn't see the door, but she was sure it was what she'd heard.

Paralyzed with fear, Kim helplessly watched as black shoes and trousers appeared and came relentlessly down the steps. Halfway they stopped. Then a figure bent down and a backlit, featureless face appeared.

"Kim?" Edward called. "Are you down here?"

Kim's first response was to let out a sigh. Until then, she hadn't been aware she'd been holding her breath. Leaning against the wall of the cell for support, since her legs felt tremulous, she called out to Edward to let him know where she was. In a few moments his large frame filled the doorway.

"You scared me," Kim said as calmly as she could manage. Now that she knew it was Edward, she was acutely embarrassed by the extent of her terror.

"I'm sorry," Edward said falteringly. "I didn't mean to frighten you."

"Why didn't you call out sooner?" Kim asked.

"I did," Edward said. "Several times. First when I came through the front door and again in the great room. I think the wine cellar must be insulated."

"I suppose it is," Kim said. "What are you doing here, anyway? I certainly didn't expect you."

"I tried to call you at your apartment," Edward said. "Marsha told me you drove out here with the idea of fixing up the old house. On the spur of the moment I decided to come. I feel responsible since I was the one who suggested it."

"That was considerate," Kim said. Her pulse was still racing.

"I'm really sorry for having scared you," Edward said.

"Never mind," Kim said. "It's my fault for letting my stupid imagination take over. I heard your footsteps and thought you were a ghost."

Edward made an evil face and turned his hands into claws. Kim playfully socked him in the shoulder and told him he wasn't funny.

They both felt relieved. The tension that existed evaporated.

"So you've started on the Elizabeth Stewart search," Edward said. He eyed the open drawer of the bureau. "Did you find anything?"

"As a matter of fact I have," Kim said. She stepped over to the bureau and handed Edward James Flanagan's letter to Ronald Stewart.

Edward carefully slipped the note from the envelope. He held it close to the light. It took him as much time to read it as it had taken Kim.

"Indian raids in Andover!" Edward commented. "Can you imagine? Life certainly was different back then."

Edward finished the letter and handed it back to Kim. "Fascinating," he said.

"Doesn't it upset you at all?" Kim asked.

"Not particularly," Edward said. "Should it?"

"It upset me," Kim said. "Poor Elizabeth had even less say about her tragic fate than I'd imagined. Her father was using her as a bargaining chip in a business deal. It's deplorable."

"I think you might be jumping to conclusions," Edward said. "Opportunity as we know it didn't exist in the seventeenth century. Life was harsher and more tenuous. People had to team up just to survive. Individual interests weren't a high priority."

"That doesn't warrant making a deal with your daughter's life," Kim said. "It sounds as if her father were treating her like a cow or some other piece of property."

"I still think you could be reading too much into it," Edward said. "Just because there was a deal between James and Ronald doesn't necessarily mean that Elizabeth didn't have any say whether she wanted to marry Ronald or not. Also, you have to consider that it might have been a great source of comfort and satisfaction for her to know that she was providing for the rest of her family."

"Well, maybe so," Kim said. "Trouble is, I know what ultimately happened to her."

"You still don't know for sure if she was hanged or not," Edward reminded her.

"That's true," Kim said. "But this letter at least suggests one reason she might have been vulnerable to being accused as a witch. From the reading I've done, people in Puritan times were not supposed to change their station in life, and if they did, they were automatically suspected of not following God's will. Elizabeth's sudden rise from a poor farmer's daughter to a comparatively wealthy merchant's wife certainly fits that category."

"Vulnerability and actually being accused are two different things," Edward said. "Since I haven't seen her name in any of the books, I'm dubious."

"My mother suggested that the reason she's not mentioned is because the family went to great lengths to keep her name out of it. She even implied the reason was because the family considered Elizabeth guilty."

"That's a new twist," Edward said. "But it makes sense in one regard. People in the seventeenth century believed in witchcraft. Maybe Elizabeth practiced it."

"Wait a second," Kim said. "Are you suggesting Elizabeth was a witch? My idea was that she was guilty of something, like changing her status, but certainly not that she considered herself a sorceress."

"I mean maybe she practiced magic," Edward said. "Back then there was white magic and black magic. The difference was that white magic was for good things, like curing a person or an animal. Black magic, on the other hand, had a malicious intent and was called witchcraft. Obviously there could have been times when it was a matter of opinion if some potion or charm represented white magic or black magic."

"Well, maybe you have a point," Kim said. She thought for a moment, then shook her head. "I don't buy it. My intuition tells me otherwise. I have a feeling Elizabeth was an entirely innocent person caught in a terrible tragedy by some insidious trick of fate. Whatever the trick was, it must have been awful, and the fact that her memory has been treated so dreadfully just compounds the injustice." Kim glanced around at the file cabinets, bureaus, and boxes. "The question is: could the explanation of whatever it was lie in this sea of documents?"

"I'd say that finding this personal letter is auspicious," Edward said. "If there's one, there's got to be more. If you're going to find the answer it will most likely be in personal correspondence."

"I just wish there were some chronological order to these papers," Kim said.

"What about the old house?" Edward asked. "Did you make any decisions about fixing it up?"

"I did," Kim said. "Come on, I'll explain it to you."

Leaving Edward's car parked at the castle, they drove over to the old house in Kim's. With great enthusiasm Kim took Edward on a tour and explained that she was going to follow his original suggestion of putting the modern conveniences in the lean-to portion. The most important bit of new information was the placement of a half-bath between the bedrooms.

"I think it will be marvelous house," Edward said as they exited the building. "I'm jealous."

"I'm excited about it," Kim said. "What I'm really looking forward to is the decorating. I think I'll arrange to take some vacation time and even personal time off in September to devote full time to it."

"You'll do it all by yourself?" Edward asked.

"Absolutely," Kim said.

"Admirable," Edward said. "I know I couldn't do it."

They climbed into Kim's car. Kim hesitated starting the engine. They could see the house through the front windshield.

"Actually I've always wanted to be an interior decorator," Kim said wistfully.

"No kidding?" Edward said.

"It was a missed opportunity," Kim said. "My main interest when I was growing up was always art in some form or fashion, especially in high school. Back then, I'd have to say, I was a whimsical artist type and hardly a member of the in-group."

"I certainly wasn't part of the in-group either," Edward said.

Kim started the car and turned it around. They headed for the castle.

"Why didn't you become an interior decorator?" Edward asked.

"My parents talked me out of it," Kim said. "Particularly my father."

"I'm confused," Edward said. "Friday at dinner you said you and your father were never close."

"We weren't close, but he still had a big effect on me," Kim said. "I thought it was my fault we weren't close. So I spent a lot of effort trying to please him, even to the point of going into nursing. He wanted me to go into nursing or teaching because he felt they were 'appropriate.' He certainly didn't think interior design was appropriate.''

"Fathers can have a big effect on kids," Edward said. "I had a similar compulsion to please my father. When I think about it, it was kind of crazy. I should have just ignored him. The problem was that he made fun of me because of my stutter and lack of ability in competitive sports. I suppose I was a disappointment to him."

They arrived at the castle, and Kim pulled up next to Edward's car. Edward started to get out, but then he sat back in the seat.

"Have you eaten?" he asked.

Kim shook her head.

"Me neither," he said. "Why don't we drive into Salem and see if we can find a decent restaurant?"

"You're on," Kim said.

They drove out of the compound and headed toward town. Kim was the first to speak. "I attribute my lack of social confidence in college directly to my relationship with my parents," she said. "Could it have been the same for you?"

"I wouldn't doubt it," Edward said.

"It's amazing how important self-esteem is," Kim said, "and it's a little scary how easily it can be undermined with children."

"Even with adults," Edward said. "And once it is undermined it affects behavior, which in turn affects self-esteem. The problem is that it can become functionally autonomous and biochemically determined. That's the argument for drugs: to break the vicious cycle."

"Are we talking about Prozac again?" Kim asked.

"Indirectly," Edward said. "Prozac can positively affect self-esteem in some patients."

"Would you have taken Prozac in college if it had been available?" Kim asked.

"I might have," Edward admitted. "It would have made a difference in my experience."

Kim glanced briefly across at Edward. She had the feeling he'd just told her something personal. "You don't have to answer this," she said, "and maybe I shouldn't ask, but have you ever tried Prozac yourself?"

"I don't mind answering," Edward said. "I did use it for a time a couple of years ago. My father died, and I became moderately depressed. It was a reaction I didn't expect considering our history. A colleague suggested I try Prozac, and I did."

"Did it help the depression?" Kim asked.

"Most definitely," Edward said. "Not immediately but eventually. But most interestingly it also gave me an unexpected dose of assertiveness. I'd not anticipated it, so it couldn't have been a placebo effect. I also liked it."

"Any side effects?" Kim asked.

"A few," Edward said. "But nothing terrible and certainly acceptable in relation to the depression."

"Interesting," Kim said sincerely.

"I hope my admission of psychotropic drug use in the face of your pharmacological Puritanism doesn't alarm you."

"Don't be silly," Kim said. "Quite the contrary. I respect your forthrightness. Besides, who would I be to judge? I've never taken Prozac, but I did have some psychotherapy during college. I'd say that makes us even."

Edward laughed. "Right!" he said. "We're both crazy!"

They found a small, popular local restaurant that served fresh fish. It was crowded, and they were forced to sit on stools at the bar. They each had baked scrod and iced mugs of draft beer. For dessert there was old-fashioned Indian pudding with ice cream.

After the boisterous publike atmosphere they both enjoyed the silence of the car as they drove back to the compound. However, as they passed through the gate, Kim sensed that Edward had become demonstrably nervous. He fidgeted, brushing his hair off his forehead.

"Is something wrong?" Kim asked.

"No," Edward said, but his stutter had returned.

Kim pulled up next to his car. She put on the emergency brake but left the engine running. She waited, knowing there was something on Edward's mind.

Edward finally blurted out: "Would you like to come over to my apartment when we get back to the city?"

The invitation threw Kim into a quandary. She sensed the courage it took for Edward to invite her, and she didn't want him to feel rejected. At the same time she thought of the needs of the patients she'd be facing in the morning. Ultimately her professionalism won out. "I'm sorry," she said. "It's a bit too late tonight. I'm exhausted; I've been up since six." In an attempt to make light of the situation she added: "Besides, it's a school night and I haven't finished my homework."

"We could turn in early," Edward said. "It is just a little after nine."

Kim was both surprised and uneasy. "I think maybe things are moving a little too swiftly for me," she said. "I've felt very comfortable with you, but I don't want to rush things."

"Of course," Edward said. "Obviously I've also felt comfortable with you."

"I do enjoy your company," Kim said. "And I'm off Friday and Saturday this week if that works with your schedule."

"How about dinner on Thursday night?" Edward said. "It won't be a school night."

Kim laughed. "It'll be a pleasure," she said. "And I'll make it a point to have all my homework done."

# 4

KIM'S EYES BLINKED OPEN. AT FIRST SHE WAS DISORI-
ented. She didn't know where she was. There were unfamiliar shutters over the windows dispersing the early
morning light. Turning her head to the side, she saw Edward's sleeping form, and it all came back to her in a flash.

Kim drew the sheet up around her neck. She felt distinctly uneasy and out of place. "You hypocrite," she silently voiced to herself. She could remember just a few
days previously telling Edward she didn't want to rush
things, and here she was waking up in his bed. Kim had
never been in a relationship which had proceeded to such
intimacy so quickly.

As quietly as possible, Kim tried to slip out of the bed
with the intention of dressing before Edward woke up. But
it was not to be. Edward's small, white, and rather nasty
Jack Russell terrier growled and bared his teeth. His name
was Buffer. He was at the foot of the bed.

Edward sat up and shooed the dog away. With a groan
he fell back against the pillow.

"What time is it?" he asked. He'd closed his eyes.

"It's a little after six," Kim said.

"Why are you awake so early?" Edward asked.

"I'm used to it," Kim said. "This is my normal wakeup
time."

"But it was almost one when we came to bed."

"It doesn't matter," Kim said. "I'm sorry. I shouldn't
have stayed."

Edward opened his eyes and looked at Kim. "Do you
feel uncomfortable?" he asked.

Kim nodded.

"I'm sorry," Edward said. "I shouldn't have talked you into it."

"It's not your fault," Kim said.

"But it was your inclination to go," Edward said. "It was my fault."

They looked at each other for a beat, then both smiled.

"This is sounding a bit repetitious," Kim said with a chuckle. "We're back to competing with each other with apologies."

"It would be funny if it weren't so pitiful," Edward said. "You'd think we would have made some progress by now."

Kim moved over and they put their arms around each other. They didn't talk for a moment as they enjoyed the embrace. It was Edward who broke the silence. "Do you still feel uncomfortable?"

"No," Kim said. "Sometimes merely talking about something really helps."

Later while Edward was in the shower, Kim called her roommate, Marsha, whom she knew would be about to leave for work. Marsha was glad to hear from her and voiced a modicum of concern that Kim had failed to come home or call the previous evening.

"I should have called," Kim admitted.

"I take it the evening was a success," Marsha said coyly.

"It was fine," Kim said. "It just got so late, and I didn't want to take the risk of waking you up."

"Oh, sure!" Marsha said with exaggerated sarcasm.

"Would you give Sheba some food?" Kim added, changing the subject. Marsha knew her too well.

"Your cat has already dined," Marsha said. "The only other news is that you got a call last night from your father. He wants you to call him when you have a chance."

"My father?" Kim questioned. "He never calls."

"You don't have to tell me," Marsha said. "I've been your roommate for years, and it was the first time I spoke with him on the phone."

After Edward got out of the shower and dressed, he surprised Kim by suggesting they go to Harvard Square for breakfast. Kim had imagined he'd want to go directly to his lab.

"I'm up two hours before I expected to be," Edward said. "The lab can wait. Also, it's been the most pleasant evening of the year and I don't want it to be over."

With a smile on her face, Kim put her arms around Edward's neck and gave him a forceful hug. She had to stand on her tiptoes in the process. He returned the affection with equal exuberance.

They used Kim's car since it had to be moved; it was illegally parked outside Edward's apartment. In the square Edward took her to a student greasy spoon where they indulged themselves with scrambled eggs, bacon, and coffee.

"What are your plans today?" Edward asked. He had to speak loudly over the general din. Summer session at the university was in full swing.

"I'm heading up to Salem," Kim said. "They've started the construction on the cottage. I want to check on the progress." Kim had decided to call the old house "the cottage" in contrast to the castle.

"When do you plan to get back?"

"Early evening," Kim said.

"How about meeting at the Harvest Bar around eight?" Edward said.

"It's a date," Kim said.

After breakfast Edward asked Kim to drop him off at the Harvard biological labs.

"You don't want me to take you home to get your car?" she asked.

"No, thanks," Edward said. "There'd be no place to park it here on the main campus. To get to work I'll take the shuttle over to the medical area. I do it frequently. It's part of the benefit of living within walking distance of the square."

Edward had Kim drop him off at the corner of Kirkland Street and Divinity Avenue. He stood on the sidewalk and waved until she was out of sight. He knew he was in love, and he loved the feeling. Turning around, he started up Divinity Avenue. He felt like singing. What made him feel so good was that he was beginning to think that Kim felt affection for him. All he could do was hope that it would last. He thought about the flowers he was having sent every day and wondered if he were overdoing it. The problem was, he didn't have a lot of experience with such things.

Arriving at the biological labs, Edward checked the time; it was before eight. As he climbed the stairs he worried he'd have to wait for Kevin Scranton. But his concerns were unfounded. Kevin was there.

"I'm glad you stopped in," Kevin said. "I was going to call you today."

"Did you find *Claviceps purpurea?*" Edward asked hopefully.

"Nope," Kevin said. "No *Claviceps.*"

"Damn!" Edward said. He slumped into a chair. There was a disappointed, sinking sensation in his stomach. He'd been banking on a positive result and was counting on it mainly for Kim's sake. He'd wanted to present it to her as a gift of science to help alleviate Elizabeth's disgrace.

"Don't look so glum," Kevin said. "There wasn't any *Claviceps,* but there was plenty of other mold. One of them that grew out morphologically resembles *Claviceps purpurea,* but it is a heretofore unknown species."

"No kidding," Edward commented. He brightened at the thought that at least they'd made a discovery.

"Of course that's not terribly surprising," Kevin said, causing Edward's face to fall again. "Currently there are approximately fifty thousand known species of fungi. At the same time some people believe that one hundred thousand to a quarter of a million species actually exist."

"So you're trying to tell me that this isn't a monumental discovery," Edward commented wryly.

"I'm not making any value judgment," Kevin said. "But it's a mold that you might find interesting. It's an ascomycete, like *Claviceps,* and it happens to form sclerotia just like *Claviceps.*"

Kevin reached across his desk and dropped several small dark objects into Edward's palm. Edward nudged them with his index finger. They appeared like dark grains of rice.

"I think you better tell me what these sclerotia are," Edward said.

"They're a type of vegetative, resting spore of certain fungi," Kevin said. "They're different than a simple, unicellular spore because sclerotia are multicellular and contain fungal filaments or hyphae as well as stored food."

"What makes you think I'd be interested in these things?" Edward asked. He thought they also looked like the seeds in rye bread. He brought one to his nose; it was odorless.

"Because it's the *Claviceps'* sclerotia that contain the bioactive alkaloids that cause ergotism," Kevin said.

"Wow!" Edward said. He sat up straight and studied the sclerotium between his fingers with additional interest. "What are the chances that this little bugger contains the same alkaloids as *Claviceps?*"

"That, I believe, is the question of the day," Kevin said. "Personally, I think the chances are reasonably good. There aren't many fungi that produce sclerotia. Obviously this new species is related to *Claviceps purpurea* on some level."

"Why don't we try it?" Edward said.

"What on earth do you mean?" Kevin asked. He eyed Edward with suspicion.

"Why don't we make a little brew with these guys and taste it?" Edward said.

"You're joking, I hope," Kevin said.

"Actually I'm not," Edward said. "I'm interested in whether this new mold makes an alkaloid that has a hallucinogenic effect. The best way to figure that out is to try it."

"You're out of your mind," Kevin said. "Mycotoxins can be quite potent, as those countless people who've suffered ergotism can testify. Science is finding new ones all the time. You'd be taking an awful risk."

"Where's your adventuresome spirit?" Edward asked teasingly. He stood up. "Can I use your lab for this little experiment?"

"I'm not sure I should be party to this," Kevin said. "But you're serious, aren't you?"

"Very much so," Edward said.

Kevin led Edward into his lab and asked him what he

needed. Edward said he needed a mortar and pestle or the equivalent, distilled water, a weak acid to precipitate the alkaloid, some filter paper, a liter flask, and a milliliter pipette.

"This is insane," Kevin said as he rounded up the materials.

Edward set to work by grinding up the few sclerotia, extracting the pulp with distilled water, and precipitating a tiny amount of white material with the weak acid. With the help of the filter paper, he isolated a few grains of the white precipitate. Kevin watched the procedure with a mixture of disbelief and wonder.

"Don't tell me you are just going to eat that?" Kevin said with growing alarm.

"Oh, come on," Edward said. "I'm not stupid."

"You could have fooled me," Kevin said.

"Listen," Edward said. "I'm interested in a hallucinogenic effect. If this stuff is going to have such an effect, it will have it at a minuscule dose. I'm talking about less than a microgram."

Edward took a speck of the precipitate on the end of a spatula and introduced it into a liter of distilled water in a volumetric flask. He shook it vigorously.

"We could screw around with this stuff for six months and still not know if it can cause hallucinations," Edward said. "Ultimately we'd need a human cerebrum. Mine is available right at the moment. When it comes to science, I'm a man of action."

"What about possible kidney toxicity?" Kevin asked.

Edward made an expression of exasperated disbelief. "At this dosage? Hell, no! We're well below by a factor of ten the toxicity range of botulinum toxin, the most toxic substance known to man. Besides, not only are we in the microgram range with this unknown, but it's got to be a soup of substances, so the concentration of any one of them is that much lower."

Edward asked Kevin to hand him the milliliter pipette. Kevin did so reluctantly.

"Are you sure you don't want to join?" Edward asked. "You could be missing out on making an interesting scientific discovery." He laughed as he filled the slender pipette.

"Thanks, but no thanks," Kevin said. "I have a comfortable understanding with my renal tubular cells that we won't abuse each other."

"To your health," Edward said as he held aloft the pipette for a moment before depositing a single milliliter on the curl of his tongue. He took a mouthful of water, swished it around, and swallowed.

"Well?" Kevin questioned nervously after a moment of silence.

"A tiny, tiny bit bitter," Edward said. He opened and closed his mouth a few times to enhance the taste.

"Anything else?" Kevin asked.

"I'm just beginning to feel mildly dizzy," Edward said.

"Hell, you were dizzy before you started," Kevin said.

"I admit this little experiment lacks scientific controls," Edward said with a chuckle. "Anything I feel could be a placebo effect."

"I really shouldn't be a part of this," Kevin said. "I'm going to have to insist that you get a urinalysis and a BUN this afternoon."

"Ohooo weee," Edward said. "Something is happening!"

"Oh, God!" Kevin said. "What?"

"I'm seeing a flood of colors that are moving around in amoeboid shapes like some kind of kaleidoscope."

"Oh, great!" Kevin said. He stared into Edward's face, which had assumed a trancelike appearance.

"Now I'm hearing some sounds like a synthesizer. Also my mouth is a bit dry. And now something else: I feel paresthesias on my arms, as if I'm being bitten or lightly pinched. It's weird."

"Should I call somebody?" Kevin demanded.

To Kevin's surprise, Edward reached out and grabbed him around the upper arms. Edward held him with unexpected strength.

"It feels like the room is moving," Edward said. "And there's a mild choking sensation."

"I'd better call for help," Kevin said. His own pulse

was racing. He eyed the phone, but Edward strengthened his grip.

"It's OK," Edward said. "The colors are receding. It's passing." Edward closed his eyes, but otherwise he didn't move. He still had hold of Kevin.

Eventually Edward opened his eyes and sighed. "Wow!" he said. Only then did he become aware he was gripping Kevin's arms. He let go, took a breath, and smoothed his jacket. "I think we got our answer," he said.

"This was idiotic!" Kevin snapped. "Your little antic terrified me. I was just about to call emergency."

"Calm down," Edward said. "It wasn't that bad. Don't get all bent out of shape over a sixty-second psychedelic reaction."

Kevin pointed up at the clock. "It wasn't sixty seconds," he said. "It was more like twenty minutes."

Edward glanced up at the clock's face. "Isn't that curious," he said. "Even my sense of time was distorted."

"Do you generally feel OK?" Kevin asked.

"Fine!" Edward insisted. "In fact I feel better than fine. I feel . . ." He hesitated while he tried to put into words his inner sensations. "I feel energized, like I'd just had a rest. And also clairvoyant, like my mind is particularly sharp. I might even feel a touch euphoric but that could be because of this positive result: we've just ascertained that this new fungus produces a hallucinogenic substance."

"Let's not be so lax with the term 'we,' " Kevin said. "You ascertained it, not me. I refuse to take any credit for this craziness."

"I wonder if the alkaloids are the same as *Claviceps?*" Edward asked. "I don't seem to have even the slightest signs of reduced peripheral vascular circulation, a frequent sign of ergotism."

"At least promise me you'll get a urinalysis and a BUN or creatinine this afternoon," Kevin said. "Even if you're not worried, I still am."

"If it will make you sleep tonight I'll do it," Edward said. "Meanwhile I want some more of these sclerotia. Is that possible?"

"It's possible now that I have figured out the medium

this fungus needs to grow, but I can't promise you a lot of sclerotia. It's not always easy to get the fungus to produce them.''

"Well, do your best," Edward said. "Remember, we'll probably get a nice little paper out of this."

As Edward hurried across campus to catch the shuttle bus to the medical area, he was thrilled with the results. He couldn't wait to tell Kim that the poison theory involving the Salem witchcraft episode was alive and well.

As excited as Kim was about seeing the progress at the compound, she was even more curious as to why her father had called her. Confident she was early enough to catch him before he left for his Boston office, Kim detoured to Marblehead.

Entering the house, she went directly to the kitchen. As she expected, she found John lingering over his coffee and his clutch of morning papers. He was a big man who'd reportedly been quite an athlete during his days at Harvard. His broad face was crowned with a full head of hair that had once been as dark and lustrous as Kim's. Over the years it had grayed in a comely fashion, giving him a stereotypically paternal appearance.

"Good morning, Kimmy," John said without taking his attention away from his paper.

Kim helped herself to the espresso machine and foamed some milk for a cappuccino.

"How's that car of yours running?" John asked. The paper crinkled loudly as he turned the page. "I hope you are having it regularly serviced like I advised."

Kim didn't answer. She was accustomed to her father treating her as if she were still a little girl and she mildly resented it. He was forever giving her instructions on how to order her life. The older she got the more she thought he shouldn't be giving anyone advice, especially considering what he'd done to his own life and marriage.

"I heard you called my apartment last night," Kim said. She sat on a window seat beneath a bay window overlooking the ocean.

John lowered his paper.

"I did indeed," he said. "Joyce mentioned that you'd become interested in Elizabeth Stewart and had been asking questions about her. It surprised me. I called you to ask why you wanted to upset your mother like that."

"I wasn't trying to upset her," Kim said. "I've become interested in Elizabeth and I just wanted to know some basic facts. Like whether or not Elizabeth truly had been hanged for witchcraft or whether it was just a rumor."

"She was indeed hanged," John said. "I can assure you of that. I can also assure you that the family made a good deal of effort to suppress it. Under the circumstances I think it is best for you to leave it alone."

"But why does it warrant such secrecy after three hundred years?" Kim asked. "It doesn't make sense."

"It doesn't matter if it makes sense to you or not," John said. "It was a humiliation then and it is today."

"Do you mean to tell me that it bothers you, Father?" Kim asked. "Does it humiliate you?"

"Well, no, not particularly," John admitted. "It's your mother. It bothers her, so it should not be a subject for your amusement. We shouldn't add to her burdens."

Kim bit her tongue. It was hard not to say something disparaging to her father under the circumstances. Instead she admitted that not only had she become interested in Elizabeth but that she'd developed a sympathy for her.

"What on earth for?" John questioned irritably.

"For one thing I found her portrait stuck away in the back of Grandfather's wine cellar," Kim said. "Looking at it emphasized that she'd been a real person. She even had the same eye color as I do. Then I remembered what had happened to her. She certainly didn't deserve to be hanged. It's hard not to be sympathetic."

"I was aware of the painting," John said. "What were you doing in the wine cellar?"

"Nothing in particular," Kim said. "Just taking a look around. It seemed like such a coincidence to come across Elizabeth's portrait, because I'd recently been doing some reading about the Salem witch trials. And what I'd learned just added to my feelings of sympathy. Within a short time of the tragedy there was an outpouring of regret and repentance. Even back then it had become evident innocent people had been killed.''

"Not everyone was innocent," John said.

"Mother intimated the same thing," Kim said. "What could Elizabeth have done for you to suggest she wasn't innocent?"

"Now you are pushing me," John said. "I don't know specifics, but I'd been told by my father it had something to do with the occult."

"Like what?" Kim persisted.

"I just told you I don't know, young lady," John snapped angrily. "You've asked enough questions."

*Now go to your room,* Kim added silently to herself. She wondered if her father would ever recognize that she'd become an adult and treat her like one.

"Kimmy, listen to me," John said in a more conciliatory and paternalistic tone. "For your own good don't dig up the past in this instance. It's only going to cause trouble."

"With all due respect, Father," Kim said, "could you explain to me how it could possibly affect my welfare?"

John stammered.

"Let me tell you what I think," Kim said with uncharacteristic assertiveness. "I believe that Elizabeth's involvement could have been a humiliation back at the time the event occurred. I also can believe it might have been considered bad for business since her husband, Ronald, started Maritime Limited, which has supported generation after generation of Stewarts, ourselves included. But the fact that the concern over Elizabeth's involvement has persisted is absurd and a disgrace to her memory. After all, she is our ancestor; if it hadn't been for her, none of us would even be here. That fact alone makes me surprised that no one has questioned over the years this ridiculous knee-jerk reaction."

"If you can't understand it from your own selfish perspective," John said irritably, "then at least think of your mother. The affair humiliates Joyce, and it doesn't matter why. It just does. So if you need some motivation to leave Elizabeth's legacy be, then there it is. Don't rub your mother's nose in it."

Kim lifted her now cool cappuccino to her lips and took a drink. She gave up with her father. Trying to have a conversation with him had never been fruitful. It only worked when the conversation was one-sided: when he told her what to do and how to do it. It was as if he mistook the role of a father to be an instructor.

"Mother also tells me you have embarked on a project at the compound," John said, assuming that Kim's silence meant she'd become reasonable about the Elizabeth issue and accepted his advice. "What exactly are you doing?"

Kim told him about her decision to renovate the old house and live in it. While she talked, John went back to glancing at his papers. When she'd finished his only question concerned the castle and his father's belongings.

"We're not going to do anything to the castle," Kim said. "Not until Brian comes home."

"Good," John said as he advanced the page of his *Wall Street Journal*.

"Speaking of Mother, where is she?" Kim asked.

"Upstairs," John said. "She's not feeling well and is not seeing anyone."

A few minutes later Kim left the house with a sad, anxious feeling that was a complicated mixture of pity, anger, and revulsion. As she climbed into her car she told herself that she hated her parents' marriage. As she started the engine she pledged to herself that she would never allow herself to be ensnared in such a situation.

Kim backed out of the driveway and headed toward Salem. As she drove she reminded herself that despite her revulsion toward her parents' relationship, she was at some risk to re-create a similar situation. That was part of the reason why she'd reacted so strongly to Kinnard's sporting trips when he'd had plans to be with her.

Kim suddenly smiled. Her gloomy thoughts were immediately overpowered by the memory of the flowers that had been arriving from Edward on a daily basis. In one way they embarrassed her; in another they were a testament to Edward's attentiveness and caring. One thing she felt quite confident about: Edward would not be a womanizer. In her mind a womanizer had to be more assertive and more competitive, like her father, or, for that matter, like Kinnard.

As frustrating as her conversation with her father had been, it had the opposite effect of what he'd intended: it only encouraged her interest in Elizabeth Stewart. Consequently, as Kim was driving through downtown Salem, she detoured to the Museum Place Mall.

Leaving her vehicle in the car park, Kim walked to the Peabody-Essex Institute, a cultural and historical association housed in a group of old refurbished buildings in the center of town. Among other functions it served as a repository for documents about Salem and the environs, including the witchcraft trials.

A receptionist in the foyer collected a fee from Kim and directed her to the library, which was reached by a few stairs directly across from the reception desk. Kim mounted the steps and passed through a heavy, windowed door. The library was housed in an early nineteenth-century building with high ceilings, decorative cornices, and dark wood molding. The main room had marble fireplaces and chandeliers in addition to darkly stained oak tables and captain's chairs. A typical library hush and a smell of old books prevailed.

A friendly and helpful librarian by the name of Grace Meehan immediately came to Kim's aid. She was an elderly woman with gray hair and a kind face. In response to a general question from Kim, she showed her how to find all sorts of papers and documents associated with the Salem witch trials including accusations, complaints, arrest warrants, depositions, hearing testimony, court records of the preliminary hearings, mittimi, and execution warrants. They were all carefully catalogued in one of the library's old-fashioned card catalogues.

Kim was surprised and encouraged by the amount of material that was so easily available. It was no wonder there were so many books on the Salem witch trials. The institute was a researcher's paradise.

As soon as the librarian left Kim on her own, Kim attacked the card catalogue. With a good deal of excitement she looked up Elizabeth Stewart. She was confident she'd be mentioned in some form or fashion. But Kim was soon disappointed. There was no Elizabeth Stewart. There were no Stewarts at all.

Returning to the librarian's desk, Kim asked the woman directly about Elizabeth Stewart.

"The name's not familiar," Grace said. "Do you know how she was connected to the trials?"

"I was told she was one of the accused," Kim said. "I believe she was hanged."

"She couldn't have been," Grace said without hesitation. "I consider myself an expert on the extant documents concerning the trials. I've never come across the name Elizabeth Stewart even as a witness, much less one of the twenty victims. Who told you she was accused?"

"It's a rather long story," Kim said evasively.

"Well, it certainly wasn't true," Grace said. "There's been too much research by too many people for one of the victims to have been missed."

"I see," Kim said. She didn't argue. Instead she thanked the woman and returned to the card-catalogue area.

Giving up on the documents associated with the trials, Kim turned her attention to another important resource of the institute: genealogical information on families from Essex County.

This time Kim found a wealth of information on the Stewarts. In fact they took up most of an entire drawer of the genealogical card catalogue. As Kim went through the material it became obvious that there were two main Stewart clans, hers and another whose history wasn't quite so old.

After a half hour Kim found a brief reference to Elizabeth Stewart. She was born on May 4, 1665, the daughter of James and Elisha Flanagan, and died on July 19, 1692, the wife of Ronald Stewart. No cause of death was given. A quick subtraction told Kim that Elizabeth died at age twenty-seven!

Kim raised her head and stared with unseeing eyes out the window. She could feel tiny gooseflesh rise up on the nape of her neck. Kim was twenty-seven, and her birthday was in May. It wasn't the fourth but rather the sixth, so it was close to Elizabeth's. Remembering their physical similarities from the portrait and considering the fact that she was planning on moving into the same house Elizabeth occupied, Kim began to wonder if there were just too many coincidences. Was this all trying to tell her something?

"Excuse me," Grace Meehan said, interrupting Kim's reverie. "Here's a list I copied for you of the people who were hanged for witchcraft. There's also the date of their execution, including the day of the week, their town of residence, their church affiliation if there was one, and their age. As you can see, it is very complete—and there is no Elizabeth Stewart."

Kim thanked the woman again and took the paper. After the woman left, Elizabeth dutifully glanced at it and was about to put it aside when she noted the date of Tuesday, July 19, 1692. Five people had been hanged that day. Looking back at Elizabeth's day of death, she noticed it was the same. Kim understood that just because the dates were the same, it didn't prove Elizabeth was hanged. But even if it were only circumstantial, it was at least suggestive.

Then Kim realized something else. Thinking back to the previous Tuesday, she remembered it had been July 19. Looking again at the paper Grace Meehan had given her, she discovered that the daily calendar was the same in 1692 as it was in 1994. Was this yet another coincidence whose meaning Kim had to ponder?

Going back to the genealogical information, Kim got a book that summarized the early history of her family. In it she looked up Ronald Stewart and quickly learned that Elizabeth had not been Ronald's first wife. Ronald had married Hannah Hutchinson in 1677, with whom he'd had a daughter, Joanna, born 1678. But then Hannah died in January 1679, with no cause of death listed. Ronald at age thirty-nine then married Elizabeth Flanagan in 1682 with whom he had a daughter Sarah, born 1682, and sons, Jonathan, born 1683, and Daniel, born 1689. Finally Ronald married Elizabeth's younger sister, Rebecca Flanagan, in 1692, with whom he had a daughter named Rachel, born in 1693.

Kim lowered the book and again stared off into space while she tried to sort out her thoughts. Mild alarm bells were going off in her head in relation to Ronald's character.

Looking back at the genealogy book, she reviewed the fact that three years after Hannah died, Ronald married Elizabeth. Then after Elizabeth died, he married her sister the same year!

Kim felt uneasy. Knowing her own father's amorous proclivities, she thought it possible that Ronald could have suffered a similar flaw and indulged it with far more disastrous consequences. It occurred to her that Ronald could have been having an affair with Elizabeth while married to Hannah, and an affair with Rebecca while married to Elizabeth. After all, Elizabeth certainly died under unusual circumstances. Kim wondered if Hannah did as well.

Kim shook her head and silently laughed at herself. She told herself that she must have watched too many soap operas, since her imagination was taking unwarranted, melodramatic leaps.

After spending a few more minutes going over the Stewart family tree, Kim learned two more facts. First she confirmed she was related to Ronald and Elizabeth through their son Jonathan. Second she learned that the name ''Elizabeth'' never reappeared in the family's three-hundred-year history. With so many generations, such a situation couldn't have happened by chance. Kim marveled at the opprobrium Elizabeth had brought on herself, and Kim's curiosity waxed concerning what Elizabeth could possibly have done to warrant it.

Finally, with her superficial genealogical inquiry, Kim descended the steps of the Peabody-Essex Institute with the idea of retrieving her car and heading out to the compound. But at the foot of the steps she hesitated. The passing question that she'd entertained about Ronald's character and the possibility of foul play on his part gave her another idea. Returning inside the institute, she asked directions for the Essex County Courthouse.

The building was on Federal Street, not far from the Witch House. It was a severe Greek Revival structure with a stark pediment and massive Doric columns. Kim entered and asked to be directed to court records.

Kim had no idea whether she would find anything at all. She didn't even know if court records were saved from so long ago, nor did she know if they did exist whether they were available to the public. Nonetheless she presented herself at the appropriate counter and asked to look at any court records of Ronald Stewart. She added that she was interested in the Ronald Stewart who'd been born in 1653.

The clerk was a sleepy-looking woman of indeterminate age. If she was surprised by Kim's request she didn't show it. Her response was to punch it up on a computer terminal. After glancing at the screen for a moment, she left the room. She'd not said a word. Kim guessed that there had been so many people researching the Salem witch trials that the town's civil servants were jaded about inquiries from that era.

Kim shifted her weight and checked her watch. It was already ten-thirty, and she'd not even been to the compound yet.

The woman reappeared with a manila pocket folder. She handed it to Kim. "You can't take this out of the room," she said. She pointed to some Formica tables and molded plastic chairs along the back wall. "You can sit over there if you like."

Kim took the folder over to an empty chair. She sat down and slipped out the contents. There was a lot of material. All of it was written in reasonably legible longhand.

At first Kim thought that the file contained only documents associated with civil suits Ronald had filed with the court for debts owed to him. But then she began to find more interesting things, like reference to a contested will involving Ronald.

Kim carefully read the document. It was a ruling in Ronald's favor involving a will contested by a Jacob Cheever. Reading on, Kim discovered that Jacob had been a child of Hannah's from a previous marriage and that Hannah had been significantly older than Ronald. Jacob had testified that Ronald had duped his mother into changing her will, thereby depriving him of his rightful inheritance. Apparently the justices disagreed. The result had been that Ronald inherited several thousand pounds, a sizable fortune in those days.

Kim marveled that life in the late seventeenth century

hadn't been as different as she'd imagined. She'd been under the delusion that at least legally it had been simpler. Reading about the contested will suggested she was wrong. It also made her think again about Ronald's character.

The next document was even more curious. It was a contract dated February 11, 1681, between Ronald Stewart and Elizabeth Flanagan. It had been drawn up and signed prior to their marriage, like a contemporary premarital agreement. But it wasn't about money or property per se. The contract merely gave Elizabeth the right to own property and enter into contracts in her own name after the marriage.

Kim read the whole document. Toward the end Ronald himself had written an explanation. Kim recognized the handwriting as the particularly graceful script she'd seen on many of the bills of lading in the castle. Ronald wrote: ''It is my intention that if actions pursuant to my mercantile endeavor require my prolonged absence from Salem Town and Maritime, Ltd, that my betrothed, Elizabeth Flanagan, may justly and legally administer our joint affairs.''

After finishing the document, Kim went back to the beginning and reread it to make sure she understood it. It amazed her. The fact that such a document was necessary in order for Elizabeth to sign contracts reminded her that the role of women had been quite different in Puritan times. Their legal rights were limited. It was the same message Kim had gotten from the letter Elizabeth's father had written to Ronald concerning Elizabeth's hand in marriage.

Laying the premarital agreement aside, Kim went back to the remaining papers in Ronald Stewart's folder. After a handful of additional debtor suits, Kim came across a truly interesting document. It was a petition by Ronald Stewart requesting a Writ of Replevin. It was dated Tuesday, July 26, 1692, a week after Elizabeth's death.

Kim had no idea what Replevin meant, but she quickly got an idea. Ronald wrote: ''I humbly beg the court in God's name to return to my possession forthwith the conclusive evidence seized from my property by Sheriff George Corwin and used against my beloved wife, Elizabeth, during her trial for witchcraft by the Court of Oyer and Terminer on 20 June 1692.''

Attached to the back of the petition was an August 3, 1692, ruling by Magistrate John Hathorne denying the petition. In his denial the magistrate said: "The Court advises said petitioner, Ronald Stewart, likewise to petition his excellency the Governor of the Commonwealth for the aforementioned evidence since, by executive order, custody of said evidence has been transferred from Essex to Suffolk County."

In one sense Kim was pleased. She'd found indirect documentary evidence of Elizabeth's ordeal: she'd been tried and evidently convicted. At the same time Kim felt frustrated that the nature of the "conclusive evidence" was never mentioned. She reread both the petition and the ruling in hopes she'd missed it. But she hadn't. The evidence was not described.

For a few minutes Kim sat at the table and tried to imagine what the evidence could have been. The only thing she could think of was something to do with the occult, and that was because of her father's vague statement. Then she got an idea. Glancing back at the petition, she wrote down the date of the trial. With the date in hand she returned to the counter and got the clerk's attention.

"I'd like to see the records of the Court of Oyer and Terminer for June 20, 1692."

The clerk literally laughed in Kim's face. Then she repeated the request and laughed again. Confused, Kim asked what was so funny.

"You're asking for something just about every Tom, Dick, and Harry would want," the clerk said. She sounded as if she'd just come from the back country of Maine. "Trouble is, no such records exist. Wish they did, but they don't. There's no record of that Court of Oyer and Terminer for all the witch trials. All there is is some scattered testimony and depositions, but the court records themselves plumb disappeared."

"How unfortunate," Kim said. "Maybe you could tell me something else. Do you happen to know what 'conclusive evidence' means?"

"I ain't no lawyer," the clerk said. "But hold your horses. Let me ask."

The clerk disappeared into an office. Seconds later she reemerged with a heavyset woman in tow. The second woman had oversized glasses balanced on a short, wide nose.

"You're interested in a definition of 'conclusive evidence,' " the woman said.

Kim nodded.

"It's pretty much self-explanatory," the woman said. "It means evidence that is incontrovertible. In other words it can't be questioned, or there is only one possible interpretation that can be drawn from it."

"That's what I thought," Kim said. She thanked the two women and went back to her material. Using a copy machine in the corner, she made a copy of the petition for a Writ of Replevin and the ruling. Then she returned the documents to their envelope and handed the envelope back to the clerk.

Finally Kim drove out to the compound. She felt a little guilty, since she'd told Mark Stevens she'd be there in the morning and already it was approaching noon. As she rounded the last bend in the road leading from the gate and broke free from the trees, she could see a handful of trucks and vans parked near the cottage. There was also a large backhoe and mounds of fresh earth. But Kim didn't see any people, not even on the backhoe.

Kim parked and got out of her car. The noontime heat and dust were oppressive, and the smell of the freshly turned earth was pungent. Kim closed the car door, and, shielding her face from the sun, she followed with her eyes the line of the trench that ran across the field toward the castle. At that moment the door to the house opened and George Harris stepped out. Sweat lined his forehead.

"Glad you could make it," George said. "I've been trying to call you."

"Is something wrong?" Kim asked.

"Sorta," George said evasively. "Maybe I'd better show you."

George motioned for Kim to follow him toward where the backhoe was parked.

"We had to stop work," George said.

"Why?" Kim asked.

George didn't answer. Instead he encouraged Kim to come over to the trench.

Hesitant to step too close to the edge for fear of its giving way, Kim stretched forward and looked in. She was impressed by the depth, which she estimated to be more than eight feet. Roots hung out of the sheer walls like miniature brooms. George directed her attention to the end, where the trench stopped abruptly fifty feet short of the cottage. Near the bottom Kim could see the damaged end of a wooden box protruding from the wall.

"That's why we had to stop," George said.

"What is it?" Kim asked.

"I'm afraid it's a coffin," George said.

"Good grief," Kim said.

"We found a headstone as well," George said. "It's an oldie." He motioned for Kim to come around the end of the trench. On the opposite side of the mound of excavated earth was a dirty white marble slab lying flat in the grass.

"It hadn't been set upright," George said. "It had been laid flat and eventually covered with earth." George bent down and wiped away the dried dirt on its face.

Kim took an involuntary gasp of air. "My God, it's Elizabeth!" she managed. She shook her head. There were too many coincidences.

"She a relative?" George asked.

"She is," Kim said. She examined the headstone. It was similar in design to Ronald's, and gave only the specifics, namely Elizabeth's birthdate and date of her death.

"Did you have any idea her grave would be here?" George asked. His tone wasn't accusatory, just curious.

"Not in the slightest," Kim said. "I only found out recently that she'd not been buried in the family plot."

"What do you want us to do?" George said. "You're supposed to have a permit to disturb a grave."

"Can't you just go around it and leave it be?" Kim asked.

"I suppose," George said. "We could just widen the trench along here. Should we be on the lookout for any others?"

"I don't think so," Kim said. "Elizabeth was a special case."

"I hope you don't mind me saying this," George said. "But you look kinda pale. Are you okay?"

"Thank you," Kim said. "I'm fine. Just a bit shocked. I guess I'm feeling a little superstitious about finding this woman's grave."

"So are we," George said. "Especially my backhoe operator. Let me go get him out here. We got to get these utilities in before we pour the basement."

George disappeared inside the house. Kim ventured back to the edge of the trench and peered down at the exposed corner of Elizabeth's coffin. The wood was in surprisingly good shape for being buried for over three hundred years. It didn't even appear rotten where the backhoe had damaged it.

Kim had no idea what to make of this unexpected discovery. First the portrait, now the grave. It was getting harder to dismiss these as fortuitous findings.

The sound of an approaching auto caught Kim's attention. Shielding her eyes once again from the noonday sun, she watched a familiar-looking car kicking up a plume of dust as it followed the dirt road across the field. She couldn't mentally place the vehicle until it pulled up next to her. Then she realized why it had been familiar. It was Kinnard's.

With some anxiety Kim walked over to the vehicle and leaned in through the passenger-side window.

"This is a surprise," Kim said. "What on earth are you doing out of the hospital?"

Kinnard laughed. "They let me out of my cage once in a while."

"What are you doing in Salem?" Kim asked. "How did you know I was here?"

"Marsha told me," Kinnard said. "I ran into her in the SICU this morning. I told her I was coming to Salem to look for an apartment since I'm rotating through Salem Hospital for August and September. There's no way I'm going to live in the hospital for two months. You do remember me telling you about my Salem Hospital rotation."

"I guess I forgot," Kim said.

"I told you several months ago," Kinnard said.

"If you say so," Kim said. She had no intention of getting into an argument. She already felt uncomfortable enough.

"You're looking good," Kinnard said. "I suppose dating Dr. Edward Armstrong agrees with you."

"How do you know whom I'm dating?" Kim asked.

"Hospital gossip," Kinnard said. "Since you've chosen a scientific celebrity, it gets around. The irony is that I know the man. I worked in his lab the year I took off to do research after my second year of medical school."

Kim could feel herself blush. She would have preferred not to show any reaction, but she couldn't help it. Kinnard was obviously trying to upset her, and as usual he was doing a good job.

"Edward is a smart man scientifically," Kinnard said, "but I'm afraid he's a little nerdy, even weird. Well . . . maybe that's unfair. Maybe I should just say eccentric."

"I find him attentive and considerate," Kim said.

"I can imagine," Kinnard said, rolling his eyes. "I heard about the daily flowers. Personally I think that's absurd. A guy has to be totally unsure of himself to go to that kind of extreme."

Kim turned a bright red. Marsha had to have told Kinnard about the flowers. Between her mother and her roommate she wondered if she had any secrets.

"At least Edward Armstrong won't irritate you by going skiing," Kinnard said. "His coordination is such that a flight of stairs can be a challenge."

"I think you are being juvenile," Kim said frostily when she found her voice. "Frankly, it doesn't suit you. I'd thought you were more mature."

"It doesn't matter." Kinnard laughed cynically. "I've gone on, as they say, to greener pastures. I'm enjoying a new burgeoning relationship myself."

"I'm happy for you," Kim said sarcastically.

Kinnard bent down so he could see out through the windshield as the backhoe started up. "Marsha told me you were fixing this place up," he said. "Is old Doc Armstrong going to move in with you?"

Kim started to deny the possibility, but caught herself. Instead she said, "We're thinking about it. We haven't decided yet."

"Enjoy yourself one way or the other," Kinnard said with equal sarcasm. "Have a nice life."

Kinnard threw his car into reverse, shot backwards, and skidded to a stop. Then he put the engine in drive and tromped on the accelerator. With a shower of dirt, small pebbles, and dust he shot across the field and disappeared through the trees.

At first Kim concentrated on shielding herself from flying stones. Once the danger was past, she watched Kinnard's car until she could no longer see it. Even though she'd known almost from the moment he'd arrived that his goal had been to provoke her, she'd not been able to prevent it. For a moment she felt emotionally frazzled. It wasn't until she walked back over to the trench that was now being widened and saw Elizabeth's coffin that she began to calm down. Comparing her troubles with Elizabeth's at the same age made hers seem trivial.

After pulling herself together emotionally, Kim set to work. The afternoon passed quickly. Most of her time was spent in Mark Stevens' office going over details of the kitchen and bathroom design. For Kim it was a supreme pleasure. It was the first time in her life that she was creating a living environment for herself. It made her wonder how she had allowed her career goals to be so easily circumvented.

By seven-thirty Mark Stevens and George Harris were both exhausted, but Kim had gotten a second wind. The men had to tell Kim their eyes were blurry before Kim admitted she had to get back to the city. As they walked her out to her car, they thanked her for coming and promised her things would move quickly.

Driving into Cambridge, Kim didn't even attempt to look for a parking place on the street. Instead she drove directly into the Charles' parking garage and walked over to the Harvest Bar. It was filled to overflowing with a Friday-night crowd, most of whom had been there through happy hour.

Kim looked for Edward but didn't immediately see him. She had to worm her way through the crowd standing five deep around the bar. Finally she found him nursing a glass of chardonnay at a table behind the bar. As soon as he saw her, his face lit up and he leaped to his feet to pull out her chair.

As Edward pushed the chair in under her, Kim remarked to herself that Kinnard would not have made the effort.

"You look like you could use a glass of white wine," Edward said.

Kim nodded. She could tell instantly that Edward was either excited or self-conscious. His stutter was more apparent than usual. She watched while he caught the waitress's attention and gave the order for two glasses of wine. Then he looked at her.

"Did you have a good day?" he asked.

"It was busy," Kim said. "What about yours?"

"It was a great day!" Edward said excitedly. "I've got some good news. The dirt samples from Elizabeth's food bins grew out a mold with hallucinogenic effects. I think we have solved the question of what at least kicked off the Salem witch trials. The only thing we don't know is whether it was ergotism or something entirely new."

Edward went on to tell Kim everything that had happened at Kevin Scranton's office.

Kim's response was concerned disbelief. "You took a drug without knowing what it was?" she asked. "Wasn't that dangerous?"

"You sound like Kevin." Edward laughed. "I'm surrounded by ersatz parents. No, it wasn't dangerous. It was too small a dose to be dangerous. But, being small, it certainly indicated the hallucinogenic power of this new fungus."

"It sounds foolhardy to me," Kim persisted.

"It wasn't," Edward said. "I even had a urinalysis and a creatinine blood test this afternoon for Kevin's sake. They were both normal. I'm fine. Believe me. In fact, I'm better than fine. I'm ecstatic. At first I was hoping this new fungus would make the same mix of alkaloids as *Claviceps* so it would prove ergotism was the culprit. Now I'm hoping it makes its own alkaloids.''

"What are alkaloids?'' Kim asked. "It's a familiar term but I couldn't define it to save my life.''

"Alkaloids are a large group of nitrogen-containing compounds found in plants,'' Edward said. "They're familiar to you because many of them are common, like caffeine, morphine, and nicotine. As you can guess, most are pharmacologically active.''

"Why are you getting so excited about finding some new ones if they are so common?'' Kim asked.

"Because I've already proven whatever alkaloid is in this new fungus, it's psychotropically active,'' Edward said. "Finding a new hallucinogenic drug can open up all sorts of doors to the understanding of brain function. Invariably they resemble and mimic the brain's own neurotransmitters.''

"When will you know if you've found new alkaloids?'' Kim asked.

"Soon,'' Edward said. "Now tell me about your day.''

Kim took a breath. Then she related to Edward everything that had happened to her, in chronological order, starting with her talk with her father and ending with the completion of the design for the new kitchen and baths for the cottage.

"Wow!'' Edward said, "you did have a busy day. I'm astounded by the discovery of Elizabeth's grave. And you said the coffin was in good shape?''

"What I could see of it,'' Kim said. "It was buried very deep, probably around eight feet down. Its end was sticking into the trench. It had been damaged by the backhoe.''

"Did finding the grave upset you?'' Edward asked.

"In a way,'' Kim said with a short mirthless laugh. "Thinking about finding it so soon after finding the portrait makes me feel weird. It gave me that feeling again that Elizabeth is trying to communicate with me.''

"Uh oh,'' Edward said. "Sounds like you are having another attack of superstition.''

Kim laughed despite her seriousness.

"Tell me something," Edward said teasingly. "Are you afraid of black cats crossing your path, or walking under ladders, or using the number thirteen?"

Kim hesitated. She was mildly superstitious, but she'd never given it much thought.

"So you *are* superstitious!" Edward said. "Now think about this! Back in the seventeenth century you could have been considered a witch since such beliefs involve the occult."

"All right, smarty pants," Kim said. "So maybe I'm a little superstitious. But there seem to be too many coincidences involving Elizabeth. I also found out today that the calendar in 1692 is the same as this year's, 1994. I also found out Elizabeth died at my age. And as if that's not enough, our birthdays are only two days apart, so we have the same astrological sign."

"What do you want me to say?" Edward asked.

"Can you explain all these coincidences?" Kim asked.

"Of course," Edward said. "It's pure chance. It's like the old cliché that if you have enough monkeys and enough typewriters, you can produce *Hamlet.*"

"Oh, I give up," Kim said with a chuckle. She took a sip of her wine.

"I'm sorry," Edward said with a shrug. "I'm a scientist."

"Let me tell you something else I learned today," Kim said. "Things were not so simple back then. Ronald was married three times. His first wife died, willing him a sizable fortune which was contested unsuccessfully by his wife's child by a previous marriage. He then married Elizabeth within a couple of years. After Elizabeth died he married her sister in the same year."

"So?" Edward said.

"Doesn't that sound a little fishy to you?" Kim asked.

"No," Edward said. "Remember life was harsh back in those days. Ronald had children to raise. Also, marrying within in-laws was not unusual."

"Well, I'm not so sure," Kim said. "It leaves a lot of questions in my mind."

The waitress appeared and interrupted their conversation

to tell them their table was ready. Kim was pleasantly surprised. She didn't know they were planning to eat at the Harvest. She was famished.

They followed the waitress out onto the terrace and were seated beneath trees filled with tiny white lights. It was a perfect temperature after having cooled down considerably from the day. There was no wind, so the candle on the table burned languidly.

While they were waiting for their food, Kim showed Edward the copy she'd made of Ronald's petition. Edward read it with great interest. When he was finished he congratulated Kim on her detective work, saying that she'd succeeded in proving Elizabeth had indeed been caught up in the witchcraft affair. Kim told him about her father's comment concerning Elizabeth's possible association with the occult.

"Which is what I suggested," Edward reminded her.

"So would you guess that the conclusive evidence had something to do with the occult?"

"I don't think there is any question," Edward said.

"That's what I thought," Kim said. "But do you have any specific ideas?"

"I don't know enough about witchcraft to be creative," Edward said.

"What about a book?" Kim questioned. "Or something she wrote?"

"Sounds good," Edward said. "I suppose it could have been something she drew as well. Or at least some kind of image."

"What about a doll?" Kim suggested.

"Good idea," Edward said. Then he paused. "I know what it must have been!"

"What?" Kim asked eagerly.

"Her broom!" Edward said. Then he laughed.

"Come on," Kim said, but she was smiling herself. "I'm being serious."

Edward apologized. He then went on to explain the background of the witch's broom, and how it had originated in medieval times with a stick that had been coated with an ointment concocted with hallucinogenic drugs. He told her that in satanic rituals it had been used to cause psychedelic experiences when placed against intimate mucous membranes.

"I've heard enough," Kim said. "I get the idea."

Their food arrived. They didn't talk until the waiter had left. Edward was the first to speak. "The problem is that the evidence could have been any one of a number of things, and there's no way of knowing specifically unless you found a description. What about looking in the court records themselves?"

"I thought of that," Kim said. "But I was told that none of the records of the special Court of Oyer and Terminer remain."

"Too bad," Edward said. "I guess that throws you back into that hopeless pile of papers in the castle."

"Yeah," Kim said without enthusiasm. "Plus there's no guarantee it would be there."

While they ate their meal the conversation shifted to more mundane issues. It wasn't until they were finishing their dessert that Edward returned to the issue of Elizabeth's grave.

"What was the state of preservation of Elizabeth's body?" he asked.

"I never saw the body," Kim said. She was shocked at such a question. "The coffin wasn't opened. The backhoe just hit the end and jarred it a little."

"Maybe we should open it," Edward said. "I'd love to get a sample—if there is anything recognizable to sample. If we could find some residue of whatever alkaloid this new fungus produces, we'd have definitive proof that the devil in Salem was a fungus."

"I can't believe you'd even suggest such a thing," Kim said. "The last thing I want to do is disturb Elizabeth's body."

"Here we go being superstitious again," Edward said. "You understand that such a position is akin to being against autopsies."

"This is different," Kim said. "She's already been buried."

"People are exhumed all the time," Edward said.

"I suppose you are right," Kim said reluctantly.

"Maybe I should take a ride up there with you tomorrow," Edward said. "We could both take a look."

"You have to have a permit to exhume a body," Kim said.

"The backhoe already did most of the job," Edward said. "Let's take a look and decide tomorrow."

The bill came and Edward paid it. Kim thanked him and told him that the next dinner was on her. Edward said they could argue about it.

Outside the restaurant there was an awkward moment. Edward asked her over to his apartment, but Kim demurred. She reminded him that she'd felt uncomfortable that morning. Ultimately they resolved the issue, at least temporarily, by agreeing to go to Edward's to discuss it.

Later, while sitting on Edward's couch, Kim asked him if he remembered a student named Kinnard Monihan, who'd done research in his lab four or five years previously.

"Kinnard Monihan," Edward said. He closed his eyes in concentration. "I have a lot of students passing through. But, yes, I remember him. As I recall he went on to the General for a surgical residency."

"That's the one," Kim said. "Do you remember much about him?"

"I remember I was disappointed when I'd heard he was taking a residency," Edward said. "He was a smart kid. I'd expected him to stay in academic research. Why do you ask?"

"We dated for a number of years," Kim said. She was about to tell Edward about the confrontation at the compound when Edward interrupted her.

"Were you and Kinnard lovers?" Edward asked.

"I suppose you can say that," Kim said hesitantly. She could tell instantly that Edward was upset. Both his behavior and speech changed dramatically. It took Kim a half hour of coaxing and convincing to get him to calm down and to understand that her relationship with Kinnard was over. Kim even apologized for bringing up his name.

In a deliberate attempt to change the subject, she asked Edward if he'd done anything about finding a new apartment. Edward admitted that he'd not had a chance. Kim warned him that September would be arriving quickly.

As the evening progressed, neither Kim nor Edward brought up the issue of whether Kim should spend the night. By not making a decision, they made a decision. She stayed. Later, as they were lying side by side in bed, Kim began to think about what she'd said to Kinnard about Edward moving in with her. It had been meant merely to provoke Kinnard, but now Kim began seriously to consider the idea. It had a definite appeal. The relationship with Edward was continuing to blossom. Besides, the cottage was more than ample, and it was isolated. It might even be lonely.

# 5

**Saturday,
July 23, 1994**

KIM AWAKENED IN STAGES. EVEN BEFORE SHE HAD opened her eyes she heard Edward's voice. At first she'd incorporated it into her dream, but then, as she'd become more conscious, she realized it was coming from the other room.

With some difficulty Kim opened her eyes. First she made sure that Edward was not in bed, then she glanced at the clock. It was 5:45 A.M.

Settling back into the pillow and feeling concerned that something was wrong, Kim tried to hear what was being said, but she couldn't. Edward's voice was unintelligible, yet from its timbre Kim could tell that he was excited.

Within a few minutes Edward returned. He was dressed in a bathrobe. As he tiptoed across the room en route to the bathroom, Kim told him she was awake. Changing directions, he came over and sat on the edge of the bed.

"I've got great news," Edward whispered.

"I'm awake," Kim repeated. "You can speak normally."

"I was just talking to Eleanor," Edward said.

"At five forty-five in the morning?" Kim questioned. "Who on earth is Eleanor?"

"She's one of my postdocs," Edward said. "She's my right-hand person in the lab."

"This seems awfully early for shop talk," Kim said. Involuntarily she thought of Grace Traters, her father's supposed assistant.

"She pulled an all-nighter," Edward said. "Kevin sent

over several more sclerotia from the new fungus last night. Eleanor stayed to prepare and run a crude sample through the mass spectrometer. The alkaloids don't seem to be the same as those in *Claviceps purpurea*. In fact they appear to be three totally new alkaloids.''

''I'm happy for you,'' Kim said. It was far too early for her to say much else.

''The most exciting thing is that I know at least one of them is psychoactive,'' Edward said. ''Hell, all *three* might be.'' He rubbed his hands excitedly as if he were about to get to work that instant.

''I can't tell you how important this could be,'' Edward continued. ''We could have a new drug here, or even a whole family of new drugs. Even if they prove not to be clinically useful, they'll undoubtedly be valuable as research tools.''

''I'm glad,'' Kim said. She rubbed her eyes; she wanted to get into the bathroom to brush her teeth.

''It's amazing how often serendipity plays a role in drug discovery,'' Edward said. ''Imagine finding a drug because of the Salem witch trials. That's even better than the way Prozac was discovered.''

''That was by accident?'' Kim asked.

''I should say.'' Edward laughed. ''The main researcher responsible was playing around with antihistamines and testing them in an experimental protocol that measured the effect on the neurotransmitter, norepinephrine. By serendipity he ended up with Prozac, which is not an antihistamine, and affects serotonin, another neurotransmitter, two hundred times more than it affects norepinephrine.''

''That's amazing,'' Kim said, but she'd not been listening. Without having had her morning coffee, her mind wasn't prepared for such intricacies.

''I can't wait to get working on these new alkaloids,'' Edward said.

''Do you want to change your mind about going up to Salem?'' Kim asked.

''No!'' Edward said without hesitation. ''I want to see that grave. Come on! As long as you're awake, let's go!'' He gave Kim a playful shake of her leg through the covers.

After showering, blow-drying her hair, and applying makeup, Kim left Edward's apartment with him for another greasy but tasty breakfast in Harvard Square. Following their meal, they stopped into one of the many bookstores in the square. Their breakfast conversation had included a discussion of Puritanism. They both realized how little they knew about it, so they bought a few appropriate books. It was well after nine by the time they were on their way to the North Shore.

Kim drove, since they were again reluctant to leave her car in the residents-only parking area in front of Edward's apartment. With no traffic they made good time and were in Salem just before ten. Following the same route they had the previous Saturday, they again passed the Witch House.

Edward reached out and grabbed Kim's arm. "Have you ever visited the Witch House?" he asked her.

"A long time ago," Kim said. "Why? Are you interested?"

"Don't laugh, but I am," Edward said. "Would you mind taking a few minutes?"

"Not at all," Kim said. She turned on Federal Street and parked near the courthouse. When they walked back they found they had to wait. The Witch House opened at ten. They also weren't the only prospective visitors. There were a number of families and several couples already standing outside the old building.

"It is amazing the appeal the Salem witch trials have," Kim commented. "I wonder if people stop to think why it interests them so much."

"Your cousin Stanton described the episode as ghoulishly seductive," Edward said.

"That sounds like Stanton," Kim said.

"He said the attraction is that it's a window on the supernatural," Edward added. "I happen to agree. Most people are a bit superstitious, and the witchcraft story titillates their imaginations."

"I agree," Kim said. "But I'm afraid there's also something perverse about the appeal. The fact that people were executed is key. Also, I don't think it was an accident that there were many more witches than wizards. There's a gender bias as well."

"Now don't get too far out on any feminist plank," Edward said. "I think there were more females involved because of the role of women in colonial culture. Obviously they were associated with birth and death, and health and disease, a lot more than men, and those aspects of life were shrouded with superstition and the occult. They simply didn't have any other explanation for them."

"I think we're both right," Kim said. "I agree with you, but I've also been impressed with the little research I've done about the lack of legal status of women in Elizabeth's time. The men were scared, and they took it out on the women. Misogyny was involved."

At that moment the door to the Witch House opened. Greeting them was a young woman in period costume. It was then that Kim and Edward learned that the visit to the house was a guided tour. Everyone trooped into the parlor and waited for the talk to begin.

"I thought we would be allowed to wander around by ourselves," Edward whispered.

"I did too," Kim replied.

They listened while the young woman described the many furnishings in the room, including a Bible box which was said to be an invariable part of a Puritan household.

"I'm losing interest," Edward whispered. "Maybe we should go."

"Fine with me," Kim said agreeably.

They exited the building. When they reached the street, Edward turned around and faced the house.

"The reason I wanted to go in was to see how much the interior resembled the cottage," Edward said. "It's amazing. It is as if they were built from the same plans."

"Well, as you said, individuality wasn't encouraged back then," Kim remarked.

They climbed back into the car and drove the rest of the way to the compound. The first thing Edward saw was the utility trench. He was amazed at its length. It now stretched from near the castle all the way to the cottage. When they stood at the edge, they could see that it had already been tunneled under the cottage's foundation.

"There's the coffin," Kim said as she pointed to the place where it protruded. At that point the trench had been significantly widened.

"What a stroke of luck," Edward said. "It looks to me like the head of the coffin. And you were right about the depth. It's at least eight feet down, maybe more."

"The trench is only deep here by the cottage," Kim pointed out. "Where it crosses the field it's much shallower."

"You're right," Edward said. He started walking away from the house.

"Where are you going?" Kim asked. "Don't you want to take a look at the headstone?"

"I'm going to take a closer look at the coffin," Edward said. As soon as he could manage it, Edward jumped into the trench, then came walking back, descending deeper with each step.

Kim watched him with growing concern. She was beginning to worry about what he had in mind.

"Are you sure this thing won't cave in?" Kim asked nervously. She could hear bits of dirt and stones fall into the crevice when she got too close to the edge.

Edward didn't answer. He was already bending down and examining the damaged end of the coffin. Scraping some of the immediately adjacent dirt into his hand, he felt it.

"This is encouraging," he said. "It's bone-dry down here and amazingly cool." He then insinuated his fingers into the partially opened joint between the head of the coffin and its side. With a sharp yank the headpiece bent to the side.

"Good God!" Kim murmured to herself.

"Would you get the flashlight from the car?" Edward said. He was looking into the open end of the coffin.

Kim did as she was told, but she wasn't happy about what was happening. She didn't like the idea of disturbing Elizabeth's grave any more than it already had been. After venturing as close to the edge of the trench as she dared, she tossed the flashlight down to Edward.

Edward shined the light into the open end of the coffin. "We're in luck," he said. "The corpse has been mummified by the cold and the dryness. Even the winding sheet is intact."

"I think we've done enough," Kim said. But she might as well have been talking to the trees. Edward wasn't listening. To her horror she watched while he put the light down and reached into the coffin. "Edward! What are you doing?"

"I'm just going to slide the body out a little way," he explained. He got hold of the head and began to pull. Nothing happened, so he put one foot against the wall of the trench and pulled harder. To his surprise the head detached suddenly, causing Edward to fall against the opposite wall of the trench. He ended up in a sitting position with Elizabeth's mummified head in his lap. A small shower of dirt dusted down onto his own head.

Kim felt weak. She had to look away.

"My gosh," Edward said as he got to his feet. He glanced at the base of Elizabeth's head. "I guess her neck must have been broken when she was hanged. That's kinda surprising since the method of death in those days was not to cause the neck to break but rather let the person dangle and die of strangulation."

Edward put the head down and bent the end of the coffin back to its original position. Using a rock, he hammered it into place. When he was convinced he'd returned it to its original appearance, he carried the head back down the trench to where he could climb out.

"I hope you don't think this is funny," Kim said when he'd joined her. She refused to look at the object. "I want that put back!"

"I will," Edward promised. "I just want to take a little sample. Let's go inside and see if we can find a box."

Exasperated, Kim led the way. She marveled how she allowed herself to get involved in such situations. Edward sensed her attitude and quickly found an appropriately sized plumbing supply box. He put the head into it and put it in the car. Coming back into the house, he said eagerly, "Okay, let's have a tour."

"I want that head put back as soon as possible," Kim said.

"I will," Edward said again. To change the subject he walked into the lean-to portion of the house and pretended to admire the studding. Kim followed him. Soon her attention was diverted. There had been significant progress in the renovation. They even discovered the cellar floor had already been poured.

"I'm glad I got my dirt samples when I did," Edward said.

When they were on the second floor inspecting the work being done to install the half-bath, Kim heard a car pull up. Looking out one of the casement windows, her heart skipped a beat. It was her father.

"Oh, no!" Kim said. An uncomfortable anxiety spread through her that brought instant moisture to her palms.

Edward sensed her discomfiture immediately. "Are you embarrassed because I'm here?" he asked.

"Heavens, no!" Kim said. "It's because of Elizabeth's grave. Please don't let on about the head. The last thing I want is to give him an excuse to interfere with this renovation project."

They descended the stairs and stepped outside. John was standing at the edge of the trench, looking down at Elizabeth's coffin. Kim made the introductions. John was polite but curt. He took Kim aside.

"It's a bloody unfortunate coincidence for George Harris to blunder onto this grave," he said. "I told him to keep it quiet, and I trust you will do the same. I don't want your mother to find out about this. It'll put her in a tailspin. She'll be sick for a month."

"There's no reason for me to tell anyone," Kim said.

"Frankly I'm surprised that it is here," John said. "I'd been told that Elizabeth had been buried in a common grave someplace west of Salem center. What about this stranger you have here? Does he know about the grave?"

"Edward is not a stranger," Kim said. "And yes, he knows about the grave. He even knows about Elizabeth."

"I thought we had an understanding that you wouldn't be telling people about Elizabeth," John said.

"I didn't tell him," Kim said. "Stanton Lewis did."

"God damn your mother's side of the family," John mumbled as he turned around and walked back to where Edward was patiently waiting.

"The story of Elizabeth Stewart is privileged information," John said to Edward. "I hope you will respect that."

"I understand," Edward said evasively. He wondered what John would say if he knew about the head in the car.

Seemingly satisfied, John diverted his attention to the cottage. At Kim's suggestion he deigned to look briefly at the construction. It was a quick tour. Back outside he hesitated as he was about to leave. Looking at Edward he said, "Kim's a fine, sensible girl. She's very warm and loving."

"I think so too," Edward said.

John got into his car and drove off. Kim watched him until the car disappeared in the trees. "He has such an uncanny ability to irritate me," Kim fumed. "The problem is he doesn't even realize how belittling it is to be treated like a teenager and called a girl."

"At least he was being complimentary," Edward said.

"Complimentary my foot!" Kim said. "That was a self-serving comment. It was his way of trying to take credit for the way I've turned out. But he had nothing to do with it. He was never there for me. He has no clue that being a real father or husband is a lot more than providing food and shelter."

Edward put his arm around Kim's shoulder. "It's not going to accomplish anything to get yourself all worked up about it now," he said.

Kim abruptly turned to Edward. "I had an idea last night," she said. "What about you moving into the cottage with me come September first?"

Edward stumbled over his words. His stutter reappeared. "That's very generous," he managed to say.

"I think it is a wonderful idea," Kim said. "This place has more than enough space, and you have to find a new apartment anyway. What do you say?"

"Thank you," Edward stammered. "I don't know quite what to say. Maybe we should talk about it."

"Talk about it?" Kim questioned. She'd not expected to be rejected. Flowers from Edward were still arriving at her apartment on a daily basis.

"I'm just afraid you are inviting me impulsively," Edward explained. "I guess I'm afraid you'll change your mind and then not know how to disinvite me."

"Is that really your reason for feeling reluctant?" Kim asked. She stood on her tiptoes and gave him a hug. "Okay," she added. "We can talk about it. But I'm not going to change my mind."

Later, when they had exhausted discussing the renovation, Kim asked Edward if he'd be willing to spend a little time up at the castle going through the old papers. She explained that his comment the previous evening about discovering the nature of the evidence used against Elizabeth had given her a renewed impetus. Edward said he didn't mind in the slightest and that he was happy to accompany her.

Arriving at the castle, Kim suggested they try the attic instead of the wine cellar. Edward was initially agreeable, but when they got up there, they discovered it was extremely hot. Even after opening the dormer windows, it was still uncomfortable. Edward quickly lost interest.

"Why do I have the feeling you're not enjoying this?" Kim said. Edward had taken a drawer over to the window, but instead of searching through it, he was staring outside.

"I guess I'm preoccupied with the new alkaloids," Edward said. "I'm eager to get to the lab to work on them."

"Why don't you drive back to town and go do your thing?" Kim said. "I'll take the train back later."

"Good idea," Edward said. "But I'll take the train."

After a mini-argument which Edward won because there was no way for Kim to get to the train station later that afternoon, they walked back to the cottage and climbed into the car. Halfway to their destination, Kim suddenly remembered Elizabeth's head in the backseat.

"No problem," Edward said. "I'm taking it with me."

"On the train?" Kim asked.

"Why not," Edward said. "It's in a box."

"I want that back up here ASAP," Kim said. "They'll be filling in that trench as soon as the utilities are in."

"I'll be finished with it in no time," Edward assured her. "I'm just hoping there's something in it to sample. If there isn't maybe I could try for the liver."

"We're not going back into that coffin for anything but to put this head back," Kim said. "Not with my father hovering around. To make matters worse, he is apparently in contact with the contractor."

Kim dropped Edward off at the top of the stairs that led down to the train station. Edward lifted the plumbing supply box off the backseat.

"Want to meet for dinner?" Edward asked.

"I think not," Kim said. "I've got to get back to my apartment. I've got laundry to do, and I've got to get up early for work."

"Let's at least talk on the phone," Edward said.

"It's a deal," Kim said.

As much as Edward relished spending time with Kim, he was glad to get back to his lab. He was especially happy to see Eleanor, whom he did not expect to be there. She'd gone home, showered, and slept, but only for four or five hours. She said she was too excited to stay away.

The first thing she did was show him the mass spectrometry results. She was now certain that they were dealing with three new alkaloids. After talking with him that morning she'd spent time researching the results; there was no way they could have been made by any known compounds.

"Are there any more sclerotia?" Edward asked.

"A few," Eleanor said. "Kevin Scranton said more will be on their way, but he didn't know when. I didn't want to sacrifice the ones we have until I'd spoken with you. How do you want to separate the alkaloids? With organic solvents?"

"Let's use capillary electrophoresis," Edward said. "If necessary we can go to micellular electrokinetic capillary chromatography."

"Should I run a crude sample like I did with the mass spec?" Eleanor asked.

"No," Edward said. "Let's extract the alkaloids with distilled water and precipitate them with a weak acid. That's what I did over at the biological labs and it worked fine. We'll get purer samples, which will make structural work easier."

Eleanor started toward her bench space, but Edward grabbed her arm. "Before you start on the extraction I want you to do something else," he said. With no preamble he opened the plumbing supply box and lifted out the mummified head. Eleanor recoiled at the ghoulish sight.

"You could have warned me," she said.

"I suppose I could have," Edward said with a laugh. For the first time he looked at the head with a critical eye. It was rather lurid. The skin was dark brown, almost mahogany in color. It had dried to a leathery texture and retracted over the bony prominences, exposing the teeth in a gruesome smile. The hair was dried and matted like steel wool.

"What is it?" Eleanor asked. "An Egyptian mummy?"

Edward told Eleanor the story. He also explained that the reason he'd brought the head to the lab was to see if there was anything in the cranial vault to sample.

"Let me guess," Eleanor said. "You want to run it through the mass spec."

"Exactly," Edward said. "It would be scientifically elegant if we could show peaks corresponding to the new alkaloids. It would be definitive proof that this woman ingested the new mold."

While Eleanor ran over to the Department of Cell Biology to borrow anatomical dissection instruments, Edward faced the graduate students and assistants who had come in for the day and were nervously biding their time waiting for his attention. He answered all their questions in turn and sent them back to their experiments. By the time he was through, Eleanor was back.

"An anatomy instructor told me we should take the whole calvarium off," Eleanor said. She held up an electric vibratory saw.

Edward set to work. He reflected the scalp and exposed

the skull. Then he took the saw and cut off a skullcap. He and Eleanor looked inside. There wasn't much. The brain had contracted to a congealed mass in the back of the skull.

"What do you think?" Edward asked. He poked the mass with the tip of a scalpel. It was hard.

"Cut out a piece and I'll get it to dissolve in something," Eleanor said.

Edward did as she suggested.

Once they had the sample, they began to try various solvents. Unsure of what they had, they began to introduce them into the mass spectrometer. By the second sample they had a match. Several of the peaks corresponded exactly with those of the new alkaloids in the crude extract that Eleanor had run the night before.

"Isn't science great?" Edward commented gleefully.

"It's a turn-on," Eleanor agreed.

Edward went over to his desk and called Kim's apartment. As he anticipated, he got the answering machine. After the beep sounded he left a message that for Elizabeth Stewart the devil in Salem had been explained scientifically.

Hanging up the phone, Edward glided back to Eleanor. He was in a rare mood.

"All right, enough of this fooling around," he said. "Let's get down to some real science. Let's see if we can separate these new alkaloids so we can figure out what we have."

"This is impossible," Kim said. She pushed the drawer of a file cabinet closed with her hip. She was hot, dusty, and frustrated. After taking Edward to the train station, she'd returned to the attic in the castle and had made a four-hour general inspection from the servants' wing all the way around to the guest wing. Not only hadn't she found anything significant, she hadn't even found any seventeenth century material at all.

"This is not going to be an easy task," Kim said. Her eyes scanned the profusion of file cabinets, trunks, boxes, and bureaus that stretched as far as she could see until the attic made a right-hand turn. She was daunted by the sheer volume of material. There was even more in the attic than there was in the wine cellar. And like the wine cellar there was no order in terms of subject matter or chronology. Sequential pages varied as much as a century, and the subject matter bounced back and forth among mercantile data, business records, domestic receipts, official governmental documents, and personal correspondence. The only way to go through it all was page by page.

Confronted by such reality, Kim began to appreciate the good luck she'd had in finding James Flanagan's 1679 letter to Ronald Stewart that Monday. It had given her the false impression that researching Elizabeth in the castle would be an enjoyable if not easy undertaking.

Finally hunger, exhaustion, and discouragement temporarily overwhelmed Kim's commitment to discover the nature of the conclusive evidence used against Elizabeth. Badly in need of a shower, Kim descended from the attic and emerged into the late afternoon summer heat. Climbing into the car, she began the trek back to Boston.

# 6

## Monday,
## July 25, 1994

EDWARD'S EYES BLINKED OPEN AFTER ONLY FOUR
hours' sleep. It was just five A.M. Whenever he got excited
about a project, his need for sleep diminished. Just now, he
was more excited than he could ever remember being. His
scientific intuition was telling him that he'd stumbled onto
something really big, and his scientific intuition had never
failed him.

Leaping out of bed, Edward set Buffer into a paroxysm
of barking. The poor dog thought there was a life-
threatening emergency. Edward had to give him a light
swat to bring him to his senses.

After speeding through his morning ritual, which included taking Buffer for a short walk, Edward drove to his
lab. It was before seven when he entered, and Eleanor was
already there.

"I'm having trouble sleeping," she admitted. Her usually carefully combed long blond hair was in mild disarray.

"Me too," Edward said.

They had worked Saturday night until one A.M. and all
day Sunday. With success in sight, Edward had even
begged off plans to see Kim Sunday evening. When he'd
explained to her how close he and Eleanor were to their
goal, Kim had been understanding.

Finally, just after midnight Sunday, Edward and Eleanor
had perfected a separation technique. The difficulties had
been mostly due to the fact that two of the alkaloids shared
many physical properties. Now all they needed was more
material, and as if an answer to a prayer, Kevin Scranton

had called saying that he'd be sending over another batch of sclerotia that morning.

"I want everything to be ready when the material arrives," Edward said.

"Aye, aye," Eleanor said as she clicked her heels and made a playful salute. Edward tried to swat her on the top of her head but she was much more agile than he.

After they had been feverishly working for more than an hour, Eleanor tapped Edward on the arm.

"Are you intentionally ignoring your flock?" she asked quietly while motioning over her shoulder.

Edward straightened up and glanced around at the students who were milling aimlessly about, waiting for him to acknowledge them. He hadn't been aware of their presence. The group had been gradually enlarging as more and more people arrived at the lab. They all had their usual questions and were in need of his advice.

"Listen!" Edward called out. "You're on your own today. I'm tied up. I'm busy with a project that can't wait."

With some grumblings the crowd reluctantly dispersed. Edward did not notice their reaction. He went right back to work, and when he worked, his powers of concentration were legendary.

A few minutes later Eleanor again tapped his arm. "I hate to be a bother," she said, "but what about your nine o'clock lecture?"

"Damn!" Edward said. "I'd conveniently forgotten that. Find Ralph Carter and send him over." Ralph Carter was one of the senior assistants.

Within a short time Ralph appeared. He was a thin, bearded fellow with a surprisingly broad red-cheeked face.

"I want you to take over teaching the basic biochem summer course," Edward said.

"For how long?" Ralph asked. He was obviously not enthused.

"I'll let you know," Edward said.

After Ralph had left, Edward turned to Eleanor. "I hate that kind of passive-aggressive nonsense. It's the first time I've ever asked anyone to stand in for me for basic chemistry."

"That's because no one else has your commitment to teaching undergraduates," Eleanor explained.

As promised, the sclerotia arrived just after nine. They came in a small glass jar. Edward unscrewed the lid and carefully spread the dark, ricelike grains onto a piece of filter paper as if they were gold nuggets.

"Kinda ugly little things," Eleanor said. "They could almost be mouse droppings."

"I like to think they look more like seeds in rye bread," Edward said. "It's a more historically significant metaphor."

"Are you ready to get to work?" Eleanor asked.

"Let's do it," Edward said.

Before noon Edward and Eleanor had succeeded in producing a tiny amount of each alkaloid. The samples were in the bases of small, conical-shaped test tubes labeled A, B, and C. Outwardly the alkaloids appeared identical. They were all a white powder.

"What's the next step?" Eleanor asked as she held up one of the test tubes to the light.

"We have to find out which are psychoactive," Edward said. "Once we find out which ones are, we'll concentrate on them."

"What should we use for a test?" Eleanor asked. "I suppose we could use *Aplasia fasciata* ganglia preparations. They would certainly tell us which ones are neuroactive."

Edward shook his head. "It's not good enough," he said. "I want to know which ones cause hallucinogenic reactions, and I want quick answers. For that we need a human cerebrum."

"We can't use paid volunteers!" Eleanor said with consternation. "That would be flagrantly unethical."

"You are right," Edward said. "But I have no intention of using paid volunteers. I think you and I will do fine."

"I'm not sure I want to be involved in this," Eleanor said dubiously. She was beginning to get the drift of Edward's intentions.

"Excuse me!" called another voice. Edward and Eleanor turned to see Cindy, one of the departmental secretaries. "I hate to interrupt, Dr. Armstrong, but a Dr. Stanton Lewis is in the office, and he'd like a word with you."

''Tell him I'm busy,'' Edward said. But as soon as Cindy started back toward the office, Edward called her back. ''On second thought,'' he said, ''send him in.''

''I don't like that twinkle in your eye,'' Eleanor said as they waited for Stanton to appear.

''It's perfectly innocent,'' Edward said with a smile. ''Of course if Mr. Lewis would like to become a principal investigator in this study I won't stand in his way. Seriously, though, I do want to talk to him about what we are doing here.''

Stanton breezed into the lab with his usual glib hellos. He was particularly pleased to get Edward and Eleanor together.

''My two favorite people,'' he said, ''but for different parts of my brain.'' He laughed at what he thought was an off-color joke. Eleanor proved to be faster than he when she said she'd not known he'd changed his sexual orientation.

''What are you talking about?'' Stanton asked. He was genuinely perplexed.

''Simply that I'm confident you are attracted to me because of my intellect,'' Eleanor said. ''That leaves your instinctual brain for Edward.''

Edward chortled. Repartee was Stanton's forte, and Edward had never seen him bested. Stanton laughed as well and assured Eleanor that her wit had always blinded him to any of her other charms.

Stanton then turned to Edward. ''All right,'' he said. ''Fun and games are over. What's the story on the Genetrix prospectus?''

''I haven't had a chance to look at it,'' Edward admitted.

''You promised,'' Stanton warned. ''Am I going to have to tell my cousin she's not to see you anymore because you're not to be trusted?''

''Who's this cousin?'' Eleanor asked, giving Edward a gentle poke in the ribs.

Edward's face blushed with color. Rarely did his mild stutter affect his speech in the lab, but it did at that moment. He did not want to discuss Kim. ''I haven't had time for any reading," he told Stanton with some difficulty. "Something has come up that might particularly interest you."

"This better be good," Stanton teased. He slapped Edward on the back and told him he was only kidding about Kim. "I would never interfere with you two love doves. I heard from my aunt that old man Stewart surprised you two up in Salem. I hope it wasn't flagrante delicto, you old rogue."

Edward coughed nervously while he motioned for Stanton to pull up a chair. He then quickly changed the subject by launching into the story about the new fungus and the new alkaloids. He told Stanton that at least one of them was psychotropic, and he told him exactly how he knew. He even handed Stanton the three test tubes, saying they'd just finished isolating the new compounds.

"Quite a story," Stanton said. He put the test tubes down on the counter. "But why did you think it might interest me in particular? I'm a practical guy. I'm not titillated by esoteric exotica which you academics thrive on."

"I think these alkaloids could have a practical payoff," Edward said. "We could be on the brink of finding a whole new group of psychotropic drugs which at the very least will have research applications."

Stanton visibly straightened up in his seat. The casual air that he affected vanished. "New drugs?" he questioned. "This does sound interesting. What do you think the possibilities are they might be clinically useful?"

"I think the chances are excellent," Edward said. "Especially considering the molecular modification techniques which are now available in modern synthetic chemistry. Also, after the psychedelic episode with the crude extract, I felt strangely energized and my mind seemed especially clear. I believe these drugs might be more than merely hallucinogenic."

"Oh, my goodness!" Stanton exclaimed. His entrepreneurial proclivity had quickened his pulse. "This could be something huge."

"That's what we have been thinking," Edward said.

"I'm talking about you seeing a major league economic reward," Stanton said.

"Our interest is primarily what a new group of psychoactive drugs can do for science,'' Edward said. ''Everyone is anticipating some new breakthrough in the understanding of brain function. Who knows? This could be it. If it were to be so, we'd have to figure out a way to finance its production on a large scale. Researchers around the world would be clamoring for it.''

''That's fine and dandy,'' Stanton said. ''I'm happy you have such lofty goals. But why not have both? I'm talking about you making some serious money.''

''I'm not concerned about becoming a millionaire,'' Edward said. ''You should know that by now.''

''Millionaire?'' Stanton questioned with a derisive chortle. ''If this new line of drugs is efficacious for depression or anxiety or some combination, you could be looking at a billion-dollar molecule.''

Edward started to remind Stanton that they had different value systems, but he stopped in midsentence. His face went slack. He asked Stanton if he'd said billion.

''I said billion-dollar molecule!'' Stanton repeated. ''I'm not exaggerating. Experience with Librium, then Valium, and now with Prozac has proved society's insatiable appetite for clinically effective psychotropic drugs.''

Edward assumed a thousand-yard stare out across the Harvard Medical School quad. When he spoke his voice had a flat, trancelike quality. ''From your point of view and experience, what would have to be done to take advantage of such a discovery?''

''Not much,'' Stanton said. ''All you'd have to do is form a company and patent the drug. It's that simple. But until you do that, secrecy is paramount.''

''There's been secrecy,'' Edward said. He was still acting distracted. ''It's only been a few days that we've known we were dealing with something new. Eleanor and I are the only ones involved.'' He didn't mention Kim's name for fear of the conversation reverting to her.

''I'd say the fewer people you tell the better,'' Stanton said. ''Also, I could just go ahead and form a company just in case things begin to look promising.''

Edward massaged his eye sockets and then his face. He took a deep breath and appeared to awaken from a trance.

"I think we are jumping the gun," he said. "Eleanor and I have a lot of work to do before we have any idea of what we might have stumbled on."

"What's the next step?" Stanton asked.

"I'm glad you asked," Edward said. He pushed away from the counter and walked over to a glassware cabinet. "Eleanor and I were just talking about that. The first thing we have to do is determine which of these compounds is psychotropic." Edward brought three flasks back to where they were sitting. He then placed a minuscule amount of each new alkaloid in each flask and filled them all with a liter of distilled water. He shook each briskly.

"How will you do that?" Stanton asked even though from Edward's story he had an idea.

Edward took three one-milliliter pipettes out of a drawer. "Anybody care to join me?" he asked. Neither Eleanor nor Stanton said a word.

"Such chickens," Edward said with a laugh. Then he added: "I'm only kidding. Actually I want you around just in case. This is my party."

Stanton looked at Eleanor. "Is this guy nuts or what?"

Eleanor eyed Edward. She knew he was not foolhardy, and she'd never met anyone as smart as he was, especially when it came to biochemistry. "You're convinced this is safe, aren't you?" she said.

"No worse than taking a few tokes on a joint," he said. "At best a milliliter will contain a few millionths of a gram. Besides, I took a comparatively crude extract with no ill effect whatsoever. In fact it was mildly enjoyable. These are relatively pure samples."

"All right!" Eleanor said. "Give me one of those pipettes."

"Are you sure?" Edward questioned. "There's no coercion here. I don't mind taking all three."

"I'm sure," Eleanor said. She took a pipette.

"What about you, Stanton?" Edward asked. "Here's your chance to participate in some real science. Plus if you really want me to read that damn prospectus, you can do me a favor as well."

"I suppose if you two screwballs think it is safe enough,

I can do it,'' Stanton said reluctantly. "But you'd better read that prospectus or you'll be hearing from some of my North End mafia friends.'' Stanton took a pipette.

"Each can choose his own poison,'' Edward said, motioning toward the flasks.

"Reword that or I'm backing out,'' Stanton said.

Edward laughed. He was enjoying Stanton's discomfiture. Too often it had been the other way around.

Stanton let Eleanor choose first, then he took one of the two remaining flasks. "This strikes me as a kind of pharmacological Russian roulette,'' he said.

Eleanor laughed. She told Stanton he was too clever for his own good.

"Not clever enough to keep myself from getting involved with you two oddballs,'' he said.

"Ladies first,'' Edward said.

Eleanor filled the pipette and placed a milliliter on her tongue. Edward encouraged her to follow it with a glass of water.

The two men watched her. No one spoke. Several minutes went by. Finally Eleanor shrugged. "Nothing,'' she said. "Except my pulse rate went up slightly.''

"That's from pure terror,'' Stanton said.

"You're next,'' Edward said, motioning to Stanton.

Stanton filled his pipette. "It's a crime what I have to go through to get you on a scientific advisory board,'' he complained to Edward. He deposited the tiny amount of liquid on his tongue, then chased it with a glass of water.

"It's bitter,'' he said. "But I don't feel anything.''

"Wait another few seconds for circulation time,'' Edward said. Edward filled his own pipette. He began to have doubts, wondering if there could have been some other water-soluble compound in the crude extract that had caused his psychedelic reaction.

"I think I'm feeling slightly dizzy,'' Stanton said.

"Good,'' Edward said. His doubts faded. He remembered dizziness had been his first symptom with the crude extract. "Anything else?''

Stanton suddenly tensed and then made a grimace as his eyes darted around the room.

"What are you seeing?" Edward asked.

"Colors!" Stanton said. "I'm seeing moving colors." He started to describe the colors in more detail, but then he interrupted himself with a cry of fear. Leaping to his feet, he began to frantically wipe off his arms.

"What's the matter?" Edward asked.

"I'm being bitten by insects," Stanton said. He continued to try to brush away imaginary pests until he began to choke.

"What's happening now?" Edward asked.

"My chest is tight!" Stanton croaked. "I can't swallow."

Edward reached out and gripped Stanton's arm. Eleanor picked up the phone and started dialing, but Edward told her it was okay. Stanton had instantly calmed down. His eyes closed and a smile spread across his face. Edward backed him up a step and sat him back down in his chair.

Stanton responded to questions slowly and reluctantly. He said he was busy and didn't want to be bothered. When asked what he was busy doing, he merely said: "Things."

After twenty minutes Stanton's smile waned. For a few minutes it appeared as if he were asleep, then his eyes slowly opened.

The first thing he did was swallow. "My mouth feels like the Gobi Desert," he said. "I need a drink."

Edward poured a glass of water and gave it to him. He drank it with gusto and had a second.

"I'd say that was a busy couple of minutes," Stanton said. "It was also kind of fun."

"It was more like twenty minutes," Edward said.

"Are you serious?" Stanton questioned.

"How do you feel generally?" Edward asked.

"Wonderfully calm," Stanton said.

"How about clairvoyant?" Edward asked.

"That's a good way to describe it," Stanton said. "I feel as if I can remember all sorts of things with startling clarity."

"That's exactly how I felt," Edward said. "What about the choking sensation?"

"What choking sensation?" Stanton asked.

"You were complaining about a choking sensation," Edward said. "You were also complaining about being bitten by insects."

"I don't remember that at all," Stanton said.

"Well, no matter," Edward said. "The point is we know that compound B is definitely hallucinogenic. Let's see about the last one."

Edward took his dose. As they did with Eleanor, they waited for several minutes. Nothing happened.

"One for three is fine with me," Edward said. "Now we know which of the alkaloids we will concentrate our efforts on."

"Maybe we should just bottle this stuff and sell it the way it is," Stanton joked. "The sixties generation would have loved it. I mean I feel great, almost euphoric. Of course, maybe I'm just reacting to the relief of the ordeal being over. I have to admit I was scared."

"I thought I experienced some euphoria as well," Edward said. "Since we both felt it, maybe it's a result of the alkaloid. One way or the other, I'm encouraged. I think we've got a psychedelic drug with some calming properties as well as some amnestic properties."

"What about this clairvoyant feeling?" Stanton asked.

"I'd like to think that is a reflection of an increase in overall brain function," Edward said. "In that sense perhaps it could have some antidepressant effect."

"Music to my ears," Stanton said. "Tell me, what's the next step with this compound?"

"First we'll concentrate on its chemistry," Edward said. "That means structure and its physical properties. Once we have the structure we will work out the drug's synthesis to obviate our reliance on extracting it from the mold. Then we'll move on to physiological function as well as toxicity studies."

"Toxicity?" Stanton questioned. He blanched.

"You had a minuscule dose," Edward reminded him. "Not to worry. You'll have no problems."

"How will you analyze the drug's physiological effects?" Stanton asked.

"It will be a multilevel approach," Edward said. "Remember, most compounds with a psychedelic effect function by imitating one of the brain's neurotransmitters. LSD, for example, is related to serotonin. Our studies will start with single-cell neurons, then move on to synaptosomes, which are ground-up, centrifuged live brain preparations, and finally involve intact neural cell systems like the ganglions of lower animals.''

"No live animals?" Stanton asked.

"Eventually," Edward said. "Mice and rats most likely. Also perhaps some monkeys. But that's down the line. We've got to look at the molecular level as well. We'll have to characterize binding sites and message transduction into the cell.''

"This sounds like a multiyear project," Stanton said.

"We've got a lot of work to do," Edward said. He smiled at Eleanor. Eleanor nodded in agreement. "It's damn exciting, though. It could be a chance of a lifetime.''

"Well, keep me informed," Stanton said. He got to his feet. He took a few tentative steps to test his balance. "I have to say, I do feel great.''

Stanton got as far as the door to the lab when he turned around and returned. Edward and Eleanor had already begun work. "Remember," he said. "You promised to read that damn prospectus, and I'm going to hold you to it no matter how busy you are.''

"I'll read it," Edward said. "I just didn't say when.''

Stanton made his hand into a pistol and put it to his head and pretended to shoot.

"Kim, you have a call on line one," the ward clerk called out.

"Take a message," Kim shouted back. She was at the bedside of a particularly sick patient, helping the nurse assigned to the case.

"Go take your call," the nurse said. "Thanks to you, things are under control here.''

"Are you sure?" Kim asked.

The nurse nodded.

Kim scooted across the center of the surgical intensive-care unit, dodging a traffic jam of beds. Patients had been coming and going all day. She picked up the phone, expecting either the chemistry lab or the blood bank. She had calls in to both places.

"I hope I'm not catching you at a bad time?" a voice asked.

"Who is this?" Kim demanded.

"George Harris, your Salem contractor. I'm returning your call."

"I'm sorry," Kim said. She'd forgotten she'd placed the call several hours earlier. "I didn't recognize your voice."

"I apologize for taking so long to get back," George said. "I've been out at the site. What can I do for you?"

"I wanted to know when the trench will be filled in," Kim said. The question had occurred to her the day before and had produced some anxiety. Her concern was what she'd do if the trench was filled in prior to Elizabeth's head being returned to her coffin.

"Probably tomorrow morning," George said.

"So soon?" Kim exclaimed.

"They're laying the utilities as we speak," George said. "Is there a problem?"

"No," Kim said quickly. "I just wanted to know. How's the work going?"

"No problems," George said.

After cutting the conversation short and hanging up, Kim called Edward immediately. Her anxiety mounted as the connection went through.

Getting Edward on the phone was no easy task. At first the secretary refused even to try to locate him, saying she'd take a message and Edward would call back. Kim insisted and finally prevailed.

"I'm glad you called," Edward said the moment he came on the line. "I've got more good news. We've not only separated the alkaloids, but we've already determined which one is psychoactive."

"I'm happy for you," Kim said. "But there is a problem. We have to get Elizabeth's head back to Salem."

"We can take it up on the weekend," Edward said.

"That will be too late," Kim said. "I just spoke with the contractor. He told me the trench is to be filled in the morning."

"Oh, jeez," Edward exclaimed. "Things are moving here at breakneck speed. I hate to take the time off. Can't they wait and fill the trench after the weekend?"

"I didn't ask," Kim said. "And I don't want to. I'd have to have a reason, and the only reason would involve the coffin. The contractor is in touch with my father, and I don't want him to have any notion that the grave has been violated."

"Damn it all," Edward said.

There was an uncomfortable pause.

"You promised you'd have that thing back ASAP," Kim said finally.

"It's just the timing," Edward said. Then, after a slight pause, he added: "Why don't you take it up yourself?"

"I don't know if I could," Kim said. "I didn't even want to look at it, much less handle it."

"You don't have to handle it," Edward said. "All you have to do is take the end of the coffin off and stick the box inside. You don't even have to open the box."

"Edward, you promised," Kim said.

"Please!" Edward said. "I'll make it up to you somehow. It's just that I am so busy at the moment. We've started to analyze the structure."

"All right," Kim said. When someone close to her asked her to do something, it was hard for her to say no. It wasn't that she minded the drive to Salem. She knew she should check the progress at the construction site as often as possible. Maybe slipping the box into the coffin wouldn't be that bad.

"How am I going to get the box?" she asked.

"I'll make it easy for you," Edward said. "I'll send it over to you by messenger so you'll have it before you finish work. How's that?"

"I'd appreciate it," Kim said.

"Call me here at the lab when you get back," Edward said. "I'll be here at least until midnight, probably longer."

Kim went back to work, but she was preoccupied. The anxiety she'd felt when she'd heard that the trench was to be filled in so soon had not abated. Knowing herself, she guessed it would remain until she'd returned the head to the coffin.

As Kim scurried back and forth between the beds caring for her patients, she felt irritated that she'd allowed Edward to take the head in the first place. The more she thought about her putting it back, the less she liked it. Although the idea of leaving it in the cardboard box had seemed reasonable when she'd been on the phone, she'd come to realize her sense of propriety wouldn't allow it. She felt obligated to return the grave to a semblance of what it had been before it had been disturbed. That meant dispensing with the box and handling the head, and she was not looking forward to that in the slightest.

The demands of Kim's job eventually pushed her concerns about Elizabeth into the back of her mind. There were patients to be taken care of, and the hours flew by. Later, as she was concentrating on a reluctant intravenous line, the ward clerk tapped her on the shoulder.

"You've got a package," he said. He pointed toward a sheepish messenger standing next to the central desk. "You've got to sign for it."

Kim looked over at the messenger. He was intimidated by the SICU's environment. A clipboard was clasped to his chest. At his elbow stood a computer paper box tied with a string. In an instant, Kim comprehended what was in the box and her heart fluttered.

"The front desk tried to get him to take it to the mail room," the clerk said. "But the messenger insisted his instructions were to deliver it to you in person."

"I'll take care of it," Kim said nervously. She started toward the desk with the clerk following at her heels. To her horror a bad situation suddenly got worse. Kinnard stood up from behind the desk where he had been writing in a chart and was looking at the receipt. She'd not seen him since their confrontation at the compound.

"What do we have here?" Kinnard said.

Kim took the clipboard from the messenger and hastily signed.

"It's a special delivery," the clerk explained.

"I can see that," Kinnard said. "I also see that it is from

Dr. Edward Armstrong's lab. The question is, what can be inside?''

"It didn't say on the receipt," the clerk said.

"Give me the box," Kim said sternly. She reached over the counter to take it from Kinnard, but Kinnard stepped back.

He smiled superciliously. "It's from one of Ms. Stewart's many admirers," he told the clerk. "It's probably candy. Pretty clever putting it in a computer paper box."

"It's the first time anyone on the staff ever got a special delivery package in the SICU," the clerk said.

"Give me the box," Kim demanded again. Her face flushed bright red as her mind's eye saw the box falling to the floor and Elizabeth's head rolling out.

Kinnard shook the box and intently listened. From across the desk Kim could hear the head distinctly thumping against the sides.

"Can't be candy unless it's a chocolate soccer ball," Kinnard said, assuming a comically confused expression. "What do you think?" He shook the package close to the clerk.

Mortified, Kim came behind the desk and tried to get hold of the package. Kinnard held it above his head, out of her reach.

Marsha Kingsley rounded the desk from the opposite end. Like most of the rest of the staff in the unit she'd seen what was happening, but unlike the others she came to her roommate's rescue. Stepping behind Kinnard, she reached up and pulled his arm down. He didn't resist. Marsha took the box and handed it to Kim.

Sensing that Kim was upset, Marsha led her into the back room. Behind them they could hear Kinnard laughing with the clerk.

"Some people's sense of humor is sick," Marsha said. "Someone should kick his Irish ass."

"Thank you for helping," Kim said. Now that she had the box in her hands she felt much better. Yet she was visibly trembling.

"I don't know what's wrong with that man," Marsha

continued. "What a bully. You don't deserve that kind of abuse."

"His feelings are hurt because I'm dating Edward," Kim said.

"So now you're defending him?" Marsha questioned. "Hell, I'm not buying the spurned lover role for Kinnard. Not in the slightest. Not that Lothario."

"Who's he dating?" Kim asked.

"The new blonde in the ER," Marsha said.

"Oh, great!" Kim said sarcastically.

"It's his loss," Marsha said. "Word has it she was the role model for those dumb-blonde jokes."

"She's also the one with the body that doesn't quit," Kim said forlornly.

"What do you care?" Marsha said.

Kim sighed. "You're right," she said. "I guess I just hate bad feelings and discord."

"Well, you sure had your share with Kinnard," Marsha said. "Look at the difference with the way Edward treats you. He doesn't take you for granted."

"You're right," Kim repeated.

After work Kim carried the computer paper box out to her car and put it in the trunk. Then she vacillated what to do. She'd had plans to visit the statehouse before the issue with Elizabeth's head came up. She considered postponing the visit until another afternoon. Then she decided there was no reason she couldn't do both, especially considering that her job at the cottage had to be done after all the workers left.

Leaving her car in the hospital garage, Kim walked up Beacon Hill and headed for the gold-domed Massachusetts Statehouse. After being cooped up all day, Kim enjoyed the outdoors. It was a warm but pleasant summer day. There was a slight sea breeze and the smell of salt in the air. Walking by the Common, she heard the complaint of sea gulls.

An inquiry at the statehouse information service directed Kim to the Massachusetts State Archives. Waiting her turn, Kim faced a heavyset male clerk. His name was William MacDonald. Kim showed him the copies she'd made of Ronald's petition and Magistrate Hathorne's negative ruling.

"Very interesting," William said. "I love this old stuff. Where'd you find this?"

"The Essex County Courthouse," Kim said.

"What can I do for you?" William asked.

"Magistrate Hathorne suggested that Mr. Stewart should petition the Governor since the evidence he sought had been transferred to Suffolk County. I'd like to find out about the Governor's response. What I'm really interested in finding out is what the evidence was. For some reason it's not described in either the petition or the ruling."

"It would have been Governor Phips," William said. He smiled. "I'm a bit of a history buff. Let's see if we can find Ronald Stewart in the computer."

William used his terminal. Kim watched his face since she couldn't see the screen. To her chagrin he kept shaking his head after each entry.

"No Ronald Stewart," he said finally. He looked again at the ruling and scratched his head. "I don't know what else to do. I've tried to cross-reference Ronald Stewart with Governor Phips, but I get nothing. The trouble is, not all the seventeenth-century petitions survived, and those that did are not all properly indexed or catalogued. There's a wealth of such personal petitions. Back then there was a hell of a lot of disagreement and discord, and people were suing each other just as much as they are today."

"What about the date?" Kim asked. "August 3, 1692. Is there some way you can use that?"

"I'm afraid not," William said. "Sorry."

Kim thanked the clerk and left the statehouse. She was mildly discouraged. With the ease she'd found the petition in Salem, she'd had high hopes of finding a follow-up ruling in Boston that would have revealed the nature of the evidence against Elizabeth.

"Why couldn't Ronald Stewart have described that damn evidence?" Kim wondered as she stalked down Beacon Hill. But then the idea occurred to her that maybe it was significant that he didn't. Maybe that was some sort of clue or message in and of itself.

Kim sighed. The more she thought about the mysterious evidence, the more curious she became. In fact at that moment she began to imagine it might be associated with the intuitive feeling she had that Elizabeth was trying to communicate with her.

Kim reached Cambridge Street and turned toward the Mass General garage. The other problem that her failure at the statehouse presented was that she was being thrown back to the impossibly large collection of papers in the castle, a daunting task at best. Yet it was apparent that if she were to learn anything more about Elizabeth, it would have to be there.

Climbing into her car, Kim headed north for Salem. But it was not an easy nor quick trip. The visit to the statehouse had put her in the height of rush-hour traffic.

As she sat in the bumper-to-bumper traffic on Storrow Drive, trying to get through Leverett Circle, she thought about the blond woman Kinnard was dating. She knew it shouldn't bother her, but it did. Yet such thoughts made her especially glad that she'd invited Edward to share the cottage with her. Not only did she truly care for Edward. She liked the message that her living with Edward would send to both Kinnard and her father.

Then Kim remembered Elizabeth's head in her trunk. The more she thought about Edward's failure to come along to Salem that evening, the more surprised she was, especially since he'd promised to take responsibility for the head and was fully aware of her distaste for handling it. It was behavior at odds with his attentiveness and, along with everything else, it disturbed her.

"What is this?" Edward asked angrily. "Do I have to hold your hand continually?" He was talking to Jaya Dawar, a brilliant new doctoral student from Bangalore, India. Jaya had been at Harvard only since the first of July, and he was struggling to find an appropriate direction for his doctorate thesis.

"I thought you could recommend to me more reading material," Jaya said.

"I can recommend an entire library," Edward said. "It's only a hundred yards away." He pointed in the general direction of the Countway Medical Library. "There comes a time in everybody's life when they have to cut the umbilical cord. Do a little work on your own!''

Jaya bowed his head and silently exited.

Edward redirected his attention to the tiny crystals he was growing.

''Maybe I should carry the burden with the new alkaloid,'' Eleanor suggested hesitantly. ''You can look over my shoulder and be the guiding light.''

''And miss all this fun?'' Edward said. He was using a binocular microscope to observe crystals forming on the surface of a supersaturated solution in the well of a microscope slide.

''I'm just concerned about your normal responsibilities,'' Eleanor said. ''A lot of people around here depend on your supervision. I also heard the undergraduate summer students complained about your absence this morning.''

''Ralph knows his material,'' Edward said. ''His teaching will improve.''

''Ralph doesn't like to teach,'' Eleanor said.

''I appreciate what you are saying,'' Edward said, ''but I'm not going to let this opportunity slip away. We've got something here with this alkaloid. I can feel it in my bones. I mean, how often does a billion-dollar molecule fall into your lap?''

''We have no idea whether this compound is going to be worth anything,'' Eleanor said. ''At this point it is purely hypothetical.''

''The harder we work, the quicker we'll know,'' Edward said. ''The students can do without my hand-holding for the time being. Who knows? Maybe it will do them some good.''

As Kim approached the compound her anxieties increased. She couldn't forget that she had Elizabeth's head in her trunk, and the longer she spent in direct proximity to it, the more she experienced a vague, uncomfortable foreboding about the course of recent events. Having stumbled onto Elizabeth's grave so quickly in the renovation process made it seem as if the witchcraft frenzy of 1692 was casting an ominous shadow over the present.

Passing through the gate, which was ajar, Kim feared that

the construction people were still there. As she emerged from the trees her suspicions were confirmed. There were two vehicles parked in front of the cottage. Kim was not happy. By that time she'd expected all of the workmen to have departed.

She parked next to the vehicles and slid out from behind the wheel. Almost simultaneously George Harris and Mark Stevens appeared at the front door. In contrast to her response, they were demonstrably pleased to see her.

"This is a pleasant surprise," Mark said. "We were hoping to get you on the phone later, but your being here is far better. We have a lot of questions."

For the next half hour Mark and George took Kim on a working tour of the renovation. The amazing progress that had been made improved her mood dramatically. To her delight Mark had brought granite samples to the site for the kitchen and the baths. With Kim's interest in interior design and her sense of color, she had no trouble making decisions. Mark and George were impressed. Kim was even impressed with herself. She knew that the ability to make such decisions was a tribute to the progress she'd made over the years with her self-confidence. When she'd first gone to college, she'd not even been able to decide on the color of her bedspread.

When they had finished with the interior, they stepped outside and began a walk around the building. Viewing the structure from the exterior, Kim told them that she wanted the new windows in the lean-to to match the small, diamond-paned windows of the main part of the house.

"They'll have to be custom," George said. "They'll be considerably more expensive."

"I want them," Kim said without hesitation.

She also told them she wanted the roof slate repaired, not replaced with a modern material, as the contractor had suggested. Mark agreed it would look far better. Kim even wanted the asphalt shingles removed from the shed and replaced with slate.

Rounding the building, they came to the utility trench. Kim glanced into its depths, where now ran a waste pipe, a water pipe, an electrical service, a phone line, and a TV cable. She was relieved to see the corner of the coffin still protruding from the wall.

"What about this ditch?" she asked.

"It'll be filled tomorrow," George said.

Kim felt an unwelcome chill descend her spine as she reluctantly imagined the terrible dilemma she would have faced had she not made the call to George that morning.

"Will all this be done by September first?" Kim asked, forcing her mind away from such disturbing thoughts.

Mark deferred to George.

"Barring any unforeseen problems we should be fine," George said. "I'll order the new casement windows tomorrow. If they're not here in time we can always hang a temporary window."

After the contractor and the architect had climbed into their respective vehicles and driven out of sight, Kim went back into the house to find a hammer. With it in hand, she opened the trunk of her car and lifted out the cardboard box.

As she followed the trench to where she could climb into it, Kim was quite astonished with her degree of nervousness. She felt like a thief in the night, and she kept stopping to listen for any approaching cars.

Once she was in the trench and had walked back to where the coffin was, a sense of claustrophobia made the ordeal even worse. The walls seemed to tower above her and from her vantage point seemed to curve out over her head, adding to her fear they might cave in at any moment.

With a tremulous hand, Kim set to work on the end of the coffin. Inserting the hammer's claws, she pried it back. Then she turned to face the box.

Now that the unpleasant task was at hand, Kim revived the debate as to what she should do in relation to the box. But she didn't debate long: hastily she untied the string. As much as she hated the idea of touching the head, she had to make an effort to restore the grave to a semblance of its original state.

Lifting the cardboard flaps, Kim reluctantly looked inside. The head was facing up, balanced on a mat of dried hair. Elizabeth was staring back at Kim with her dried, sunken eyeballs partially exposed. For an uncomfortable moment, Kim tried vainly to reconcile the gruesome face with the pleasing portrait that she was having restored, re-lined, and reframed. The images were such stark opposites that it seemed inconceivable they were the same person.

Holding her breath, Kim reached in and lifted the head. Touching it gave her renewed shivers, as if she were touching death itself. Kim also found herself wondering anew about what had really happened three hundred years previously. What could Elizabeth have done to bring on such a cruel fate?

Turning around carefully to avoid tripping over any of the pipes and cables, Kim extended the head into the coffin. Gingerly she set it down. She could feel her hands touch fabric and other firmer objects, but she didn't try to look in to see what they were. Hastily she bent the end of the coffin back to its original position and hammered it home.

Picking up the empty box and string, Kim hurried back up the trench. She didn't begin to relax until she'd put the trash back in her trunk. Finally she took a deep breath. At least it was over.

Walking back to the trench, she looked down at the end of the coffin just to make sure she'd not left some telltale evidence behind. She could see her footprints, but she didn't think that was a problem.

With her hands on her hips, Kim's eyes left the coffin and looked up at the quiet, cozy cottage. She tried to imagine what life had been like back in those dark days of the witchcraft scare, when poor Elizabeth was unknowingly ingesting the poisonous, mind-altering grain. With all the books Kim had been reading on the witchcraft ordeal, she'd learned quite a lot. For the most part the young women who presumably had been poisoned with the same contaminant as Elizabeth were the "afflicted," and they were the ones who "called out against" the witches.

Kim looked back at the coffin. She was confused. The young afflicted women had not been thought of as witches themselves, as Elizabeth had been. The exception had been Mary Warren, who had been both one of the afflicted and one of the accused, yet she'd been released and not executed. What made Elizabeth different? Why wasn't she just one of the afflicted? Could it have been that she was afflicted but refused to accuse anyone of afflicting her? Or could she have been practicing the occult, as her father had intimated?

Kim sighed and shook her head. She didn't have any answers. It all seemed to come back to the mysterious conclusive evidence and what it could have been. Kim's gaze wandered to the lonely castle, and in her mind's eye she saw the innumerable file cabinets, trunks, and boxes.

She glanced down at her watch. There were still several hours of daylight. Impulsively, she walked over to her car, climbed in, and drove up to the castle. With the mystery of Elizabeth so prominent in her mind, she thought she'd spend a little more time on the daunting task of looking through the papers.

Kim pushed through the front door of the castle and whistled to keep herself company. At the base of the grand staircase she hesitated. The attic was certainly more agreeable than the wine cellar, but her last visit to the attic had been singularly unsuccessful. She'd found nothing from the seventeenth century despite almost five hours of effort

Reversing her direction, Kim walked into the dining room and opened the heavy oak door of the wine cellar. She flipped on the sconces and descended the granite steps. Walking along the central corridor, she peered into successive individual cells. Recognizing that there was no order to the material, she thought it important that she develop some rational plan. Vaguely she thought that she would start in the very farthest cell and begin to organize the papers according to subject matter and age.

Passing one particular cell, Kim did a double take. Returning to it, she gazed in at the furniture. There was the usual complement of file cabinets, bureaus, trunks, and boxes But there was also something different. On top of one of the bureaus was a wooden box that looked familiar to Kim. It closely resembled the Bible box which the Witch House tour guide had described as an invariable part of a Puritan home.

Stepping over to the bureau, Kim ran her fingers along the top of the box, leaving parallel trails in the dust. The wood was unfinished yet perfectly smooth. There was no doubt the box was old. Placing her hands at either end, Kim opened the hinged lid.

Inside, appropriately enough, was a worn Bible bound in thick leather. Lifting the Bible out, Kim noticed that beneath it were some envelopes and papers. She carried the Bible out to the hall where the light was better. Folding back the cover and flyleaf, she looked at the date. It was printed in London in 1635. She thumbed through the text in hopes that some sheets of paper might have been stuck in the pages, but there was nothing.

Kim was about to return to the Bible box when the back cover of the Bible fell open in her hands. Written on the endpaper was: *Ronald Stewart his book 1663.* The handwriting resembled the graceful cursive script Kim recognized to be Ronald's. She guessed he'd written in the Bible as a boy.

Turning the back flyleaf, Kim found a series of blank pages with the word *Memorandum* printed at the top. On the first memorandum page following the Bible text she found more of Ronald's handwriting. Here he had recorded each of the marriages, births, and deaths of his family. With her index finger keeping her oriented on the page, Kim read off each of the dates until she came to the date of Ronald's marriage to Rebecca. It had been Saturday, October 1, 1692.

Kim was appalled. That meant that Ronald had married Elizabeth's sister just ten weeks after Elizabeth's death! That seemed much too quick to Kim, and once again she found herself questioning Ronald's behavior. She couldn't help but wonder if he'd had something to do with Elizabeth's execution. With such haste to remarry it was difficult for Kim to imagine that Ronald and Rebecca hadn't been having an affair.

Encouraged by her discovery, Kim returned to the Bible box and lifted out the envelopes and papers. Eagerly she opened the envelopes, hoping for personal correspondence, but each was a disappointment. All the enclosed material was business-related and from a period from 1810 to 1837.

Kim turned to the papers. She went through them sheet by sheet, and although they were older, they were not any more interesting until she came to one that was folded in thirds. Unfolding the multipage document, which had traces of a wax seal, Kim found a deed to a huge tract of land called Northfields Property.

Turning to the second page of the deed, Kim found a map. It was not difficult for her to recognize the area. The tract included the current Stewart compound as well as the land presently occupied by the Kernwood Country Club and the Greenlawn Cemetery. It also crossed the Danvers River, which was labeled the Wooleston River, to include property in Beverly. To the northwest it ran into present-day Peabody and Danvers, which in the deed was called Salem Village.

Turning the page, Kim found the most interesting part of the deed. The buyer's signature was Elizabeth Flanagan Stewart. The date was February 3, 1692.

Kim pondered the fact that Elizabeth was the buyer and not Ronald. It seemed strange although she did recall the premarital document she'd seen in the Essex County Courthouse giving Elizabeth the right to enter into contracts in her own name. But why was Elizabeth the buyer, especially since it was such a huge tract and must have cost a fortune?

Attached to the back of the deed was a final sheet of paper which was smaller in size and written by a different hand. Kim recognized the signature. It was Magistrate Jonathan Corwin, the original occupant of the Witch House.

Holding the document up to the light since it was difficult to read, Kim learned that it was a ruling by Magistrate Corwin denying a petition by Thomas Putnam, who wanted the Northfields purchase contract declared null and void because of the illegality of Elizabeth's signature.

To conclude the ruling, Magistrate Corwin wrote: "The legality of the signature of the aforesaid contract stands on the contract bound by Ronald Stewart and Elizabeth Flanagan dated 11th February 1681."

"My goodness," Kim murmured. It was as if she were peeking through a window on the late seventeenth century. From her general reading she knew that name Thomas Putnam. He was one of the principal characters in the factional strife that had engulfed Salem Village prior to the witchcraft frenzy and that many historians felt had been the hidden social cause of the affair. It had been Thomas Putnam's afflicted wife and daughter who'd made many of the witch-craft accusations. Obviously Thomas Putnam had not been aware of the premarital contract between Ronald and Elizabeth when he filed his petition.

Kim slowly folded the deed and the ruling. She had learned something that might be important for her understanding of what happened to Elizabeth. Obviously Thomas Putnam had been upset about Elizabeth's purchase of the land, and considering his role in the witchcraft saga, his enmity had to have been significant. It could very well have catapulted Elizabeth into the middle of the tragedy.

For a few moments Kim pondered the possibility that the evidence used against Elizabeth in her trial had something to do with Thomas Putnam and the purchase of the North-fields tract. After all, such a purchase by a woman would have been a disturbing act in Puritan times considering the accepted role of women. Perhaps the evidence had been something that was considered compelling proof Elizabeth was a virago and therefore unnatural. But try as she might, Kim couldn't think of anything.

Kim placed the deed and the attached ruling on top of the Bible, and examined the rest of the papers from the Bible box. To her delight she found one more seventeenth-century document, but when she read it she was less excited. It was a contract between Ronald Stewart and Olaf Sagerholm of Göteborg, Sweden. The contract directed Olaf to build a ship of a new and swift frigate design. The ship was specified to be 128 feet in length, 34 feet 6 inches in beam, and 19 feet 3 inches in draft when fully loaded with 276 last. The date was 12 December 1691.

Kim put the Bible and the two seventeenth-century documents back in the Bible box and carried the box to a console table at the base of the steps leading up to the dining room. She planned to use the box as a repository for any papers she found that related to Elizabeth or Ronald. To that end she went into the cell where she'd found the letter from James Flanagan and brought the letter back to put it with the other materials.

With that accomplished, Kim returned to the room where she'd found the Bible box and began a search through the bureau on which the Bible box sat. After several hours of diligent work, she straightened up and stretched. She'd found nothing interesting. A quick glance at her watch told her it was nearing eight and time for her to head back to Boston.

Slowly climbing the stairs, she realized how exhausted she was. It had been a busy day at work, and she found searching through the papers tiring even if it wasn't physically demanding.

The drive back to Boston was far easier than the drive out to Salem. There was little traffic until she entered Boston proper. Getting on Storrow Drive for what normally was only a short stretch, Kim changed her mind and drove on to the Fenway exit. She had the sudden idea to pay a visit to Edward in his lab rather than phone him. Since the task of replacing Elizabeth's head had been so complication-free, she felt guilty she'd been so upset anticipating it.

Passing through the Medical School security with the help of her MGH identity card, Kim mounted the stairs. She'd briefly visited the lab with Edward after one of their dinners, so she knew the way. The departmental office was dark, so Kim knocked on a frosted-glass door that she knew led directly into the lab.

When no one responded, Kim knocked again a bit louder. She also tried the door, but it was locked. After a third knock, Kim could see someone approaching through the glass.

The door opened, and Kim confronted an attractive, slim, blond woman whose curvaceous figure was apparent despite an oversized white lab coat.

"Yes?" Eleanor questioned perfunctorily. She looked Kim up and down.

"I'm looking for Dr. Edward Armstrong," Kim said.

"He's not seeing visitors," Eleanor said. "The department office will be open tomorrow morning." She started to close the door.

"I think he might be willing to see me," Kim said hesitantly. In truth she wasn't entirely sure and for a moment wondered if she should have called.

"Really, now?" Eleanor questioned haughtily. "What's your name? Are you a student?"

"No, I'm not a student," Kim said. The question seemed absurd since she was still in her nurse's uniform. "My name is Kimberly Stewart."

Eleanor didn't say anything before closing the door in Kim's face. Kim waited. She shifted her weight and wished she hadn't come. Then the door reopened.

"Kim!" Edward exclaimed. "What on earth are you doing here?"

Kim explained that she thought it better to visit than to merely call. She apologized if she'd caught him at a bad time.

"Not at all," Edward said. "I'm busy but that doesn't matter. In fact I'm more than busy. But come in." He stepped back out of the doorway.

Kim entered, then followed Edward as he headed toward his desk area.

"Who was it who opened the door?" Kim asked.

"Eleanor," Edward said over his shoulder.

"She wasn't terribly friendly," Kim said, unsure if she should mention it.

"Eleanor?" Edward questioned. "You must be mistaken. She gets along with everyone. Around here I'm the only bear. But both of us are worn a little thin. We're on a roll. We've been working nonstop since late Saturday morning. In fact Eleanor has been working that way since Friday night. Both of us have hardly slept."

They arrived at Edward's desk. He lifted a stack of periodicals off a straight-backed chair, tossed them in the corner, and motioned for Kim to sit. Edward sat in his desk chair.

Kim studied Edward's face. He seemed to be in overdrive, as if he'd drunk a dozen cups of coffee. His lower jaw was dancing nervously up and down while he chewed gum. There were circles under his cool blue eyes. A two-day stubble dotted his cheeks and chin.

"Why all this frantic activity?" Kim asked.

"It's the new alkaloid," Edward said. "We're already beginning to learn something about it and it looks awfully good."

"I'm pleased for you," Kim said. "But why all the rush? Are you under some sort of deadline?"

"It's purely an anticipatory excitement," Edward said. "The alkaloid could prove to be a great drug. If you've never done research it's hard to comprehend the thrill you get when you discover something like this. It's a real high, and we've been reexperiencing that high on an hourly basis. Everything we learn seems positive. It's incredible."

"Can you say what you've been learning?" Kim asked. "Or is it some kind of secret?"

Edward moved forward in his chair and lowered his voice. Kim glanced around the lab but saw no one. She wasn't even sure where Eleanor was.

"We've stumbled onto an orally effective, psychoactive compound that penetrates the blood-brain barrier like the proverbial knife through butter. It's so potent it is effective in the microgram range."

"Do you think this is the compound that affected the people in the Salem witchcraft affair?" Kim asked. Elizabeth was still in the forefront of her mind.

"Without doubt," Edward said. "It's the Salem devil incarnate."

"But the people who ate the infected grain were poisoned," Kim said. "They became the 'afflicted' with horrid fits. How can you be so excited about that kind of drug?"

"It is hallucinogenic," Edward said. "There's no doubt about that. But we think it's a lot more. We have reason to believe it calms, invigorates, and may even enhance memory."

"How have you learned so much so quickly?" Kim asked.

Edward laughed self-consciously. "We don't know anything for certain yet," he admitted. "A lot of researchers would find our work so far less than scientific. What we've been doing is attempting to get a general idea of what the alkaloid can do. Mind you, these are not controlled experiments by any stretch of the imagination. Nevertheless, the results are terribly exciting, even mind-boggling. For instance we found that the drug seems to calm stressed rats better than imipramine, which is the benchmark for antidepressant efficacy."

"So you think it might be an hallucinogenic antidepressant?" Kim said.

"Among other things," Edward said.

"Any side effects?" Kim asked. She still didn't understand why Edward was as excited as he was.

Edward laughed again. "We haven't been worrying about hallucinations with the rats," he said. "But seriously, apart from the hallucinations we've not seen any problems. We've loaded several mice with comparatively huge doses and they're as happy as pigs in the poke. We've plopped even larger doses into neuronal cell cultures with no effect on the cells. There doesn't seem to be any toxicity whatsoever. It's unbelievable."

As Kim continued to listen to Edward, she became progressively disappointed that he did not ask her about her visit to Salem and about what happened to Elizabeth's head. Finally Kim had to bring it up herself when there was a pause in Edward's exuberant narrative.

"Good," Edward said simply when she told him the head had been replaced. "I'm glad that's over."

Kim was about to describe how the episode had made her feel when Eleanor breezed into view and immediately monopolized Edward's attention with a computer printout. Eleanor did not even acknowledge Kim's presence nor did Edward introduce them. Kim watched as they had an animated discussion over the information. It was obvious Edward was pleased with the results. Finally Edward gave Eleanor some suggestions along with a pat on the back, and Eleanor vanished as quickly as she'd appeared.

"Now where were we?" Edward said, turning to Kim.

"More good news?" Kim asked, referring to Eleanor's printout.

"Most definitely," Edward said. "We've started on determining the compound's structure, and Eleanor has just confirmed our preliminary impression that it is a tetracyclic molecule with multiple side chains."

"How on earth can you figure that out?" Kim asked. In spite of herself she was impressed.

"You really want to know?" Edward asked.

"Provided you don't go too far over my head," Kim said.

"The first step was to get an idea of molecular weight with standard chromatography," Edward said. "That was easy. Then we broke the molecule apart with reagents that rupture specific types of bonds. Following that we try to identify at least some of the fragments with chromatography, electrophoresis, and mass spectrometry."

"You're already beyond me," Kim admitted. "I've heard those terms, but I don't really know what the processes are."

"They're not that complicated," Edward said. He stood up. "The basic concepts are not difficult to comprehend. It's the results that can be difficult to analyze. Come on, I'll show you the machines." He took Kim's hand and pulled her to her feet.

Edward enthusiastically dragged a reluctant Kim around his lab, showing her the mass spectrometer, the high-performance liquid chromatography unit, and the capillary electrophoresis equipment. The whole time he lectured about how they were used for fragment separation and identification. The only thing Kim understood completely was Edward's obvious bent for teaching.

Opening up a side door, Edward gestured inside. Kim glanced within. In the center of the room was a large cylinder about four feet high and two feet wide. Cables and wires emerged from it like snakes from Medusa's head.

"That's our nuclear magnetic resonance machine," Edward said proudly. "It's a crucial tool with a project like this. It's not enough to know how many carbon atoms, hydrogen atoms, oxygen atoms, and nitrogen atoms there are in a compound. We have to know the three-dimensional orientation. That's what this machine can do."

"I'm impressed," Kim said, not knowing what else to say.

"Let me show you one other machine," Edward said, oblivious to Kim's state of mind. He led her to yet another door. Opening it, he again gestured inside.

Kim looked in. It was a hopeless tangle of electronic

equipment, wires, and cathode ray tubes. "Interesting," she said.

"You know what it is?" Edward asked.

"I don't think so," Kim said. She was reluctant to let Edward know how little she knew about what he did.

"It's an X-ray defraction unit," Edward said with the same degree of pride he'd evinced with the NMR unit. "It complements what we do with the NMR. We'll be using it with the new alkaloid because the alkaloid readily crystallizes as a salt."

"Well, you do have your work cut out for you," Kim said.

"It's work but it's also extraordinarily stimulating," Edward said. "Right now we're using everything in our investigative arsenal, and the data is pouring in. We'll have the structure in record time, especially with the new software that is available with all these instruments."

"Good luck," Kim said. She'd derived only a sketchy idea of what Edward had explained, but she had certainly gotten a taste of his enthusiasm.

"So what else happened up in Salem?" Edward asked suddenly. "How's the renovation going?"

Kim was momentarily nonplussed by Edward's question. With his preoccupation involving his own work, she didn't think he was currently interested in her puny project. She'd been just about to excuse herself.

"The renovation is going well," she said. "The house is going to be darling."

"You were gone quite a while," Edward said. "Did you delve back into the Stewart family papers?"

"I spent a couple of hours," Kim admitted.

"Find anything more about Elizabeth?" he asked. "I'm getting more and more interested in her myself. I feel as if I owe her an enormous debt. If it hadn't been for her, I never would have come across this alkaloid."

"I did learn some things," Kim said. She told Edward about going to the statehouse prior to driving to Salem and that there was no follow-up petition concerning the mysterious evidence. She then told him about the Northfields deed with Elizabeth's signature, and how it had angered Thomas Putnam.

"That might be the most significant piece of information you've learned so far," Edward said. "From the little reading I've done, I don't think Thomas Putnam was the right person to irritate."

"I had the same thought," Kim said. "His daughter, Ann, was one of the first of the girls to be afflicted, and she accused many people of witchcraft. The problem is, I can't relate a feud with Thomas Putnam with the conclusive evidence."

"Maybe these Putnam people were malicious enough to plant something," Edward suggested.

"That's a thought," Kim said. "But it doesn't answer what it could have been. Also, if something were planted, does it make sense that it was conclusive? I still think it had to be something Elizabeth made herself."

"Maybe so," Edward said. "But the only hint you have is Ronald's petition stating it was seized from his property. I don't think it could have been anything indubitably associated with witchcraft."

"Speaking of Ronald," Kim said. "I learned something about him that's reawakened my suspicions. He remarried only ten weeks after Elizabeth's death. That's an awfully short grieving period, to say the least. It makes me think he and Rebecca might have been having an affair."

"Perhaps," Edward said without enthusiasm. "I still think that we have no idea how difficult life was back then. Ronald had four children to raise and a burgeoning business to run. He probably didn't have a lot of choice. I'd bet a long grieving period was a luxury he could not afford."

Kim nodded, but she wasn't sure she agreed. At the same time she wondered how much her suspicious attitude toward Ronald was influenced by her father's behavior.

Eleanor appeared just as abruptly as she had earlier and again enlisted Edward in a private yet animated discussion. When she left, Kim excused herself.

"I'd better be on my way," she said.

"I'll walk you out to your car," Edward offered.

While descending the stairs and walking across the quadrangle, Kim detected a gradual change in Edward's demeanor. As he'd done in the past, he became noticeably more nervous. From previous experience Kim guessed he was about to say something. She didn't try to encourage him. She'd learned it didn't help.

Finally when they reached her car he spoke: "I've been thinking a lot about your offer to come to live with you in the cottage," he said while toying with a pebble with his toe. He paused. Kim waited impatiently, unsure what he would say. Then he blurted: "If you're still thinking positively about it, I'd like to come."

"Of course I'm thinking positively," Kim said with relief. She reached up and gave him a hug. He returned the gesture.

"We can go up on the weekend and talk about furniture," Edward said. "I don't know if there is anything from my apartment you'd want to use."

"It'll be fun," Kim said.

With some awkwardness they separated, and Kim climbed into her car. She opened the passenger-side window and Edward leaned in.

"I'm sorry I'm so preoccupied about this alkaloid," he said.

"I understand," Kim said. "I can see how excited you are. I'm impressed with your dedication."

After they said their goodbyes, Kim drove toward Beacon Hill feeling a lot happier than she had just a half hour earlier.

# 7

## Friday,
## July 29, 1994

Edward's excitement escalated as the week progressed. The database on the new alkaloid grew at an exponential rate. Neither he nor Eleanor slept more than four or five hours each night. Both were living in the lab for all practical purposes and working harder than they had in their lives.

Edward insisted on doing everything himself, which meant he even reproduced Eleanor's work in order to be one hundred percent certain of no mistakes. In like manner he had Eleanor check his results.

As busy as Edward was with the alkaloid, he had no time for anything else. Despite Eleanor's advice to the contrary and despite mounting rumblings from the undergraduate students, he'd given no lectures. Nor had he devoted any time to his bevy of graduate students, many of whose research projects were now stalled without his continual leadership and advice.

Edward was unconcerned. Like an artist in a fit of creation, he was mesmerized by the new drug and oblivious to his surroundings. To his continued delight the structure of the drug was emerging atom by atom from the mists of time in which it had been secreted.

By early Wednesday morning, in a superb feat of qualitative organic chemistry, Edward completely characterized the four-ringed structural core of the compound. By Wednesday afternoon all of the side chains were defined both in terms of their makeup and point of attachment to the core. Edward jokingly described the molecule as an apple with protruding worms.

It was the side chains that particularly fascinated Edward. There were five of them. One was tetracyclic like the core and resembled LSD. Another had two rings and resembled a drug called scopolamine. The last three resembled the brain's major neurotransmitters: norepinephrine, dopamine, and serotonin.

By the wee hours of Thursday morning, Edward and Eleanor were rewarded by the image of the entire molecular structure appearing on a computer screen in virtual three-dimensional space. The achievement had been the product of new structural software, supercomputer capability, and hours of heated argument between Edward and Eleanor as each played devil's advocate with the other.

Hypnotized by the image, Edward and Eleanor silently watched as the supercomputer slowly rotated the molecule. It was in dazzling color, with the electron clouds represented by varying shades of cobalt blue. The carbon atoms were red, the oxygen green, and the nitrogen yellow.

After flexing his fingers as if he were a virtuoso about to play a Beethoven sonata on a Steinway grand piano, Edward sat down at his terminal, which was on-line with the supercomputer. Calling upon all his knowledge, experience, and intuitive chemical sense, he began to work the keyboard. On the screen the image trembled and jerked while maintaining its slow rotation. Edward was operating on the molecule, chipping away at the two side chains he instinctively knew were responsible for the hallucinogenic effect: the LSD side chain and the scopolamine side chain.

To his delight, he was able to remove all but a tiny two-carbon stump of the LSD side chain without significantly affecting either the three-dimensional structure of the compound or its distribution of electrical charges. He knew altering either of these properties would dramatically affect the drug's bioactivity.

With the scopolamine side chain it was a different story. Edward was able to amputate the side chain partially, leaving a sizable portion intact. When he tried to remove more, the molecule folded on itself and drastically changed its three-dimensional shape.

After Edward had removed as much of the scopolamine

side chain as he dared, he downloaded the molecular data to his own lab computer. The image now wasn't as spectacular, but was in some respects more interesting. What Edward and Eleanor were looking at now was a hypothetical new designer drug that had been formed by computer manipulation of a natural compound.

Edward's goal with the computer manipulations was to eliminate the drug's hallucinogenic and antiparasympathetic side effects. The latter referred to the dry mouth, the pupillary dilation, and partial amnesia both he and Stanton had experienced.

At that point Edward's true forte, synthetic organic chemistry, came to bear. In a marathon effort from early Thursday to late Thursday night, Edward ingeniously figured out a process to formulate the hypothetical drug from standard, available reagents. By early Friday morning he produced a vialful of the new drug.

"What do you think?" Edward asked Eleanor as the two of them gazed at the vial. They were both exhausted, but neither had any intention of sleeping.

"I think you've accomplished an amazing feat of chemical virtuosity," Eleanor said sincerely.

"I wasn't looking for a compliment," Edward said. He yawned. "I'm interested to know what you think we should do first."

"I'm the conservative member of this team," Eleanor said. "I'd say let's get an idea of toxicity."

"Let's do it," Edward said. He heaved himself to his feet and lent Eleanor a hand. Together they went back to work.

Empowered by their accomplishments and impatient for immediate results, they forgot scientific protocol. As they had done with the natural alkaloid, they dispensed with controlled, careful studies to get a rapid, general data to give them an idea of the drug's potential.

The first thing they did was add varying concentrations of the drug to various types of tissue cultures, including kidney and nerve cells. With even relatively large doses they were happy to see no effect. They put the cultures in an incubator so that they could periodically access them.

Next they prepared a ganglion preparation from *Aplasia fasciata* by inserting tiny electrodes into spontaneously firing nerve cells. Connecting the electrodes to an amplifier, they created an image of the cells' activity on a cathode ray tube. Slowly they added their drug to the perfusing fluid. By watching the neuronal responses, they determined that the drug was indeed bioactive although it didn't depress or increase the spontaneous activity. Instead the drug appeared to stabilize the rhythm.

With mounting excitement, since everything they did yielded positive results, Eleanor began feeding the new drug to a new batch of stressed rats while Edward added the new drug to a fresh synaptosome preparation. Eleanor was the first to get results. She was quickly convinced the modified drug had even more calming effect on the rats than the unaltered alkaloid.

It took Edward a little longer to get his results. He found that the new drug affected the levels of all three neurotransmitters, but not equally. Serotonin was affected more than norepinephrine, which was affected more than dopamine. What he didn't expect was that the drug seemed to form a loose covalent bond with both glutamate and gamma-aminobutyric acid, two of the major inhibitory agents in the brain.

''This is all fantastic!'' Edward exclaimed. He picked up the papers from his desk that recorded all their findings and allowed them to rain down like massive sheets of confetti. ''This data suggests that the potential of the drug is monumental. I'm willing to bet it's both an antidepressant and an anxiolytic, and as such it could revolutionize the field of psychopharmacology. It might even eventually be compared with the discovery of penicillin.''

''We still have the worry about it being hallucinogenic,'' Eleanor said.

''I sincerely doubt it,'' Edward said. ''Not after removing that LSD-like side chain. But I agree we have to be sure.''

''Let's check the tissue cultures,'' Eleanor said. She knew Edward would want to take the drug. It was the only way to determine if it was hallucinogenic.

They retrieved their tissue cultures from the incubator and examined them under a low-power microscope. One after another they appeared healthy. There was no sign of cellular damage from the new drug, even those subjected to high doses.

"There doesn't seem to be any toxicity at all," Edward said with glee.

"I wouldn't have believed it if I hadn't seen it," Eleanor said.

They went back to Edward's bench area and made up several solutions of increasing strength. The starting point was a concentration that yielded a dose approximating the dosage of the unmodified alkaloid that Stanton had received. Edward was the first to try it, and when nothing happened, Eleanor took it. Again nothing happened.

Encouraged by these negative results, Edward and Eleanor gradually increased their dosages up to a full milligram, knowing that LSD was psychedelic at 0.05 milligrams.

"Well?" Edward questioned a half hour later.

"No hallucinogenic effect as far as I can tell," Eleanor said.

"But there is an effect," Edward said.

"Most definitely," Eleanor said. "I'd have to describe it as calm contentment. Whatever it is, I like it."

"I also feel as if my mind is particularly sharp," Edward said. "It has to be drug-related because twenty minutes ago I was a basket case, thinking my ability to concentrate was nil. Now I'm energized as if I'd had a night's rest."

"I have a sense my long-term memory has been awakened from a slumber," Eleanor said. "Suddenly I remember my home phone number when I was a child of six. It was the year my family moved to the West Coast."

"What about your senses?" Edward asked. "Mine seem particularly acute, especially my sense of smell."

"I wouldn't have thought of it until you mentioned it," Eleanor said. She put her head back and sniffed the air. "I never realized the lab was such a cacophony of odors."

"There's something else I'm feeling that I wouldn't have even been sensitive to if I hadn't taken a course of Prozac,"

Edward said. "I feel socially assertive, like I could walk into a group of people and do whatever I wanted. The difference is that it took three months of Prozac before I felt that way."

"I can't say I feel anything like that," Eleanor said. "But I can say my mouth is a little dry. Is yours?"

"Perhaps," Edward admitted. Then he looked directly into Eleanor's deep blue eyes. "Your pupils also might be a bit dilated. If they are, it must be the scopolamine side chain we couldn't totally eliminate. Check your near vision."

Eleanor picked up a reagent bottle and read the tiny print on the label. "No problem," she said.

"Anything else?" Edward said. "Any trouble with your circulation or breathing?"

"Everything is fine," Eleanor said.

"Excuse me," a voice called.

Eleanor and Edward turned to see one of the second-year doctorate students had approached them. "I need some help," she said. Her name was Nadine Foch. She was from Paris. "The NMR is not functioning."

"Perhaps it would be best to talk to Ralph," Edward said. He smiled warmly. "I'd like to help, but I'm rather involved at the moment. Besides, Ralph knows the machine better than I, particularly from a technical point of view."

Nadine thanked them and went to find Ralph.

"That was rather civil of you," Eleanor said.

"I feel rather civil," Edward said. "Besides, she's a nice person."

"Perhaps this is a good time for you to resume your normal activities," Eleanor said. "We've made fantastic progress."

"It's only a harbinger of what's to come," Edward said. "It's good of you to worry about my teaching and supervisory responsibilities, but I assure you that they can slide for several weeks without causing anybody irreparable damage. I'm not about to forfeit any of this excitement with this new drug. Meanwhile I want you to start computerized molecular modeling to create a family of compounds from our new drug by substituting side chains."

While Eleanor went off to work at her computer terminal, Edward walked back to his desk and picked up the phone. He called Stanton Lewis.

"Are you busy tonight?" Edward asked his old friend.

"I'm busy every night," Stanton said. "What's on your mind? Did you read that prospectus?"

"How about having dinner with me and Kim?" Edward said. "There's something you should know."

"Ah ha, you old rogue," Stanton said. "Is this going to be some sort of a major social announcement?"

"I believe I'd rather discuss it in person," Edward said smoothly. "What about dinner? It will be my treat!"

"This is sounding serious," Stanton said. "I have a dinner reservation at Anago Bistro on Main Street in Cambridge. The reservation is for two, but I'll see that it gets changed to four. It's for eight P.M. I'll call back if there is a problem."

"That's perfect," Edward said. Then he hung up before Stanton could ask any more questions. Edward dialed Kim at work in the SICU.

"Busy?" he asked when Kim came on the line.

"Don't ask," Kim said.

"I made dinner plans with Stanton and his wife," Edward said excitedly. "It will be at eight unless I hear back from Stanton. I'm sorry it's such short notice. I hope it's OK for you."

"You're not working tonight?" Kim asked with surprise.

"I'm taking the evening off," Edward said.

"What about tomorrow?" Kim asked. "Are we still going up to Salem?"

"We'll talk about it," Edward said noncommittally. "What about dinner?"

"I'd rather eat just with you," Kim said.

"You're sweet to say that," Edward said. "And I'd rather eat just with you. But I have to talk with Stanton, and I thought we could make a little party out of it. I know I haven't been so much fun this week."

"You sound buoyant," Kim said. "Did something good happen today?"

"It's all been good," Edward said. "And that's why this

meeting is important. After the dinner just you and I can spend some time together. We'll take a walk in the square like we did the evening we first met. How about it?''

"You've got a date," Kim said.

Kim and Edward arrived at the restaurant first, and the hostess, who was also one of the owners, sat them at a cozy table wedged into a nook next to the window. The view was out over a portion of Main Street with its collection of pizza joints and Indian restaurants. A fire truck sped by with all its bells and sirens screaming.

"I'd swear the Cambridge fire company uses their equipment to go for coffee," Edward said. He laughed as he watched the truck recede. "They're always out riding around. There can't be that many fires."

Kim eyed Edward. He was in a rare mood. Kim had never seen him so talkative and jovial, and although he looked tired, he was acting as if he'd just had several espressos. He even ordered a bottle of wine.

"I thought you told me you always let Stanton order the wine," Kim said.

Before Edward could answer, Stanton arrived, and true to character breezed into the restaurant as if he were an owner. He kissed the hostess's hand, which the hostess endured with thinly disguised impatience.

"OK, you guys," Stanton said to Edward and Kim as he tried to help Candice into her chair. The table was narrow, and each couple had to sit side-by-side. "What's the big news between you two? Do I have to pop for a bottle of Dom Pérignon?"

Kim looked at Edward for some explanation.

"I've already ordered some wine," Edward said. "It will do nicely."

"You ordered wine?" Stanton questioned. "But they don't serve Ripple here." Stanton laughed heartily as he sat down.

"I ordered an Italian white," Edward said. "A cool dry wine goes nicely with hot summer weather."

Kim lifted her eyebrows. This was a side of Edward she'd not seen.

"So what is it?" Stanton said. He eagerly leaned forward with his elbows on the table. "Are you two getting married?"

Kim blushed. With some embarrassment she wondered if Edward had told Stanton about their plans to share the cottage. It wasn't a secret as far as she was concerned, but she would have liked to tell her family herself.

"I should be so lucky," Edward said with a laugh of his own. "I've got some news—but it's not that good."

Kim blinked and looked at Edward. She was impressed he dealt so adroitly with Stanton's inappropriate comment.

The waitress arrived with the wine. Stanton made a production of examining the label before allowing it to be opened. "I'm surprised, old boy," he said to Edward. "Not a bad choice."

Once the wine was poured, Stanton started to make a toast, but Edward quieted him.

"It's my turn," Edward said. He held out his glass toward Stanton. "To the world's cleverest medical venture capitalist," he said.

"And I thought you never noticed," Stanton said with a laugh. Then they all took a drink.

"I have a question for you," Edward said to Stanton. "Were you serious when you said recently that a new, effective psychotropic drug could potentially be a billion-dollar molecule?"

"Absolutely," Stanton said. His demeanor instantly became more serious. "Is this why we're here? Do you have some new information about the drug that sent me on my psychedelic trip?"

Both Candice and Kim questioned what psychedelic trip Stanton was referring to. When they heard what had happened they were appalled.

"It wasn't half bad," Stanton said. "I rather enjoyed it."

"I've got a lot of information," Edward said. "All of it is superlative. We eliminated the hallucinogenic effect by altering the molecule. Now I think we have created the next-generation drug to the likes of Prozac and Xanax. It seems to be perfect. It's nontoxic, effective orally, has fewer side effects and probably a broader therapeutic capability. In fact, because of its unique side chain structure capable of alteration and substitution, it might have unlimited therapeutic capability in the psychotropic arena.''

''Be more specific,'' Stanton said. ''What do you think this drug can do?''

''We believe it will have a general, positive impact on mood,'' Edward said. ''It seems to be antidepressant and anxiolytic, meaning it lowers anxiety. It also seems to function as a general tonic to combat fatigue, increase contentment, sharpen the senses, and encourage clear thinking by enhancing long-term memory.''

''My God!'' Stanton exclaimed. ''What *doesn't* it do? It sounds like Soma from *Brave New World*.''

''That analogy might have merit,'' Edward said.

''One question,'' Stanton said. He lowered his voice and leaned forward. ''Will it make sex better?''

Edward shrugged. ''It might,'' he said. ''Since it enhances the senses, sex could be more intense.''

Stanton threw up his hands. ''Hell,'' he said. ''We're not talking about a billion-dollar molecule; we're talking about a five-billion-dollar molecule.''

''Are you serious?'' Edward asked.

''Let's say a billion plus,'' Stanton said.

The waitress interrupted their conversation. They ordered their dinners. After she'd left, Edward was the first to speak. ''We haven't proven any of this,'' he said. ''There's been no controlled experiments.''

''But you're pretty confident,'' Stanton said.

''Very confident,'' Edward said.

''Who knows about this?'' Stanton asked.

''Only me, my closest assistant, and the people at this table,'' Edward said.

''Do you have any idea how the drug works?'' Stanton asked.

''Only a vague hypothesis,'' Edward said. ''The drug seems to stabilize the concentrations of the brain's major neurotransmitters and in that way works on a multilevel basis. It affects individual neurons but also whole networks of cells as if it were an autocoid or brain hormone.''

''Where did it come from?'' Candice asked.

Edward summarized the story by explaining the association between Kim's forebear, the Salem witch trials, and the theory the accusers in Salem had been poisoned by a mold.

"It was Kim's question whether the poison theory could be proved which got me to take some samples of dirt," Edward said.

"I don't deserve any credit," Kim said.

"But you do," Edward said. "You and Elizabeth."

"Such irony," Candice said. "Finding a useful drug in a dirt sample."

"Not really," Edward said. "Many important drugs have been found in dirt like cephalosporins or cyclosporine. In this case the irony is the drug is coming from the devil."

"Don't say that," Kim said. "It gives me the creeps."

Edward laughed teasingly. He hooked his thumb at Kim and told the others that she was wont to have occasional attacks of superstition.

"I don't think I like the association either," Stanton said. "I'd rather consider it a drug from heaven."

"The association with the witch frenzy doesn't bother me at all," Edward said. "In fact I like it. Although finding this drug can't justify the death of twenty people, at least it might give their sacrifice some meaning."

"Twenty-one deaths," Kim corrected. She explained to the others that Elizabeth's execution had been overlooked by the historians.

"I wouldn't care if the drug were related to the biblical flood," Stanton said. "It sounds like an extraordinary discovery." Then, looking at Edward, he asked, "What are you going to do?"

"That's why I wanted to see you," Edward said. "What do you think I should do?"

"Exactly what I already told you," Stanton said. "We should form a company and patent the drug and as many clones as possible."

"You really think this could be a billion-dollar situation?" Edward asked.

"I know what I'm talking about," Stanton said. "This is my area of expertise."

"Then let's do it," Edward said. "Let's form a company and go for it."

Stanton stared into Edward's face for a beat. "I think you are serious," he said.

"You bet I'm serious," Edward said.

"All right, first we need some names," Stanton said. He took out a small notebook and pen from his jacket pocket. "We need a name for the drug and a name for the company itself. Maybe we should call the drug Soma for the literary set."

"There's already a drug called Soma," Edward said. "How about Omni, in keeping with its potentially wide range of clinical applications?"

"Omni just doesn't sound like a drug," Stanton said. "In fact it sounds more like a company. We could call it Omni Pharmaceuticals."

"I like it," Edward said.

"How about 'Ultra' for the drug," Stanton said. "I can see that working well for advertising."

"Sounds good," Edward said.

The men looked at the women for their reaction. Candice hadn't been listening, so Stanton had to repeat the names. After he did she said they were fine. Kim had been listening, but she didn't have an opinion; she was a bit taken aback by the discussion. Edward had shown no awkwardness in this sudden and unexpected interest in business.

"How much money can you raise?" Edward asked.

"How long would you estimate it would take before you were ready to market this new drug?" Stanton asked.

"I don't think I can answer that question," Edward said. "Obviously I can't even be one hundred percent sure it will ever be marketable."

"I know that," Stanton said. "I'm just looking for a best-guess estimate. I know that the average duration from discovery of a potential drug to its FDA approval and marketing is about twelve years, and the average cost is somewhere around two hundred million dollars."

"I wouldn't need twelve years," Edward said. "And I wouldn't need anywhere near two hundred million dollars to do it."

"Obviously the shorter the development time and the less money needed means more equity we can keep for ourselves."

"I understand," Edward said. "Frankly I'm not interested in giving away much equity at all."

"How much money do you think you would need?" Stanton asked.

"I'd have to set up a state-of-the-art lab," Edward said, beginning to think out loud.

"What's the matter with the lab you already have?" Stanton asked.

"The lab belongs to Harvard," Edward said. "I have to get the Ultra project away from Harvard because of a participation agreement I signed when I accepted my position."

"Is this going to cause us some problems?" Stanton asked.

"No, I don't think so," Edward said. "The agreement concerns discoveries made on company time using company equipment. I'll argue that I discovered Ultra on my own time, which is technically correct although I've done the preliminary separation and synthesis on company time. Anyway, the bottom line is that I'm not afraid of some legal harassment. After all, Harvard doesn't own me."

"How about the development period?" Stanton asked. "How much shorter do you think you could make that?"

"A lot," Edward said. "One of the things about Ultra that has impressed me is how unbelievably nontoxic it appears to be. I believe this fact alone will make FDA approval a breeze since characterizing specific toxicities is what takes so damn much time."

"So you're talking about getting FDA approval years sooner than the average," Stanton said.

"Without doubt," Edward said. "Animal studies will be accelerated if there's no toxicity to worry about, and the clinical portion can be collapsed by combining phase II and phase III with the FDA's expedited schedule."

"The expedited plan is for drugs targeted for life-threatening diseases," Kim said. From her experience in the SICU she knew something about experimental drug testing.

"If Ultra is as efficacious for depression as I think it will prove to be," Edward said, "I'm confident we can make a case for it in relation to some serious illness."

"What about western Europe and Asia?" Stanton asked. "FDA approval is not needed to market a drug in those areas."

"Very true," Edward said. "The USA is not the only pharmaceutical market."

"I'll tell you what," Stanton said. "I can easily raise four to five million without having to give up more than a token amount of equity since most of it would come from my own resources. How does that sound?"

"It sounds fantastic," Edward said. "When can you start?"

"Tomorrow," Stanton said. "I'll start raising the money and organizing the legal work to set up the corporation as well as to start the patent applications."

"Do you know if we can patent the core of the molecule?" Edward asked. "I'd love the patent to cover any drug formulated with the core."

"I don't know, but I can find out," Stanton said.

"While you're seeing to the financial and legal aspects," Edward said, "I'll start the process of setting up the lab. The first question will be where to site it. I'd like to have it someplace handy because I'll be spending a lot of time there."

"Cambridge is a good location," Stanton said.

"I want it away from Harvard," Edward said.

"How about the Kendall Square area?" Stanton suggested. "It's far enough away from Harvard and yet close enough to your apartment."

Edward turned to Kim and their eyes met. Kim guessed what he was thinking so she nodded. It was a gesture imperceptible to the Lewises.

"Actually I'm moving out of Cambridge at the end of August," Edward said. "I'm moving to Salem."

"Edward is coming to live with me," Kim said, knowing

it would quickly get back to her mother. "I'm renovating the old house on the family compound."

"That's wonderful," Candice said.

"You old rogue," Stanton said as he reached across the table and gave Edward a light punch in the shoulder.

"For once in my life my personal life is going as well as my professional life," Edward said.

"Why don't we site the company somewhere on the North Shore?" Stanton suggested. "Hell, commercial rents up there must be a fraction of what they are in the city."

"Stanton, you've just given me a great idea," Edward said. He turned sideways to look at Kim. "What about that mill-turned-stables on the compound? It would make a perfect lab for this kind of project because of its isolation."

"I don't know," Kim stammered. She'd been caught totally unawares by the suggestion.

"I'm talking about Omni renting the space from you and your brother," Edward said, warming to the idea. "As you've mentioned, the compound is a burden. I'm sure some legitimate rent could be a real help."

"It's not a bad idea," Stanton said. "The rent could be totally written off, so it would be tax free. Good suggestion, old sport."

"What do you say?" Edward asked.

"I'd have to ask my brother," Kim said.

"Of course," Edward said. "When? I mean the sooner the better."

Kim looked at her watch and calculated that it was about two-thirty in the morning in London, just about the time Brian would be getting down to work. "I could call him any evening," Kim said. "I suppose I could even call him now."

"That's what I like to hear," Stanton said. "Decisiveness." He pulled his cellular phone from his pocket and pushed it across to Kim. "Omni will even pay for the call."

Kim stood up.

"Where are you going?" Edward asked.

"I feel self-conscious calling my brother in front of everyone," Kim said.

"Perfectly understandable," Stanton said. "You go on into the ladies' room."

"I think I prefer to step outside," Kim said.

After Kim had left the table Candice congratulated Edward on the progress of his relationship with Kim.

"We've been enjoying each other's company," Edward said.

"How much personnel would you need at the lab?" Stanton asked. "Hefty salaries can eat up capital like nothing else."

"I'd keep the number to a minimum," Edward said. "I'd need a biologist to handle the animal studies, an immunologist for the cellular studies, a crystallographer, a molecular modeler, a biophysicist for nuclear magnetic resonance, a pharmacologist, plus myself and Eleanor."

"Jesus Christ!" Stanton exclaimed. "What the hell do you think you are creating, a university?"

"I assure you this is a minimum for the kind of work we'll be doing," Edward said calmly.

"Why Eleanor?"

"She's my assistant," Edward said. "She's the person I work with the closest, and she's crucial to the project."

"When can you start to assemble this team?" Stanton asked.

"As soon as you have the money," Edward said. "We'll have to have first-class people, so they won't come cheap. I'll be enticing them away from coveted academic appointments and lucrative positions in private industry."

"That's exactly what I'm afraid of," Stanton said. "Many new biomedical companies go belly-up from a hemorrhage of capital from overly generous salaries."

"I'll keep that in mind," Edward said. "When can you have money available for me to draw on?"

"I can have a million available by the beginning of the week," Stanton said.

The first courses of their dinner arrived. Since Candice and Stanton were having hot appetizers, Edward insisted they start. But no sooner had they picked up their forks when Kim returned. She sat down and handed Stanton his phone.

"I've good news," she said. "My brother is delighted with the idea of paying tenants in the old mill building, but he insisted that we will not pay for any improvements. That will have to be up to Omni."

"Fair enough," Edward said. He picked up his glass in preparation for another toast. He had to nudge Stanton, who was momentarily lost in thought. "To Omni and to Ultra," Edward said. They all drank.

"This is how I think we should set the company up," Stanton said as soon as he put his glass down. "We'll capitalize with four and a half million and value the stock at ten dollars a share. Out of the four hundred and fifty thousand shares we'll each hold one hundred and fifty thousand, leaving one hundred and fifty thousand for future financing and for attracting the best people by offering some equity. If Ultra turns out to be anything like it's been described tonight, each share of the stock will end up being ungodly valuable."

"I'll drink to that," Edward said, raising his wineglass yet again. They all clinked their glasses and drank, particularly Edward, who found himself enjoying the wine selection he'd made. He'd never had better white wine, and he took a moment to savor its vanilla bouquet and slightly apricot finish.

After the dinner was over and goodbyes had been said, Kim and Edward climbed into Edward's car in the restaurant's parking lot.

"If you wouldn't mind, I'd like to skip the walk in the square," Edward said.

"Oh?" Kim questioned. She was mildly disappointed. She was also surprised, but then the whole evening had been a surprise. She'd not expected Edward to have been willing to take an evening off, and on top of that, his behavior had been exceptional from the moment he'd picked her up.

"There's some phone calls I'd like to make," Edward said.

"It's after ten," Kim reminded him. "Isn't it a little late to be calling people?"

"Not on the West Coast," Edward said. "There's a couple of people at UCLA and Stanford who I'd like to see on the Omni staff."

"I gather you are excited about this business venture," Kim commented.

"I'm ecstatic," Edward said. "My intuition told me I was onto something important the moment I learned we'd stumbled onto three previously unknown alkaloids. I just didn't know it was going to be this big."

"Aren't you a little worried about the participation agreement you signed with Harvard?" Kim asked. "I've heard about similar situations leading to serious trouble in this town, like during the 1980s, when academia and industry became much too cozy."

"It's a problem I will leave to the lawyers," Edward said.

"I don't know," Kim said, unconvinced. "Whether lawyers are involved or not, it could affect your academic career." Knowing how much Edward valued teaching, Kim was worried that his sudden entrepreneurial enthusiasm was clouding his better judgment.

"It's a risk," Edward admitted. "But I'm more than willing to take it. The opportunity Ultra offers is a once-in-a-lifetime proposition. It's a chance to make a mark in this world and to earn some real money while doing it."

"I thought you said you weren't interested in becoming a millionaire," Kim said.

"I wasn't," Edward said. "But I hadn't thought about becoming a billionaire. I didn't realize the stakes were that high."

Kim wasn't sure there was that much difference, but she didn't say anything. It was an ethical question that she didn't feel like debating at the moment.

"I'm sorry about making the suggestion of converting the Stewart stables to a lab without discussing it with you beforehand," Edward said. "It's not like me to blurt something like that out on the spur of the moment. I guess the excitement of talking with Stanton got the best of me."

"Your apology is accepted," Kim said. "Besides, my brother was intrigued with the idea. I suppose the rent will be helpful in paying the taxes on the property. They're astronomical.''

"One nice thing is that the stables are far enough away from the cottage so the lab's presence won't bother us,'' Edward said.

They turned off Memorial Drive and headed into the quiet, residential back streets of Cambridge. Edward pulled into his parking spot and turned off the engine. Then he hit his forehead with the palm of his hand.

"Stupid me,'' he said. "We should have driven back to your place to get your things.''

"You want me to stay tonight?''

"Of course,'' Edward said. "Don't you want to?''

"You've been so busy lately,'' Kim said. "I didn't know what to expect.''

"If you stay it will make heading up to Salem in the morning that much easier,'' Edward said. "We can get an early start.''

"You definitely want to go?'' Kim asked. "I had the sense you won't want to take the time.''

"I do now that we are siting Omni there,'' Edward said. He restarted the car and backed out. "Let's go back and get you a change of clothes. Of course that's assuming you want to stay—which I hope you do.'' He smiled broadly in the half-light.

"I suppose,'' Kim said. She was feeling indecisive and anxious without knowing exactly why.

# 8

## Saturday,
## July 30, 1994

KIM AND EDWARD DID NOT GET AN EARLY START AS Edward had suggested the night before. Instead Edward had spent half the morning on the phone. First he'd called Kim's contractor and architect about expanding the work at the compound to include the new lab. They'd agreed with alacrity and offered to meet at the compound at eleven. Next Edward had called a series of representatives of laboratory equipment manufacturers and scheduled them to show up at the same time as the contractor and architect.

After a quick call to Stanton to be sure the money he'd promised would be immediately forthcoming, Edward phoned a series of people whom he wanted to consider recruiting for Omni's professional staff. Edward and Kim did not get into the car for the drive north until well after ten.

By the time Edward parked in front of the stables in the Stewart compound there was a small crowd of people waiting. They had all introduced themselves, so Edward was spared the task. Instead he waved for them to gather by the padlocked sliding door.

The building was a long, single-story stone structure with infrequent windows set high under the eaves. Since the terrain fell off sharply toward the river, the back was two stories, with separate entrances to each stall on the lower level.

Kim tried multiple keys before finding the correct one to open the heavy padlock. After sliding it open, everyone entered what was the ground floor from the front and the second story from the rear.

The interior was a huge, undivided long room with a cathedral ceiling. On the rear side of the building there were multiple shuttered openings. One end of the room was filled with bales of hay.

"At least the demolition will be easy," George said.

"This is perfect," Edward said. "My idea of a lab is one big space so that everyone interfaces with everyone else."

The stairway leading down to the lower level was constructed of rough-hewn oak and pegged together with dowels an inch in diameter. Downstairs they found a long hall with stalls to the right and tack rooms to the left.

Kim tagged along and listened to the plans to convert the barn rapidly into a state-of-the-art biological and pharmacological laboratory. Downstairs there were to be quarters for a menagerie of experimental animals including rhesus monkeys, mice, rats, and rabbits. There was also to be space for tissue- and bacterial-culture incubators along with containment facilities. And finally there were to be specially shielded rooms for the NMR and X-ray crystallography.

The upstairs would house the main laboratory space as well as a shielded, air-conditioned room for a large mainframe computer. Every laboratory bench would have its own terminal. To power all the electronic equipment a huge electrical service would be brought in.

"Well, there you have it," Edward said when they had finished the tour. He turned to the contractor and architect. "Can you see any problems with all this?"

"I don't think so," Mark said. "The building is sound. But I would suggest we design an entrance with a reception area."

"We won't be having many visitors," Edward said. "But I see your point. Go ahead and design it. What else?"

"I can't see that we'll have any trouble with permits," George said.

"Provided we don't say anything about the animal aspect," Mark said. "My advice is just not to mention it. It could create problems that would take a long time to resolve."

"I'm more than happy to leave the civic relations to you experienced men," Edward said. "The fact is, I'm interested in expediting this project, so I'd like to take full advantage of your expertise. And to speed completion I'm willing to give a ten percent bonus above time, materials, and fees."

Enthusiastic and eager smiles appeared on Mark's and George's faces.

"When can you start?" Edward asked.

"We can start immediately," Mark and George said in unison.

"I hope my little job isn't going to suffer with this newer and bigger project," Kim said, speaking up for the first time.

"No need to worry," George said. "If anything it will speed work up at the cottage. We'll be bringing a big crew in here with all the trades represented. If we need a plumber or an electrician for some small task on your job, they'll already be on site."

While Edward, the contractor, the architect, and the various medical-equipment reps settled down to work out the details for the new lab, Kim wandered outside the stables. She squinted her eyes against the hazy but intense noontime sun. She knew she wasn't contributing to the planning of the lab, so she hiked across the field toward the cottage to check on the renovation.

As she neared the building she noticed the trench had been filled in. She also noticed that the workmen had reset Elizabeth's headstone into the ground above the grave. They'd laid it flat just as they'd found it.

Kim entered the cottage. It seemed tiny after being in the stables. But the work was progressing well, especially in the kitchen and the bathrooms. For the first time she could imagine what they would be like when they were finished.

After touring the cottage, Kim wandered back to the stables, but there was no suggestion that Edward and the others were anywhere near finishing their impromptu conference. Kim interrupted long enough to let Edward know she'd be up in the castle. Edward told her to enjoy herself and immediately went back to some problem involving the NMR machine.

Stepping from the bright sunshine into the somber, heavily draped interior of the castle was like stepping into another world. Kim stopped and listened to the creaks and groans of the house as it adjusted to the heat. For the first time she realized she couldn't hear the sound of the birds, which outside was loud, particularly the cry of sea gulls.

After a short debate she mounted the grand staircase. Despite her recent success finding seventeenth-century material in the wine cellar, she thought she'd give the attic another chance, especially since it was so much more pleasant.

The first thing she did was open many of the dormer windows to let in the breeze from the river. Stepping away from the last window she opened, she noticed stacks upon stacks of clothbound ledgers. They were arranged along one side of the dormer.

Taking one of the books in her hand, Kim looked at the spine. Handprinted in white ink on a black background were the words *Sea Witch.* Curious about what the book was, Kim cracked it open. At first she thought it was someone's diary because all the handwritten entries began with the day of the month followed by a narrative involving detailed descriptions of the weather. She soon realized that it wasn't a personal diary but rather a ship's log.

Turning to the front of the book, Kim learned that it covered the years 1791 through 1802. Kim put the log back and glanced at the spines of the other books in the stack, reading the names. There were seven books with the name *Sea Witch.* Checking them all, she learned the oldest went from 1737 to 1749.

Wondering if there could be any from the seventeenth century, Kim looked at the books in other stacks. In a small pile near the window she noticed that there was one with a worn leather spine and no name. She got it out.

The book had an old feel much like the Bible Kim had found in the wine cellar. She opened to the title page. It was the ship's log for a brig called the *Endeavor,* and it covered the years from 1679 to 1703. Delicately turning the aged pages, Kim advanced through the book year by year until she got to 1692.

The first entry for the year was on the 24th of January. It described the weather as cold and clear with a good westerly wind. It went on to say that the ship had embarked with the tide and was bound for Liverpool with a load of whale oil, timber, ship's stores, fur, potash, and dried cod and mackerel.

Kim sucked in a mouthful of air as her eyes stumbled onto a familiar name. The next sentence in the entry stated that the ship was carrying a distinguished passenger, Ronald Stewart, Esquire, the ship's owner. Hastily Kim read on. The log explained that Ronald was en route to Sweden to supervise the outfitting and take possession of a new ship to be called the *Sea Spirit*.

Quickly Kim scanned the subsequent entries for the voyage. Ronald's name was not mentioned again until he disembarked in Liverpool after an uneventful crossing.

With some excitement, Kim closed the book and descended from the attic to the wine cellar. Opening the Bible box, she took out the deed she'd found on her last visit and checked the date. She'd been correct! The reason Elizabeth's signature was on the deed was because Ronald had been at sea when the deed was signed.

Solving even a small mystery involving Elizabeth gave Kim a sense of satisfaction. She put the deed back in the Bible box and was in the process of adding the ship's log to her small collection when three envelopes tied with a thin ribbon slipped out from beneath the back cover.

Kim picked up the slim packet with trembling fingers. She could see that the top one was addressed to Ronald Stewart. After untying the ribbon she discovered they were all addressed to Ronald. With great excitement she opened the envelopes and removed the contents. There were three letters, dated October 23rd, October 29th, and November 11th, 1692.

The first was from Samuel Sewall:

Boston

My Dear Friend,
I understand that you are troubled in spirit although
I hope in God's name that your recent marriage may
ease your disquietude. I also understand your wish to
contain the knowledge of your late wife's unfortunate
association with the Prince of Darkness, but I must in
good faith advise you to forebear petitioning the Governor for a Writ of Replevin in regards to the conclusive evidence used to convict your aforesaid wife of
abominable witchcraft. To the like purpose I would
have you apply to and beseech Reverend Cotton
Mather in whose cellar you espied your wife's infernal
doings. It has come into my knowledge that official
custody of the evidence has been granted in perpetuity
to Reverend Mather according to his request.

I remain your Friend,
Samuel Sewall.

Frustrated that she'd found another reference to the mysterious evidence without its being described, Kim turned to
the second letter. It was written by Cotton Mather.

Saturday 29th October
Boston

Sir:
I am in receipt of your recent letter and your reference
to our being fellow graduates of Harvard Colledge which
gives me the hope that your disposition to the venerable
institution is one of loving solicitude so that you will be
amenable of mind and spirit to what I and my esteemed father hath decided is the proper place for Elizabeth's handiwork. You recall when we met at my home in July I had
worried concern that the good people of Salem could very
well be excited to a state of unruly and turbulent spirit in
regards to the Devil's presence so clearly defined by Elizabeth's actions and infernal works. It is most unfortunate

that my fervent concerns have come to pass and despite
my urging of a very critical and exquisite caution in the
use of spectral evidence since the Father of Lies could
conceivably assume the outward shape of an innocent person, innocent people's good reputation can be sullied despite the sedulous endeavors of our honorable judges who
are so eminent for their justice, wisdom, and goodness. I
fully comprehend your honorable wish to shield your family from further humiliation but it is my belief that Elizabeth's evidence should be preserved for the benefit of
future generations in their eternal combat with the forces
of evil as a prime example of the type of evidence needed
to objectively determine a true covenant with the Devil
and not mere maleficium. In this regard I have had much
discours with my father, the Good Reverend Increase
Mather who is currently justly serving as the President of
Harvard Colledge. We together in like mind have decided
that the evidence should be preserved at the Colledge for
the edification and instruction of future generations
whereof vigilance is important to thwart the work of the
Devil in God's New Land.

Your servant in God's name,
Cotton Mather.

Kim wasn't certain she understood the entire letter, but
the gist was easy enough to comprehend. Feeling even
more frustrated about the mysterious evidence, she turned
to the final letter. Glancing at the signature, she saw it was
from Increase Mather.

11th November 1692
Cambridge

Sir:
I am in complete empathy for your wish for the
aforesaid evidence to be returned for your private disposition, but I have been informed by the tutors William Brattle and John Leverett that the evidence has
been received by the students with diligent interest and
has stimulated impassioned and enlightening debate

with the effect of convincing us it is God's will that Elizabeth's legacy be left at Harvard to stand as an important contribution to establishment of objective criteria for Ecclesiastic Law in association with witchcraft and the damnable work of the Devil. I beg of you to understand the importance of this evidence and agree that it indeed should remain with our collections. If and when the esteemed Fellows of the Corporation of Harvard deem to found a school of law it will at that time be sent to that institution.

I remain your servant,<br>Increase Mather.

"Damn it!" Kim said after reading the third letter. She could not believe that she'd been lucky enough to find so many references to Elizabeth's evidence yet still not know what it was. Thinking she might possibly have missed something, she read the letters again. The strange syntax and orthography made reading them somewhat difficult, but when she got to the end of the second reading she was sure she'd not missed anything.

Stimulated by the letters, Kim again tried to imagine the nature of the incontrovertible evidence used against Elizabeth. From Kim's continued general reading that week on the Salem witch trials, she'd become more convinced that it had to have been some kind of book. Back in the days of the trials the issue of the Devil's Book had come up frequently. The method that a supposed witch established a covenant with the devil was by writing in the Devil's Book.

Kim looked back at the letters. She noticed the evidence was described as "Elizabeth's handiwork." Perhaps Elizabeth had made a book with an elaborately tooled leather cover? Kim laughed at herself. She knew she was taxing her imagination, but nothing else came to mind.

In Increase Mather's letter, Kim noted that the evidence had elicited "impassioned and enlightening" debate among the students. She thought that description not only gave weight to the idea of the evidence being a book, but tended to suggest it was the contents that were important, not its appearance.

But then Kim thought again about the evidence being some kind of doll. Just that week she'd read that a doll with pins in it had been used in the trial of Bridget Bishop, the first person to be executed in the Salem ordeal.

Kim sighed. She knew that her wild speculations as to the nature of the evidence was not accomplishing anything. After all, the evidence could have been anything to do with the occult. Instead of wild speculation she had to stick to the facts that she had, and the three letters she'd just found gave her a very significant fact, namely that the evidence, whatever it was, had been given to Harvard University in 1692. Kim wondered what the chances were that she could find reference to it at the institution today, and if she were to try, whether they would laugh at her.

"Ah, there you are," Edward called down from the top of the wine cellar stair. "Having any luck?"

"Strangely enough I have," Kim yelled back. "Come down and take a look at these."

Edward climbed down the stairs and took the letters. "My goodness," he exclaimed when he saw the signatures. "These are three of the most famous Puritans. What a find!"

"Read them," Kim said. "They're interesting but frustrating for my purposes."

Edward leaned against a bureau to take advantage of the light from one of the wall sconces. He read the letters in the same order that Kim had.

"They're marvelous," he said when he was finished. "I love the wording and the grammar. It lets you know that rhetoric was a major course of study in those days. Some of it's above my head: I don't even know what the word 'sedulous' means."

"I think it means diligent," Kim said. "I didn't have any difficulty with definitions. What gave me trouble was how the sentences ran on and on."

"You're lucky these letters weren't written in Latin," Edward said. "Back in those days you had to read and write Latin fluently to get into Harvard. And speaking of Harvard, I'd bet Harvard would be interested in these, especially the one from Increase Mather.''

''That's a good point,'' Kim said. ''I was thinking about going to Harvard and asking about Elizabeth's evidence. I was afraid they might laugh at me. Maybe I could make a trade.''

''They wouldn't laugh at you,'' Edward said. ''I'm sure someone in the Widener Library would find the story intriguing. Of course they wouldn't turn down a gift of the letter. They might even offer to buy it.''

''Does reading these letters give you any better idea what the evidence could have been?'' Kim asked.

''Not really,'' Edward said. ''But I can understand what you mean by their being frustrating. It's almost funny how many times they mention the evidence without describing it.''

''I thought Increase Mather's letter gave more weight to the idea it was some kind of book,'' Kim said. ''Especially the part where he mentioned it stimulated debate among the students.''

''Perhaps,'' Edward said.

''Wait a second,'' Kim said suddenly. ''I just had another idea. Something I hadn't thought about. Why was Ronald so keen to get it back? Doesn't that tell us something?''

Edward shrugged. ''I think he was interested in sparing his family further humiliation,'' he said. ''Often entire families suffered when one member was convicted of witchcraft.''

''What about the possibility it could have been self-implicating?'' Kim said. ''What if Ronald had something to do with Elizabeth's being accused and convicted of witchcraft? If he did, then maybe he wanted to get the evidence back so he could destroy it.''

''Whooo, hold on!'' Edward said. He backed away a step as if Kim were a threat. ''You're too conspiratorially inclined; your imagination is working overtime.''

''Ronald married Elizabeth's sister ten weeks after Elizabeth's death,'' Kim said heatedly.

''I think you are forgetting something,'' Edward said. ''The test I ran on Elizabeth's remains suggests that she'd been chronically poisoned by the new fungus. She'd probably been having psychedelic trips on a regular basis, which had nothing to do with Ronald. In fact he might have been having his own if he were ingesting the same grain. I still think the evidence had to do with something Elizabeth made while under the hallucinogenic effect of the mold. Like we said, it could have been a book, or a picture, or a doll, or anything they thought related to the occult."

"You have a point," Kim conceded. She took the letters from Edward and put them in the Bible box. She glanced down the wine cellar's long hall with its complement of furniture filled with paperwork. "Well, back to the drawing board. I'll just have to keep looking in hopes of finding the evidence described."

"I finished my meetings," Edward said. "Everything is going smoothly regarding the new lab. I have to compliment you on your contractor. He's going to start today by digging the utility trench. He said his only concern was finding more graves! I think finding Elizabeth's spooked him. What a character."

"Do you want to go back to Boston?" Kim asked.

"I do," Edward admitted. "There are a lot of people I want to talk to now that Omni is soon to be a reality. But I don't mind taking the train like I did the last time. If you want to stay working here on your project, I think you should."

"Well, if you wouldn't mind," Kim said. Finding the letters had at least encouraged her.

# 9

## Friday,
## August 12, 1994

AUGUST BEGAN HOT, HAZY, AND HUMID. THERE HAD been little rain all through July, and the drought continued into the following month without remittance until the grass on the Boston Common in front of Kim's apartment changed from green to brown.

At work, August brought some relief for Kim. Kinnard had started his two-month rotation at Salem Hospital, so she didn't have the anxiety of facing him daily in the SICU. Kim had also concluded negotiations with the department of nursing to give her the entire month of September free. It was put together with a combination of accumulated vacation time plus personal time off without pay. The nursing office hadn't been happy with the request, but they had compromised in order not to lose Kim altogether.

The beginning of the month also provided Kim with some time on her hands because Edward was away constantly. He was busy flying around the country on secret recruitment missions for Omni Pharmaceuticals. But he did not forget her. Despite his pressing schedule, he phoned every night around ten, just before Kim went to sleep. He also kept up the daily flowers although on a more modest scale. Now the deliveries were a single rose a day, which Kim felt was much more appropriate.

Kim had no trouble filling her time. In the evenings she continued her background reading on the Salem witch trials and Puritan culture. She also made it a point to visit the compound every day. Construction was proceeding at an extremely rapid rate. The crew at the lab was more numerous than the one working on the cottage. Nonetheless, progress at the cottage did not slow, and finish painting was begun even before all the cabinetwork had been completed.

To Kim, the biggest irony of the construction project was that her father was thoroughly impressed with her because of the work on the lab. Kim did not let on that she was not involved in that part of the renovation, and that it had not been her idea.

On every visit to the compound Kim spent at least some time in the castle, painstakingly sifting through the hoard of dusty documents and books. The results were disappointing. Although she'd been encouraged by the discovery of the three letters, twenty-six hours of subsequent search had yielded nothing of comparable value. Consequently, on Thursday the 11th she decided to follow the lead she had, and she brought the letter from Increase Mather to Boston, having built up the courage to approach Harvard.

After leaving work on August 12th, Kim walked to the corner of Charles and Cambridge streets and climbed the stairs to the MTA station. After the experience at the statehouse, which she now knew was a totally hopeless venture since Ronald had never petitioned the Governor, Kim was not optimistic about finding the evidence against Elizabeth at Harvard. Not only did she think the chances of the university still having such material in its possession slim, she fully expected people at the university to think of her as some kook. Who else would come on a quest for a three-hundred-year-old object, the nature of which was never specified in what few tangible references to it she had?

While waiting for the train, Kim almost turned back several times, but each time she reminded herself that this was her only lead. Consequently she felt impelled to follow up on it, no matter what response it might elicit.

Exiting the underground station, Kim found herself in the usual bustle of Harvard Square. But once she'd crossed Massachusetts Avenue and entered the campus, the noise of the traffic and crowds was muffled with startling rapidity. As she walked along the tranquil, tree-shaded walkways and ivy-covered red brick walls, she wondered what the campus had looked like in the seventeenth century, when Ronald Stewart had attended. None of the buildings she was passing looked quite that old.

Recalling Edward's comment about the Widener Library, Kim had decided to try there first. She mounted the broad steps and passed between its impressive columns. She was feeling nervous and had to encourage herself to continue. At the information desk she made a vague request about speaking with someone concerning very old objects. She was sent to Mary Custland's office.

Mary Custland was a dynamic woman in her late thirties, stylishly dressed in a dark blue suit, white blouse, and colorful scarf. She hardly fit Kim's stereotypical image of a librarian. Her title was Curator of Rare Books and Manuscripts. To Kim's relief she was gracious and warm, immediately asking how she could be of help.

Kim produced the letter, handed it to Mary, and mentioned that she was a descendant of the addressee. She started to explain what she wanted, but Mary interrupted her.

"Excuse me," she said. She was startled. "This letter is from Increase Mather!" As she spoke, she reverentially moved her fingers to the very periphery of the page.

"That's what I was explaining," Kim said.

"Let me get Katherine Sturburg in here," Mary said. She carefully laid the letter on her blotter and picked up the phone. While she was waiting for the connection to go through, she told Kim that Katherine specialized in seventeenth-century material and was particularly interested in Increase Mather.

After making her call, Mary asked Kim where she'd gotten the letter. Kim again started to explain, but then Katherine arrived. She was an older woman with gray hair; a pair of reading glasses resided permanently on the end of her nose. Mary introduced them and then showed the letter to Katherine.

Katherine used just the tip of her finger to move the letter around so she could read it. Kim was immediately embarrassed by her own cavalier handling of it.

"What do you think?" Mary asked when Katherine was finished reading.

"It's definitely authentic," Katherine said. "I can tell by both the handwriting and the syntax. It's fascinating. It references both William Brattle and John Leverett. But what is this evidence he's discussing?"

"That's the question," Kim said. "That's why I'm here. I'd started out trying to learn something about my ancestor Elizabeth Stewart, and that goal has evolved to solving this puzzle. I was hoping Harvard could help, since the evidence, whatever it was, was left here."

"What is the association with witchcraft?" Mary asked.

Kim explained that Elizabeth had been caught up in the witchcraft trials in Salem and that the evidence—whatever it was—had been used to convict her.

"I should have guessed about the Salem connection when I saw the date," Katherine said.

"The second time Mather refers to it, he describes it as 'Elizabeth's legacy,'" Mary pointed out. "That's a curious phrase. It suggests to me something Elizabeth either made herself or acquired with some degree of effort or wealth."

Kim nodded. She then explained her idea about its being a book or writings although she admitted it could have been anything associated in those days with sorcery or the occult.

"I suppose it could have been a doll," Mary said.

"I'd thought of that," Kim said.

The two librarians conferred as how best to access the enormous resources of the library. After a short discussion, Mary sat down at her terminal and entered the name ELIZABETH STEWART.

For a minute no one spoke. The only movement in the room was the blinking of the cursor in the blank screen as the computer searched the extensive data banks. When the monitor flashed alive with multiple listings, Kim's hopes rose. But they were short-lived. All the Elizabeth Stewarts listed were in the nineteenth and twentieth centuries and bore no relation to Kim.

Mary then tried RONALD STEWART, but got similar results. There were no seventeenth-century references. Next Mary tried to cross-reference with INCREASE MATHER.

There was a wealth of material, but no intersections with the Stewart family listed.

"I'm not surprised," Kim said. "I wasn't optimistic coming here. I hope you didn't find this a bother."

"Quite the contrary," Katherine said. "I'm pleased you showed us this letter. We'd certainly like to make a copy of it for our files, if you wouldn't mind."

"Of course not," Kim said. "In fact, when I'm finished with my mini-crusade I'll be happy to donate the letter to the library."

"That would be very generous," Mary said.

"As the archivist most interested in Increase Mather I'll be happy to go over my extensive files for the name of Elizabeth Stewart," Katherine promised. "Whatever the object was, there should be some reference to it, since Mather's letter confirms it was given to Harvard. The debate about spectral evidence in the Salem witchcraft trials had been ferocious, and we have extensive material on it. I have a feeling that's what Mather is indirectly referring to in your letter. So there is still a chance I could find something."

"I'd appreciate any effort you made," Kim said. She gave her phone number both at work and at home.

The librarians exchanged knowing glances. Mary then spoke up. "I don't want to be a pessimist," she said, "but we should warn you that the chances of finding the evidence itself are minuscule, no matter what it was. There was a great tragedy here at Harvard on January 24, 1764. At that time Old Harvard Hall was being used by the General Court because of a smallpox epidemic in Boston. Unfortunately a fire left in the library on that cold, snowy night sparked a conflagration that destroyed the building and all its priceless contents. That included all the portraits of the college's presidents and benefactors as well as most of its five-thousand-volume library. I know a lot about the episode because it was the worst disaster in the library's history. And not only did the library lose books: there was also a collection of stuffed animals and birds and, most curious of all, a collection that was referred to as 'a repository of curiosities.' "

"That sounds like it could have included objects associated with the occult," Kim said.

"Most definitely," Mary said. "There's a very good chance what you are seeking was part of that mysterious collection. But we might never know. The catalogue of the collection was lost as well."

"But that still doesn't mean I can't find some reference to it," Katherine said. "I'll give it my best shot."

As Kim descended the library's front steps, she reminded herself that she'd not expected to be successful so that she shouldn't be discouraged. At least no one had laughed at her, and the librarians had been genuinely interested in the letter. Kim was confident they would continue looking for references to her forebear.

Kim took the subway back to Charles Street and got her car from the hospital garage. She'd intended to go to her apartment to change clothes, but the trip to Harvard had taken more time than she expected. Instead she headed to the airport to pick up Edward, who was due back from the West Coast.

Edward arrived on schedule, and since he had not checked a bag, they bypassed the baggage area and headed directly to the parking lot.

"Things couldn't be going any better," Edward said. He was in a buoyant mood. "There's only been one person who I wanted for Omni who declined to come on board. Otherwise everybody I talk to is wildly enthusiastic. They all think Ultra is going to break the bank."

"How much do you tell them?" Kim asked.

"Almost nothing until they commit," Edward said. "I'm not taking any chances. But even with generalities they're all so eager that I haven't had to give up much equity. So far I've committed only forty thousand unvested shares."

Kim didn't know what that meant, and she didn't ask. They got to the car. Edward put his carry-on bags in the trunk. They climbed in and drove out of the garage.

"How are things going up at the compound?" Edward asked.

"Well," Kim said without inflection.

"Do I detect that you are a little down?" Edward asked.

"I suppose," Kim said. "I got up the courage to go to Harvard this afternoon about Elizabeth's evidence."

"Don't tell me they gave you a hard time," Edward said.

"No, they were very helpful," Kim said. "The problem was they didn't have good news. There was a big fire at Harvard in 1764 that destroyed the library and consumed a collection they called 'the repository of curiosities.' To make matters worse, they lost the index as well, so at this point no one knows what the collection contained. I'm afraid that Elizabeth's evidence literally went up in smoke."

"I guess that throws you back to the repository at the castle," Edward said.

"I suppose," Kim said. "The trouble is I've lost some of my enthusiasm."

"How come?" Edward asked. "Finding those letters from the Mathers and Sewall should have been a great incentive."

"They were," Kim said. "But the effect has started to wear off. I've spent almost thirty hours since then and haven't even found one paper from the sixteen hundreds."

"I told you it wasn't going to be easy," Edward reminded her.

Kim didn't say anything. The last thing she needed at that point was Edward saying "I told you so."

When they arrived at Edward's apartment, he was on the phone with Stanton before he'd taken his suit jacket off. Kim listened vaguely to Edward's end of the conversation as he related his successful efforts at recruitment.

"Good news on both ends," Edward said after hanging up. "Stanton already has most of the four and a half million in the Omni coffers and has started the patent proceedings. We're cooking with gas."

"I'm happy for you," Kim said. She smiled and sighed at the same time.

# 10

## Friday,
## August 26, 1994

THE LATTER DAYS OF AUGUST FLEW BY. WORK CONTIN-
ued at the compound at a furious rate, particularly at the
lab, where Edward already spent most of his time. Pieces
of scientific equipment were arriving on a daily basis, causing a flurry of effort to get them properly housed, installed,
and shielded, if necessary.

Edward was a whirlwind of activity, wearing many hats.
One minute he was an architect, the next an electronics
engineer, and finally a general contractor as he single-
handedly directed the emergence of the lab. The drain on
his time was enormous, and as a consequence he devoted
even less time to his duties at Harvard.

The conflicting demands as a researcher and a teacher
came to a head due to actions of one of Edward's postdocs.
He'd had the temerity to complain to the Harvard administration about Edward's lack of availability. When Edward
heard, he'd become furious and dismissed the student sum-
marily.

The problem did not end there. The student was equally
incensed and again sought redress from the administration.
The administration contacted Edward, but he refused to
apologize or accept the student back into his lab. As a result, relations between Edward and the administration became increasingly acrimonious.

To add to Edward's headaches, the Harvard Licensing
Office got wind of his involvement in Omni. It also had
heard a disturbing rumor of a patent application on a new
class of molecules. In response, the licensing office had sent
a slew of inquiry letters, which Edward chose to ignore.

Harvard found itself in a difficult situation. The university did not want to lose Edward, one of the brightest rising stars of postmodern biochemistry. At the same time, the university could not let a bad situation get worse since principles as well as precedents were involved.

The tension was taking its toll on Edward, especially when combined with the stresses of the excitement of Omni, the promise of Ultra, and the daily problems at the construction site.

Kim was aware of the escalating pressures and attempted to compensate by trying to make Edward's life a little bit easier. She'd begun staying at his apartment most evenings, where she'd assumed more domestic responsibility without being asked: fixing dinner, feeding Edward's dog, and even doing some cleaning and laundry.

Unfortunately, Edward was slow to recognize Kim's efforts. The flowers had stopped as soon as she began staying at Edward's on a regular basis, a cessation she thought was reasonable. But she missed the attentiveness they represented.

As Kim left work on Friday, August 26, she pondered the situation. Adding to the stress was the fact that she and Edward had not yet made moving plans even though both of them had to be out of their respective apartments in five days. Kim had been afraid to raise the issue with Edward until he'd had a less-stressful day. The problem was, he didn't have any.

Kim stopped at the Bread and Circus grocery store and bought food for dinner. She picked something she was confident Edward would particularly like. She even got a bottle of wine as a treat.

When Kim got to Edward's apartment she picked up magazines and newspapers and generally straightened up. She fed the dog. Then she made the dinner and had it ready for seven, which was when Edward had told her he'd be home.

Seven came and went. Kim turned off the heat from the rice. At seven-thirty she covered the salad with plastic wrap and put it into the refrigerator. Finally at eight Edward walked in.

"Damn it all to hell!" he said as he kicked the door closed. "I take back all the nice things I've ever said about your contractor. The guy is an ass. I could have hit him this afternoon. He promised me there'd be electricians there today and there weren't."

Kim told him what they were having for dinner. He grunted and went into the bathroom to wash his hands. Kim heated up the rice in the microwave.

"The goddamn lab could be functional in no time if these lunkheads would get their act together," Edward yelled from inside the bathroom.

Kim poured two glasses of wine. She carried them into the bedroom and handed one to Edward as he emerged from the bathroom. He took it and sipped it.

"All I want to do is to get started on a controlled investigation of Ultra," he said. "It seems that everybody wants to thwart me by putting obstacles in my way."

"This might not be the best time to bring this up," Kim said hesitantly, "but there's never a good time. We still don't have any formal moving plans, and the first of the month is almost here. I've been meaning to talk to you for a couple of weeks."

Edward exploded. In a moment of uncontrolled fury he hurled his full wineglass into the fireplace, where it shattered, and yelled: "The last thing I need is pressure from you!"

Edward hovered over Kim. His eyes had dilated and his veins stood out on his temples. His jaw muscles were quivering and he was clasping and unclasping his hands.

"I'm sorry," Kim blurted. For a moment she didn't move. She was terrified. She'd not seen this side of Edward. As big as he was, she knew his strength and guessed what he could do to her if he were inclined.

As soon as she could, Kim ran from the room. She went into the kitchen and busied herself. As soon as the immediate shock lessened, she decided to leave. Turning from the stove, she started toward the living room and the front door, but she immediately stopped. Edward was in the doorway. To Kim's relief, his face was totally transformed; instead of rage it reflected confusion, even sadness.

"I'm sorry," he said. His stutter made getting the words out an ordeal. "I don't know what came over me. I guess it's been the pressure, although that's not an adequate excuse. I'm embarrassed. Forgive me."

Kim was immediately taken by his sincerity. She stepped over to him and they hugged. Then they went into the living room and sat on the couch.

"I'm finding this period terribly frustrating," he said. "Harvard is driving me crazy, and I desperately want to get back to work on Ultra. Eleanor has been continuing work on the drug as best she can and is getting continually good results. It's aggravating not to be able to help her, but the last thing I want to do is take my frustrations out on you."

"I've been on edge as well," Kim admitted. "Moving has always made me nervous. On top of that I'm afraid this Elizabeth thing has become something of an obsession."

"I certainly haven't been giving you any support," Edward said. "I'm sorry about that too. Let's make a pact to be more sensitive to each other."

"That's a wonderful idea," Kim said.

"I should have said something about moving myself," Edward said. "It's not solely your responsibility. When do you want to move?"

"We have to be out of our apartments by the first of September," Kim said.

"So how about the thirty-first?" Edward said.

## Wednesday, August 31, 1994

Moving day was hectic from the first hours of daylight when Kim got up. The van arrived at Kim's apartment at seven-thirty and loaded her things first. Then it went to Cambridge to get Edward's belongings. By the time the last chair was put in, the truck was full.

Kim and Edward drove to the compound in their own cars, with their own pets. When they arrived, Sheba and Buffer met for the first time. Since they were approximately the same size, the confrontation ended in a standoff. From then on they ignored each other.

As the movers began bringing things into the cottage, Edward surprised Kim by suggesting they take separate bedrooms.

"Why?" Kim questioned.

"Because I'm not acting like myself," Edward explained. "I haven't been sleeping well with everything that has been going on. If we have separate bedrooms I can turn on the light and read if I need to calm myself down."

"That wouldn't bother me," Kim insisted.

"You've been sleeping at your apartment the last few nights," Edward said. "Haven't you been sleeping better?"

"No," Kim said.

"Well, then, we're just a little different," Edward said. "I've been sleeping better. Knowing I'm not bothering you makes me more relaxed. Anyway, it will be a temporary arrangement. As soon as the lab opens and things settle down, the pressure will be off. Then we'll move in together. You can understand, can't you?"

"I suppose," Kim said, trying to hide her disappointment.

The unloading of the moving van went considerably faster than its loading, and soon the cottage was filled to overflowing with boxes and haphazardly placed furniture. When the truck was empty, the movers picked up their gear and the boxes that had been unpacked and stowed them in the truck. Kim then signed the moving documents and watched the movers drive away.

No sooner had the truck disappeared from view than Kim saw a Mercedes emerge from the trees and speed toward her. She recognized the car. It was Stanton's. She called up to Edward to tell him that he had company before going to the door and opening it.

"Where's Edward?" Stanton demanded without so much as a greeting.

"He's upstairs," Kim said, pointing over her shoulder.

Stanton pushed past her and yelled for Edward to come down. He stood in the foyer with his hands on his hips, tapping his right foot. He was clearly agitated.

Kim's pulse quickened. Knowing Edward's fragile mental state, she was worried that Stanton would set him off.

Stanton always operated as if he had no regard for other people's feelings.

"Come down here, Edward," Stanton yelled again. "We've got to talk."

Edward appeared at the turn of the stairs. He was descending slowly. "What's the problem?" he asked.

"Oh, nothing much," Stanton said sarcastically. "It's just that your burn-rate on our capital is out of control. This lab of yours is costing an ungodly amount of money. What are you doing, paving the johns with diamonds?"

"What exactly are you referring to?" Edward asked warily.

"The whole thing," Stanton said. "I'm beginning to think you used to work for the Pentagon, since everything you order is the most expensive available."

"To do first-class experiments you need a first-class facility," Edward said. "I made that clear when we talked about forming Omni. I hope you don't think you can buy such labs at garage sales."

Kim watched the two men bicker. The longer they argued the less concern she had. Edward was angry but not out of control.

"All right," Stanton said. "Let's leave the cost of the lab alone for a moment. Instead I want you to give me a timetable for FDA approval of Ultra. I must know so I can estimate when we might see money coming in instead of going out."

Edward threw up his hands in exasperation. "We haven't even opened the doors to the lab and you're talking about a deadline. We discussed the FDA issue at the restaurant before we agreed to form the company. Have you forgotten?"

"Listen, smartass," Stanton shot back. "The burden to keep this operation afloat falls on my shoulders. Unfortunately it ain't going to be an easy task with the rate you are going through our capital."

Stanton turned to Kim, who was standing against the parlor wall. "Kim," he said, "tell this thickheaded dork that fiscal responsibility is a prime requirement of startup companies."

"Leave her out of it!" Edward snarled.

Stanton apparently sensed that he'd pushed Edward too far because he quickly assumed a more conciliatory tone.

"Let's all be calm," Stanton said, lifting his hands in supplication. "You have to recognize the reasonableness of my request. I have to have some vague outline of what you are going to do in this gold-plated lab so that I can try to anticipate and provide for our financial needs."

Edward exhaled noisily and visibly relaxed a degree. "Asking about what we will be doing in the lab is a far different question than bursting in here and demanding a date for FDA approval," he said.

"I'm sorry I'm not more diplomatic," Stanton said. "Give me an idea of your plan of attack."

"As soon as possible we'll be launching a crash course to learn everything there is to know about Ultra," Edward said. "First we must complete our knowledge of its basic chemistry, such as its solubility in various solvents, and its reactivity with other compounds. Then we have to commence controlled biological studies to understand metabolism, excretion, and toxicity. The toxicological studies will have to be done in vitro as well as in vivo on individual cells, groups of cells, and intact organisms. We'll have to start with viruses, then bacteria, and finally higher animals. We'll have to formulate assays. On a molecular level we'll have to determine binding sites and methods of action. We'll have to test under all sorts of conditions of temperature and pH. We'll have to do all this before we file an investigational new drug application with the FDA, which is what you have to do before you can even start the clinical phase."

"Good Lord." Stanton moaned. "You're making me dizzy. This sounds like decades of work."

"It's not decades," Edward said. "But it *is* years. I told you that already. At the same time I told you that it would be significantly shorter than the twelve-year average development time for a drug."

"How about six years?" Stanton questioned.

"I can't say until we begin work and start getting some

data," Edward said. "All I can say is that it will be more than three years and less than twelve."

"There's a chance it could be three years?" Stanton asked hopefully.

"It would be a miracle," Edward admitted. "But it is possible. But there is another factor you have to consider. The rapid spending of capital has been for the lab, and now that the lab is almost done, spending will drop considerably."

"I wish I could count on that," Stanton said. "But I can't. Soon we will be paying the enormous salaries you promised your Ultra team."

"Hey, I had to give big salaries to get the best people," Edward said. "Also, I preferred giving higher salaries rather than more stock. I didn't want to give away too much equity."

"The equity isn't going to be worth anything if we go bankrupt."

"But we're ahead of the game," Edward said. "Most biotech and pharmaceutical companies are formed with no drug on the horizon. We've already got the drug."

"I'm aware of that," Stanton said. "But I have the jitters. I've never invested all my money in one company and then watched it being spent so quickly."

"You've invested it wisely," Edward said. "We're both going to be billionaires. Ultra is that good, I'm sure of it. Come on. Let me show you the lab. It will reassure you."

Kim breathed a sigh of relief as she watched the two men walk toward the lab. Stanton even had his hand draped on Edward's shoulder.

Once they were gone, Kim surveyed the room. To her surprise her thoughts were not on the ungodly mess the moving had created. Instead the sudden silence brought an intense sense of Elizabeth's presence and a strong recurrence of her feeling that Elizabeth was trying to communicate with her. But try as she might, Kim could hear no words. Nevertheless, at that moment, Kim was acutely aware that some of Elizabeth existed in the core of her being. And what was now Kim's home was still in some way Elizabeth's.

Kim was not entirely comfortable with these thoughts. Somehow she detected an element of distress and urgency in Elizabeth's message.

Turning her back on what should have been more pressing tasks, Kim hastily unwrapped the newly restored portrait of Elizabeth and hung it over the fireplace. With the repainting of the walls, the portrait's silhouette had vanished. Kim had to guess how high it had hung. She was following an urge to replace the painting in the exact position it had occupied three hundred years previously.

Kim stepped away and turned to face the mantel. When she did, she was shocked by how lifelike the painting appeared. In better light Kim had thought it was rather primitive. Hanging in the afternoon twilight of the cottage gave a completely different effect. Elizabeth's green eyes were hauntingly penetrating as they shone through the shadows.

For a few mesmerizing minutes Kim stood rooted in the center of the room, staring at a picture that in some respects was like looking into a mirror. Gazing into Elizabeth's eyes, Kim felt even stronger the sense that her ancestor was trying to communicate with her across the centuries. Kim again strained to hear the words, but there was only silence.

The mystical feeling radiating from the painting sent Kim back to the castle. Despite the many boxes to unpack, and despite having spent so many frustratingly fruitless hours searching through the castle's papers, Kim had a sudden irresistible urge to return. Elizabeth's portrait had renewed her motivation to learn what she could about her mysterious ancestor.

As if driven by a preternatural force, Kim mounted the stairs and headed for the attic. Once inside, she didn't hesitate nor did she take the time to open the windows. Instead she marched directly to what looked like an old sea trunk. Opening the lid, she found the usual mix of papers, envelopes, and a few ledgers.

The first book was an inventory of ships' stores. The date was 1862. Directly beneath it was a larger, primitively bound notebook with a letter tied to it. Kim gulped. She could see that the letter was addressed to Ronald Stewart.

Kim reached into the trunk and lifted out the notebook.

After untying the string, she opened the envelope and slid out the letter. Recalling how carefully the Harvard archivists handled the Mather letter, Kim tried to do the same. The aged paper resisted being unfolded. It was a short note. Kim looked at the date and her anticipation lessened. It was from the eighteenth century.

16th April 1726
Boston

Dearest father,
In response to your query I esteem it to be in the meete interests of the family and the business to forebear transposing mother's grave to the family plot since the required permit would cause much disquietude in Salem town and awaken the whole affair which you suppressed with great diligence and effort.

Your loving son,
Jonathan.

Kim carefully folded the note and replaced it in its envelope. Thirty-four years after the witchcraft affair Ronald and his son were still concerned about its effect on the family despite a public apology and a day of mourning ordered by the colonial government.

Turning her attention to the notebook, whose binding was crumbling, Kim folded back the cloth cover only to have it detach in her hand. Then her heart skipped a beat. On the flyleaf was written: *Elizabeth Flanagan, her book, December 1678.*

Kim carefully leafed through the book and realized to her utter joy that it was Elizabeth's diary! The fact that the entries she saw were short and not consecutive didn't lessen her excitement.

Clasping the book with both hands for fear of its coming apart, Kim hurried over to a dormered window for better light. Starting from the back, she noticed that there were a number of blank pages. Coming to the last entry, Kim noticed that the diary stopped prior to what she would have preferred. The date was Friday 26th February 1692.

There is no end to this cold. More snow on this day. The Wooleston River is now thick with ice to support a person to the Royal Side. I am much distracted. A sickness has weakened my spirit with cruel fits and convulsions as described by Sarah and Jonathan in like manner as those I have observed with poor Rebecca, Mary, and Joanna and the same that Ann Putnam suffered on her visit.

How have I offended almighty God that he would visit such torments on his dutiful servant? I hath no memory of the fits yet before I see colors that now affright me and hear strange sounds not of this world as I feel as if to faint. On the sudden I am restored to my senses to discover I am on the floor and have thrashed about and said unintelligible mutterings or so have said my children Sarah and Jonathan who, praise the Lord, are still unafflicted. How I wish Ronald be here and not on the high seas. These molestations commenced with the purchase of the Northfields tract and the spiteful quarrel with the Thomas Putnam family. Doctor Griggs is mystified for all and hath purged me to no avail. Such a cruel winter and travail for all. I fear for Job who is so innocent as I fear the Lord seeth to take away my life and my work is not done. I have endeavored to do God's work in his land to aid the congregation by baking the rye grain to extend our stores taxed by cruel weather and poor harvest, and refugees from Indian raids in the north whom I have encouraged the brethren accept into their hearth as family as I have done with Rebecca Sheafe and Mary Roots. I have taught the older children in the manner of constructing dolls for the surcease of the torment of the orphaned infants whose trust the Lord hath given us. I pray for Ronald's speedy return to help us with these terrible molestations before the sap runs.

Kim closed her eyes and took a deep breath. She was overwhelmed. Now it was truly as if Elizabeth were speaking to her. Kim could feel the force and character of Elizabeth's personality through her anguish: caring, empathetic, generous, assertive, and courageous; all the traits Kim wished she had herself.

Kim opened her eyes and reread sections of the entry. She wondered who Job was, or if Job were a biblical reference and not a person. She reread the part about doll-making and wondered again if the evidence that convicted Elizabeth had been a doll rather than a book.

Fearing she might have missed something, Kim reread the entire entry and became impressed with the tragic irony that Elizabeth's generosity might have caused her to spread the poisonous mold. Perhaps the unspecified evidence somehow proved Elizabeth's responsibility.

For several minutes Kim stared out the window, pondering this new line of thinking. But try as she might, she couldn't think of any way Elizabeth could have been implicated. At the time, no way existed to connect the mold with the fits.

Kim looked back at the diary. Carefully, she turned individual pages and glanced at other entries. Most were short: only a few sentences for each day, which included a terse description of the weather.

Kim closed the book and then reopened it from the front. The first entry was 5th December 1678, and was written in a larger, more hesitant script than the last entry fourteen years later. It merely described the day as cold and snowy and gave Elizabeth's age: thirteen.

Kim closed the book. She wanted to savor the experience. Clutching it to her chest as if it were a treasure, Kim returned to the cottage. Moving a table and a chair to the middle of the room, she sat down. In full view of the portrait she randomly leafed through the pages. On 7 January 1682 Kim found a longer entry.

Elizabeth described the weather as being warm for the season of the year and cloudy. She then matter-of-factly mentioned that she'd been married that day to Ronald Stewart. That short sentence was followed by a long description of the fine carriage she rode from Salem Town. Elizabeth then related her joy and amazement at moving into such a fine house.

Kim smiled. As she read relatively lengthy descriptions of the rooms and their contents she understood that Elizabeth was relating her reactions to moving into the same house Kim was currently moving into. It was a charming coincidence to have found the book on such a day, and it made the three-hundred-year interval that separated Elizabeth and Kim seem suddenly short.

Kim made a quick subtraction and realized that Elizabeth had been only seventeen when she married. Kim could not imagine herself getting married at such an age, especially considering the emotional problems she had during the first few years of college.

Looking ahead in the diary, Kim learned that Elizabeth became pregnant only a few months later. Kim sighed. What would she have done with a child at that age? It was a frightening concept yet obviously Elizabeth had dealt with it admirably. It was also a stark reminder to Kim that birth control had not been available to Elizabeth, and how little control Elizabeth had over her destiny.

Reversing her direction in the notebook, Kim glanced at entries prior to Elizabeth's marriage to Ronald. She stopped at another relatively long entry for 10 October 1681. Elizabeth recorded that on that hot, sunny day her father returned from Salem Town with an offer of marriage. Elizabeth went on to write:

> I was at first troubled in spirit at such a strange affair since I know nothing of this gentleman yet father speaks well of him. Father says the gentleman espied me in September when he visited our land for purposes of timber for masts and spars for his ships. My father says it is for me to decide but that I should know the gentleman has offered most graciously to move us one and all to Salem Town where my father shall work in his company and my dear sister Rebecca should go to school.

A few pages on Elizabeth wrote:

> I have told my father I shall accept the proposal of marriage. How can I not? Providence beckons as we have been living these years on poor land in Andover at constant threat of attack by red savages. Our neighbors on both sides have suffered such grave misfortune and many have been killed or taken captive in a most cruel way. I have tried to explain to William Paterson but he does not understand and I fear that he is now ill disposed toward me.

Kim paused and raised her eyes to Elizabeth's portrait. She was moved by the realization she was reading the thoughts of a seventeen-year-old selfless girl willing to give up a teenage love and to take a chance with fate for the benefit of her family. Kim sighed and wondered when the last time was she had done something completely unselfish.

Looking back at the diary, Kim searched for a record of Elizabeth's first meeting with Ronald. She found it on 22 October 1681, a day of sunshine and falling leaves.

> I met today in our common room Mr. Ronald Stewart who proposes to be my husband. He is older than I supposed and has already a young daughter from a wife who died with the pox. He appears to be a good man, strong of mind and body albeit a hint of a choleric disposition when he heard that the Polks, our neighbors to the north had been attacked two nights before. He insists we move forthwith in our sundry plans.

Kim felt a twinge of guilt concerning some of her earlier suspicions of Ronald with this revelation of the cause of Ronald's first wife's death. Flipping ahead in the diary to 1690, Kim read more about fears of smallpox and Indian raids. Elizabeth wrote that the pox was rampant in Boston and that devastating raids from the red savages were occurring a mere fifty miles north of Salem.

Kim shook her head in awe. Reading about such tribulations brought to mind Edward's remarks about how tenuous life's threads were back in the seventeenth century. It had to have been a difficult and stressful life.

The sound of the door banging open startled Kim. She looked up to see Edward and Stanton returning from their visit to the nearly complete lab. Edward was carrying blueprints.

"This place looks as bad as when I left," Edward said in a disgruntled tone of voice. He was looking for a spot to put down his plans. "What have you been doing, Kim?"

"I've had a wonderful bit of luck," Kim said excitedly. She scraped back her chair and brought the notebook over to Edward. "I found Elizabeth's diary!"

"Here in the cottage?" Edward asked with surprise.

"No, in the castle," Kim said.

"I think we should be making more progress getting the house in order before you go back to your paper chase," Edward said. "You'll have the whole month to indulge yourself up there."

"This is something even you will find fascinating," Kim said, ignoring Edward's remarks. She carefully opened the notebook to the last entry. Handing it to Edward and indicating the passage, she told him to read.

Edward put his blueprints on the game table Kim had been using. As he read the entry his face gradually changed from vexation to surprised interest.

"You're right," he said eagerly. He gave the book to Stanton.

Kim told them both to be more careful with it.

"That will make a great introduction to the article I plan to write for *Science* or *Nature* about the scientific causes of the afflictions in the Salem witch trials," Edward said. "It's perfect. She even talks specifically about using the rye. And the description of the hallucinations is right on target. Putting that diary entry together with the results of the mass spec on her brain sample closes the case. It's elegant."

"You're not writing an article about the new mold until the patent situation is more secure," Stanton said. "We're not about to take any chances so you can amuse yourself with your research colleagues."

"Of course I won't," Edward said. "What do you think I am? An economic two-year-old?"

"You said it, I didn't," Stanton said.

Kim took the diary from Stanton and pointed out to Edward the part about Elizabeth teaching others to make dolls. She asked him if he thought that was significant.

"You mean in relation to the missing evidence?" he asked.

She nodded.

"Hard to say," Edward said. "I suppose it is a little suspicious. . . . You know, I'm famished. What about you, Stanton? Could you eat something?"

"I can always eat," Stanton said.

"How about it, Kim?" Edward said. "How about throwing something together. Stanton and I still have a lot to go over."

"I'm hardly set up for entertaining," Kim said. She'd not even ventured to glance into the kitchen.

"Then order in," Edward said. He began unrolling his blueprints. "We're not picky."

"Speak for yourself," Stanton said.

"I suppose I could make some spaghetti," Kim said as she mentally reviewed what she'd need. The one room that was reasonably organized was the dining room; before the renovation it had been the old kitchen. The dining table and chairs and breakfront were all in place.

"Spaghetti would be perfect," Edward said. He had Stanton hold the blueprints while he weighted the corners with books.

With a sigh of relief, Kim slipped between her crisp, clean sheets for her first night's rest in the cottage. From the moment she'd started making the spaghetti to a half hour previously when she'd stepped into the shower, she'd not stopped working. There was still a lot to do, but the house was in reasonable order. Edward had worked equally as hard once Stanton finally left.

Kim lifted Elizabeth's diary off her night table. She fully intended to read more of it, but as she lay back into her bed, she became aware of the sounds of the night. The most notable was the remarkably loud symphony of nocturnal insects and frogs that inhabited the surrounding forest, marshes, and fields. There were also the gentle creaks from the aged house as it radiated off the heat absorbed during the day. Finally there was the subtle moan of the breeze from the Danvers River wafting through the casement windows.

As her mind calmed, Kim realized that the mild anxiety she'd felt when she'd first arrived at the house that afternoon still lingered. It had merely been overwhelmed by her subsequent intense activity. Although Kim guessed there were several sources of her unease, one was obvious: Edward's unexpected request to sleep apart. Although she understood his point of view better now than when the subject had first come up, Kim was still disturbed and disappointed.

Putting Elizabeth's diary aside, Kim climbed back out of bed. Sheba flashed her an exasperated look, since she'd been fast asleep. Kim slipped her feet into her mules and crossed to Edward's bedroom. His door was slightly ajar and his light was still on. Kim pushed the door open only to be confronted by a deep growl from Buffer. Kim gritted her teeth; she was learning to dislike the ungrateful mutt.

"Is there a problem?" Edward asked. He was propped up in bed with the lab blueprints spread around him.

"Only that I miss you," Kim said. "Are you sure about this idea of sleeping apart? I'm feeling lonely, and it's not very romantic to say the least."

Edward beckoned her over. He cleared the bed of the plans and patted the edge for her to sit down.

"I'm sorry," he said. "It is all my fault. I take full responsibility. But I still think it is best for now. I'm like a piano wire about to break. I even lost my cool with Stanton, as you saw."

Kim nodded while examining her hands tucked into her lap. Edward reached out and raised her chin.

"Are you OK?" he asked.

Kim nodded again, yet she was struggling with her emotions. She guessed she was overtired.

"It's been a long day," Edward said.

"I guess I also feel a little uneasy," Kim said.

"What about?"

"I'm not entirely sure," Kim admitted. "I suppose it has something to do with what happened to Elizabeth and with this being Elizabeth's house. I can't forget the fact that some of my genes are also Elizabeth's genes. Anyway, I sense her presence."

"You're exhausted," Edward reminded her. "When you're tired your imagination can do crazy things. Besides, this is a new place and that's bound to upset you to a degree. After all, we're all creatures of habit."

"I'm sure that's part of it," Kim said, "but it's not all."

"Now don't start getting weird on me," Edward said with a chuckle. "I mean, you don't believe in ghosts, do you?"

"I never have in the past, but now I'm not so sure."

"You're kidding?"

Kim laughed at his seriousness. "Of course I'm kidding," she said. "I don't believe in ghosts, but I am changing my opinion about the supernatural. The way I found Elizabeth's diary gives me chills when I think about it. I'd just hung up Elizabeth's portrait when I felt compelled to go back to the castle. And once I got there I didn't have to look very hard. It was in the first trunk I opened."

"People get a sense of the supernatural just being here in Salem," Edward said with a laugh of his own. "It has to do with that old witchcraft nonsense. But if you want to believe some mystical force guided you up to the castle, that's fine. Just don't ask me to subscribe to it."

"How else can you explain what happened?" Kim said fervently. "Prior to today I'd spent thirty-plus hours without so much as finding something from the sixteen hundreds much less Elizabeth's diary. What made me look in that specific trunk?"

"OK!" Edward said soothingly. "I'm not going to try to talk you out of it. Calm down. I'm on your side."

"I'm sorry," Kim said. "I didn't mean to get all worked up. I just came in here to tell you that I missed you."

After a lingering goodnight kiss, Kim left Edward to his blueprints and stepped from the room. After closing Edward's door she was bathed in moonlight coming through the half-bath window. From where she was standing she could see the black brooding mass of the castle silhouetted against the night sky. She shuddered; the scene reminded her of the backdrop of classic Dracula movies which used to terrify her as a teenager.

After descending the dark, enclosed staircase that took a full one-hundred-and-eighty-degree turn, Kim navigated through a sea of empty boxes that filled the foyer. Stepping into the parlor, she looked up at Elizabeth's portrait. Even in the dark Kim could see Elizabeth's green eyes glowing as if they had an inner light.

"What are you trying to tell me?" Kim whispered to the painting. The instant she'd looked at it the feeling that Elizabeth was trying to give her a message came back in a rush along with a clear understanding that whatever the message was, it wasn't in the diary. The diary was only a tease to goad Kim to further effort.

A sudden movement out of the corner of Kim's eye brought a stifled scream to her lips, and her heart leaped in her chest. She raised her arms by reflex to protect herself, but then quickly lowered them. It was only Sheba leaping onto the game table.

Kim supported herself for a moment against the table. Her other hand was over her chest. She was embarrassed about the degree of her terror. It also indicated to her how tense she really was.

# 11

## Early September 1994

THE LAB WAS FINISHED, STOCKED WITH REAGENTS, AND opened during the first full week in September. Kim was glad. Although she had the month off and was available to sign receipts for the hundreds of daily deliveries, she was glad to be relieved of the duty. The person who relieved her was Eleanor Youngman.

Eleanor was the first person to start work officially in the lab. Several weeks previously she'd given her notice to Harvard that she was relinquishing her postdoctorate position, but it had taken her almost two weeks to wrap up all her projects and move to Salem.

Kim's relationship with Eleanor improved but not drastically. It was cordial but stiff. Kim recognized that there was animosity on Eleanor's part born of jealousy. At their first meeting Kim had intuitively sensed that Eleanor's reverence for Edward included an unexpressed longing for a more personal relationship. Kim was amazed that Edward was blind to it. It was also a point of minor concern for her given her father's history of licentious relationships with his so-called assistants.

The next occupants to arrive at the lab were the animals. They came midweek in the dead of the night. Edward and Eleanor supervised the unloading of the unmarked trucks and getting the menagerie of animals into the appropriate cages; Kim preferred to watch from the window of the cottage. She couldn't see much of what was going on, but that was fine with her. Animal studies bothered her even though she understood their necessity.

Heeding the advice of the contractor and architect, Edward had established a policy that the less the community knew about what went on at the lab the better. He did not want any trouble with zoning laws or animal rights groups. This policy was aided by the natural insulation the compound enjoyed: a dense forest ringed with a high fence separated it from the surrounding community.

Toward the end of the first full week in September the other researchers began to arrive. With Edward and Eleanor's assistance they secured rooms at the various bed and breakfast establishments sprinkled in and around Salem. Part of the contractual agreement with the researchers was that they come alone; they left their families temporarily behind to ease the stress of working around the clock for several months. The incentive was that everyone would become a millionaire once their stock was vested.

The first out-of-town member of the team to arrive was Curt Neuman. It was midmorning and Kim was in the cottage, preparing to leave for the castle, when she heard the muffled roar of a motorcycle. Going to the window, she saw a cycle glide to a stop in front of the house. A man of approximately her age dismounted and lifted the visor of his helmet. A suitcase was strapped to the back of the bike.

"Can I help you?" Kim called out through the window. She assumed it was a delivery person who'd missed the turnoff to the lab.

"Excuse me," he said in an apologetic voice that had a mild Germanic timbre. "Perhaps you can help me locate the Omni lab."

"You must be Dr. Neuman," Kim said. "Just a minute. I'll be right out." Edward had mentioned an accent when he'd told Kim he was expecting Curt that day. She hadn't expected the renowned researcher to arrive by motorcycle.

Kim quickly closed some fabric sample books left open on the game table and picked up several days' worth of newspapers strewn over the couch in anticipation of inviting Curt Neuman in. Checking herself briefly in the foyer mirror, she opened the door.

Curt had removed his helmet and was cradling it in his arm like a medieval knight. But he wasn't looking in Kim's direction. He was looking toward the lab. Edward had apparently heard the motorcycle and was barreling along the dirt road in his car on his way to the cottage. He pulled up, jumped out, and embraced Curt as if they were long-lost brothers.

The two men talked briefly about Curt's metallic-red BMW motorcycle until Edward realized Kim was standing in the doorway. He then introduced Kim to Curt.

Kim shook hands with the researcher. He was a large man, two inches taller than Edward, with blond hair and cerulean blue eyes.

"Curt's originally from Munich," Edward said. "He trained at Stanford and UCLA. Many people, including myself, think he's the most talented biologist specializing in drug reactions in the country."

"That's enough, Edward," Curt managed to say as his face blushed red.

"I was lucky to steal him away from Merck," Edward continued. "They wanted him to stay so badly that they offered to build him his own lab."

Kim watched in sympathy as poor Curt squirmed in the face of Edward's encomium, reminding her of their own reactions to Stanton's praise during the dinner when they'd first met. Curt seemed surprisingly bashful for his commanding size, model-like good looks, and reputed intelligence. He avoided eye contact with Kim.

"Enough of this blabber," Edward said. "Come on, Curt! Follow me with that death-wish machine of yours. I want you to see the lab."

Kim watched them caravan across the field toward the lab before she went back inside the house to finish what she had to do before heading up to the castle.

Later that day, just as Kim and Edward were finishing a light lunch, the second out-of-town researcher arrived. Edward heard the car drive up. Pushing back from the table, he went outside. Shortly afterward he returned with a tall, thin, but muscular man in tow. He was swarthy and handsome and appeared to Kim more like a professional tennis player than a researcher.

Edward introduced them. His name was François Leroux. To Kim's surprise he made a motion to kiss the back of her hand, but he didn't actually do it. All she felt was the light caress of his breath on her skin.

As he'd done with Curt, Edward gave Kim a brief but highly complimentary summary of François's credentials. But unlike Curt, François had no trouble hearing Edward's praise. While Edward went on and on, he'd locked his dark, piercing eyes on Kim in a manner that made her squirm.

"The fact of the matter is that François is a genius," Edward was saying. "He's a biophysicist originally from Lyons, France, who trained at the University of Chicago. What sets him off from his colleagues is that he has managed to specialize in both NMR and X-ray crystallography. He's managed to combine two technologies which are usually competitive."

Kim noticed a slight smile had appeared on François's face at this point in Edward's accolade. He also bowed his head in Kim's direction as if to emphasize that he was everything Edward was saying and more. Kim looked away. She had the feeling that François was a bit too sophisticated and forward for her taste.

"François will be responsible for our saving a lot of time with the Ultra research," Edward continued. "We're truly lucky to have him. It's France's loss and our gain."

A few minutes later Edward led François from the house to take him to the lab. He was eager for François to see the facility and meet Curt. Kim watched them climb into Edward's car from the window. She couldn't help marvel how such widely disparate personalities could end up doing such similar work.

The last two of the core researchers arrived Saturday, September 10. They arrived by train from Boston. Edward and Kim went together as a welcoming committee and were standing on the platform as the train pulled into the station.

Edward saw them first and waved to get their attention. As they walked toward Edward and Kim, Kim jokingly asked Edward if physical attractiveness had been one of the requirements for employment at Omni.

"What in the devil are you talking about?" Edward asked.

"All your people are so good-looking," Kim said.

"That's something I hadn't noticed," Edward said.

When the two groups came together Edward did the introductions. Kim met Gloria Hererra and David Hirsh, and she shook hands with each.

Gloria, like Eleanor, did not fit Kim's stereotypical image of a female academic researcher. But that was their only similarity. They were complete opposites in coloring and manner. In contrast to Eleanor's fairness, Gloria was olive complected with hair as dark as Kim's and dark eyes almost as penetrating as François's. In contrast to Eleanor's cool reserve, Gloria was warm and forthright.

David Hirsh reminded Kim of François. He too was tall and slender, with a panache like an athlete. He was dark but not quite as swarthy as François. His demeanor was equally as urbane but more pleasant since he wasn't as bold and had a demonstrable sense of humor along with a pleasing smile.

On the drive to the station Edward described Gloria and David's accomplishments with similar detail and accolades as he'd done with Curt and François. Both Gloria and David assured Kim that Edward was exaggerating. They then turned the conversation around to talk about Edward. In the end all Kim was certain of was that Gloria was a pharmacologist and David was an immunologist.

At the compound Kim was dropped off at the cottage. As the car pulled away en route to the lab, Kim could hear more laughter. Kim was happy for Edward. She was confident that Gloria and David would be good additions to the atmosphere of the lab.

The following day, September 11, Edward and the other five researchers had a brief celebration to which Kim was invited. They uncorked a bottle of champagne, clinked glasses, and toasted Ultra. A few minutes later they fell to work at a furious pace.

Over the next few days, Kim visited the lab often to lend moral support as well as to make sure there were no problems she could help solve. She thought of her position as somewhere between hostess and landlord. By midweek she slowed the frequency of her visits considerably. By the end of the week she rarely went since every time she did, she'd been made to feel as if she were intruding.

Edward did not help. On the previous Friday he told her outright that he'd prefer her not to come too often since her visits interrupted their collective concentration. Kim didn't take the rebuff personally because she was well aware of the pressure they were under to produce results as quickly as possible.

Besides, Kim was content with her own activities. She'd adjusted nicely to living in the house and found it pleasant. She still felt twinges of Elizabeth's presence but not nearly so disturbingly intense as that first night. Indulging her interest in interior design, Kim had obtained dozens of books on wall and floor covering, drapery design, and colonial furniture. She'd brought in scores of samples which she had littered about the house in the areas she considered using the materials. As an added treat she'd spent many an hour rummaging through the area's many antique shops hunting for period colonial furniture.

Kim also invested significant time back in the castle, either in the attic or the wine cellar. The discovery of Elizabeth's diary had been a great incentive to her. It had also wiped away the discouragement built up by so many previously fruitless hours.

In the very beginning of September during Kim's first trip back to the castle after finding Elizabeth's diary, she'd found another significant letter. It had been in the same sea trunk as the diary. It was addressed to Ronald and was from Jonathan Corwin, the magistrate who originally occupied the Witch House.

20th July 1692
Salem Town

Dear Ronald:
I esteemed it prudent to draw your attention that your removal of Elizabeth's body from its interment on Gallows Hill hath been espied by Roger Simmons who in like manner did see the son of Goodwife Nurse remove his mother's body to the same end as yourself. I

beg of you my friend not to flaunt this act in these unruly turbulent times lest you bring more molestation to
yourself and your family for raising the departed is
seen by many as witch's work. Nor would I in the
mood of the public call attention to a grave for the
likewise reason that it result in you being wrongfully
accused. I hath spoke with said Roger Simmons and he
hath sworn to me that he will speak of your deed to no
man except a magistrate if he be deposed. God be with
you.

Your servant and friend,<br>
Jonathan Corwin.

After finding the Corwin letter Kim entered a two-week
period of finding nothing related to Ronald or Elizabeth.
But it did not dampen her enthusiasm for spending time in
the castle. Belatedly recognizing that almost all of the documents in the attic and the wine cellar had historical significance, Kim decided to organize the papers rather than
merely look through them for seventeenth-century material.

In both the attic and the wine cellar she designated areas
for storing papers according to half-century periods. In each
area she separated the material into business, government,
and personal categories. It was a monumental task but it
gave her a sense of accomplishment even if she wasn't
adding to her collection of documents relating to her seventeenth-century ancestors.

Thus the first half of September passed comfortably, with
Kim dividing her time between decorating the cottage and
searching and organizing the castle's disordered archives.
By midmonth she avoided the lab altogether and rarely saw
any of the researchers. She even began to see less of Edward as he came home progressively later each evening and
left earlier in the morning.

# 12

## Monday,
## September 19, 1994

IT WAS A GORGEOUS FALL DAY WITH BRIGHT WARM SUN-shine that quickly brought the temperature to nearly eighty. To Kim's delight some of the trees in the low-lying marshy areas of the forest already had a hint of their fall splendor, and the fields surrounding the castle were a rich blanket of goldenrod.

Kim had not seen Edward at all. He'd gotten up before she did at seven and had left for the lab without breakfasting. She could tell because there were no soiled dishes in the sink. Kim wasn't surprised since Edward had told her several days previously that the group had begun taking their meals together in the lab to save time. He'd said they were making amazing progress.

Kim spent the morning in the cottage with her decorating project. After a week's indecision she was able to decide on the fabric for the bedspreads, the bed hangings, and the curtains for both upstairs bedrooms. It had been a difficult choice, but having finally made it, Kim felt relieved. With the fabric number in hand she called a friend at the design center in Boston and had her place the order.

After a pleasant lunch of salad and iced tea, Kim walked up to the castle for her afternoon of searching and organizing. Once inside the mansion she had her usual debate between spending the afternoon in the wine cellar or the attic. The attic won out because of the sunshine. She reasoned there would be plenty of gloomy, rainy days when the wine cellar would be a relief.

Moving all the way around to the distant point of the attic over the servants' wing, Kim set to work on a series of black file cabinets. Using empty cardboard moving boxes that had brought Edward's books to the cottage, Kim separated the documents as she'd been doing the previous weeks. The papers were mostly business-related from the early nineteenth century.

Kim had become adept at reading the handwritten pages and could file them in the proper box after a mere glance at the title page, if there was one, or at the first paragraph if there wasn't. By late afternoon she'd come to the last file cabinet. She was in the next-to-last drawer, going through a collection of shipping contracts, when she found a letter addressed to Ronald Stewart.

After having gone so long without finding such a document, Kim was momentarily stunned. She looked at the letter as if her eyes were deceiving her. Finally, she reached into the drawer and lifted it out. She held it with just the tips of her fingers the way Mary Custland had handled the Mather letter. Looking at the signature, her hopes rose. It was another letter from Samuel Sewall.

8th January 1697
Boston

My Dear Friend,
    As you are undoubtedly aware the Honorable Lieutenant-Governor, Council, and Assembly of his Majesty's Province of the Massachusetts Bay, in General Court did command and appoint Thursday the fourteenth of January next be observed as a day of fasting in repentance for any and all sins done against innocent people as perpetrated by Satan and his Familiars in Salem. In like manner I being sensible of my complicity serving with the late Commission of Oyer and Terminer wish to make public my blame and shame of it and shall do so in The Old South Church. But to you my friend I know not what to say to surcease your burden. That Elizabeth was involved with the Forces of Evil I have no doubt but be she possessed or in covenant I know not nor do I wish to conjecture in view of my past errors of judgement. As to your inquiry in regards

to the records of the Court of Oyer and Terminer in general and to Elizabeth's trial in particular, I can attest that they are in the possession of Reverend Cotton Mather who has sworn to me that they will never fall into the wrong hands to impugn the character of the justices and magistrates who served to the best of their ability albeit in error in many cases. I believe although I dared not ask nor do I wish to know that Reverend Mather intends to burn the aforesaid records. As for my opinion in regards to the offer Magistrate Jonathan Corwin made to give you all records of Elizabeth's case including initial complaint, arrest warrant, mittimus, and preliminary hearing testimony, I think you should take them and dispose of them in like manner for then future generations of your family will not suffer public exposure of this tragedy in Salem brought on or abetted by Elizabeth's actions.

Your Friend in Christ's name,<br>Samuel Sewall.

"For Godsake!" Edward snapped. "Sometimes you can be so blasted hard to find."

Kim looked up from the Sewall letter to see Edward standing over her. She was partially hidden behind one of the black filing cabinets.

"Is something wrong?" Kim asked nervously.

"Yes, there is," Edward said. "I've been looking for you for a half hour. I'd guessed you were up here in the castle, and I'd even come all the way up here to the attic and yelled. When you didn't answer I went down and searched the wine cellar. When you weren't there, I came back here. This is ridiculous. If you're going to spend this much time up here at least put in a phone."

Kim scrambled to her feet. "I'm sorry," she said. "I never heard you."

"That's obvious," Edward said. "Listen, there's a problem. Stanton is up in arms again about money, and he's on his way driving out here to Salem. We all hate to take the time out to meet with him, especially in the lab, where he'll want explanations about what everybody is doing. And to make matters worse everyone is on edge from overwork. There's a lot of bickering for stupid reasons like who has the most space and who's closer to the goddamn water cooler. It's gotten to the point I feel like a den mother for a bunch of bratty Cub Scouts and Brownies. Anyway, to make a long story short, I want to have the meeting in the cottage; it'll be good to get everybody out of the hostile environment. To save time I thought we could eat as well. So could you throw something together for dinner?"

At first Kim thought Edward was joking, but when she realized he wasn't, she glanced at her watch. "It's after five," she reminded him.

"It would have been four-thirty if you hadn't effectively hidden yourself away," Edward said.

"I can't make dinner for eight people at this time in the afternoon," Kim said.

"Why not?" Edward questioned. "It doesn't have to be a feast, for chrissake. It can be take-out pizza for all I care. That's what we've been living on anyway. Just something to fill their bellies. Please, Kim. I need your help. I'm going nuts."

"All right," Kim said against her better judgment. She could tell Edward was stressed. "I can do better than take-out pizza but it surely won't be gourmet." Kim gathered her things including the Sewall letter and followed Edward out of the attic.

As they were descending the stairs she handed the letter to him, explaining what it was. He handed it back.

"I don't have time for Samuel Sewall at the moment."

"It's important," Kim said. "It explains how Ronald was able to eliminate Elizabeth's name from the historical record. He didn't do it alone. He had help from Jonathan Corwin and Cotton Mather."

"I'll read the letter later," Edward said.

"There's a part that you might find interesting," Kim said. They had reached the landing of the grand staircase. Edward paused beneath the stained glass rose window. The yellow light made him appear particularly pale. Kim thought he looked almost ill.

"All right," Edward said impatiently. "Show me what you think I might find interesting."

Kim gave him the letter and pointed to the very last sentence, where Sewall mentioned that the Salem tragedy was either brought on or abetted by Elizabeth's actions.

Edward looked up at Kim after reading it. "So?" he questioned. "We already know that."

"We do," Kim agreed, "but did they? I mean, did they know about the mold?"

Edward looked back at the letter and read the sentence a second time. "They couldn't have," he said when he'd finished. "Scientifically it was impossible. They didn't have the tools or the understanding."

"Then how do you explain the sentence?" Kim said. "In the earlier part of the letter Sewall was admitting he made mistakes with the other convicted witches, but not with Elizabeth. They all knew something we don't."

"Then it comes back to the mysterious evidence," Edward said. He handed her back the letter. "It's interesting but not for my purposes, and truly I don't have time for this stuff now."

They continued down the stairs.

"I'm sorry I'm so preoccupied," Edward said. "On top of all the other pressures I'm under, Stanton is turning out to be a royal pain in the ass, almost as bad as Harvard. Between the two of them I'm ready to be committed."

"Is all this effort worth it?" Kim questioned.

Edward eyed Kim with disbelief. "Of course it is," he said irritably. "Science requires sacrifice. We all know that."

"This is sounding less like science than economics," Kim said. Edward didn't respond.

Outside, Edward went directly to his car. "We'll be at the house at seven-thirty sharp," he called over his shoulder just before climbing in behind the wheel. He started the engine and sprayed sand and dirt from beneath the wheels as he sped off toward the lab.

Kim got into her own car and drummed her fingers on the steering wheel while she mulled the problem of what to do for dinner. Now that Edward had left and she had a moment to think, she was irritated and disappointed in herself for having accepted this unexpected and unreasonable burden.

Kim recognized her behavior, and she didn't like it. By being so compliant she was reverting to more childlike conduct of appeasement, just as she had years before, whenever her father was concerned. But recognizing what she was doing and doing something about it were two very different things. As with her father, she wanted to please Edward since she desired and needed his esteem. Besides, Kim reasoned, Edward was under a lot of pressure and needed her.

Kim started the car and headed toward town for food shopping. As she drove she thought more about her situation. She certainly didn't want to lose Edward, yet over the last several weeks it had seemed as if the harder she tried to please him and the more understanding she tried to be, the more demanding he'd become.

With such short notice Kim decided on a simple dinner of barbecue-grilled steaks accompanied by salad and hot rolls. The beverage was to be either jug wine or beer. For dessert she got fresh fruit and ice cream. By six forty-five she had the steaks trimmed, the salad prepared, and the rolls ready for the oven. She even had the fire going in the outside grill.

Dashing into the bathroom, Kim took a quick shower. Then she went upstairs to put on fresh casual clothes before returning back to the kitchen to get out napkins and flatware. She was setting the table in the dining room when Stanton's Mercedes pulled up to the front of the house.

"Greetings, cousin," Stanton said as he came through the door. He gave Kim a peck on her cheek.

Kim welcomed him and asked if he'd like a glass of wine. Stanton accepted and followed her into the kitchen

"Is that the only wine you have?" Stanton questioned with disdain as Kim unscrewed the cap.

"I'm afraid so," Kim said.

"I think I'll have beer."

While Kim continued with the dinner preparations Stanton perched himself on a stool and watched her work. He didn't offer to help, but Kim didn't mind. She had everything under control.

"I see you and Buffer get along okay," Stanton commented. Edward's dog was under Kim's feet as she moved about the kitchen. "I'm impressed. He's a nasty son-of-a-bitch."

"Me get along with Buffer?" Kim questioned cynically. "That's a joke. He's certainly not here because of me; it's because of all this steak. He's usually with Edward at the lab."

Kim checked the warming temperature on the oven and slipped in the rolls.

"How are you enjoying living in this cottage?" Stanton asked.

"I like it," Kim said. Then she sighed. "Well, mostly. The lab situation is unfortunately dominating things. With all the pressure, Edward has been on edge."

"Don't I know," Stanton commented.

"Harvard is giving him a hard time," Kim said. She purposely didn't add that so was Stanton.

"I warned him about Harvard from the beginning of this venture," Stanton said. "I knew from past experience that Harvard wouldn't be apt to roll over and play dead, not when they got wind of the potential earnings involved. Universities have become very sensitive to this kind of situation, especially Harvard."

"I'd hate to see him jeopardize his academic career," Kim said. "Before Ultra, teaching was his first love."

Kim began to dress the salad.

Stanton watched her work and didn't say anything until he'd caught her eye. "Have you guys been getting along okay?" he asked. "I don't mean to be nosy, but since I've been working with him on this project, I've found that Edward is not the easiest person to deal with."

"It's been a bit stressful of late," Kim admitted. "Moving up here hasn't been as smooth as I'd anticipated, but of course I hadn't taken into account Ultra and Omni. As I said, Edward's been under a lot of pressure."

"He's not the only one," Stanton said.

The front door opened and Edward and the researchers

trooped in. Kim went out to greet them to make the best of the situation, but it wasn't easy. They were all in an irritable mood, even Gloria and David. It seemed that no one had wanted to come to the cottage for dinner. Edward had to order them to attend.

The worst response was from Eleanor. As soon as she got wind of the menu she announced petulantly that she did not eat red meat.

"What do you normally eat?" Edward asked her.

"Fish or chicken," she said.

Edward looked at Kim and raised his eyebrows as if to say: "What are we going to do?"

"I can get some fish," Kim said. She got her car keys and went out and got in the car. It was certainly a rude response on Eleanor's part, but in actuality Kim liked getting out of the house for a few minutes. The mood in there was depressing.

There was a market which sold fresh fish within a short drive, and Kim bought several salmon filets in case someone besides Eleanor preferred fish. On the drive back, Kim wondered with some trepidation what she would be encountering on her return.

Entering the cottage, she was pleasantly surprised. The atmosphere had improved. It still wasn't a joyous gathering by any stretch of the imagination, but it was less strained. In her absence the wine and beer had been opened and drunk with more gusto than she'd expected. She was glad she'd bought as much as she had.

Everyone was sitting in the parlor, grouped around the trestle table, with the portrait of Elizabeth staring down at them. Kim nodded to those who looked in her direction and proceeded directly into the kitchen. She washed the fish and put it on a platter next to the meat.

With her own glass of wine in her hand, Kim walked back to the parlor. Stanton had stood up while she'd been in the kitchen and given everyone a handout. He was now standing in front of the fireplace, directly below the portrait.

"What you are looking at is a forecast of how quickly we will run out of money at the present burn-rate," he said. "Obviously that's not a good situation. Thus I need some idea when each of you will get to various milestones in order to best advise how to raise more capital. There are three choices: go public, which I doubt would work, at least not to our advantage until we have something to sell—''

''But we *do* have something to sell!'' Edward interrupted. ''We've got the most promising drug since the advent of antibiotics, thanks to the Missus.'' Edward raised his beer bottle to Elizabeth's portrait. ''I'd like to make a toast to the woman who may yet become Salem's most famous witch.''

Everyone except Kim raised their drinks. Even Stanton joined after getting his beer from where he'd placed it on the end of the mantel. After a moment of silence they all drank eagerly.

Kim squirmed uncomfortably, half expecting Elizabeth's expression in the portrait to change. She felt Edward's comments were disrespectful and in bad taste. Kim wondered how Elizabeth would feel if she were there to see these talented people maneuvering for personal gain in her house from a discovery related to her misfortune and untimely death.

''I'm not denying we have a potential product,'' Stanton said after putting his beer back down. ''We all know that. But we don't have a currently marketable product. So trust me, in the current economic climate, it is not the time for a public offering. What we could do is a private offering, which has the benefit of less loss of control. The last alternative is to approach additional venture capitalists. Of course this approach would require the most sacrifice of stock and hence equity. In fact we'd have to dilute what we already hold.''

A murmur of dissatisfaction arose from the researchers.

''I don't want to give away any more stock,'' Edward said. ''It's going to be too valuable when Ultra hits the market. Why can't we just borrow the money?''

''We don't have any collateral to secure such a loan,'' Stanton said. ''Borrowing the kind of money we'll need without collateral means paying exorbitant interest since it will not come from the usual sources. And since it's not from the usual sources, the people you have to deal with don't allow any hiding behind a corporate shield should things go sour. Do you understand what I'm saying, Edward?''

"I get the drift," Edward said. "But investigate the possibility anyway. Let's not leave any stone unturned that would avoid giving up any more equity. It would be a shame, because Ultra is such a sure thing.''

"Are you as confident of that as you were when we formed the company?" Stanton asked.

"More so," Edward said. "Every day I'm more convinced. Things are going very well, and if they continue as they are we might be in a position to file an IND—an Investigative New Drug application—within six to eight months, which is far different than the usual three and a half years.''

"The faster you move, the better the financial situation becomes," Stanton said. "It would be even better if you could pick up the pace."

Eleanor let out a short, derisive laugh.

"We are all working at maximum velocity," François said.

"It's true," Curt said. "Most of us are sleeping less than six hours a night."

"There's one thing that I haven't started doing," Edward said. "I've not yet contacted the people I know at the FDA. I want to start laying the groundwork to get Ultra at least considered for the expedited track. What we'll do eventually is try the drug on severe depression as well as AIDS and maybe even terminal cancer patients."

"Anything that saves time helps," Stanton said. "I can't stress that fact enough."

"I think we get the message," Edward said.

"Any better idea of Ultra's mode of action?" Stanton asked.

Edward asked Gloria to tell Stanton what they'd just discovered.

"Just this morning we found low levels of a natural enzyme in the brains of rats that metabolize Ultra," Gloria said.

"Is that supposed to excite me?" Stanton asked sarcastically.

"It should," Edward said, "provided you remember anything from the four years you wasted at medical school."

"It strongly suggests that Ultra could be a natural brain molecule, or at least structurally very close to a natural molecule," Gloria said. "Additional support for this theory is the stability of the binding of Ultra to neuronal membranes. We're beginning to think the situation could be somewhat akin to the relationship between morphine-like narcotics and the brain's own endorphins."

"In other words," Edward said, "Ultra is a natural brain autocoid, or internal hormone."

"But the levels are not the same throughout the brain," Gloria said. "Our initial PET scans suggests Ultra concentrates in the brain stem, the midbrain, and the limbic system."

"Ah, the limbic system," Stanton said. His eyes lit up. "That I remember. That's the part of the brain associated with the animal inside us and his basic drives: like rage, hunger, and sex. See, Edward, my medical education wasn't a complete waste."

"Gloria, tell him how we think it works," Edward said, ignoring Stanton's comment.

"We think it buffers the levels of the brain's neurotransmitters," Gloria said. "Something similar to the way a buffer maintains the pH of an acid-base system."

"In other words," Edward said, "Ultra, or the natural molecule if it is different than Ultra, functions to stabilize emotion. At least that was its initial function. It was to bring emotion back from extremes created by a disturbing event like seeing a saber-tooth tiger in your cave. Whether the extreme emotion is fear or anger or whatever, Ultra buffers the neurotransmitters, allowing the animal or primitive human being to quickly return to normal to face the next challenge."

"What do you mean by 'initial function'?" Stanton asked.

"With our latest work we believe the function has

evolved as the human brain has evolved,'' Edward said. ''Now we believe the function has gone from merely stabilizing emotion to bringing it more into the realm of voluntary control.''

Stanton's eyes lit up again. ''Wait a second,'' he said as he struggled to understand. ''Are you saying that if a depressed patient were to be given Ultra, all he'd have to do is desire not to be depressed?''

''That's our current hypothesis,'' Edward said. ''The natural molecule exists in the brain in minute amounts but plays a major role in modulating emotion and mood.''

''My God!'' Stanton said. ''Ultra could be the drug of the century!''

''That's why we're working nonstop,'' Edward said.

''What are you doing now?'' Stanton asked.

''We're doing everything,'' Edward said. ''We're studying the molecule from every vantage point possible. Now that we know it binds to a receptor, we want to know the binding protein. We want to know the binding protein's structure or structures since we suspect Ultra binds with different side chains in different circumstances.''

''When do you think we can start marketing in Europe and Japan?'' Stanton asked.

''We'll have some idea once we start clinical trials,'' Edward said. ''But that won't happen until we get the IND from the FDA.''

''We've got to speed the process up somehow,'' Stanton said. ''This is crazy! We've got a billion-plus drug and we could go bankrupt.''

''Wait a second,'' Edward said suddenly, drawing everyone's attention. ''I just got an idea. I just thought of a way to save some time. I'll start taking the drug myself.''

For a few minutes there was absolute silence in the room save for the ticking of a clock on the mantel and the raucous cry of sea gulls down by the river.

''Is that a wise move?'' Stanton asked.

''Damn right it is,'' Edward said, warming to the idea. ''Hell, I don't know why I didn't think of it before. With the results of the toxicity studies we've already done, I'm confident to take Ultra without the slightest qualm.''

"It's true we've seen no toxicity whatsoever," Gloria said.

"Tissue cultures seem to thrive on the stuff," David said. "Particularly neural cell cultures."

"I don't think taking an experimental drug is a good idea," Kim said, speaking up for the first time. She was standing in the doorway to the foyer.

Edward flashed her a scowl for interrupting. "I think it is a masterful idea," he said.

"How will it save time?" Stanton asked.

"Hell, we'll have all the answers before we even begin clinical trials," Edward said. "Think how easy it will make designing the clinical protocols."

"I'll take it as well," Gloria said.

"Me too," Eleanor said.

One by one the other researchers agreed that it was a fabulous idea and offered to participate.

"We can all take different dosages," Gloria said. "And six people will even give us a modicum of statistical significance when trying to evaluate the results."

"We can do the dosage levels blindly," François suggested. "That way we won't know who's on the highest dose and who's on the lowest."

"Isn't taking an unapproved investigational drug against the law?" Kim asked.

"What kind of law?" Edward asked with a laugh. "An institutional review board law? Well, as far as Omni goes, *we* are the institutional review board as well as every other committee, and we haven't passed any laws at all."

All the researchers laughed along with Edward.

"I thought the government had guidelines or laws about such things," Kim persisted.

"The NIH has guidelines," Stanton explained. "But they are for institutions receiving NIH grants. We're certainly not getting any government money."

"There must be some applicable rule against human use of a drug before the animal trials are completed," Kim said. "Just plain intuition tells you that it is foolhardy and dangerous. What about the thalidomide disaster? Doesn't that worry you people?"

"There is no comparison with that unfortunate situation," Edward said. "There wasn't any question of thalidomide being a natural compound, and it was generally far more toxic. But, Kim, we're not asking you to take Ultra. In fact you can be the control."

Everyone laughed anew. Kim blushed self-consciously and left the parlor for the kitchen. She was amazed how the atmosphere of the meeting had changed. From its strained beginning it had become buoyant. It gave Kim the uncomfortable feeling that some degree of group hysteria was occurring due to a combination of overwork and heightened expectations.

In the kitchen Kim busied herself with getting the rolls from the oven. From the parlor she heard continued laughter and loud, excited talk about building a science center with some of the billions they foresaw in their futures.

While she was transferring the rolls to a breadbasket, Kim sensed that someone had come into the kitchen behind her.

"I thought I'd offer to help," François said.

Kim turned and glanced at the man, but then looked quickly away, surveying the kitchen. She made it seem as if she were thinking about what he could do. In reality the man disturbed her with his forwardness, and she was still uncomfortable from the episode in the parlor.

"I think everything is under control," she said. "But thank you for asking."

"May I fill my wineglass?" he asked. He already had his hand wrapped around the neck of the wine jug.

"Of course," Kim said.

"I'd love to see some of the environs when the work calms down," François said as he poured the wine. "Perhaps you could show me some of the sights. I hear Marblehead is charming."

Kim hazarded another quick glance at François. As she expected, he was regarding her with his intense stare. When he caught her eye he smiled wryly, giving Kim the uncomfortable feeling that he was flirting with her. It also made her question what Edward had said to him about their relationship.

"Perhaps your family will be here by then," Kim said.
"Perhaps," François answered.

After Kim finished her usual bedtime routine, she purpose-fully left her door completely ajar so that she could see into the half-bath the two bedrooms shared. Her intention was to stay awake to talk with Edward when he came back from the lab to sleep. Unfortunately she didn't know what time that might be.

Sitting up comfortably against her pillows, Kim took Eli-zabeth's diary off her night table and opened it to where she was currently reading. The diary hadn't proven to be what she'd originally expected: except for the last entry it had been a disappointment. For the most part Elizabeth merely recorded the weather and what happened each day instead of expressing her thoughts, which Kim would have found much more interesting.

Despite her attempt to stay awake, Kim fell fast asleep around midnight with her bedside light still on. The next thing she was aware of was the sound of the toilet flushing. Opening her eyes, she could see Edward in the half-bath.

Kim rubbed her sleep-filled eyes and tried to concentrate on the clock. It was after one in the morning. With some effort she got herself out of bed and into her robe and slippers. Feeling a bit more awake, she padded into the half-bath. Edward was busy brushing his teeth.

Kim sat on the closed toilet seat and hugged her knees to her chest. Edward gave her a questioning look but didn't say anything until he'd finished with his teeth.

"What on earth are you doing up at this hour?" Edward asked. He sounded concerned, not irritated.

"I wanted to talk to you," Kim said. "I wanted to ask you if you really intend to take Ultra."

"Sure do," he said. "We're all going to start in the morning. We set up a blind system so no one will know how much they are taking compared to the others. It was François's idea."

"Do you really think this is a wise move?"

"It's probably the best idea I've had in ages," Edward said. "It will undoubtedly speed up the whole drug-evaluation process and Stanton will be off my back."

"But there must be a risk," she said.

"Of course there is a risk," Edward said. "There is always a risk, but I'm confident it is an acceptable risk. Ultra is not toxic, that we know for sure."

"It makes me feel very nervous," Kim said.

"Well, let me reassure you of one significant point," Edward said. "I'm no martyr! In fact I'm basically a chicken. I wouldn't be doing this if I didn't feel it was perfectly safe, nor would I allow the others. Besides, historically we'll be in good company. Many of the greats in the history of medical research used themselves as the first experimental subjects."

Kim raised her eyebrows questioningly. She wasn't convinced.

"You're just going to have to trust me," Edward said. He vigorously washed his face, then began to towel it dry.

"I have another question," Kim said. "What have you told people at the lab about me?"

Edward lowered the towel from his face and looked at Kim. "What are you talking about? Why would I be telling the people at the lab anything about you?"

"I mean about our relationship," Kim said.

"I don't recall specifically," Edward said with a shrug. "I suppose I might have said you were my girlfriend."

"Does that mean lover or does that mean friend?" Kim asked.

"What's going on here?" Edward questioned with annoyance. "I haven't divulged any personal secrets, if that's what you are implying. I've never gone into intimate details with anyone about us. And why am I getting the third degree at one o'clock in the morning?"

"I'm sorry if you feel I'm interrogating you," Kim said. "That wasn't my intention. I was just curious what you've said, since we're not married and I assume they've talked with you about their families."

Kim had started to explain about François, but she'd thought better of it. At the moment Edward was too temperamental for such a conversation, with his fatigue and anxious preoccupation with Ultra. Besides, Kim was reluctant to cause any potential rift between him and François because she couldn't be a hundred percent sure of what François's intentions had been.

Kim stood up. "I hope I haven't upset you," she said. "I know how tired you must be. Good night." She stepped from the bathroom and started toward her bed.

"Wait," Edward called out. He emerged from the bathroom. "I'm overreacting again," he said. "I'm sorry. Instead of making you feel badly I should be thanking you. I really appreciated your putting the dinner together. It was perfect and turned out to be a big hit with everyone. It was the kind of break we all needed."

"I appreciate your saying something," Kim said. "I have been trying to help. I think I know the pressure you're under."

"Well, it should get better with Stanton temporarily mollified," Edward said. "Now I can concentrate on Ultra and Harvard."

# 13

## Late September 1994

EDWARD'S RECOGNITION OF KIM'S EFFORTS AT PUTTING together the dinner on such short notice encouraged Kim to think that things would improve between herself and Edward. But it was not to be. During the week immediately after the Monday-night dinner, things seemed to get worse. In fact Kim did not see Edward at all. He'd come in late at night long after she'd gone to bed and would be up and out before she awoke. He made no effort to communicate with her at all even though she left numerous Post-It messages for him.

Even Buffer seemed to be nastier than usual. He appeared unexpectedly around dinnertime Wednesday night while Kim was preparing her food. He acted hungry, so Kim filled a dish with his food and extended it toward him, intending to put it on the floor. Buffer reacted by baring his teeth and snapping at her viciously. Kim put the food down the disposal.

With no contact whatsoever with anyone in the lab, Kim began to feel more estranged from what was happening in the compound than she had earlier in the month. She even began to feel lonely. To her surprise she started to look forward to returning to work the following week, a feeling she never expected to have. In fact, when she'd left work at the end of August, she'd thought returning to work would be difficult.

By Thursday, September 22, Kim was aware that she was feeling mildly depressed and the resulting anxiety scared her. She'd had a brush with depression in her sophomore year of college and the experience had left an enduring scar. Fearing that her symptoms might get worse, Kim called Alice McMurray, a therapist at MGH whom she'd seen a number of years previously. Alice graciously agreed to give up half her lunch hour the following day.

Friday morning Kim got up feeling a little better than she had on previous mornings. She guessed it was the excitement of having made plans to go into the city. Without her parking privileges at the MGH, she decided to take the train.

Kim arrived in Boston a little after eleven. With plenty of time to spare, she walked from North Station to the hospital. It was a pleasant fall day of intermittent clouds and sunshine. In contrast to Salem, the leaves on the city trees had yet to begin changing.

It felt good for Kim to be in the familiar hospital environment, especially when she ran into several colleagues who teased her about her tan. Alice's office was in a professional building owned by the hospital corporation. Kim entered from the hall and found the reception desk deserted.

Almost immediately the inner door opened, and Alice appeared.

"Hi," she said. "Come on in." She motioned with her head toward the secretary's desk. "Everyone is at lunch in case you were wondering."

Alice's office was simple but comfortable. There were four chairs and a coffee table grouped in the center of the room on an oriental rug. A small desk was against the wall. By the window stood a potted palm. On the walls were Impressionist prints and a few framed diplomas and licenses.

Alice was an ample-bodied woman whose compassionate manner radiated from her like a magnetic field. As Kim knew from Alice's own admission, she had been fighting a weight problem all her life. Yet the struggle had added to Alice's effectiveness by giving her extra sensitivity to other people's problems.

"Well, what can I do for you?" Alice asked once they were seated.

Kim launched into an explanation of her current living situation. She tried to be honest and fully admitted her disappointment that things had not gone as she'd anticipated. As she spoke she began to hear herself assuming most of the blame. Alice heard it too.

"This is sounding like an old story," Alice said in a nonjudgmental way. Alice then inquired about Edward's personality and social skills.

Kim described Edward, and with the help of Alice's presence, she immediately heard herself defending him.

"Do you think there is any resemblance between the relationship you had with your father and the relationship you have with Edward?" Alice asked.

Kim thought for a moment and then admitted her behavior in regard to the recent dinner party had suggested some analogy.

"It sounds to me that they are superficially quite similar," Alice said. "I can remember your describing similar frustration about trying to please your father. Both of these men appear to have an overriding interest in their business agendas that supersedes their personal lives."

"It's temporary with Edward," Kim said.

"Are you sure about that?" Alice questioned.

Kim thought for a moment before answering: "I guess you can never be sure about what another person is thinking."

"Precisely," Alice said. "Who knows, Edward could be changing. Nevertheless, it sounds like Edward needs your social support and you are giving it. There's nothing wrong with that except I sense that your needs aren't currently being met."

"That's an understatement," Kim admitted.

"You should be thinking about what is good for you and act accordingly," Alice said. "I know that is easy to say and difficult to do. Your self-esteem is terrified to lose his love. At any rate at least give it serious thought."

"Are you saying I shouldn't be living with Edward?" Kim asked.

"Absolutely not," Alice said. "That's not for me to say. Only you can say that. But as we discussed in the past, I think you should give thought to issues of codependency."

"Do think there are codependent issues here?" Kim asked.

"I just would like it to enter into your thinking," Alice said. "You know there is a tendency for people who were abused as children to re-create the circumstances of the abuse in their own domestic situations."

"But you know I wasn't abused," Kim said.

"I know you weren't abused in the general sense of the term," Alice said. "But you didn't have a good relationship with your father. Abuse can come in many different forms because of the vast difference in power between the parent and the child."

"I see what you mean," Kim said.

Alice leaned forward and put her hands on her knees. She smiled warmly. "It sounds to me like we have some things that we should talk about. Unfortunately our half hour is up. I wish I could give you more time, but on such short notice this is the best I can do. I hope I've at least got you thinking about your own needs."

Kim got to her feet. Glancing at her watch, she was amazed at how quickly the time had gone. She thanked Alice profusely.

"How is your anxiety?" Alice asked. "I could give you a few Xanax if you think you might need it."

Kim shook her head. "Thanks, but I'm okay," she said. "Besides, I still have a couple of those you gave me years ago."

"Call if you'd like to make a real appointment," Alice said.

Kim assured her that she'd give her more notice in the future and then left. As she walked back to the train station, Kim thought about the short session she'd had. It had seemed she was just getting started when it was over. Yet Alice had given her a lot to think about, and that was precisely why Kim had wanted to see her.

As she rode back to Salem, Kim stared out the window and decided that she had to talk to Edward. She knew it would not be an easy task because such confrontations were extremely difficult for her. Besides, with the pressure Edward was under he was hardly in the mood for such emotionally laden issues like whether they should currently be living together. Yet she knew she had to have a conversation with him before things got worse.

Driving onto the compound, Kim glanced at the lab building and wished she had the assertiveness to go over there directly and demand to talk to Edward immediately. But she knew she couldn't. In fact, she knew she couldn't even talk to him even if he showed up at the cottage that afternoon unless he also did something to make her feel he was ready to talk. With a degree of resignation, Kim knew she'd have to wait for Edward.

But Kim did not see Edward Friday evening, nor all day Saturday. All she'd find was scant evidence that he came in sometime after midnight and left prior to sunrise. With the knowledge she had to talk to him hanging over her like a dark cloud, Kim's anxiety gradually increased.

Kim spent Sunday morning keeping herself busy in the castle's attic, sorting documents. The mindless task provided a bit of solace and for a few hours took her mind away from her unfulfilling living situation. At quarter to one her stomach told her it had been a long time since her morning coffee and bowl of cold cereal.

Emerging from the musty interior of the castle, Kim paused on the faux drawbridge and let her eyes feast on the fall scene spread out around her. Some of the tree colors were beautiful, but they were hardly of the intensity they would assume in several more weeks. High above in the sky several sea gulls lazily rode the air currents.

Kim's eyes roamed the periphery of the property and stopped at the point of entry of the road. Just within the shadow of the trees she could see the front of an automobile.

Curious as to why the car was parked there, Kim struck out across the field. As she neared, she approached the car warily from the side, trying to get a glimpse of the driver. She was surprised to see it was Kinnard Monihan.

When Kinnard caught sight of Kim, he leaped from the car and did something Kim could not remember his ever having done. He blushed.

"Sorry," he said self-consciously. "I don't want you to think I'm just lurking here like some Peeping Tom. The fact is I was trying to build up my courage to drive all the way in.''

"Why didn't you?'' Kim asked.

"I suppose because I was such an ass the last couple of times we saw each other,'' Kinnard said.

"That seems a long time ago,'' Kim said.

"I suppose in some ways,'' Kinnard said. "Anyway I hope I'm not disturbing you.''

"You're not disturbing me in the slightest.''

"My rotation here at Salem Hospital is over this coming week,'' Kinnard said. "These two months have flown by. I'll be back working at MGH a week from tomorrow.''

"I'll be doing the same,'' Kim said. She explained that she'd taken the month of September off from work.

"I've driven out here to the compound on a few occasions,'' Kinnard admitted. "I just never thought it appropriate to stop by and your phone's unlisted.''

"I'd wondered how your rotation was going every time I drove near the hospital,'' Kim said.

"How did the renovations turn out?'' Kinnard asked.

"You can decide for yourself,'' Kim said. "Provided you'd like to see.''

"I'd like to see very much,'' Kinnard said. "Come on, get in. I'll give you a lift.''

They drove to the cottage and parked. Kim gave Kinnard a tour. He was interested and complimentary.

"What I like is the way you've been able to make the house comfortable yet maintain its colonial character,'' Kinnard said.

They were upstairs, where Kim was showing Kinnard how they had managed to put in a half-bath without disturbing the historical aspect of the house. Glancing out the window, Kim did a double take. Looking again, she was shocked to see Edward and Buffer walking across the field on their way to the cottage.

Kim was immediately gripped with a sense of panic. She had no idea what Edward's reaction to Kinnard's presence would be, especially with Edward's cantankerous mood of late and especially since she'd not seen him since Monday night.

"I think we'd better go downstairs," Kim said nervously.

"Is something wrong?" Kinnard asked.

Kim didn't answer. She was too busy castigating herself for not considering the possibility of Edward's appearing. She marveled how she managed to get herself into such situations.

"Edward is coming," Kim finally said to Kinnard as she motioned for him to step into the parlor.

"Is that a problem?" Kinnard asked. He was confused.

Kim tried to smile. "Of course not," she said. But her voice was not convincing and her stomach was in a knot.

The front door opened and Edward entered. Buffer headed for the kitchen to check for food that might have inadvertently been dropped on the floor.

"Ah, there you are," Edward said to Kim when he caught sight of her.

"We have company," Kim said. She had her hands clasped in front of her.

"Oh?" Edward questioned. He stepped into the parlor.

Kim introduced them. Kinnard moved forward and extended his hand, but Edward didn't move. He was thinking.

"Of course," Edward said while clicking his fingers. He then reached out and pumped Kinnard's hand with great enthusiasm. "I remember you. You worked in my lab. You're the fellow who went on to the MGH for a surgical residency."

"Good memory," Kinnard said.

"Hell, I even remember your research topic," Edward said. He then tersely summarized Kinnard's year-long project.

"It's humbling to hear you remember it better than I do," Kinnard said.

"How about a beer?" Edward asked. "We've got Sam Adams on ice."

Kinnard nervously glanced between Kim and Edward. "Maybe I'd better leave," he said.

"Nonsense," Edward said. "Stay if you can. I'm sure Kim could use some company. I have to get back to work. I've only come over here to ask her a question."

Kim was as bewildered as Kinnard. Edward was not behaving as she'd feared. Instead of being irritable and possibly throwing a temper tantrum, he was in a delightful mood.

"I don't know how best to word this," Edward said to Kim, "but I want the researchers to bunk in the castle. It will be infinitely more convenient for them to sleep on the property since many of their experiments require round-the-clock data collection. Besides, the castle is empty and has so many furnished rooms that it's ridiculous for them to stay in their respective bed-and-breakfasts. And Omni will pay."

"Well, I don't know . . ." Kim stammered.

"Come on, Kim," Edward said. "It will only be temporary. In no time their families will be coming and they'll be buying homes."

"But there are so many family heirlooms in the building," Kim said.

"That's not a problem," Edward said. "You've met these people. They are not going to touch anything. Listen, I'll personally guarantee that there won't be any difficulties whatsoever. If there are, out they go."

"Let me think about it," Kim said.

"What is there to think about?" Edward persisted. "These people are like family to me. Besides, they only sleep from about one to five, just like me. You won't even know they are there. You won't hear them and you won't see them. They can stay in the guest wing and the servants' wing."

Edward winked at Kinnard and added: "It's best to keep the women and the men apart because I don't want to be responsible for any domestic strife."

"Would they be content to use the servants' and the guest wing?" Kim asked. She was finding it hard to resist Edward's outgoing, friendly assertiveness.

"They will be thrilled," Edward said. "I can't tell you how much they will appreciate this. Thank you, my sweet! You are an angel." Edward gave Kim a kiss on the middle of her forehead and a hug.

"Kinnard!" Edward said, breaking away from Kim.

"Don't be a stranger now that you know where we are. Kim needs some company. Unfortunately I'm a bit preoccupied for the immediate future."

Edward gave a high-pitched whistle which made Kim cringe. Buffer trotted out from the kitchen.

"See you guys later," Edward said with a wave. A second later the front door banged shut.

For a moment Kim and Kinnard merely looked at each other.

"Did I agree or what?" Kim questioned.

"It happened kind of fast," Kinnard admitted.

Kim stepped to the window and watched Edward and Buffer crossing the field. Edward threw a stick for the dog.

"He's a lot more friendly than when I worked in his lab," Kinnard said. "You've had a big effect on him. He was always so stiff and serious. In fact he was downright nerdy."

"He's been under a lot of pressure," Kim said. She was still watching from the window. Edward and Buffer seemed to be having a marvelous time with the fetching game.

"You'd never guess, the way he's acting," Kinnard said.

Kim turned to Kinnard. She shook her head and rubbed her forehead nervously. "Now what have I gotten myself into?" she asked. "I'm not completely comfortable with Edward's people staying in the castle."

"How many are there?" Kinnard questioned.

"Five," Kim said.

"Is the castle empty?" Kinnard asked.

"No one is living there if that's what you mean," Kim said. "But it surely isn't empty. You want to see?"

"Sure," Kinnard said.

Five minutes later Kinnard was standing in the center of the two-storied great room. A look of disbelief dominated his face.

"I understand your concern," he said. "This place is like a museum. The furniture is incredible, and I've never seen so much fabric for drapes."

"They were made in the twenties," Kim said. "I was told it took a thousand yards."

"Jeez, that's over a half mile," Kinnard said with awe.

''My brother and I inherited this from our grandfather,'' Kim explained. ''We haven't the slightest idea what to do with it all. Still, I don't know what my father or brother will say about five strangers living in here.''

''Let's look at where they would stay,'' Kinnard said.

They inspected the wings. There were four bedrooms in each, and each had its own stairway and door to the exterior.

''With separate entrances and stairs they won't have to traverse the main part of the house,'' Kinnard pointed out.

''Good point,'' Kim said. They were standing in one of the servants' bedrooms. ''Maybe it won't be so bad. The three men can stay in this wing and the two women over in the guest wing.''

Kinnard poked his head into the connecting bath. ''Uh oh,'' he said. ''Kim, come in here!''

Kim joined him. ''What's the problem?''

Kinnard pointed to the toilet. ''No water in the bowl,'' he said. He leaned over the sink and turned on the faucet. Nothing came out. ''Some kind of plumbing problem.''

They checked the other bathrooms in the servants' wing. None of them had water. Crossing to the guest wing, they found that the problem, whatever it was, was confined to the servants' wing.

''I'll have to call the plumber,'' Kim said.

''It could be something simple like the water has just been turned off,'' Kinnard said.

Leaving the guest wing, they walked through the main part of the house again.

''The Peabody-Essex Institute would love this place,'' Kinnard said.

''They'd love to get their hands on the contents of the attic and the wine cellar,'' Kim said. ''Both are filled with old papers, letters, and documents that go back three hundred years.''

''This I gotta see,'' Kinnard said. ''Do you mind?''

''Not at all,'' Kim said. They reversed directions and climbed the stairs to the attic.

Kim opened the door and gestured for Kinnard to enter. ''Welcome to the Stewart archives,'' she said.

Kinnard walked down the central aisle looking at all the files. He shook his head. He was floored. "I used to collect stamps when I was a boy," he said. "Many a day I dreamed of finding a place like this. Who knows what you could find?"

"There's an equal amount in the basement," Kim said. Kinnard's delight gave her pleasure.

"I could spend a month in here," Kinnard said.

"I practically have," Kim said. "I've been searching for references to one of my ancestors named Elizabeth Stewart who'd been caught up in the witchcraft frenzy in 1692."

"No kidding," Kinnard said. "I find all that stuff fascinating. Remember, my undergraduate major was American History."

"I'd forgotten," Kim said.

"I visited most of the Salem witchcraft sites while I've been out here on rotation," Kinnard said. "My mom came for a visit and we went together."

"Why didn't you take the blonde from the ER?" Kim asked before she had a chance to think about what she was saying.

"I couldn't," Kinnard said. "She got homesick and went back to Columbus, Ohio. How are things going for you? It looks like your relationship with Dr. Armstrong is alive and well."

"It's had its ups and downs," Kim said vaguely.

"How was your ancestor involved in the witchcraft episode?" Kinnard asked.

"She was accused as a witch," Kim said. "And she was executed."

"How come you never told me that before?" Kinnard said.

"I was involved in a cover-up," Kim said with a laugh. "Seriously, I had been conditioned by my mother not to talk about it. But that's changed. Now getting to the bottom of her case has become a mini-crusade with me."

"Have you had any luck?" Kinnard said.

"Some," Kim said. "But there is a lot of material here and it has been taking me longer than I'd anticipated."

Kinnard put his hand on the handle of a file drawer and glanced at Kim. ''May I?'' he asked.

''Be my guest,'' Kim said.

Like most of the drawers in the attic it was filled with an assortment of papers, envelopes, and notebooks. Kinnard rummaged through but didn't find any stamps. Finally he picked up one of the envelopes and slipped out the letter. ''No wonder there's no stamps in here,'' he said. ''Stamps weren't invented until the end of the nineteenth century. This letter is from 1698!''

Kim took the envelope. It was addressed to Ronald.

''You lucky son of a gun,'' Kim said. ''This is the kind of letter I've been breaking my back to find, and you just walk in here and pluck it out like there was nothing to it.''

''Glad to be of assistance,'' Kinnard said. He handed the letter to Kim.

Kim read the letter aloud:

12th October 1698
Cambridge

Dearest Father,
I am deeply grateful for the ten shillings as I have been in dire need during these troublesome days of acclimation to colledge life. Ever so humbly I should like to relate that I have had complete success in the endeavor about which we had much discours prior to my matriculation. After lengthy and arduous inquiry I located the evidence used against my Dearly Departed Mother in the chambers of one of our esteemed tutors who had taken a fancy to its gruesome nature. Its prominent display caused me some disquietude but Tuesday last during the afternoon bever when all were retired to the buttery I chanced a visit to the aforesaid chambers and changed the name as you instructed to the fictitious Rachel Bingham. To a like purpose I entered the same in the catalogue in the library of Harvard Hall. I hope Dear Father that now you find solace that the surname Stewart has been freed from its most grievous molestation. In consideration of my studies I can with some felicity relate that

my recitations have been well received. My chamber-mates are hale and of a most agreeable nature. Apart from the fagging about which you aptly forewarned me, I am well and content and

I remain your loving Son,
Jonathan.

"Damn it all," Kim said when she'd finished the letter.

"What's the matter?" Kinnard asked.

"It's this evidence," Kim said, pointing it out in the letter. "It refers to the evidence used to convict Elizabeth. In a document I found at the Essex County Courthouse it was described as conclusive evidence, meaning it incontrovertibly convicted her. I've found several other references to it but it is never described. Figuring out what it was has become the chief object of my crusade."

"Do you have any idea what it could be?" Kinnard asked.

"I believe it has something to do with the occult," Kim said. "Probably it was a book or a doll."

"I'd say this letter favors its being a doll," Kinnard said. "I don't know what kind of book would have been considered 'gruesome.' The gothic novel wasn't invented until the nineteenth century."

"Maybe it was a book describing some witch's potion that used body parts as ingredients," Kim suggested.

"I hadn't thought of that," Kinnard said.

"Doll-making was mentioned in Elizabeth's diary," Kim said. "And dolls helped convict Bridget Bishop. I suppose a doll could be 'gruesome' either by being mutilated or perhaps sexually explicit. I imagine with the Puritan morality many things associated with sex would have been considered gruesome."

"It's a misconception of sorts that the Puritans were all hung up on sex," Kinnard said. "I remember from my history courses that they generally considered sins associated with premarital sex and lust as lesser sins than lying or the promotion of self-interest, since the latter had to do with breaking the sacred covenant."

"That means things have certainly turned around since

Elizabeth's day,'' Kim said with a cynical chuckle. ''What the Puritans thought were terrible sins are accepted and often lauded activities in present-day society. All you have to do is watch a government hearing.''

''So you hope to solve the mystery of the evidence by going through all these papers?'' Kinnard said, making a sweeping motion with his hand around the attic.

''Here and in the wine cellar,'' Kim said. ''I did take a letter from Increase Mather to Harvard since in the letter he said that the evidence had become part of the Harvard collections. But I didn't have any luck. The librarians couldn't find any reference to Elizabeth Stewart in the seventeenth century.''

''According to Jonathan's letter you should have been looking for 'Rachel Bingham,' '' Kinnard said.

''I realize that now,'' Kim said. ''But it wouldn't have made any difference. There was a fire in the winter of 1764 that consumed Harvard Hall and its library. Not only did all the books burn, but also what was called a 'repository of curiosities,' plus all the catalogues and indexes. Unfortunately no one even knows what was lost. I'm afraid Harvard can't be any help to me.''

''I'm sorry,'' Kinnard said.

''Thanks,'' Kim said.

''At least you still have a chance with all these papers,'' Kinnard said.

''It's my only hope,'' Kim said. She showed him how she was organizing all the material in terms of chronology and subject matter. She even took him to the area where she'd been working that morning.

''Quite a task,'' Kinnard said. Then he looked at his watch. ''I'm afraid I have to go. I've got to round on my patients this afternoon.''

Kim accompanied him down to his car. He offered to give her a ride back to the cottage, but she declined. She said she intended to put in a few more hours in the attic. She said she particularly wanted to search the drawer where he'd so easily found Jonathan's letter.

''Maybe I shouldn't ask this,'' Kinnard said. He had the

door to his car open. "But what is Edward and his team of researchers doing up here?"

"You're right," Kim said. "You shouldn't ask. I can't tell you the details because I've been sworn to secrecy. But what is common knowledge is that they are doing drug development. Edward built a lab in the old stables."

"He's no fool," Kinnard said. "What a fabulous place for a research lab."

Kinnard started to climb into his car when Kim stopped him. "I have a question for you," she said. "Is it against the law for researchers to take an experimental drug that has yet to reach clinical testing?"

"It's against FDA rules for volunteers to be given the drug," Kinnard said. "But if the researchers take it, I don't think the FDA has any jurisdiction. I can't imagine that they would sanction it, and it might cause trouble when they attempt to get an Investigational New Drug application."

"Too bad," Kim said. "I was hoping it might be against the law."

"I suppose I don't have to be a rocket scientist to guess why you are asking," Kinnard said.

"I'm not saying anything," Kim said. "And I'd appreciate it if you didn't either."

"Who am I going to tell?" Kinnard questioned rhetorically. He hesitated a moment and then asked: "Are they all taking the drug?"

"I really don't want to say," Kim said.

"If they are, it would raise a significant ethical issue," Kinnard said. "There would be the question of coercion with the more junior members."

"I don't think there is any coercion involved," Kim said. "Maybe some group hysteria, but no one is forcing anyone to do anything."

"Well, regardless, taking an uninvestigated drug is not a smart idea," Kinnard said. "There is too much risk of unexpected side effects. That's the reason the rules were promulgated in the first place."

"It was nice seeing you again," Kim said, changing the subject. "I'm glad to feel that we are still friends."

Kinnard smiled. "I couldn't have said it better myself."

Kim waved as he drove away. She waved again just before his car disappeared in the trees. She was sorry to see him go. His unexpected visit had been a welcome relief.

Returning inside the castle, Kim climbed the stairs on her way to the attic. She was still enjoying the warmth generated by Kinnard's visit when she found herself marveling over the episode with Edward. She could distinctly remember back to when she had first started dating Edward that he had reacted jealously to the mere mention of Kinnard's name. That made his response that afternoon even more surprising. It also made Kim wonder if the next time she saw Edward alone he would react with a belated temper tantrum.

By late in the day Kim was ready to give up the search. She stood up and stretched her achy muscles. To her chagrin she'd not found any other related material in the drawer, file cabinet, or even in the immediate vicinity where Kinnard had found Jonathan's letter. It made Kinnard's feat that much more impressive.

Leaving the castle behind, she started out across the field toward the cottage. The sun was low in the western sky. It was already fall and winter wouldn't be far behind. As she walked she vaguely thought about what to make for dinner.

Kim was almost to the cottage when she heard the distant sound of excited voices. Turning around, she saw that Edward and his research team had emerged from their isolation in the lab.

Kim was immediately intrigued: she stood and watched the group approach. Even from a distance she could tell that they were acting frolicsome and exuberant like a group of schoolchildren let out for recess. She could hear laughter and yelling. The men, except for Edward, were throwing a football back and forth.

The first thought that went through Kim's mind was that they had made some monumental discovery. The closer they got the more sure she became. She'd never seen them in such good spirits. But when they were within shouting distance, Edward proved her wrong.

"Look what you've done to my team!" he called out to

Kim. "I just told them about your offer to let them stay in the castle and they've gone berserk."

When the group got near to Kim they let out a cheer: "Hip hip, hurray!" they repeated three times and then collapsed in laughter.

Kim found herself smiling in return. Their exuberance was contagious. They were like collegians at a pep rally

"They really are touched by your hospitality," Edward explained. "They recognize that it is a real favor you are doing for them. Curt had even been sleeping on the floor of the lab a few nights."

"I like your outfit," Curt said to Kim.

Kim looked down at her leather vest and jeans. It certainly wasn't special. "Thank you," she said.

"We'd like to reassure you about the furnishings in the castle," François said. "We understand that they are family heirlooms, and we will treat them with the utmost respect."

Eleanor stepped forward and gave Kim an unexpected hug. "I'm touched by your selfless contribution to the cause," she said. She squeezed Kim's hand and looked her in the eye. "Thank you so much."

Kim nodded. She didn't know what to say. She was embarrassed she'd been against the idea.

"By the way," Curt said, angling himself in front of Eleanor. "I've been meaning to ask you if the noise from my motorcycle ever bothers you. If it does, I'll be happy to park it outside the compound."

"I've not been aware of any noise," Kim said.

"Kim!" Edward called out as he came around to her other side. "If it's convenient the group would like you to take them to the castle so that you can show them which rooms you want them to sleep in."

"I guess it's as good a time as any," Kim said.

"Perfect," Edward said.

Retracing her steps, Kim led the animated group in the direction of the castle. David and Gloria made it a point to catch up with her and walk alongside. They were full of questions about the castle such as when it had been built and whether Kim had ever lived in it.

When they entered the mansion there were a lot of ohs

and ahs, especially in the massive great room and the formal dining room, with its heraldic flags.

Kim showed them the guest wing first, suggesting the women stay there. Eleanor and Gloria were pleased and chose connecting bedrooms on the second floor.

"We can wake each other up if we oversleep," Eleanor said.

Kim showed everyone how each wing had a separate entrance and stair.

"This is perfect," François said. "We won't have to go into the main part of the house at all."

Moving across to the servants' wing, Kim explained about the plumbing problem but assured them that she would call a plumber in the morning. She then showed them a bathroom in the main part of the house they could use in the interim.

The men chose rooms without any disagreement although some of the rooms were obviously more desirable than others. Kim was impressed with their amicability.

"I can have the phone turned on as well," Kim said.

"Don't bother," David said. "We appreciate you offering, but it's not necessary. We'll only be here to sleep, and we're not sleeping that much. We can use the phone in the lab."

After the tour was over they all left the castle by the exit in the servants' wing and then walked around to the front. They discussed the issue of keys, and it was decided to leave the doors to the wings unlocked for the time being. Kim would have keys made as soon as she had an opportunity.

After a round of fervent handshakes and hugs and thank you's, the researchers headed off to their respective bed-and-breakfasts to gather their belongings. Kim and Edward walked to the cottage.

Edward was in a great mood and thanked Kim over and over for her generosity.

"You've really contributed to changing the whole atmosphere of the lab," Edward said. "As you could see for yourself, they are ecstatic. And, as important as mental state is, I'm certain their work will reflect their mood. So you've positively impacted the whole project.''

''I'm glad I could contribute,'' Kim said, making her feel even more guilty that she'd been against the idea from the start.

They arrived at the cottage. Kim was surprised when Edward accompanied her inside. She'd thought he'd head directly back to the lab.

''It was nice of that Monihan fellow to drop by,'' Edward said.

Kim's mouth dropped open. She had to make a conscious effort to close it.

''You know, I could use a beer,'' Edward said. ''How about you?''

Kim shook her head. For the moment she'd lost her voice. As she followed Edward into the kitchen, she struggled to summon the courage to talk to him about their relationship. He was in a better mood than he'd been in for ages.

Edward went to the refrigerator. Kim sat on a stool. Just when she was about to broach the subject, Edward popped the top from the beer and shocked her again.

''I want to apologize to you for having been such a bear for the last month or so,'' he said. He took a drink from his beer, burped, and excused himself. ''I've been giving it some thought over the last couple of days, and I know I've been difficult, inconsiderate, and unappreciative. I don't mean this as an excuse or to absolve myself of responsibility, but I have been under enormous pressure from Stanton, Harvard, the researchers, and even myself. Yet I never should have let such issues come between us. Once again, I want to ask you to forgive me.''

Kim was taken aback by Edward's admission. It was a totally unexpected development.

''I can tell you are upset,'' Edward said. ''And you don't have to say anything immediately if you don't want to. I can well imagine you could be harboring some ill will toward me.''

''But I do want to talk,'' Kim said. ''I've been wanting

to talk, particularly since Friday when I went into Boston to see a therapist I'd seen years ago.''

''I applaud your initiative,'' Edward said.

''It made me think a lot about how we've been relating to one another,'' Kim said. She looked down at her hands. ''It made me wonder if perhaps living together right at the moment is not the best thing for either of us.''

Edward put down his beer and took her hands. ''I understand how you must feel,'' he said. ''And your feelings are appropriate in light of my most recent behavior. But I can see my mistakes, and I think I can make it up to you.''

Kim started to say something, but Edward interrupted her.

''All I ask is to allow the status quo to remain for a few weeks with me staying here in my room and you in yours,'' he said. ''If you feel we shouldn't be staying together at the end of this trial period, I'll move up to the castle with the others.''

Kim contemplated what Edward had said. He had impressed her with his remorse and his insight. His offer seemed reasonable.

''All right,'' she said finally.

''Wonderful!'' Edward said. He reached out and gave her a long hug.

Kim held herself back a little. It was hard for her to change emotional directions so quickly.

''Let's celebrate,'' Edward said. ''Let's go out to dinner—just you and me.''

''I know you can't take the time,'' Kim said. ''But I appreciate the offer.''

''Nonsense!'' Edward said. ''I'm taking the time! Let's go back to that dive we went to on one of our first trips up here. Remember the scrod?''

Kim nodded. Edward drained his beer.

As they drove from the compound and Kim glanced at the castle, she thought about the researchers and commented about how exuberant they had seemed.

''They couldn't be any happier,'' Edward said. ''Things are going well at the lab, and now they won't have to commute.''

"Did you start taking Ultra?" Kim asked.

"We sure did," Edward said. "We all started Tuesday."

Kim contemplated telling Edward about Kinnard's thoughts on the subject but hesitated because she knew that Edward would be upset that she'd spoken to anybody about their project.

"We've already learned something interesting," Edward said. "The tissue level of Ultra can't be critical because all of us are experiencing equally positive results even though we're on widely different dosages."

"Could the euphoria you and the others are enjoying have anything to do with the drug?" Kim asked.

"I'm sure it does," Edward said. "Indirectly if not directly. Within twenty-four hours of our first dose all of us felt relaxed, focused, confident, and even—" Edward struggled for a word. Finally he said: "Content. All of which is a far cry from the anxiety, fatigue, and contentiousness we'd been experiencing before Ultra."

"What about side effects?"

"The only side effect that we've all had was some initial dryness of the mouth," Edward said. "Two of the others reported some mild constipation. I was the only one who had some difficulty with near vision, but it only lasted for twenty-four hours and I'd been experiencing the problem prior to taking Ultra, particularly when I got tired."

"Maybe you should stop taking the drug now that you've learned as much as you have," Kim suggested.

"I don't think so," Edward said. "Not when we are getting such positive results. In fact, I brought some for you in case you want to try it."

Edward reached into his jacket pocket and pulled out a vial of capsules. He extended it toward Kim. She shrank back.

"No, thank you," she said.

"For God's sake, at least take the container."

Reluctantly Kim allowed Edward to drop the vial into her hands.

"Just think about it," Edward said. "Remember that discussion we had a long time ago about not feeling socially connected? Well, you won't feel that way with Ultra. I've been on it less than a week, and it's allowed the real me to emerge; the person that I've wanted to be. I think you should try it. What do you have to lose?''

"The idea of taking a drug for a personality trait bothers me,'' Kim said. ''Personality is supposed to come from experience not chemistry.''

"This is sounding like a conversation we've already had,'' Edward said with a laugh. ''I guess as a chemist I'm bound to feel differently. Suit yourself, but I guarantee you'd feel more assertive if you try it. And that's not all. We also think it enhances long-term memory and alleviates fatigue and anxiety. I had a good demonstration of this latter effect just this morning. I got a call from Harvard announcing they've instituted suit against me. It infuriated me, but the outrage only lasted a few minutes. Ultra smoothed my anger out, so instead of pounding the walls I was able to think about the situation rationally and make appropriate decisions.''

"I'm glad you are finding it so helpful,'' Kim said. ''But I still don't want to take it.'' She tried to give the container back to Edward. He pushed her hand away.

"Keep it,'' he said. ''All I ask is that you give it some serious thought. Just take one capsule a day and you'll be amazed at who you are.''

Understanding that Edward was adamant, Kim dropped the vial into her bag.

Later at the restaurant, while Kim was in the ladies' room standing in front of the mirror, she caught sight of the vial in her bag. Removing it, she undid the cap. With her thumb and index finger she lifted out one of the blue capsules and examined it. It seemed incredible it could do all the things Edward claimed.

Glancing in the mirror, she admitted to herself how much she'd like to be more assertive and less fearful. She also admitted how tempting it would be to deal so easily with her low-level but nagging anxiety. She looked back down at the capsule. Then she shook her head. For a moment she'd wavered, but as she put the capsule back into the container, she reaffirmed that drugs were not her answer.

As Kim returned to the restaurant proper she reminded

herself that she'd always been suspicious of quick and easy solutions. Over the years she'd developed the opinion that the best way to deal with her problems was the old-fashioned way with introspection, a little pain, and effort.

Later that night, while Kim was comfortably reading in bed, she heard the front door slam shut. It made her jump. Glancing at the clock, she saw it was before eleven.

"Edward?" she called out nervously.

"It's just me," Edward called back as he came up the stairs two at a time. He poked his head into Kim's bedroom. "I hope I didn't scare you," he said.

"It's so early," Kim said. "Are you okay?"

"Couldn't be better," Edward said. "I even feel energetic, which is amazing since I've been up since five this morning."

He went into the half-bath and began brushing his teeth. While he did so he managed to maintain a lively chatter about humorous incidents that occurred in the lab that evening. It seemed that the researchers were playing harmless practical jokes on each other.

As Edward spoke, Kim reflected on how different her own mood was from everyone else's at the compound. Despite Edward's apparent turnaround, she still was uptight, vaguely anxious, and even still a bit depressed.

After Edward was finished in the bathroom he returned to Kim's room and sat on the edge of her bed. Buffer followed him in and, to Sheba's chagrin, tried to jump up as well.

"No, you don't, you rascal," Edward said as he scooped the dog up and held him in his lap.

"Are you going to bed already?" Kim asked.

"I am indeed," Edward said. "I've got to be up at three-thirty instead of the usual five to deal with an experiment I'm running. Out here in Salem I don't have any postdocs to do my dirty work."

"That's not much sleep," Kim said.

"It's been adequate," Edward said. Then he changed the subject abruptly. "How much money did you inherit along with the compound?"

Kim blinked. Edward seemed to be surprising her every time he opened his mouth. The inappropriateness of this new question was completely out of character for him.

"You don't have to tell me if you feel uncomfortable," Edward said when he saw Kim's hesitancy. "The reason I'm asking is because I'd be willing to let you have some equity in Omni. I haven't wanted to sell any more of the stock, but you're different. You'll get a monumental return on your investment if you are interested."

"My portfolio is fully invested," Kim managed to say.

Edward put Buffer down and held up his hands. "Don't misinterpret me," he said. "I'm not playing salesman. I'm just trying to do you a favor for what you've done for Omni by allowing the lab to be built here."

"I appreciate the offer," Kim said.

"Even if you choose not to invest I'm still going to give you some stock as a gift," Edward said. He gave her leg a pat through the covers and stood up. "Now I've got to get to bed. I'm looking forward to four solid hours of sleep. I tell you, ever since I started taking Ultra I've been sleeping so soundly that four hours is plenty. I never knew sleep could be so enjoyable."

With a spring in his step, Edward went back into the bathroom and began brushing his teeth again.

"Aren't you overdoing that?" Kim called out.

Edward stuck his head back into Kim's bedroom. "What are you talking about?" he said while keeping his lower lip over his lower teeth.

"You already brushed your teeth," Kim said.

Edward looked at his toothbrush as if it were to blame. Then he shook his head and laughed. "I'm becoming the absentminded professor," he said. He went back into the bathroom to rinse his mouth.

Kim looked down at Buffer, who'd stayed behind, positioning himself in front of her night table. He was vigorously begging for some biscotti she'd brought up earlier from the kitchen.

"This dog of yours is acting awfully hungry," Kim yelled to Edward, who was now in his bedroom. "Did he get fed tonight?"

Edward appeared at the door. "I honestly can't remember," he said. Then he disappeared again.

With resignation Kim got up, slipped on her robe, and descended to the kitchen. Buffer followed close at her heels as if he understood what had been said. Kim got out the dog food and scooped a portion onto a plate. Buffer was beside himself with excitement and was both growling and barking. It was obvious that he'd not been fed, maybe even for more than one day.

To avoid being bitten, Kim closed the dog in the bathroom while she put his food on the floor. When she reopened the door, Buffer went past her like a white blur and began wolfing the food down so quickly he sounded as if he were gagging.

When Kim climbed back up the stairs, she saw that Edward's light was still on. Wanting to tell him about Buffer, she stuck her head into his room only to find he was already fast asleep. He'd seemingly lain down and fallen asleep before he'd even had a chance to turn out the light.

Kim walked over to his bedside and marveled at his stertorous breathing. Knowing the schedule he'd been keeping, she wasn't surprised at the depth of his sleep. He had to be exhausted. Kim turned out his light then went back to her own room.

# 14

WHEN KIM FINALLY OPENED HER EYES SHE WAS SUR-
prised to see it was nearly nine o'clock. That was later than
she'd been getting up during the last month. Climbing out
of bed, she glanced into Edward's room, but he had been
long gone. His empty room appeared neat and orderly. Edward had the commendable habit of making his bed in the
morning.

On her way to the bathroom to shower, Kim placed a
call to the plumber, Albert Bruer, who'd worked on both
the cottage and the lab. She left her number on his answering machine.

Albert called back within a half hour, and by the time
Kim had finished breakfast he was at her door. Together
they drove up to the castle in his truck.

"I think I already know the problem," Albert said. "In
fact I knew about it when your grandfather was alive. It's
the soil pipes. They're cast-iron and some of them have
rusted."

Albert took Kim into each of the bathrooms in the servants' wing and took off the fronts of the access panels. In
each he pointed out the rusted pipes.

"Can it be fixed?" Kim asked.

"Of course it can," Albert said. "But it will take some
doing. It might take me and my boy a week."

"Do it," Kim said. "I've got some people staying in
here."

"If that's the case I can get water to the bathroom on
the third floor. Those pipes look pretty good. Maybe no
one lived up there."

After the plumber left, Kim walked over to the lab to let the men know about the third-floor bathroom. She'd not been to the lab for some time and was not looking forward to the visit. They'd never made her feel welcome.

"Kim!" David called out excitedly. He was the first to see her come through the door that led from the vacant reception area into the lab proper. "What a nice surprise," David yelled out to the others that she was there. Everyone, including Edward, dropped what they were doing and came over to greet her.

Kim felt herself blush. She did not relish being the center of attention.

"We have fresh coffee and donuts," Eleanor said. "Can I get you some?"

Kim declined but thanked her, explaining she'd just had breakfast. She apologized to the group for bothering them and quickly told the men about the resolution of the plumbing problem.

The men were pleased and assured her that using the bathroom on the third floor was not an imposition. They even tried to talk her out of bothering to make any repairs.

"I don't think it should be left the way it is," Kim said. "I'd prefer it be fixed."

Kim then started to leave, but they wouldn't allow it. They insisted on showing her what each one of them was doing.

David was first. He took Kim to his lab bench and had her peer through a dissecting microscope while he explained that she was looking at an abdominal ganglion preparation that he'd taken from a mollusk called *Aplasia fasciata*. Then he showed her printouts of how Ultra modulated the spontaneous firing of certain neurons of the ganglion. Before Kim could even figure out what she was looking at, David took the printouts from her hands and led her into the tissue-culture incubator. There he explained how he evaluated the tissue cultures for signs of toxicity.

Then it was Gloria's and Curt's turn. They took Kim downstairs to the animal area. They showed her some pitiful creatures: stressed rats and stressed monkeys that had been raised to have severe anxiety. Then they showed her similar animals that had been treated with Ultra and imipramine.

Kim tried to appear interested, but animal experiments disturbed her.

François took over from Gloria and Curt and led Kim into the shielded room where the NMR machine was isolated. He tried to explain exactly how he was attempting to determine the structure of the binding protein for Ultra. Unfortunately, Kim understood little of his explanation. She merely nodded her head and smiled whenever he paused.

Eleanor then took over and led Kim back upstairs to her computer terminal. She gave Kim a lengthy explanation of molecular modeling and how she was attempting to create drugs that were permutations of Ultra's basic structure and that would potentially share some of Ultra's bioactivity.

As Kim was whisked around the lab, she began to notice that not only were the researchers friendly, they were also patient and respectful of each other. Although they were assertively eager to please her, they were content to wait their turn.

"This has been most interesting," Kim said when Eleanor finally finished her lecture. Kim started to back toward the door. "Thank you all for taking so much of your valuable time to show me around."

"Wait!" François said. He dashed to his desk, picked up a sheaf of photographs, and ran back. Breathlessly he showed them to Kim and asked her what she thought of them. They were brightly colored PET scans.

"I think they are—" Kim searched for a word that wouldn't make her sound foolish. She finally said: "Dramatic."

"They are, aren't they?" François said, cocking his head to the side to regard them from a slightly different angle. "They're like modern art."

"What exactly do they tell you?" Kim asked. She would have preferred to leave, but with everyone watching, she felt obligated to ask a question.

"The colors refer to concentrations of radioactive Ultra," François said. "The red is the highest concentration. These scans show quite clearly that the drug localizes maximally to the upper brain stem, the midbrain, and the limbic system.''

"I remember Stanton's referring to the limbic system at the dinner party,'' Kim said.

"He did indeed,'' François said. "As he suggested, it's part of the more primitive, or reptilian, parts of the brain and is involved with autonomic function, including mood, emotion, and even smell.''

"And sex,'' David said.

"What do you mean, 'reptilian'?'' Kim asked. The word had an ugly connotation to her. She'd never liked snakes.

"It's used to refer to the parts of the brain that are similar to the brains of reptiles,'' François said. "Of course it is an oversimplification, but it does have some merit. Although the human brain evolved from some common distant ancestor with current-day reptiles, it's not like taking a reptile brain and sticking a couple of cerebral hemispheres on top.''

Everybody laughed. Kim found herself laughing as well. The general mood was hard to resist.

"As far as basic instincts are concerned,'' Edward said, "we humans have them just like reptiles. The difference is ours are covered by varying degrees of socialization and civilization. Translated, that means that the cerebral hemispheres have hard-wired connections that control reptilian behavior.''

Kim looked at her watch. "I really have to be going,'' she said. "I've got a train to catch into Boston.''

With such an excuse Kim was finally able to break free from the obliging clutches of the researchers although they all encouraged her to come back. Edward walked her outside.

"Are you really on your way to Boston?'' Edward asked.

"I am,'' Kim said. "Last night I decided to go back to Harvard for one more try. I'd found another letter that included a reference to Elizabeth's evidence. It gave me another lead.''

"Good luck,'' Edward said. "Enjoy yourself.'' He gave her a kiss and then went back into the lab. He didn't ask about Kim's latest letter.

Kim walked back to the cottage, feeling strangely numb from the researchers' intense congeniality. Maybe something was wrong with her. She hadn't liked how aloof they'd been, but now she found she didn't like them sociable either. Was she impossible to please?

The more Kim thought about her response, the more she realized that it had a lot to do with their sudden uniformity. When she'd first met them she'd been struck by their eccentricities and quirks. Now their personalities had become blended into an amiable but bland whole that shrouded their individuality.

As Kim changed clothes for her trip into Boston, she couldn't stop mulling over what was happening at the compound. She felt her misgiving—the very anxiety that had driven her to see Alice—on the increase again.

Ducking into the parlor to retrieve a sweater, Kim paused beneath Elizabeth's portrait and looked up into her ancestor's feminine yet forceful face. There was not a hint of anxiety in Elizabeth's visage. Kim wondered if Elizabeth had ever felt as out of control as she did.

Kim got into her car and headed for the train station, unable to get Elizabeth out of her mind. It suddenly occurred to her that there were striking similarities between her world and Elizabeth's despite the enormous gap in time. Elizabeth had to live with the continual threat of Indian attack, while Kim was conscious of the ever-present peril of crime. Back then there had been the mysterious and frightful menace of smallpox while today it was AIDS. In Elizabeth's time there was a breakdown of the Puritan hold on society, with the emergence of unbridled materialism; today it was the passing of the stability of the Cold War with the emergence of fractious nationalism and religious fundamentalism. Back then there was a confusing and changing role for women; today it was the same.

"The more things change, the more they stay the same," Kim said, voicing the old adage.

Kim wondered if all these similarities could have anything to do with the message she'd come to believe Elizabeth was trying to send her over the centuries. With a shudder, Kim wondered if a fate similar to Elizabeth's was

in store for her. Could that be what Elizabeth was trying
to tell her? Could it be a warning?

Increasingly upset, Kim made a conscious effort to stop
ruminating obsessively. She was successful until she got on
the train. Then the thoughts came tumbling back.

''For goodness' sake!'' Kim said aloud, causing the
woman sitting next to her to eye her with suspicion.

Kim turned to face out the window. She chided herself
for allowing her active imagination too much free rein. After all, the differences between her life and Elizabeth's were
far greater than any similarities, particularly in the area of
control. Elizabeth had had very little control over her destiny. She had been essentially coerced at a young age into
what was actually an arranged marriage, and she did not
have access to birth control. In contrast, Kim was free to
choose whom she would marry, and was free to control her
body insofar as reproduction was concerned.

This line of thinking kept Kim comfortable until the train
neared North Station in Boston. Then she began to wonder
if she was as free as she'd like to believe. She reviewed
some of the major decisions in her life, such as becoming
a nurse instead of pursuing a career in art or design. Then
she reminded herself that she was living with a man in a
relationship that was becoming disturbingly similar to the
one she'd had with her father. On top of that, she reminded
herself that she was saddled with a research lab on her
property and five researchers living in the family house—
none of which had been her idea.

The train lurched to a stop. Mindless of her immediate
environment, Kim walked to the subway. She knew what
the problem was. She could almost hear Alice's voice in
the background, telling her it was her personality. She
didn't have appropriate self-esteem; she was too pliant; she
thought of other people's needs and ignored her own. And
all these conspired to constrain her freedom.

Such an irony, Kim thought. Elizabeth's personality,
with her assertiveness and decisiveness, would have been
perfect for today's world whereas in her own time it undoubtedly contributed to her untimely death. Kim's personality, on the other hand, which was more dutiful and

submissive rather than assertive and decisive, would have been fine in the seventeenth century but was not working out so well today.

With renewed resolve to unravel Elizabeth's story, Kim boarded the subway and traveled to Harvard Square. Within fifteen minutes of her arrival she was back in Mary Cust-land's office in the Widener Library, waiting for Mary to finish reading Jonathan's letter.

"This house of yours must be a treasure of memorabilia," Mary said, looking up from the page. "This letter is priceless." She immediately called Katherine Sturburg to her office and had her read it.

"What a delight," Katherine said when she was finished.

Both women told Kim that the letter was from a period of Harvard history of which there was scant material. They asked if they could copy it, and Kim gave them permission.

"So we have to find a reference to 'Rachel Bingham,' " Mary said, sitting down at her terminal.

"That's what I'm hoping," Kim said.

Mary entered the name while Kim and Katherine looked over her shoulder. Kim found herself with crossed fingers without having been conscious of doing it.

Two Rachel Binghams flashed onto the screen, but both were from the nineteenth century and could have had no association with Elizabeth. Mary tried a few other tricks, but there was nothing.

"I'm awfully sorry," Mary said. "Of course you realize that even if we did find a reference, the problem of the 1764 fire would still be a rather insurmountable difficulty."

"I understand," Kim said. "I really didn't expect to find anything, but, as I said on my first visit, I feel obligated to follow up on any new leads."

"I'll be sure to go through my sources with the new name," Katherine said.

Kim thanked both women and left. She took the subway back to North Station and had to wait for a train to Salem. As she stood on the platform she vowed to redouble her efforts at sorting the impossible jumble of papers in the castle over the next couple of days. Once she started back to work she'd have little opportunity to work on it except on her days off.

Arriving back at the compound, Kim intended to drive directly to the castle, but as she cleared the trees, she saw a Salem police car parked in front of the cottage. Curious as to what that could mean, she headed in its direction.

As she approached, Kim spotted Edward and Eleanor standing and conversing with two policemen in the middle of the grassy field about fifty yards from the house. Eleanor had her arm around Edward's shoulder.

Kim parked next to the patrol car and got out. The group in the field either hadn't heard her arrive or were too preoccupied to notice her.

Curious, Kim started walking toward them. As she approached she could see that there was something in the grass that had their collective attention.

Kim gasped when she saw what had their attention. It was Buffer. The poor dog was dead. What made the scene particularly gruesome was that some of the dog's flesh from its hindquarters was gone, exposing bloodied bones.

Kim cast a sorrowful look at Edward, who greeted her with composure, suggesting to her that he'd recovered from the initial shock. She could see dried tears on his cheeks. As nasty as the dog was, she knew he cared for him.

"It might be worth it to have the bones looked at by a medical examiner," Edward was saying. "There's a chance someone could recognize the teethmarks and tell us what species of animal could have done this."

"I don't know how the medical examiner's office would respond to a call about a dead dog," one of the officers said. His name was Billy Selvey.

"But you said you've had a couple of similar episodes during the last few nights," Edward said. "I think it behooves you to find out what kind of animal is involved. Personally, I think it was either another dog or a raccoon."

Kim was impressed with Edward's rationality in the face of his loss. He'd recovered enough to have a technical discussion about potential teethmarks on the exposed bone.

"When was the last time you saw the dog?" Billy asked.

"Last night," Edward said. "He usually slept with me,

but maybe I let him out. I can't remember. Occasionally the dog stayed out all night. I'd never thought it was a problem since the compound is so big, and the dog wouldn't bother anyone anyway.''

"I fed the dog around eleven-thirty last night," Kim said. "I left him in the kitchen eating.''

"Did you let him out?'' Edward asked.

"No, as I said, I left him in the kitchen,'' Kim said.

"Well, I didn't see him when I got up this morning,'' Edward said. "I didn't think anything about it. I just assumed he'd show up at the lab.''

"Do you people have one of those pet doors?'' Billy asked.

Both Kim and Edward said no at the same time.

"Anybody hear anything unusual last night?'' Billy asked.

"I was dead to the world,'' Edward said. "I sleep very soundly, especially lately.''

"I didn't hear anything either,'' Kim said.

"There's been some talk down at the station about these incidents being due to a rabid animal,'' the other officer said. His name was Harry Conners. "Do you people have any other pets?''

"I have a cat,'' Kim said.

"We advise you to keep it on a short leash for the next few days,'' Billy said.

The police put away their notepads and pens, said goodbye, and started toward their cruiser.

"What about the carcass?'' Edward called out. "Don't you want to take it to the medical examiner?''

The two officers looked at each other, hoping the other one would respond. Finally Billy yelled back that they thought it best not to take it.

Edward waved them away good-naturedly. "I gave them a great tip and what do they do?'' he said. "They walk away.''

"Well, I've got to get back to work,'' Eleanor said, speaking up for the first time. She looked at Kim. "Don't forget, you promised to come back to the lab real soon.''

"I'll be there," Kim promised. She was amazed Eleanor cared, yet she seemed sincere.

Eleanor started off toward the lab.

Edward stood looking down at Buffer. Kim averted her eyes. The sight was grisly and made her stomach turn.

"I'm very sorry about Buffer," Kim said, putting her hand on Edward's shoulder.

"He had a good life," Edward said cheerfully. "I think I'll disarticulate the back legs and send them to one of the pathologists I know at the medical school. Maybe he could tell us what kind of animal we should be looking for."

Kim swallowed hard hearing Edward's suggestion. Further mutilating the poor dog was hardly what she'd expected from him.

"I've got an old rag in the back of my car," Edward said. "I'll get it to wrap the carcass in."

Not sure what she should do, Kim stayed by Buffer's remains while Edward went for the old towel. She was rattled by Buffer's cruel fate even if Edward seemingly wasn't. Once Buffer was wrapped in the towel, she accompanied Edward back to the lab.

As they neared the lab a disturbing possibility occurred to Kim. She stopped Edward. "I just thought of something," she said. "What if Buffer's death and mutilation had something to do with sorcery?"

Edward looked at her for a beat, then threw his head back with howls of laughter. It took him several minutes to get himself under control. Meanwhile Kim found herself laughing with him as well, embarrassed at having suggested such a thing. "Wait just one minute," Kim protested. "I can remember reading someplace about black magic and animal sacrifice going hand in hand."

"I find your melodramatic imagination wonderfully entertaining," Edward managed amid renewed laughter. When he finally got himself under control, he apologized for laughing at her. At the same time he thanked her for a moment of comic relief.

"Tell me," he said, "do you really think that after three hundred years the devil has decided to return to Salem and that witchcraft is being directed at me and Omni?"

"I just made the association between animal sacrifice and sorcery," Kim said. "I really didn't think too much about it. Nor did I mean to imply that I believed in it, just that somebody did."

Edward put Buffer down and gave Kim a hug. "I think maybe you've been spending too much time hidden in the castle going through the old papers. Once things are really under control with Omni, we should go on a vacation. Someplace hot where we can lie in the sun. What do you say?"

"It sounds fun," Kim said although she wondered what kind of time frame was in Edward's mind.

Kim did not care to watch Edward dissect Buffer, so she stayed outside the lab when he went in to do it. He came back out in a few minutes, carrying a shovel, with the carcass still wrapped in the towel. He dug a shallow grave near the entrance of the lab. When he was finished burying Buffer, he told Kim to wait a moment since he had forgotten something. He disappeared back inside the lab.

Reemerging, Edward showed Kim a chemical reagent bottle he had retrieved. With a flamboyant gesture he placed the bottle at the head of Buffer's grave.

"What's that?" Kim asked.

"It's a chemical buffer called TRIS," Edward said. "A buffer for Buffer." Then he laughed almost as heartily as he had with Kim's suggestion of sorcery.

"I'm impressed how you are handling this unfortunate incident," Kim told him.

"I'm certain it has something to do with Ultra," Edward said, still chuckling over the pun. "When I first heard what had happened I was crushed. Buffer was like family to me. But the awful sorrow I felt passed quickly. I mean, I'm still sorry he's gone, but I don't feel that awful emptiness that accompanies grief. I can rationally recognize that death is a natural complement of living. After all, Buffer did have a good life for a dog, and he didn't have the world's best disposition."

"He was a loyal pet," Kim said. She wasn't about to tell him her true feelings about the dog.

"This is another example of why you should give Ultra

a chance,'' Edward said. ''I guarantee it will calm you down. Who knows, maybe it would clear your mind enough to help you with your quest to learn the truth about Elizabeth.''

''I think only hard work can possibly do that,'' Kim said.

Edward gave her a quick kiss, thanked her effusively for her moral support, and disappeared back into the lab. Kim turned around and started for the castle. She'd only gone a short distance when she started to worry about Sheba. Suddenly she remembered letting the cat out the night before, after she'd fed Buffer, and she hadn't seen her that morning.

Reversing her direction, Kim headed for the cottage. As she walked she gradually increased her pace. Buffer's death had added to her general anxiety. She couldn't imagine how devastated she'd be if Sheba had succumbed to a similar fate as Buffer.

Entering the house, Kim called for Sheba. She quickly climbed the stairs and went into her bedroom. To her relief she saw the cat curled up in a ball of fur in the middle of the bed. Kim rushed over and snuggled with the animal. Sheba gave her one of her disdainful looks for being disturbed.

After petting the cat for several minutes, Kim went to her bureau. With tremulous fingers she picked up the container of Ultra she'd put there the night before. Once again she removed one of the blue capsules and examined it. She yearned for relief. She debated with herself the idea of trying the drug for twenty-four hours, just to see what it could do for her. Edward's ability to deal so well with Buffer's death was an impressive testimonial. Kim went so far as to get a glass of water.

But she did not take the capsule. Instead she began to wonder if Edward's response was too modulated. From her reading as well as her intuition Kim knew that a certain amount of grieving was a necessary human emotion. That made her consider whether blocking the normal process of grieving might exact a price in the future.

With that thought in mind, Kim replaced the capsule in the vial and hazarded another visit to the lab. Fearing being entrapped by more interminable demonstrations by Edward's team, Kim literally sneaked into the building.

Luckily, only Edward and David were on the upper floor and they were at opposite ends of the huge room. Kim was able to surprise Edward without the others knowing she was there. When Edward saw her and started to respond, Kim shushed him with her finger to her lips. Taking his hand, she led him from the building.

Once the door to the lab had closed behind them, Edward grinned and asked, ''What on earth has gotten into you?''

''I just want to talk to you,'' Kim explained. ''I had a thought that maybe you could include in the clinical protocol of Ultra.''

Kim explained to Edward what she'd thought about grief and expanded the notion to include anxiety and melancholy, saying that moderate amounts of these emotionally painful feelings play a positive role as motivators of human growth, change, and creativity. She concluded by saying, ''What I'm worried about is that taking a drug like Ultra that modulates these mental states may have a hidden cost and could cause a serious negative side effect that would not be anticipated.''

Edward smiled and slowly nodded his head. He was impressed. ''I appreciate your concern,'' he said. ''It's an interesting thought you have, but I don't share it. You see, it's based on a false premise, namely that the mind is somehow mystically apart from the material body. That old hypothesis has been debunked by recent experience that shows that the mind and the body are one even in regards to mood and emotion. Emotion has been proved to be biologically determined by the fact that it is affected by drugs like Prozac, which alter levels of neurotransmitters. It has revolutionized ideas about brain function.''

''That kind of thinking is dehumanizing,'' Kim complained.

''Let me put it another way,'' Edward said. ''What about pain? Do you think drugs should be taken for pain?''

''Pain is different,'' Kim said, but she could see the philosophical trap Edward was laying for her.

''I don't think so,'' Edward said. ''Pain, too, is biological. Since physical pain and psychic pain are both biological, they should both be treated the same, namely with well-designed drugs that target only those parts of the brain responsible.''

Kim felt frustrated. She wanted to ask Edward where the world would be if Mozart and Beethoven had been on drugs for anxiety or depression. But she did not say anything. She knew it was no use. The scientist in Edward blinded him.

Edward gave Kim an exuberant hug and reiterated how much he appreciated her interest in his work. He then patted the top of her head.

''We'll talk more about this issue if you'd like,'' he said. ''But now I better get back to work.''

Kim apologized for bothering him and started back for the cottage.

# 15

## Thursday,
## September 29, 1994

OVER THE NEXT SEVERAL DAYS KIM WAS AGAIN
tempted on several occasions to give Ultra a try. Her gradually mounting anxiety had begun to affect her sleep. But
each time she was on the brink of taking the drug, she
pulled back.

Instead Kim tried to use her anxiety as a motivator. Each
day she spent more than ten hours working in the castle
and quit only when it became difficult for her to see well
enough to read the handwritten pages. Unfortunately, her
increased efforts were to no avail. She began to wish that
she would find some seventeenth-century material, even if
it had no association with Elizabeth, just to encourage her.

The presence of the plumbers turned out to be a pleasant
diversion rather than an imposition. Whenever Kim took a
break she at least had someone to talk with. She even
watched them work for a time, intrigued with the use of
the blowtorch for soldering copper tubing.

The only indication that Kim noticed that the researchers
were sleeping in the castle was dirt tracked in from both
entrances to the wings. Although some soiling was to be
expected, she thought the amount involved suggested surprising inconsiderateness.

Edward's assertive, happy, and caring mood continued.
With a gesture reminiscent of their initial dating days, Edward even had a large bouquet sent to the house on Tuesday
with a note that said, *In Loving Gratitude.*

The only alteration in his behavior occurred on Thursday
morning when Kim was just about to leave the cottage for

the castle. Edward came through the front door in a huff. Obviously irritated, he slammed his address book down on the table next to the telephone, putting Kim immediately on edge. "Is something wrong?" she asked.

"Damn right something is wrong," he said. "I have to come all the way up here to use the phone. When I use one at the lab every one of those twits listens to my conversation. It drives me nuts."

"Why didn't you use the phone in the empty reception area?" Kim asked.

"They listen when I go there too," he said.

"Through the walls?" she questioned.

"I've got to call the goddamn head of the Harvard Licensing Office," Edward complained, ignoring Kim's comment. "That jerk has launched a personal vendetta against me." Edward opened his address book to find the number.

"Could it be that he's just doing his job?" Kim asked, knowing this was an ongoing controversy.

"You think he's doing his job by getting me suspended?" Edward yelled. "It's incredible! I never would have guessed the little dick-headed bureaucrat had the nerve to pull off such a stunt."

Kim felt her heart pounding. Edward's tone reminded her of the glass-throwing episode in his apartment. She was afraid to say anything else.

"Ah, well," Edward said in a completely calm tone of voice. He smiled. "Such is life. There's always these little ups and downs." He sat down and dialed his number.

Kim allowed herself to relax a degree, but she didn't take her eyes off Edward. She listened while he had a civilized conversation with the man he'd just railed against. When he got off the phone he said that the man was quite reasonable after all.

"As long as I'm here," Edward said, "I'll dash upstairs and get the dry cleaning together that you asked me to take care of yesterday."

Edward started for the stairs.

"But you already got the dry cleaning together," Kim said. "You must have done it this morning, because I found it when I got up."

Edward stopped and blinked as if he were confused. "I did?" he asked. Then he added: "Well, good for me! I should be getting right back to the lab anyway."

"Edward?" Kim called to him before he went out the front door. "Are you all right? You've been forgetting little things lately."

Edward laughed. "It's true," he said. "I've been a bit forgetful. But I've never felt better. I'm just preoccupied. But there's light at the end of the tunnel, and we're all about to be extremely rich. And that includes you. I spoke to Stanton about giving you some stock, and he agreed. So you'll be part of the big payoff."

"I'm flattered," Kim said.

Kim went to the window and watched Edward walk back to the lab. She watched him the whole way, pondering his behavior. He was now more congenial toward her on the whole, but he was also unpredictable.

Impulsively Kim got her car keys and headed into town. She needed to talk to someone professional whose opinion she valued. Conveniently, Kinnard was still in the area. Using the phone at the information desk in the Salem Hospital, she had him paged.

A half hour later he met her in the coffee shop. He was dressed in surgical scrub clothes, having come directly from surgery. She had been nursing a cup of tea.

"I hope I'm not bothering you terribly," Kim said the moment he sat down across from her.

"It's good to see you," Kinnard said.

"I needed to ask a question," she said. "Could forgetfulness be a side effect of a psychotropic drug?"

"Absolutely," he said. "But I have to qualify that by saying that a lot of things can affect short-term memory. It's a very nonspecific symptom. Should I assume that Edward is having such a problem?"

"Can I count on your discretion?" she asked.

"I've already told you as much," Kinnard said. "Are Edward and his team still taking the drug?"

Kim nodded.

"They're crazy," Kinnard said. "They're just asking for trouble. Have you noticed any other effects?"

Kim gave a short laugh. "You wouldn't believe it," she said. "They're all having a dramatic response. Before they started the drug they were bickering with each other and sullen. Now they are all in great moods. They couldn't be any happier or more content. They act as if they're having a ball even though they continue to work at the same feverish pace."

"That sounds like a good effect," Kinnard said.

"In some respects," Kim admitted. "But after you've been with them for a while you sense something weird, like they are all too similar and tedious despite their hilarity and their industriousness."

"Now it sounds a little like *Brave New World*," Kinnard said with a chuckle.

"Don't laugh," Kim said. "I thought of the same thing. But that's more of a philosophical issue, and it's not my immediate concern. What has me worried is the forgetfulness Edward has been exhibiting with silly everyday things. And it seems to be getting worse. I don't know if the other people are experiencing it or not."

"What are you going to do?" Kinnard asked.

"I don't know," Kim said. "I was hoping you could either definitively confirm my fears or dispel them. I guess you can't do either."

"Not with any degree of certainty," Kinnard admitted. "But I can say something you can think about. Perceptions are extraordinarily influenced by expectations. That's why double-blind studies have been instituted in medical research. There is a possibility that your expectation to see negative effects from Edward's drug is affecting what you see. I know Edward is extraordinarily smart, and it doesn't make much sense to me that he would take any unreasonable risk."

"You have a point," Kim said. "It's true that at the moment I don't know what I'm seeing. It could all be in my head, but I don't think so."

Kinnard glanced at the wall clock and had to excuse himself to do a case. "I'm sorry to cut this short," he said, "but I'm here for the next few days if you want to talk more. Otherwise I'll see you in the SICU in Boston."

The moment they parted, Kinnard gave her hand a squeeze. She squeezed back and thanked him for listening to her.

Arriving back at the compound, Kim went directly to the castle. She had a few words with the plumbers, who insisted they were making good progress but that they'd need another three days or so to finish. They also suggested they should check the guest wing for the same problem. Kim told them to do whatever was needed.

Before going down to the wine cellar, Kim inspected the two entrances to the wings. She was appalled when she saw the one to the servants' quarters. Not only was there dirt on the stairs, but there were also some sticks and leaves. Even an empty container for Chinese take-out food was in the corner near the door.

Swearing under her breath, Kim went to the cleaning closet, got out a mop and a bucket, and cleaned the stairway. The dirt had been tracked up to the first landing.

After she'd cleaned everything up, Kim walked to the front door, picked up the outdoor mat, and carried it around to the entrance to the servants' wing. She thought about putting up a note, but then thought the mat should be message enough.

Finally Kim descended into the depths of the wine cellar and got to work. Although she did not find any documents even close to the seventeenth century, her concentration served to free her mind from her concerns, and she slowly began to relax.

At one o'clock Kim took a break. She went back to the cottage and let Sheba out while she had some lunch. Before she returned to the castle she made sure the cat was back in the house. At the castle she chatted with the plumbers for a few minutes and watched Albert deftly make some seals on water-supply pipes with his blowtorch. Finally she got back to work, this time in the attic.

Kim was again becoming discouraged when she found a whole folder of material from the era she was interested in. With excitement she carried it over to one of the dormered windows.

She was not surprised when the papers turned out to be business-related. A few of them were in Ronald's easily recognizable script. Then Kim caught her breath. Out of the customs documents and bills of lading she pulled a piece of personal correspondence. It was a letter to Ronald from Thomas Goodman.

17th August 1692
Salem Town

Sir:
Many are the villainies that have plagued our God fearing town. It has been a matter of great affliction for me whereby I have been unwillingly involved. I am sore of heart that you have thought ill of me and my duty as a convenanted member of our congregation and hath refused to converse with me in matters of joint interest. It is true that I in good faith and in God's name did testify against your departed wife at her hearing and at her trial. At your request I did visit your home on occasion to offer aid if it be needed. On that fateful day I found your door ajar yet a frigid chill be on the land and the table laden with food and sustenance as if a meal interrupted yet other objects upside down or sharply broken with blood droplets on the floor. I did fear for an Indian raid and the safety of your kin. But the children both natural and the refugee girls I espied cowering in fear upstairs with word that your Goodwife fell into a fit while eating and not be of her normal self and having run to the shelter of your livestock. With trepidation I took myself there and called her name in the darkness. She came at me like a wild woman and affrighted me greatly. Blood was on her hands and her frock and I saw her handiwork. With troubled spirit I did quiet her at risk to my own well being. To a like purpose I did likewise with your livestock which were all affrighted yet all were safe. To these things I spoke the truth in God's name.

I remain your friend and neighbor,
Thomas Goodman.

"These poor people," Kim murmured. This letter came the closest to anything she'd read so far in communicating to her the personal horror of the Salem witch ordeal, and Kim felt empathy for all involved. She could tell that Thomas was confused and dismayed at being caught between friendship and what he thought was the truth. And Kim's heart went out to poor Elizabeth, who'd been rendered out of her mind with the mold to the point of terrorizing her own children. It was easy for Kim to understand how the seventeenth-century mind would have ascribed such horrifying and inexplicable behavior to witchcraft.

In the middle of Kim's empathy she realized that the letter presented something new and disturbing. It was the mention of blood with its implication of violence. Kim didn't even want to imagine what Elizabeth could have been doing in the shed with the livestock, yet she had to admit it might be significant.

Kim looked back at the letter. She reread the sentence where Thomas described that all the livestock was safe despite the presence of blood. That seemed confusing unless Elizabeth had done something to herself. The thought of self-mutilation made Kim shudder. Its possibility was enhanced by Thomas's mention of droplets of blood on the floor in the house. But the blood in the house was mentioned in the same sentence with broken objects, suggesting the blood could have come from an inadvertent wound.

Kim sighed. Her mind was a jumble, but one thing was clear. The effect of the fungus was now associated with violence, and Kim thought that was something Edward and the others should know immediately.

Clutching the letter, Kim hastened from the castle and half-ran to the lab. She was out of breath when she entered. She was also immediately surprised: she'd walked into the middle of a celebration.

Everyone greeted Kim with great merriment, pulling her over to one of the lab benches where they had uncorked a bottle of champagne. Kim tried to refuse a beakerful but they wouldn't hear of it. Once again she felt as if she were with a bunch of frolicsome collegians.

As soon as Kim was able, she worked her way over to Edward's side to ask him what was going on.

"Eleanor, Gloria, and François have just pulled off an

amazing feat of analytic chemistry," Edward explained. "They've already determined the structure of one of Ultra's binding proteins. It's a huge leap forward. It will allow us to modify Ultra if need be or to design other possible drugs that will bind at the same site."

"I'm happy for you," Kim said. "But I want to show you something that I think you ought to see." She handed him the letter.

Edward quickly scanned the letter. When he looked up at Kim he winked at her. "Congratulations," he said. "This is the best one yet." Then, turning to the group he called out: "Listen up, you guys. Kim has found the greatest bit of proof that Elizabeth had been poisoned with the fungus. It will be even better than the diary entry for the article for *Science.*"

The researchers eagerly gathered around. Edward gave them the letter and encouraged them all to read it.

"It's perfect," Eleanor said, passing it on to David. "It even mentions she'd been eating. It's certainly a graphic description how fast the alkaloid works. She'd probably just taken a bite of bread."

"It's a good thing you eliminated that hallucinogenic side-chain," David said. "I wouldn't want to wake up and find myself out with the cows."

Everyone laughed except Kim. She looked at Edward and, after waiting for him to stop laughing, asked him if the suggestion of violence in the letter bothered him.

Edward took the letter back and read it more carefully. "You know, you have a good point," he told Kim when he was finished the second time. "I don't think I should use this letter for the article after all. It might cause some trouble we don't need. A few years ago there was an unfortunate rumor fanned by TV talk shows that associated Prozac with violence. It was a problem until it was debunked statistically. I don't want anything like that to happen to Ultra."

"If the unaltered alkaloid caused violence, it had to have been the same side chain that caused the hallucinations," Gloria said. "You could mention that in the article."

"Why take the chance?" Edward said. "I don't want to

give some rabid journalist even a tidbit that might raise the specter of violence.''

''Perhaps the concern for violence should be included in the clinical protocols,'' Kim suggested. ''Then if the question ever were to arise, you'd already have data.''

''You know, that's a damn good idea,'' Gloria said.

For several minutes the group favorably discussed Kim's suggestion. Encouraged that people were listening to her, she suggested they should include short-term-memory lapses as well. To make her case she cited Edward's recent episodes.

Edward laughed good-naturedly along with everyone else. ''So what if I brush my teeth twice?'' he said, bringing on more laughter.

''I think including short-term-memory loss in the clinical protocols is an equally good idea as including violence,'' Curt said. ''David's been similarly forgetful. I've noticed, since we're immediate neighbors in the castle.''

''You should talk,'' David said with a chuckle. He then told the group that just the night before, Curt had called his girlfriend twice because he'd forgotten he'd called her the first time.

''I bet that went over well with her,'' Gloria said.

Curt gave David a playful punch in the shoulder. ''The only reason you noticed was because you'd done the exact same thing the night before with your wife.''

As Kim watched Curt and David playfully spar, she noticed Curt's hands and fingers were marred by cuts and scratches. Her reflex response as a nurse was one of concern. She offered to look at them.

''Thank you, but they aren't as bad as they look,'' Curt said. ''They don't bother me in the slightest.''

''Did you fall off your motorcycle?''

Curt laughed. ''I hope not,'' he said. ''I don't remember how I did it.''

''It's an occupational hazard,'' David said, showing his hands, which appeared similar although not as bad. ''It just proves we're all working our fingers to the bone.''

''It's the pressure of working nineteen hours a day,''

François said. "It's amazing we have been functioning as well as we have."

"It seems to me that short-term-memory loss must be a side effect of Ultra," Kim said. "It sounds like you all are experiencing it."

"I haven't," Gloria said.

"Neither have I," Eleanor said. "My mind and memory are demonstrably better since I've been on Ultra."

"Same with me," Gloria said. "I think François is right. We're just working too hard."

"Wait a second, Gloria," Eleanor said. "You *have* been forgetful. What about the morning before last when you left your bathrobe in the bathroom and then two minutes later had a fit when it wasn't hanging behind your door in the bedroom?"

"I didn't throw a fit," Gloria contradicted good-naturedly. "Besides, that's different. I've been misplacing my robe way before I've been on Ultra."

"Regardless," Edward said. "Kim is right. Short-term memory lapse could be related to Ultra, and as such it should be included in the clinical protocols. But it's not something we need to lose any sleep over. Even if it proves to occur on occasion, it will surely be an acceptable risk in light of the drug's enhancement of mental function in general."

"I agree," Gloria said. "It's the equivalent of Einstein forgetting little everyday matters while he was formulating the Theory of Relativity. The mind makes value judgments of what to keep in the processor, and how many times you brush your teeth isn't that important."

The sound of the outer door closing got everyone's attention since the lab got few visitors. All eyes turned to the door to the reception area. It opened and in walked Stanton.

A spontaneous triple cheer arose from the researchers. A confused Stanton stopped in his tracks. "What on earth is going on here?" he questioned. "Nobody working today?"

Eleanor rushed him a beaker of champagne.

"A little toast," Edward said, lifting his drink. "We'd like to drink to your heckling nature that motivated us to start taking Ultra. We're reaping the benefits on a daily basis.''

Amid giggles everyone took a drink including Stanton.

''It really has been a boon,'' Edward said. ''We've been drawing blood on each other and saving urine to test.''

''All of us except François,'' Gloria said, teasing the Frenchman. ''He forgets more than half the time.''

''We did have a slight problem with compliance in that regard,'' Edward admitted. ''But we solved it by taping the toilet seats down and putting up a sign saying HOLD IT.''

They all laughed again. Gloria and David had to put their drinks down for fear of spilling them.

''You certainly are a happy group,'' Stanton commented.

''We have reason to be,'' Edward said. He then told Stanton the good news about discovering the structure of the binding protein. He gave partial credit to Ultra for sharpening everyone's mental acuity.

''This is marvelous news indeed!'' Stanton exclaimed. He made it a point to walk around and shake Gloria's, Eleanor's, and François's hands individually. Then he told Edward he wanted to talk with him.

Using Stanton's arrival as an opportunity to excuse herself, Kim left. She felt good about her visit to the lab; she had the feeling she'd accomplished something by suggesting violence and short-term-memory loss should be included in the clinical evaluation of Ultra.

Kim headed back toward the castle. The first thing she wanted to do was put Thomas Goodman's letter into the Bible box with the other memorabilia pertaining to Elizabeth. As she neared the mansion she saw a Salem police car emerge from the trees. Evidently the driver saw her, because the cruiser immediately turned onto the road to the castle, heading in her direction.

Kim stopped and waited. The car pulled to a stop, and the same two officers who'd responded to the call about Buffer got out.

Billy touched the rim of his visored hat in a kind of salute while he and Kim exchanged greetings.

''I hope we're not bothering you,'' Billy said.

''Is something wrong?'' Kim questioned.

"We wanted to ask if you'd had any more trouble since the death of the dog," Billy said. "There's been a rash of vandalism in the immediate area, as if Halloween had come a month early."

"Halloween's big here in Salem," Harry said. "It's the time of year we law-enforcement officers have learned to hate."

"What kind of vandalism?" Kim questioned.

"The usual nonsense," Billy said. "Trash cans turned over, garbage spread around. Also more pets have disappeared and some of the carcasses have turned up across the road in the Greenlawn Cemetery."

"We're still concerned about the possibility of a rabid animal in the neighborhood," Harry said. "You'd better keep that cat of yours indoors, especially considering the size of your property and all its wooded areas."

"We think some local kids have joined the fray, so to speak," Billy said. "They're imitating what the animal has been doing. There's been too much for one animal. I mean, how many trash cans can a raccoon do in a night?" He snickered.

"I appreciate your coming by to warn me," Kim said. "We haven't had any trouble since the dog's death, but I'll be sure to continue to keep my cat close to home."

"If you have any problems please give us a call," Harry said. "We'd like to get to the bottom of this before it gets out of hand."

Kim watched while the police car made a U-turn and headed out of the compound. She was about to enter the castle when she heard Stanton call. Turning, she saw him coming from the lab.

"What the devil were the police doing here?" he asked as soon as he was within talking distance.

Kim told him about the concern of there being a rabid animal in the area.

"It's always something," Stanton said. "Listen, I want to talk to you about Edward. Do you have a minute?"

"Of course," Kim said, wondering what this could be about. "Where would you like to talk?"

"Here's fine," Stanton said. "Where to start?" He

stared off for a minute then looked Kim in the eye. "I'm a bit bewildered by Edward lately and the others as well. Every time I pop into the lab I feel like the odd man out. A couple of weeks ago it was like a morgue in there. Now it's eerie the way they are enjoying themselves. It's become like a vacation retreat only they're working as hard or harder than they did before. Their repartee is difficult to follow since they are all so damn smart and witty. In fact, it makes me feel dumb to hang around." Stanton laughed wryly before continuing. "Edward has become so outgoing and pushy that he reminds me of me!"

Kim put her hand to her mouth but laughed through her fingers at Stanton's self-deprecating insightfulness.

"It's not funny," Stanton complained, but he was laughing himself. "The next thing that Edward will want to be is a venture capitalist. He's gotten carried away with the business stuff, and unfortunately we don't see eye to eye. Now we're at loggerheads over how to raise more capital. The good doctor has become so greedy he will not sacrifice any equity. He's metamorphosed overnight from an avowed ascetic academician to an insatiable capitalist."

"Why are you telling me this?" Kim questioned. "I have nothing to do with Omni nor do I want to have."

"I was just hoping that you could talk to Edward," Stanton said. "I cannot in good conscience condone borrowing money from dirty sources through foreign banks, and I'm even sorry that I mentioned the possibility. There's just too much risk, and I'm not talking about financial risk. I'm talking about risk to life and limb. It just ain't worth it. I mean, the financial aspect of this venture should be left up to me, just like the scientific stuff should be left up to Edward."

"Does Edward seem forgetful to you?" Kim asked.

"Hell, no!" Stanton said. "He's as sharp as a tack. He's just innocent when it comes to the ways of the financial world."

"He's been forgetful around me," Kim said. "Just little everyday things. And most of the other researchers have admitted to being just as absentminded."

"I haven't noticed any absentmindedness with Edward,"

Stanton said. "But he did seem a little paranoid. Just a few minutes ago we had to go outside to talk so we wouldn't be overheard."

"Overheard by whom?" Kim asked.

Stanton shrugged. "The other researchers, I assume. He didn't say and I didn't ask."

"This morning he came all the way to the house to make a call so that he wouldn't be overheard," Kim said. "He was afraid to use the phone in the reception area because he thought someone would listen through the walls."

"Now that sounds even more paranoid," Stanton said. "But in his defense I've drilled it into him that secrecy is important at this stage."

"Stanton, I'm getting worried," Kim said.

"Don't say that," Stanton complained. "I came to you to relieve my anxieties not increase them."

"I'm concerned that the forgetfulness and paranoia are side effects from the Ultra," Kim said.

"I don't want to hear this," Stanton said as he cupped his hands over his ears.

"They shouldn't be taking the drug at this stage," Kim said. "And you know it. I think you should stop them."

"Me?" Stanton said. "I just told you a minute ago I'm in finances. I don't meddle with the science side, especially when they have told me that taking the drug will speed up its evaluation process. Besides, this mild paranoia and forgetfulness are probably due to how hard they are working. Edward knows what he is doing. My God, he's tops in his field."

"I'll make you a deal," Kim said. "If you try to convince Edward to stop taking the drug, I'll try to convince him that the finances should be left to you."

Stanton made a face as if he had been stabbed in the back. "This is ridiculous," he said. "I've got to negotiate with my own cousin."

"It sounds reasonable to me," Kim said. "We'll be helping each other."

"I can't promise anything," Stanton said.

"Nor can I," Kim said.

"When will you talk with him?" Stanton asked.

"Tonight," Kim said. "What about you?"

"I suppose I could just go back and talk with him now," Stanton said.

"Do we have a deal?" Kim asked.

"I suppose so," Stanton said reluctantly. He stuck out his hand and Kim shook it.

Kim watched as Stanton started back toward the lab. In contrast to his usual sprightly step his gait was plodding, with his arms hanging straight down like he was lugging heavy weights in both hands. Kim couldn't help but feel sorry for him since she knew that he was distressed. The problem was he'd put all his money into Omni, violating one of his own cardinal rules of investing.

After climbing up to the attic, Kim walked over to one of the dormer windows that faced in the direction of the lab. She was just in time to see Stanton disappear into the building. Kim didn't have high hopes that Stanton would be successful getting Edward to stop taking Ultra, but at least she could feel that she'd tried.

That night Kim made it a point to stay awake until Edward came in just after one in the morning. She was reading when she heard the front door close, followed by Edward's footfalls on the old stairs.

"My goodness," he said, sticking his head into her bedroom. "That must be one hell of a book to keep you awake until this hour."

"I'm not tired," Kim said. "Come in."

"I'm exhausted," Edward said. He stepped into the room and absently petted Sheba while he yawned. "I can't wait to get into bed. It hits me just after midnight like clockwork. The amazing thing is how quickly I fall asleep once the tiredness comes. I have to be careful if I sit down. If I lie down, forget it."

"I noticed that," Kim said. "Sunday night you didn't even turn out your light."

"I suppose I should be aggravated with you," Edward said. He was smiling. "But I'm not. I know you only have my best interests at heart."

"Are you going to tell me what you are talking about?" Kim asked.

"As if you didn't know," Edward said teasingly. "I'm talking about Stanton's sudden concern for my well-being. I knew you were behind it the moment he opened his mouth. It's not like him to be so sympathetic."

"Did he tell you about our deal?" Kim said.

"What kind of deal?" Edward asked.

"He agreed to try to get you to stop taking Ultra if I would convince you that Omni's finances should be left up to him."

"Et tu Brute," Edward said jokingly. "This is a fine state of affairs. The two people I think I'm closest to are scheming behind my back."

"As you said, we've only your best interests at heart," Kim said.

"I think I'm capable of deciding what's best for me," Edward said amiably.

"But you've changed," Kim said. "Stanton said you've changed so much that you're becoming like him."

Edward laughed heartily. "That's great!" he said. "I've always wanted to be as outgoing as Stanton. Too bad my father passed away. Maybe he'd finally be pleased with me."

"This isn't a joking matter," Kim said.

"I'm not joking," Edward said. "I enjoy being socially assertive instead of shy and bashful."

"But it's dangerous taking an untested drug," Kim said. "Besides, don't you question the ethics of acquiring character traits from a drug rather than from experience? I think it's fake and like cheating."

Edward sat on the edge of Kim's bed. "If I fall asleep call a tow truck to get me into my bed," he said with a chuckle. He then had another extended yawn that he tried to cover with his fist. "Listen, my dearest," he said. "Ultra is not un tested; it's just not fully tested. But it's nontoxic and that's the important thing. I'm going to continue taking it unless a serious side effect occurs, which I sincerely doubt. As to your second point, it's clear to me that undesirable character traits, like in my case my shyness, can become entrenched by experience. Prozac, to an extent, and now Ultra, to a greater extent, have unlocked the real me, the person whose personality had been submerged by an unfortunate series of life experiences that made me the socially awkward person I'd become. My personality right now hasn't been invented by Ultra and isn't fake. My current personality has been allowed to emerge despite a haze of facilitated neural responses that I'd call a 'bum network.' "

Edward chuckled as he gave Kim's leg a reassuring pat through her covers. "I assure you, I've never felt better in my life. Trust me. My only concern now is how long I have to take Ultra before this current 'me' has been facilitated so that when I stop taking Ultra I won't relapse into my shy, socially awkward old self."

"You make it sound so reasonable," Kim complained.

"But it is," Edward said. "This is the way I want to be. Hell, this is the way I probably would have been if my father hadn't been such a bore."

"But what about the forgetfulness and the paranoia?" Kim said.

"What paranoia?" Edward asked.

Kim reminded him of his coming to the house that morning to use the phone and having to go out of the lab to talk with Stanton.

"That wasn't paranoid," Edward said indignantly. "Those characters down in the lab have become the worst gossip hounds I've ever been around. I'm just trying to protect my privacy."

"Both Stanton and I thought it seemed paranoid," Kim said.

"Well, I can assure you it wasn't," Edward said. He smiled. The twinge of irritation he'd felt at being accused of paranoia had already passed. "The forgetfulness I'll admit to but not the other."

"Why not stop the drug and start it again during the clinical phase?"

"You are a hard person to convince," Edward said. "And unfortunately I'm out of energy. I can't keep my eyes open. I'm sorry. We'll continue this tomorrow if you'd like since it is an extension of a previous discussion. Right now I have to go to bed."

Edward bent over, gave Kim a kiss on her cheek, and then walked unsteadily out of her room. She heard him moving about his bedroom for only a few minutes. Then she heard the deep heavy respiration of someone already fast asleep.

Amazed at the rapidity of the transformation, Kim got out of bed. After slipping on her robe, she walked through the connecting hall to Edward's bedroom. A trail of discarded clothes led across the room, and Edward was spread-eagled on top of his bed, clothed only in his underwear. Just as what happened Sunday night, his bedside lamp was still on.

Kim walked to the light and switched it off. Standing next to him, she was amazed at how loud his snoring was. She wondered why it had never awakened her when they slept together.

Kim retreated to her own bed. She turned out the light and tried to go to sleep. But it was impossible. Her mind would not turn off, and she could hear Edward as if he were in her room.

After a half hour, Kim got back out of bed and went into the bathroom. She found the old vial of Xanax she'd been saving for years and took one of the pink, boat-shaped pills. She didn't like the idea of taking the drug, but she thought she needed it; there would be no sleep if she didn't.

Coming out of the bathroom, she closed both Edward's door and her own. Getting back into bed, she could still hear Edward but at least it was muffled. Within fifteen minutes she felt a welcome serenity drift over her. A little while later she fell into her own deep sleep.

# 16

## *Friday,*
## *September 30, 1994*

$A$T NEARLY THREE A.M. THERE WAS LITTLE TRAFFIC ON the darkened streets of Salem, and Dave Halpern felt as if he owned the world. Since midnight he'd been aimlessly cruising in his '89 red Chevy Camaro. He'd been to Marblehead twice and even up to Danvers and around through Beverly.

Dave was seventeen and a junior at Salem High. He'd gotten the car thanks to an after-school job at a local McDonald's and a sizable loan from his parents, and it was the current love of his life. He reveled in the sense of freedom and unadulterated power the car gave him. He also liked the attention it evoked from his friends, particularly Christina McElroy. Christina was a sophomore and had a great body.

Dave checked the dimly illuminated clock set into the center console on the dash. It was just about time for the rendezvous. Turning onto Dearborn Street, where Christina lived, Dave hit the lights and turned off the engine. He slowed and glided to a silent stop beneath the canopy of a large maple.

He didn't have to wait long. Christina appeared out of the hedges that ran alongside her clapboard house, rushed to the car, and jumped in. The whites of her eyes and teeth glistened in the half-light. She was tremulous with excitement.

She slid across the vinyl seat so that her tightly denimed thigh pressed against Dave's.

Trying to project an air of insouciance, as if this middle-of-the-night rendezvous were an everyday occurrence, Dave didn't speak. He merely reached forward and started his machine. But his hand shook and rattled the keys. Fearing he'd given himself away, he cast a furtive look in Christina's direction. He caught a smile and worried that she thought he wasn't cool.

When Dave reached the corner he switched on his headlights. Instantly the nightscape lit up, revealing blowing leaves and deep shadows.

"Have any problems?" Dave asked, keeping his mind on the road.

"It was a breeze," Christina said. "I can't understand why I was so scared to sneak out of the house. My parents are unconscious. I mean I could have just walked out the front door instead of climbing out the window."

They drove down a street lined with dark houses.

"Where are we going?" Christina asked nonchalantly.

"You'll see," Dave said. "We'll be there in a sec."

They were now cruising past the dark, expansive Greenlawn Cemetery. Christina pressed up against Dave and looked over his shoulder into the graveyard with its stubble of headstones.

Dave slowed the car, and Christina sat bolt upright. "We're not going in there," she said defiantly.

Dave smiled in the darkness, exposing his own white teeth. "Why not?" he said. Almost as soon as the words left his mouth he pulled the wheel to the left, and the car bumped over the threshold into the cemetery. Dave quickly doused the headlights and slowed to a speed approximating a slow jog. It was hard to see the road beneath the foliage.

"Oh, my God!" Christina said as her head pivoted and her wide eyes scanned the immediate area on both sides of the car. The headstones loomed eerily in the night. Some of them gave off sudden splinters of ambient light from their highly polished surfaces.

Instinctively Christina moved even closer to Dave's side, with one hand gripping the inside of his thigh. Dave grinned with satisfied contentment.

They rolled to a stop beside a silent, still pond bordered

by droopy willows. Dave turned off the engine and locked the doors. "Can't be too careful," he said.

"Maybe we should crack the windows," Christina suggested. "Otherwise it will be an oven in here."

Dave took the suggestion but voiced the hope that there wouldn't be any mosquitoes.

The two teenagers eyed each other for a moment of awkward hesitation. Then Dave tentatively leaned toward Christina, and they gently kissed. The contact instantly fueled the fires of their passion, and they fell into a wild, libidinous embrace. Clumsily they groped for each other's physical secrets as the windows steamed up.

Despite the power of their youthful, teenage hormones, both Dave and Christina sensed a movement of the car that was not of their making. Simultaneously they glanced up from their endeavors and looked out through the misty windshield. What they saw instantly terrified them. Hurling at them through the night air was a pale white specter. Whatever the preternatural creature was, it collided with a jarring impact against the windshield and then rolled off the passenger side of the car.

"What the hell?" Dave yelled as he frantically struggled with his pants, which had worked their way halfway down his thighs.

Christina then shrieked as she battled to fend off a filthy hand that thrust itself through her cracked window and tore away a handful of her hair.

"Holy crap!" Dave yelled as he gave up on his pants to fight a hand that came in through his side. Fingernails sank into the skin of his neck and ripped off a piece of his T-shirt, leaving rivulets of blood to run down his back.

In a panic Dave started the Camaro. Jamming the car in reverse, he shot backward, bouncing over the rocky terrain. Christina screamed again as her head hit the roof of the car. The car slammed into a headstone that snapped off at its base and thudded to the ground.

Dave threw the car into drive and gunned the engine. He wrestled with the wheel as the powerful engine hurled the car forward. Christina ricocheted off the door and was

thrown into Dave's lap. He pushed her away just in time
to miss another marble monument.

Dave snapped on the headlights as they careened around
a sharp turn in the road that meandered through the cemetery. Christina recovered enough to start crying.

"Who the hell were they?" Dave shouted.

"There were two of them," Christina managed through
her tears.

They reached the street and Dave turned toward town,
laying a patch of rubber on the street. Christina's crying
lessened to whimpering with an occasional sob. Turning
the rearview mirror in her direction, she inspected the damage to her hair. "My cut's been ruined," she cried.

Dave readjusted the mirror and glanced behind them to
be certain no one was following. He wiped his neck with
his hand and looked at the blood with disbelief.

"What the devil were they wearing?" Dave asked angrily.

"What difference does it make?" Christina cried.

"They were wearing white clothes or something," Dave
said. "Like a couple of ghosts."

"We never should have gone there," Christina bawled.
"I knew it from the start."

"Give me a break," Dave said. "You didn't know anything."

"I did," she said. "You just didn't ask me."

"Bull," Dave said.

"Whoever they were, they must be sick," Christina said.

"You're probably right," Dave said. "Maybe they're
from Danvers State Hospital. But if they are, how do they
get all the way down here to Greenlawn Cemetery?"

Christina put her hand to her mouth and mumbled, "I'm
going to be sick."

Dave jammed on his brakes and pulled over to the side
of the road. Christina cracked her door and vomited in the
street. Dave said a silent prayer that it all went out of the
car.

Christina pushed herself back to a sitting position. She
laid her head against the headrest and closed her eyes.

"I want to go home," she said miserably.

''We'll be there in a sec,'' Dave said. He drove away from the curb. He could smell the sour aroma of vomit, and he worried that his lovely car had been ruined.

''We can't tell anybody about this,'' Christina said. ''If my parents find out I'll be grounded for six months.''

''All right,'' Dave said.

''You promise?''

''Sure, no problem.''

Dave hit the lights when he turned onto Christina's street. He stopped several doors down from her house. He hoped she didn't expect him to kiss her and was glad when she got right out.

''You promised,'' she said.

''Don't worry,'' Dave said.

He watched her run across the lawns and disappear into the same hedge from which she'd emerged.

Under a nearby streetlight, Dave got out and inspected his car. In the back there was a dent on the bumper where he'd knocked over the headstone, but it wasn't bad. Going around to the passenger side, he opened the door and cautiously sniffed. He was relieved when he didn't smell any vomit. Closing the door, he walked around the front of the car. That was when he noticed the windshield wiper on the passenger side was gone.

Dave gritted his teeth and swore under his breath. What a night, and he didn't even get anything. Climbing back into his car, he wondered if he'd be able to rouse George, his best friend, from sleep. Dave couldn't wait to tell him about what had happened. It was so weird it was like some old horror movie. In a way, Dave was thankful about the broken wiper. If it hadn't happened George probably wouldn't believe the story.

Having taken the Xanax around one-thirty that morning, Kim slept much later than usual, and when she got up she felt mildly drugged. She didn't like the feeling, but she was convinced it was a small price to pay for getting some sleep.

Kim spent the first part of the day getting her uniform ready for Monday, when she was scheduled to start back to work. It amazed her how much she was looking forward to it. And it wasn't just because of the mounting anxieties about the lab and what was happening in it. During the last two weeks she'd become progressively weary of the isolated and lonely life she'd been leading in Salem, especially once she'd finished decorating the cottage.

The main problem on both counts was Edward, despite the better mood he was in while taking Ultra. Living with him had hardly been what she'd expected, although when she thought about it, she wasn't sure what she did expect since she'd invited him to come and live with her on impulse. But she certainly had expected to see more of him and share more with him than she had. And she certainly hadn't expected to be worrying about him taking an experimental drug. All in all, it was a ridiculous situation.

Once Kim had her uniform in order, she hiked over to the castle. The first thing she did was see Albert. She'd hoped the plumbing work would be finishing that day, but Albert said it was impossible with the additional work in the guest wing. He told her they'd need another two days tops. He asked her if they could leave their tools in the castle over the weekend. Kim told him he could leave whatever he wanted.

Kim went down the stairs in the servants' wing and checked the entrance. To her great disappointment it was again filthy. Glancing outside, she noticed the mat was in pristine shape, almost as if they purposefully ignored it.

Getting the mop once again, Kim scolded herself for not mentioning the problem to the researchers the day before, when she'd been at the lab.

Crossing the courtyard, Kim checked the entrance to the guest wing. There was less dirt than in the servants' wing, but there was some, and in some respects it was worse. The stairs in the guest wing were carpeted. To clean them Kim had to cart over an old vacuum cleaner from the servants' wing. When she was finished she vowed to herself that she would talk to the researchers about it this time.

After putting away the cleaning paraphernalia, Kim contemplated walking over to the lab. But she decided against it. The irony was that in the beginning of the month she'd not wanted to visit the lab because they'd made her feel unwelcome. Now she was reluctant to go because they were too friendly.

Finally Kim climbed the stairs and fell to work in the attic. Finding the Thomas Goodman letter the day before had kindled her enthusiasm. The hours passed quickly, and before she knew it, it was time for lunch.

Walking back to the cottage, Kim eyed the lab and again debated stopping by and again decided against it. She thought she'd wait rather than make a special trip. She knew she was procrastinating, but she couldn't help it. She even considered telling Edward about the dirt problem and having him talk to the researchers.

After lunch Kim returned to the attic, where she worked all afternoon. The only thing she came across from the time period she was interested in was Jonathan Stewart's college evaluation. Reading it, Kim learned that Jonathan was only an average student. According to one of the more verbally colorful evaluating tutors, Jonathan was "more apt at swimming in Fresh Pond or skating on the Charles River according to season than in logic, rhetoric, or ethics."

That evening while Kim was enjoying fresh fish grilled outdoors accompanied by a mixed green salad, she saw a pizza delivery service drive onto the compound and head to the lab. She marveled that Edward and his team existed on junk food. Twice a day there was a delivery of fast food such as pizza, fried chicken, or Chinese take-out. Back in the beginning of the month Kim had offered to make dinner for Edward each evening, but he had declined, saying he thought he should eat with the others.

In one sense Kim was impressed with their dedication, while in another sense she thought they were zealots and a little crazy.

Around eleven Kim took Sheba outside. She stood on the porch while her pet wandered around in the grass. Keeping one eye on the cat, Kim looked over at the lab and saw the light spilling from the windows. She wondered how long they would keep up their insane schedule.

When she felt Sheba had had adequate outdoor time, Kim carried her back inside. The cat wasn't happy, but with what the police had told her, she surely wasn't about to let the animal roam freely.

Upstairs Kim prepared for bed. She read for an hour, but like the evening before, her mind would not turn off. In fact, lying in bed seemed to augment her anxiety. Getting out of bed, Kim went into the bathroom and took another Xanax tablet. She didn't like taking it, but she reasoned that until she started back to work, she needed the respite it provided.

# 17

## Saturday,
## October 1, 1994

KIM PULLED HERSELF FROM THE DEPTHS OF A MINOR stupor caused by the Xanax. Once again she was surprised she'd slept as long as she had. It was almost nine.

After showering and dressing, Kim took Sheba outside. Feeling guilty that she'd been denying the animal her normal wandering, Kim was patient with the cat and allowed her to go wherever she wanted. Sheba chose to go around the house. Kim followed.

As Kim rounded the back of the house she suddenly stopped, angrily put her hands on her hips, and let out an expletive. She had discovered she'd been targeted by the vandals or the animal which the police had warned her about. Both her trash containers had been tipped over and emptied. The trash had been strewn around the yard.

Ignoring Sheba for the moment, Kim righted the two plastic garbage cans. As she did so she discovered that both had been torn at their top edges, presumably when their covers had been forcibly removed.

"What a pain!" Kim exclaimed as she carried the two containers back to where they normally stood next to the house. Looking at them more closely, she realized that she'd have to replace them since their covers would no longer be secure.

Kim rescued Sheba just before she was about to take off into the woods, and carried her back into the house. Remembering that the police had asked to be called if she had any trouble, Kim called the station. To her surprise they insisted on sending someone out.

Using a pair of gardening gloves, Kim went back outside and spent a half hour picking up all the trash. Temporarily she put it back into the two broken containers. She was just finishing when the Salem police car arrived.

It was a single officer this time who Kim thought looked about her age. His name was Tom Malick. He was a serious fellow and asked to see the crime scene. Kim thought he was making more of the incident than it deserved, but took him around behind the house and showed him the containers. She had to explain that she'd just finished picking everything up.

"It would have been better if you left everything the way you found it until we'd seen it," Tom said.

"I'm sorry," Kim said. She couldn't imagine what difference it would have made.

"Your situation here fits the same scenario that we've been seeing in the general area," Tom said. He squatted down next to the containers and examined them carefully. Then he looked at the lids.

Kim watched him with mild impatience.

He stood up. "This was done by the animal or animals," he said. "It wasn't the kids. I believe there are teethmarks along the lips of the covers. Do you want to see?"

"I suppose," Kim said.

Tom lifted up one of the covers and pointed to a series of parallel grooves.

"I think you should get more secure containers," Tom said.

"I was planning on replacing them," Kim said. "I'll see what's available."

"You might have to go out to Burlington to find them," Tom said. "There's been a run on them in town."

"It sounds like this is developing into a real problem," Kim said.

"You'd better believe it," Tom said. "The town is in an uproar. Didn't you watch the local news this morning?"

"No, I didn't," Kim said.

"Up until last night the only deaths we've had with this affair have been dogs and cats," Tom said. "This morning we found our first human victim."

"That's awful," Kim said, catching her breath. "Who was it?"

"He was a vagrant who was fairly well known in town," Tom said. "His name was John Mullins. He was found not far from here, near the Kernwood Bridge. The gruesome thing was that he'd been partially eaten."

Kim's mouth went dry as her mind unwillingly called up the horrid image of Buffer lying in the grass.

"John did have an ungodly blood alcohol level," Tom said, "so he might have been dead before the animal got to him, but we'll know more after a report from the medical examiner. The body went to Boston in hopes that we can get a lead on what kind of animal we're dealing with from toothmarks on bones."

"It sounds horrible," Kim said with a shudder. "I didn't realize how serious this was."

"Initially we were thinking about a raccoon," Tom said. "But with this human victim, and the amount of vandalism going on, we're thinking of a bigger animal, like a bear. There's been a marked increase in the bear population of New Hampshire so it's not out of the question. But whatever it is, it's got our Salem witch industry loving it. Of course they're saying it's the devil and all that kind of nonsense, trying to get people to think it's 1692 all over again. Trouble is, they're doing a pretty good job, and their business is brisk. So is ours."

After a strong warning for Kim to be careful because of all the forest land on her property which could certainly conceal a bear, Tom left.

Before going all the way to Burlington, Kim went into the house and called the hardware store in Salem where she did most of her business. Contrary to what Tom had said, they assured her they had a full selection of trash containers available since they'd just gotten a shipment the day before.

Happy to have an errand that took her to town, Kim left as soon as she'd had something to eat. She drove straight to the hardware store. The clerk told her she was wise to have come directly. Since he'd spoken with her an hour previously, they'd sold a good portion of the trash container shipment.

"This animal really gets around," Kim said.

"You'd better believe it," the clerk said. "They're starting to have the same problems over in Beverly. Everybody's talking about what kind of animal it is. There's even odds in case you want to bet some money. But it's been great for us. Not only have we been selling a ton of garbage cans; there's been a fire sale on ammo and rifles in our sporting goods section."

While Kim was waiting by the register to pay for her purchases, she could hear other customers talking about the same subject. There was excitement in the air that was almost palpable.

Leaving the store, Kim had an uncomfortable feeling. She was worried that if hysteria broke out about this creature now that a human death was involved, innocent people could get hurt. She shuddered to think of trigger-happy people hiding behind their curtains just waiting to hear something or somebody toying with their trash. Since kids were apparently getting involved, it could easily turn into a tragedy.

Back at the house, Kim transferred the trash from the damaged containers to the new ones with their lids secured by an ingenious compression mechanism. She put the old ones in the back of the shed to use for collecting leaves. As she worked, she longed for the city, nostalgically remembering life there as being simple in comparison. She'd had to worry about muggers but not bears.

With the garbage problem taken care of, Kim walked across the field to the lab. She wasn't excited about going, but with this new development of her garbage being ransacked and a body being found nearby she felt she had no choice.

Before she went inside she checked the bins where the lab's garbage was stored. They were two heavy industrial-sized steel boxes that were lifted by the garbage truck. The lids were heavy. Kim could barely push them up. Looking inside, she could see that the lab's trash had been undisturbed.

At the front door Kim hesitated, trying to think up an excuse to use in case she was waylaid by the congenial researchers. Lunch was the only thing she could think of. She also girded herself to bring up the subject of the dirt being tracked into the castle.

Kim passed through the reception area and entered the lab proper. Once again she was surprised. On her last visit it had been a celebration, this time it was an impromptu meeting that had to be about something important. The gay, festive atmosphere that she was learning to expect at the lab was gone. In its place was a solemnity that was almost funereal.

"I'm terribly sorry if I'm interrupting," Kim said.

"It's quite all right," Edward said. "Did you want something in particular?"

Kim told them about the problem with her garbage and the visit by the police. She then asked if anybody heard or saw anything out of the ordinary during the night.

Everyone looked at each other expectantly. No one responded at first, then they all shook their heads.

"I sleep so soundly I doubt I'd hear an earthquake," Curt said.

"You sound like an earthquake," David joked. "But you're right, I sleep equally as soundly."

Kim glanced around at the faces of the researchers. The somber mood she'd detected when she'd first entered already seemed to be improving. She then told them that the police thought the culprit might be a rabid bear, but that kids had been taking advantage of the situation in the name of fun. She also described the excitement that bordered on hysteria that gripped the town.

"Only in Salem could something like this get so blown out of proportion," Edward said with a chuckle. "This town is never going to recover completely from 1692."

"Some of their concern is justified," Kim said. "The problem has recently taken on a new dimension. A dead man was found this morning not too far away from here, and his body had been gnawed."

Gloria blanched. "How grotesque!" she exclaimed.

"Have they determined how the man died?" Edward asked.

"Not exactly," Kim said. "They've sent the body to Boston to be examined. There's a question about whether or not the man had been dead prior to being attacked by the animal."

"Then the animal would have been only acting as a scavenger," Edward said.

"That's true," Kim said. "But I still thought it was important to warn you all. I know that you walk late at night. Maybe you should drive the short distance to the castle until this problem has been taken care of. Meanwhile, keep your eye out for either a rabid animal or teenagers."

"Thanks for warning us," Edward said.

"One other thing," Kim said, forcing herself to switch subjects. "There's been a minor problem at the castle. There's been some dirt tracked in through the entrances to the wings. I wanted to ask that you all wipe your feet."

"We're terribly sorry," François said. "It's dark when we get there and dark when we leave. We'll have to be more careful."

"I'm sure you will," Kim said. "Well, that's all I had. Sorry to bother you."

"No problem at all," Edward said. He accompanied her to the door. "You be careful too," he told her. "And watch out for Sheba."

Edward walked back to the group after seeing Kim off. He looked at each face in turn. They were all concerned.

"A human body puts this all in a different perspective," Gloria said.

"I agree," Eleanor said.

There was silence for a few minutes while everyone thought about the situation. David finally spoke: "I guess we have to face the fact that we could be responsible for some of the problems in the area."

"I still think the idea is absurd," Edward said. "It flies in the face of reason."

"How do you explain my T-shirt?" Curt said. He pulled it from a drawer where he'd stuffed it when Kim had suddenly arrived. It was torn and stained. "I ran a test spot of one of these stains. It's blood."

"But it was your blood," Edward said.

"True. But still," Curt said, "how did it happen? I mean, I don't remember."

"It's also hard to explain the cuts and bruises we have on our bodies when we wake up in the morning," François said. "There were even sticks and dead leaves strewn about my floor."

"We must be sleepwalking or the equivalent," David said. "I know we don't want to admit it."

"Well, *I* haven't been sleepwalking," Edward said. He glared at the others. "I'm not entirely sure this isn't some elaborate practical joke after all the playing around you guys have been doing."

"This is no joke," Curt said as he folded up his damaged shirt.

"We've seen nothing with any of the experimental animals that would even suggest a reaction like you're suggesting," Edward said belligerently. "It doesn't make scientific sense. There'd be some corollary. That's why we do animal studies."

"I agree," Eleanor said. "I've not found anything in my room nor do I have any cuts or bruises."

"Well, I'm not hallucinating," David said. "I've got real cuts here." He stuck out his hands so everybody could see them all. "As Curt says, this is no joke."

"I haven't had any cuts, but I've awakened with my hands all dirty," Gloria said. "And I don't have a nail worth mentioning left. They've all broken off."

"There's something wrong despite the fact it hasn't shown up with the animals," David insisted. "I know that no one wants to suggest the obvious, but I will! It must be the Ultra."

Edward's jaws visibly tightened and his hands closed into fists.

"It's taken me a couple of days to admit it even to myself," David continued. "But it's pretty clear I've been out at night without any recollection of going. Nor do I know what I've been up to, except that I'm filthy in the morning when I wake up. And I assure you, I've never done anything like this in my life."

"Are you suggesting that it's not an animal that has been

causing problems around the neighborhood?" Gloria asked timidly.

"Oh, be serious," Edward complained. "Let's not let our imaginations go haywire."

"I'm not suggesting anything other than I've been out and I don't know what I've been doing," David said.

A ripple of fear spread through the group as they began to face the reality of the situation. But it became immediately apparent there were two groups. Edward and Eleanor feared for the future of the project while the others feared for their well-being.

"We have to think about this rationally," Edward said.

"Without doubt," David agreed.

"The drug has been so perfect," Edward said. "We've had nothing but good responses. We've reason to believe it's a natural substance, or close to a natural substance, that already exists in our brains. The monkeys have shown no tendency toward somnambulism. And I personally like the way I feel on Ultra."

Everyone immediately agreed.

"In fact, I think it is a tribute to what Ultra can do that allows us to even think rationally under these circumstances," Edward said.

"You're probably right," Gloria said. "A minute ago I was beside myself with worry and disgust. I already feel more composed."

"That's exactly my point," Edward said. "This is a fantastic drug."

"But we still have a problem," David said. "If the sleepwalking we've suggested is occurring, and if it is caused by the drug, which I think is the only explanation, it has to be a side effect that we couldn't possibly have anticipated. It has to be doing something in our brains that is unique."

"Let me get my PET scans," François said suddenly. He went down to his cluttered workspace but quickly returned. He began laying out a series of brain scans of a monkey that had been given radioactively tagged Ultra.

"I wanted to show everybody something that I just noted this morning," he said. "I really haven't had time to think too much about it, and I wouldn't have noticed it except the computer picked it up when these images were in digital form. If you look carefully, the concentration of the Ultra in the hindbrain, midbrain, and limbic system slowly builds from the first dose, then, when it gets to a certain level, the concentration goes up markedly, meaning there's no steady state reached.''

Everyone bent over the photographs.

"Maybe the point where the concentration increases markedly is at the point that the enzymatic system that metabolizes it is overwhelmed," Gloria suggested.

"I think you are right," François said.

"That means we should look at the key that tells us how much Ultra each of us has been taking," Gloria said.

They all looked at Edward.

"Seems reasonable," Edward said. He walked over to his desk and removed a small locked box. Inside was a three-by-five card with the code that matched dosages.

The group quickly learned that Curt was on the highest dose followed by David on the next highest. On the other end of the scale, Eleanor had the lowest with Edward just behind her.

After a lengthy, rational discussion, they came up with a theory of what was happening. They reasoned that when the concentration of Ultra got to a certain point, it progressively blocked the normal variation of serotonin levels that occurred during sleep, ironing them out and altering sleep patterns.

It was Gloria who suggested that when the concentration got even higher, perhaps to the point where the sharp upward swing of the curve occurred, then the Ultra blocked the radiations from the lower, or reptilian, brain to the higher centers in the cerebral hemispheres. Sleep, like other autonomous function, was regulated by the lower brain areas where the Ultra was massing.

The group was quiet for a time while everyone pondered this hypothesis. Despite their emotional recovery, they all found this idea disturbing.

"If this were the case," David said, "what would happen if we were to wake up while this blockage was in place?''

"It would be as if we'd experienced retroevolution," Curt said. "We'd be functioning on our lower-brain centers alone. We'd be like carnivorous reptiles!''

The shock of this statement quieted everyone with its horrid connotations.

"Wait a minute, everybody," Edward said, trying to cheer himself as well as the others. "We're jumping to conclusions that are not based on fact. This is all complete supposition. We have to remember that we've seen no problems with the monkeys, who we all agree have cerebral hemispheres, although smaller than humans', at least most humans.''

Everyone except Gloria smiled at Edward's humor.

"Even if there is a problem with Ultra," Edward reminded them, "we have to take into consideration the good side of the drug, and how it has positively affected our emotions, mental abilities, acuity of our senses, and even long-term memory. Perhaps we have been taking too much of the drug and we should cut down. Maybe we should cut down to Eleanor's level since all she's experienced are the positive psychological effects.''

"I'm not cutting back," Gloria said defiantly. "I'm stopping as of this minute. It horrifies me to think of the possibility of some primitive creature lurking inside my body without my even being aware and sneaking out to forage in the night.''

"Very colorfully said," Edward remarked. "You are welcome to stop the drug. That goes without saying. No one is going to force anyone to do anything they don't want to do. You all know that. Each person can decide whether to continue taking the drug or not, and here's what I suggest: for an added cushion of safety I think we should halve Eleanor's dose and use that as an upper limit, dropping subsequent doses in one-hundred-milligram steps.''

"That sounds reasonable and safe to me," David said.

"To me as well," Curt said.

"And me," François said.

"Good," Edward said. "I'm absolutely confident that if

the problem is as we've theorized, it has to be dose related, and there has to be a point where the chances of causing the problem is an acceptable risk.''

"I'm not taking it," Gloria restated.

"No problem," Edward said.

"You won't be irritated with me?" Gloria asked.

"Not in the slightest," Edward said.

"I'll be able to be a control," Gloria said. "Plus I'll be able to watch over the others at night."

"Excellent idea," Edward said.

"I have a suggestion," François said. "Perhaps we should all take radioactively tagged Ultra so I can follow the buildup and chart concentrations in our brains. The ultimate dose of Ultra might be that dose which merely maintains a specific level of Ultra without continually increasing it."

"I'd agree to that idea," Curt said.

"One other thing," Edward said. "I'm sure I don't have to remind all you professionals, but this meeting must be kept secret from everyone, including your families."

"That goes without saying," David said. "The last thing any of us wants to do is compromise Ultra's future. We might have a little growing pains here and there, but it's still going to be the drug of the century."

Kim had intended to spend some time in the castle during the morning, but when she got back to the cottage she realized it was already lunchtime. While she was eating, the phone rang. To her surprise it was Katherine Sturburg, the archivist at Harvard who had a particular interest in Increase Mather.

"I might have some potentially good news for you," Katherine said. "I've just found a reference to a work by Rachel Bingham!"

"That's marvelous," Kim said. "I'd given up hope of help from Harvard."

"We do the best we can," Katherine said.

"How did you happen to find it?" Kim asked.

"That's the best part," Katherine said. "What I did was go back and reread the letter you let us copy from Increase Mather. Because of his reference to a law school, I accessed the Law School library data bank, and the name popped up. Why it's not cross-referenced in our main data bank I have yet to figure out. But the good news is the work seemed to have survived the 1764 fire.''

"I thought everything was burned," Kim said.

"Just about everything," Katherine said. "Fortunately for us, about two hundred books out of the five thousand-volume library survived because they were out on loan. So someone must have been reading the book you are looking for. At any rate, the reference I found indicated that it was transferred to the Law School from the main library in Harvard Hall in 1818, a year after the Law School was founded."

"Did you find the book itself?" Kim asked excitedly.

"No, I haven't had time," Katherine said. "Besides, I think it would be better if you took it from here. What I recommend is that you give Helen Arnold a call. She's an archivist at the Law School. I'll call her first thing Monday morning so that she'll expect a call or a visit."

"I'll go right after work on Monday," Kim said eagerly. "I get off at three."

"I'm sure that will be fine," Katherine said. "I'll let Helen know."

Kim thanked Katherine before they disconnected.

Kim felt ecstatic. She'd totally given up hope that Elizabeth's book had survived the Harvard fire. Then Kim questioned why Katherine had been so sure it was a book. Had it said as much on the reference?

Kim went back to the phone and tried to call Katherine right back. Unfortunately she wasn't able to reach her. A secretary said that Katherine had rushed out to a luncheon meeting and wouldn't be back to the office until Monday.

Kim hung up the phone. She was disappointed but didn't remain so for long. The idea that on Monday afternoon she would finally learn the nature of the evidence used against Elizabeth was a source of great satisfaction. Whether it was a book or not did not matter.

Despite this good news, Kim still went to the castle to work. In fact, she attacked the jumble of papers with new enthusiasm.

Halfway through the afternoon she paused long enough to try to estimate how much longer she thought it would take for her to finish sorting the material. After counting all the remaining trunks and boxes and assuming about the same number existed in the wine cellar, she figured out it would take another week if she were to work for eight hours a day.

The reality of that fact robbed Kim of some of her enthusiasm. Now that she was about to start back to work at the hospital, it wasn't going to be so easy to find the time. She was about to give up for the afternoon when she surprised herself by pulling off a stunt reminiscent of Kinnard's. She opened a drawer at random and pulled out a letter addressed to Ronald!

Sitting on a trunk by a window, Kim took the letter from its envelope. It was another letter from Samuel Sewall. Looking at the date, Kim could tell that it had been sent just days before Elizabeth's execution.

15th July 1692
Boston

Sir,

I have come from a comfortable supper with the most Reverend Cotton Mather and we did indeed discours upon the sorry plight of your wife and we are much in troubled spirit for you and your children. In a most gracious way Reverend Mather agreed to accept your distracted wife into his household to cure her as he most successfully did with the much afflicted Goodwin girl if only Elizabeth will confess and repent in publique the covenant she'd entered with the Prince of Lies. Reverend Mather is strongly convinced that Elizabeth can furnish with evidence and argument as a critical eye witness to confute the sadducism of this troubled age. Failing that Reverend Mather cannot and will not intervene in carrying out of the sentence of the court. Be advised that there is no time to waste. Reverend Mather is eager and believes that your wife can teach us all about matters of the invisible world that doth threaten our country. God bless your endeavors and I remain

Your Friend,
Samuel Sewall.

For a few minutes Kim stared out the window. The day had started cloudless and blue, but now dark clouds were blowing in from the west. From where she was sitting she could see the cottage sitting among its birch trees whose leaves had become bright yellow. The combination of the old house and the letter transported Kim back three hundred years, and she could feel the utter panic brought on by the impending reality of Elizabeth's execution. Although the letter she'd just read had been to Ronald rather than from him, she got the impression it was a response from a letter Ronald had written in desperation to save his wife's life.

Kim's eyes filled up with tears. It was hard for her to imagine the agony Ronald must have experienced. It made Kim feel guilty that she'd had suspicions of Ronald back when she'd first started to learn the truth about Elizabeth.

Kim finally got up. Replacing the letter in its envelope, she carried it downstairs to the wine cellar and deposited it with the other material in the Bible box. Then she left the castle and started back toward the cottage.

Kim got halfway and slowed her pace. Glancing toward the lab, she stopped walking. She looked at her watch. It was not quite four. All at once the idea occurred to her that it would be a nice gesture to make an attempt at improving the researchers' diet. They'd seemed depressed when she'd stopped in that morning, and she imagined they must be sick of pizza. Kim reasoned she could easily repeat the steak-and-fish dinner she'd made somewhat less than a fortnight previously.

With this thought in mind, Kim changed her direction and headed for the lab. As she passed through the reception area she felt mild apprehension since she never quite knew what to expect. Entering the lab proper, Kim let the door close behind her. No one came running over to greet her.

Kim set off toward Edward's area. She passed David, who greeted her pleasantly but with hardly the buoyancy he had a few days previously. Kim said hello to Gloria, who, like David, immediately turned her attention back to her work.

Kim continued on her way, but she felt progressively wary. Although David's and Gloria's behavior was probably the most normal Kim had experienced since they had arrived, it represented another change.

Edward was so engrossed in his work that Kim had to tap his shoulder twice to get his attention. She noticed that he was making new Ultra capsules.

"Is there a problem?" he asked. He smiled and acted reasonably happy to see her.

"I wanted to make you and the others an offer," Kim said. "How about a repeat of the dinner that we had a few weeks ago. I'd be happy to run into town and get the food."

"That's very sweet of you," Edward said. "But not tonight. We can't take the time. We'll just order in some pizza."

"I promise you wouldn't have to take much time," Kim said.

"I said no!" Edward hissed between clenched teeth, causing Kim to take a step back. But Edward immediately regained his composure and smiled again. "Pizza will do just fine."

"If that's how you feel," Kim said with a mixture of confusion and apprehension. It had been as if Edward had momentarily teetered on the edge of control for a few seconds. "Are you all right?" she asked hesitantly.

"Yes!" he snapped, but then quickly smiled again. "We're all a little preoccupied. We had a minor setback but it's under control."

Kim took several more steps backward. "Well, if you change your mind in the next hour or so I can still go into town," she said. "I'll be at the cottage. Just call."

"We're really much too busy," Edward said. "You go ahead and eat, but thanks for offering. I'll let everyone know you were thinking of them."

As Kim departed, none of the researchers acknowledged her or even looked up from their work. When she got outside she sighed and shook her head. She was amazed at how changeable the atmosphere in the lab was and wondered how the people could live with themselves. Kim was coming to the conclusion that she had little in common with the scientific personality.

After dinner there was still plenty of light to go back to the castle, but Kim couldn't get herself to return. Instead she vegetated in front of the TV. She'd hoped that watching several mindless sitcoms would get the experience in the lab out of her mind, but the more she thought about her interaction with Edward and the others, the more disturbed she became.

Kim tried to read, but she couldn't concentrate. Instead she found herself wishing she'd been able to follow up that afternoon on the lead involving the Law School. Feeling progressively more nervous as the evening dragged on, Kim began to think about Kinnard. She wondered who he was with and what he was doing. She also wondered if he ever thought about her.

Kim awakened with a start despite having again taken a Xanax to slow her churning mind. It was pitch black in her bedroom, and a glance at her clock told her she'd been asleep only for a short time. Settling back into her pillow, she listened to the night sounds of the house, trying to decide what could have awakened her so abruptly.

Then she heard several dull thumps coming from the back of the house that sounded like her new rubberized trash cans hitting up against the clapboard. Kim stiffened as she thought of a black bear or a rabid raccoon trying to get at her garbage, which she knew contained chicken skin and bones.

After switching on her bedside light, Kim got out of bed. She put on her robe and slipped her feet into her slippers. She gave Sheba a reassuring pat. Kim was thankful she'd been keeping the animal inside.

Hearing the thumping yet again, Kim hurried through the short hall into Edward's room. Switching on the light, she discovered that Edward's bed was empty. Thinking he must still be in the lab, and concerned about his walking back in the dark, Kim went back into her bedroom and dialed the lab number. After ten rings she gave up.

Kim took out the flashlight she kept in her bedside table

and started down the stairs. Her intention was to shine the light out the kitchen window where the trash cans were stored, hoping to scare away whatever animal was out there.

As Kim rounded the turn in the stairs, giving her a view of the foyer, she froze. She saw something that made her blood run cold. The front door was wide open.

At first Kim could not move. She was paralyzed with the terrorizing thought that the creature, whatever it was, had come into her house and was that moment stalking her through the darkness.

Kim listened intently, but all she could hear was the chorus of the last tree frogs of the season. A cool wet breeze wafted in through the open doorway and swirled around Kim's bare legs. Outside, a light rain was falling.

The house was deathly silent, giving her the hope that the animal had not come in. Kim descended the steps one at a time. After each step she hesitated and strained to hear some telltale sound of an animal intruder. But the house remained quiet.

Kim reached the open door and grasped the knob. Looking back and forth from the darkened dining room to the parlor, she began to close the door. She was fearful of moving too quickly lest she provoke an attack. She had the door almost closed when she glanced outside. She gasped.

Sheba was sitting about twenty feet away from the front of the house in the middle of the flagstone walkway. She was blissfully ignoring the drizzle while calmly licking her paw and rubbing it over the top of her head.

At first Kim could not believe her eyes since she thought she'd just seen the cat on her bed. Obviously Sheba had sensed the front door was open while Kim was checking on Edward, and had come down to take advantage of the opportunity to get outside.

Kim took several deep breaths to try to rid herself of the heavy, drugged feeling that clouded her brain. Terrified about what was possibly lurking in the nearby shadows, she was reluctant to call out to the animal, who probably would have ignored her anyway.

Sensing she had little choice, Kim slipped through the

door. After a quick scan of the immediate area, she dashed to the cat, snatched it from the ground, and turned, only to see the front door closing.

Screaming a silent "no," Kim lunged for the door, but she was too late. It shut with a heavy thud followed by a sharp metallic click of the bolt engaging the striker plate.

Kim vainly tried the handle. It was locked as she'd expected. She pushed the door ineffectually with her shoulder, but it was of no use.

Hunching her shoulders against the cold rain, Kim slowly turned to face the blackness of the night. She shivered with fear and cold, marveling at her desperate circumstance. She was in her robe and pajamas, locked out of her house on a rainy night with a disgruntled cat in one hand and an ineffectual flashlight in the other, facing an unknown nocturnal creature lurking somewhere in the shrubbery.

Sheba struggled to be put down and audibly complained. Kim shushed her. Stepping away from the house, Kim scanned the front casement windows, but all were shut. She knew they were locked. Turning around, she gauged the distance to the lab, where the lights were finally off. Then she looked at the castle. The castle was farther away, but she knew the doors to the wings were unlocked. She didn't know about the door to the lab.

Suddenly Kim heard the sound of a large creature moving in the gravel along the right side of the house. Knowing she could not stay where she was, she ran in the opposite direction, going around the left side of the house, away from the approaching bear or whatever animal had been at her new trash containers.

Desperately Kim tried the kitchen door. But it was locked, as she was sure it would be. Using her shoulder, she hit it several times, but it was no use. All she managed to do was make the cat howl.

Turning from the house, she spied the shed. Clutching the cat closer to her chest and holding the flashlight like a club, Kim ran as quickly as her backless mules would allow. When she got to the shed, she undid the hook that held the door closed, opened it, and squeezed into the shed's inner blackness.

Kim pulled the door shut behind her. Just to the right of the door was a tiny, dirty window that afforded a meager view of the yard behind the cottage. The only illumination came from a pool of light spilling from her bedroom window and the luminous glow of the low swirling cloud cover.

As she watched, a hulking figure rounded the house from the same direction she had come. It was a person, not an animal, but he was acting in a most peculiar fashion. Kim watched him pause to smell the wind just as an animal might do. To her dismay he turned in her direction and appeared to be staring at the shed. In the darkness she could see no features, just his dark silhouette.

Dismay turned to horror as Kim watched the figure lurch toward her with a slow, dragging gait, still sniffing the air as if following a scent. Kim held her breath and prayed the cat would be still. When the figure was a mere ten feet away, Kim shrank back into the dark recess of the shed, pushing against tools and bicycles.

She could now hear his footfalls in the gravel. They came closer, then stopped. There was an agonizing pause. Kim held her breath.

Suddenly the door was rudely yanked open. Losing control, Kim screamed. Sheba answered with her own scream and leaped from Kim's arms. The man screamed as well.

Kim grasped the flashlight in both hands and turned it on, flashing the beam directly into the man's face. He shielded himself from the unexpected blast of light with his hands and forearms.

Kim's mouth clamped shut in surprised relief. She recognized it was Edward!

"Thank God," she said, lowering the flashlight.

Scrambling from her position wedged among bikes, lawnmower, and old trash containers, Kim burst from the shed and threw her arms around Edward. The beam of her flashlight played hapazardly in the trees.

For a moment Edward did not move. He looked down on her with a blank expression.

"I can't tell you how glad I am to see your face," Kim

said, leaning back so she could look into his dark eye sockets. "I've never been so scared in my life."

Edward did not respond.

"Edward?" Kim asked, moving her head to try to see him better. "Are you all right?"

Edward exhaled noisily. "I'm fine," he said at last. He was angry. "No thanks to you. What in the hell are you doing out here in the shed in the middle of the night, dressed in your robe, scaring me half out of my wits?"

Kim apologized effusively, stumbling over her words as she realized how much she must have frightened him. She explained what had happened. By the time she was finished, she could see that Edward was smiling.

"It's not funny," she added. But now that she was safe, she smiled too.

"I can't believe you'd risk life and limb for that lazy old cat," he said. "Come on! Let's get in out of this rain."

Kim went back into the shed and with the aid of the flashlight located Sheba. The cat was hiding in the far corner behind a row of yard tools. Kim enticed her into the open and picked her up. Then she and Edward went into the house.

"I'm freezing," she said. "I need something hot like herbal tea. Would you like some?"

"I'll sit with you for a moment," Edward said.

While Kim put the water on to boil, Edward explained his side of the story. "I had intended to work all night," he said. "But by one-thirty I had to admit it was impossible. My body is so accustomed to going to sleep around one, I couldn't keep my eyes open. It was all I could do to walk from the lab to the cottage without lying down in the grass. When I got to the house I opened the door and then remembered I was carrying a bag full of the remains of our pizza dinner which I was supposed to put in the Dumpster at the lab. So I went around back to put it into our trash. I guess I left the door open, which I shouldn't have done if only because of mosquitoes. Anyway, I couldn't get the goddamn covers off the trash containers, and the harder I tried the more frustrated I became. I even hit them a couple of times."

"They're new," Kim explained.

"Well, I hope they came with directions," Edward said.

"It's easy in the light," Kim said.

"I finally gave up," Edward said. "When I came back around the house, the door was closed. I also thought I smelled your cologne. Since I've been taking Ultra, my sense of smell has improved remarkably. I followed the scent around the house and eventually to the shed."

Kim poured herself a mug of the hot tea. "Are you sure you don't want any?" she asked.

"I couldn't," Edward said. "Just sitting here is a strain. I've got to go to sleep. It's as if my body weighs five tons, including my eyelids." Edward slipped off the stool and staggered. Kim reached out and steadied him.

"I'm okay," he said. "When I'm this tired it takes me a second to get my bearings."

Kim listened to him struggle up the stairs while she put away the tea and the honey. Picking up her mug, she followed him. At the head of the stairs she looked into his room. He was on his bed asleep with his clothes half off.

Kim went into the room, and with a great deal of difficulty got his pants and shirt all the way off and put him under the covers. She turned out his light. She felt jealous how easily he could fall asleep. It was such a contrast with herself.

# 18

## Sunday,
## October 2, 1994

IN THE MISTY PREDAWN LIGHT EDWARD AND THE RE-searchers met halfway between the cottage and the castle and trooped silently through the wet grass to the lab. They were all in a somber mood. Inside, they poured themselves cups of morning coffee.

Edward was considerably more dour than the others, and he had improved from a half hour earlier when he'd first awakened. As he'd gotten out of bed he'd been shocked to find a carcass of a chicken on the floor that looked as if it had come from someone's garbage. It was encrusted with coffee grounds. Then he'd noticed his fingernails were filthy, as if he'd been digging dirt. In the bathroom he'd looked in the mirror and saw that his face and undershirt were both smeared with filth.

Everyone carried their coffee to the area of the lab they used for their meetings. François was the first to speak. "Even though my dose of Ultra was more than halved, I was still out last night," he said gloomily. "When I woke up this morning I was as dirty as I'd ever been. I must have been crawling in the mud. I had to wash my sheets! And look at my hands." He extended his hands, palms up, to show a myriad of shallow cuts and scratches. "My pajamas were so dirty I had to dispose of them."

"I was out too," Curt admitted.

"I'm afraid I was as well," David said.

"What do you think the chances are we wander off the property?" François asked.

"There's no way to know," David said. "But it's onc

hell of a disturbing thought. What if we had something to do with that vagrant?''

"Don't even bring up the possibility," Gloria snapped. "It's beyond contemplation."

"The immediate problem could be the police or some local inhabitant," François said. "If everyone in the town is as worked up as Kim says they are, one of us might be confronted if we go beyond the fence."

"It's certainly a concern," David said. "I suppose there's no way to know how we'd react."

"If we're functioning on our reptilian brains, I think we can imagine," Curt said. "It would be a survival instinct. We'd undoubtedly fight back. I don't think we should delude ourselves. We'd be violent."

"This has got to stop," François said.

"Well, I certainly wasn't out," Eleanor said. "So it's got to be dose-related."

"I agree," Edward said. "Let's halve our doses again. That will take the maximum to one fourth of Eleanor's original dose."

"I'm afraid that might not be enough," Gloria said. Everyone swung around to look at her. "I didn't take any Ultra yesterday, and I'm afraid I still went out. I'd intended to stay awake to make sure no one else did, but I found it virtually impossible to keep from falling asleep no matter what I did."

"Falling asleep quickly is something I've been doing since I began taking Ultra," Curt said. "I thought it was due to the level of activity it caused during the day. Maybe it has something to do with the drug itself."

Everyone agreed with Curt and added that when they awoke in the morning they'd had the feeling they had had a particularly good night's sleep.

"I even feel rested this morning," François said. "I find that especially surprising with the evidence that I'd been out running around in the rain."

For a few minutes everyone was silent as they pondered the dilemma posed by Gloria's revelation that even though she'd stopped taking the drug, she'd still experienced somnambulism.

Edward finally broke the silence. "All our studies show that Ultra is metabolized at a reasonable rate, certainly a lot faster than Prozac," he said. "Gloria's experience only indicates that the concentration in her lower brain is still higher than the threshold for this unfortunate complication. Maybe we should cut our doses even more, like even a factor of a hundred."

François again held out his hands for everyone to see. "These cuts are telling me something," he said. "I don't want to take this risk anymore. Obviously I'm out wandering around with no comprehension of what I'm doing. I don't want to get shot or run over because I'm acting like an animal. I'm stopping the drug."

"I feel the same," David said.

"It's only reasonable," Curt said.

"All right," Edward said reluctantly. "You all have a point. It's unconscionable for us to take any chances with our safety or the safety of anyone else. We all liked to think of ourselves as animals while we were in college, but I guess we've outgrown the urge."

Everyone smiled at Edward's humor.

"Let's stop the drug and reevaluate in a few days," Edward said agreeably. "As soon as the drug is out of our systems, we can contemplate starting again at much lower dosages."

"I'm not going to take the drug until we find an animal system that mimics this somnambulistic effect," Gloria said. "I think it should be studied completely before any more human use is considered."

"We respect your opinion," Edward said. "As I've always indicated, self-medication is totally voluntary. I should remind you that it was my intention for me to take the drug alone in the first place."

"What are we going to do in the interim for safety?" François asked.

"Perhaps we should run EEGs while we're sleeping," Gloria suggested. "We could rig them with a computer to wake us if the normal sleep patterns change."

"Brilliant idea," Edward said. "I'll see that the equipment is ordered on Monday."

"What about tonight?" François asked.

Everyone thought for a few moments.

"Hopefully there won't be a problem," Edward said. "After all, Gloria was on the second-highest dose and probably had significantly high blood levels in relation to her body weight. I think we should all check our blood levels with hers. If they're lower, maybe we'll be okay. Probably the only person who poses a significant risk is Curt."

"Thanks a lot," he said with a laugh. "Why don't you just put me in one of the monkey cages?"

"Not a bad idea," David said.

Curt took a playful swipe at David's head.

"Perhaps we should sleep in shifts," François said. "We can watch over each other."

"Sleeping in shifts is a good idea," Edward said. "Plus, if we do blood levels today we'll be able to correlate them with any episodes of somnambulism tonight."

"You know, this might all turn out for the best," Gloria said. "By stopping Ultra we'll have a great opportunity to follow blood and urine levels and relate them to residual psychological effects. Everybody should be sensitive to any 'depressive' symptoms in case there's a rebound phenomenon. The monkey studies have suggested there are no withdrawal symptoms, but that must be confirmed."

"We might as well make the best of it," Edward agreed. "Meanwhile we've got an enormous amount of work to do. And it goes without saying that everything we've been discussing must remain a highly guarded secret until we've had a chance to isolate the problem and eliminate it."

Kim looked at the clock and blinked. She couldn't believe her eyes. It was almost ten o'clock. She'd slept later than she had since she'd been in college.

Sitting on the edge of the bed, she suddenly recalled the scary episode in the shed. It had truly terrified her. After the event she'd found herself so wound up that she'd not been able to fall back asleep. She'd tried for almost two hours before she gave up and took another half Xanax. Finally she'd been able to calm down, but when she did, she found herself thinking about Thomas Goodman's letter that had described

Elizabeth's flight to the shed, no doubt under the influence of poisonous mold. Kim felt it was another coincidence that in her panic she'd run to the very same shed.

Kim showered, dressed, and had breakfast in hopes of reviving enough to enjoy the day. Her attempt was only partially successful. She felt sluggish from the double dose of medication. She also felt anxious. The sheer unpleasantness of what had happened during the night, combined with her general agitation, was too much for the medication. She needed something more, and sorting old documents in the castle wasn't going to be adequate. Kim needed some human contact, and she missed the convenience and resources of the city.

Sitting down at the phone, Kim tried a number of friends in Boston. But she did not have much luck. All she got was answering machines. She left her number on some of them but did not expect a call back until evening. Her friends were active people, and there was a lot to do on a fall Sunday in Boston.

Feeling a strong urge to get away from the compound, Kim called Kinnard's number. As the call went through, she almost hoped he wouldn't answer; she wasn't sure what she would say to him. As luck would have it, he picked up on the second ring.

They exchanged pleasantries. Kim was nervous. She tried to hide it, but not very successfully.

"Are you okay?" Kinnard asked after a pause. "You sound a little strange."

Kim struggled to think of something to say, but she couldn't. She felt confused, embarrassed, and suddenly emotional.

"Just not answering is telling me something," Kinnard said. "Can I help somehow? Is something wrong?"

Kim took a deep breath to get herself under control. "You can help," she said finally. "I need to get away from Salem. I've called several girlfriends, but no one is home. I had it in mind to come into town and spend the night since I have to be at work in the morning."

"Why don't you stay here?" Kinnard asked. "I'll just move my exercise bike and eighty thousand copies of the

*New England Journal of Medicine* out of my guest room, and it's all yours. Besides, I've got the day off. I'm sure we could have some fun.''

"Do you honestly think it's a good idea?"

"I'll behave myself if that's your worry," Kinnard said with a laugh.

Kim wondered if she was more worried about behaving herself.

"Come on," Kinnard encouraged. "It sounds like it will do you good to get out of suburbia for a day and an evening."

"All right," Kim said with sudden determination.

"Great!" Kinnard said. "What time will you be here?"

"What about in an hour?" Kim said.

"See you then," Kinnard said.

Kim replaced the receiver. She wasn't sure what she was doing, but it felt right. Getting up, she climbed the stairs and got her things together, remembering her uniform for work. In the kitchen she put extra food out for Sheba and changed the Kitty Litter box by the back door.

After putting her things in the car, Kim drove over to the lab. Just before she entered the building she paused to think about whether she should specifically mention that she was staying with Kinnard. She decided she wouldn't bring it up, but she'd tell Edward if he asked.

The atmosphere in the lab was even more intense than on her previous visit. Everyone was absorbed in their work, and although they acknowledged her, they did it perfunctorily.

Kim didn't mind. In fact she preferred it. The last thing she needed at the moment was a long lecture on some arcane experiment.

She found Edward at his printer. His computer was busy spilling out data. He smiled at her, but the smile was fleeting. In the next second his mind was back on what was coming out of the printer.

"I'm going into Boston for the day," Kim said brightly.

"Good," Edward said.

"I'll be spending the night," Kim said. "I could leave a number if you'd like."

"It won't be necessary," Edward said. "If there's any problem, call me. I'll be here as usual."

Kim said goodbye and started for the door. Edward called to her. She stopped.

"I'm really sorry I'm so preoccupied," Edward said. "I wish we weren't so busy. We've got an emergency of sorts."

"I understand," Kim said. She looked at Edward's face. There was a hint of awkwardness she'd not seen for some time.

Kim hurried from the lab and got in her car. She drove out of the compound with Edward's demeanor on her mind. It was as if the old persona of Edward were reemerging: the persona she'd been attracted to when they'd first met.

It didn't take long for Kim to begin to relax, and the farther south she drove, the better she felt. The weather helped. It was a hot, Indian summer day with bright sunshine and fall clarity. Here and there were trees tinted with a hint of their dazzling fall foliage. The sky was so blue, it looked like one vast celestial ocean.

Sunday was not a difficult day for parking, and Kim found a spot within easy walking distance of Kinnard's apartment on Revere Street. She was nervous when she rang his bell, but he immediately made her feel comfortable. He helped carry her things into his guest room, which he'd obviously taken the time to clean.

Kinnard took Kim on an invigorating walk around the city, and for a number of blissful hours she forgot about Omni, Ultra, and Elizabeth. They started in the North End with lunch at an Italian restaurant followed by espressos in an Italian café.

For an entertaining interlude they ducked into Filene's Basement for a quick scouting of the merchandise. Both were experienced Filene's Basement shoppers. Kim surprised herself by finding a great skirt originally from Saks Fifth Avenue.

After their shopping they strolled around the Boston Gardens and enjoyed the fall foliage and flowers. They sat for a while on one of the park benches and watched the swan boats glide around the lake.

"I probably shouldn't say this," Kinnard said, "but you do look a bit tired to me."

"I'm not surprised," Kim said. "I haven't been sleeping well. Living in Salem hasn't been particularly idyllic."

"Anything you want to talk about?" Kinnard said.

"Not at the moment," Kim said. "I suppose I'm confused about a lot of things."

"I'm glad you came for a visit," Kinnard said.

"I want to make sure you understand that I'm definitely staying in the guest room," Kim said quickly.

"Hey, relax," Kinnard said, lifting up his hands as if to defend himself. "I understand. We're friends, remember?"

"I'm sorry," Kim said. "I must seem hyper to you. The fact of the matter is that I'm the most relaxed I've been in weeks." She reached over and gave Kinnard's hand a squeeze. "Thank you for being my friend."

After leaving the park, they walked down Newbury Street and window-shopped. Then they indulged in one of Kim's favorite Boston pastimes. They went into Waterstone's Booksellers and browsed. Kim bought a paperback Dick Francis novel while Kinnard bought a travel book on Sicily. He said it was a place he always wanted to go.

Late in the afternoon they stopped into an Indian restaurant and had a delicious tandoor-style dinner. The only problem was that the restaurant lacked a liquor license. Both agreed the spicy food would have been far better with cold beer.

From the Indian restaurant they walked back to Beacon Hill. Sitting on Kinnard's couch, they each had a glass of cold white wine. Kim soon felt herself getting sleepy.

She turned in early in anticipation of having to get up at the crack of dawn for work. She did not need any Xanax when she slipped between Kinnard's freshly laundered sheets. Almost immediately she fell into a deep, restful sleep.

# 19

## Monday,
## October 3, 1994

KIM HAD ALMOST FORGOTTEN HOW HARD A NORMAL day was in the SICU. She was the first to acknowledge that after a month's vacation she was out of shape for both the physical and emotional stamina that was needed. But as the day drew to a close, she had to admit that she'd truly enjoyed the intensity, the challenge, and the sense of accomplishment of helping people in dire need, not to mention the comradeship of shared endeavor.

Kinnard had appeared several times during the day with patients coming from surgery. Kim made it a point to be available to help. She thanked him again for the best night's sleep she'd had in weeks. He told her that she was welcome anytime, even that night, despite the fact that he was on call and would be spending the night in the hospital.

Kim would have liked to stay. After her isolation at the compound, she'd enjoyed being in Boston, and she'd become nostalgic for the time she'd lived there. But she knew she had to get back. She wasn't under any delusion that Edward would be available, but she still felt a strong obligation to be there.

As soon as Kim's shift was over, she walked to the corner of Charles and Cambridge streets and caught the Red Line to Harvard Square. The trains were frequent at that hour, and after only twenty minutes she was walking northwest on Massachusetts Avenue on her way to the Harvard Law School.

Kim slowed her pace when she realized she was perspiring. It was another hot Indian summer day, without the previous day's crystalline clarity. There was no breeze whatsoever, and a hazy, muggy canopy was stalled over the city, making it seem more like summer than fall. The weatherman warned of possible violent thunderstorms.

Kim got directions to the Law Library from a student. She found it with no difficulty. The air-conditioned interior was a relief.

Another inquiry directed her to Helen Arnold's office. Kim gave her name to a secretary and was told she'd have to wait. No sooner had Kim sat down when a tall, slender, and strikingly attractive black woman appeared in a connecting doorway and waved her in.

"I'm Helen Arnold, and I've got some good news for you," the woman said enthusiastically. She led Kim into her office and motioned for her to sit down.

Kim was struck by the woman's appearance. It wasn't what she expected at a law school library. Her hair was done in the most exquisite cornrows Kim had ever seen, and her dress was a brilliantly colored silk chemise loosely gathered at the waist with a gold chain belt.

"I spoke this morning, quite early if you must know, with Ms. Sturburg, who is a wonderful woman by the way, and she told me all about your interest in a work by Rachel Bingham."

Kim nodded through this dialogue which Helen delivered in rapid-fire.

"Have you found it?" Kim asked as soon as Helen paused.

"Yes and no," Helen said. She smiled warmly. "The good news is that I confirmed Katherine Sturburg's belief that the work survived the fire of 1764. I am absolutely sure of this. Mark my word. Apparently it had been rather permanently housed in the chambers of one of the tutors who'd lived outside Old Harvard Hall. Isn't that good news?"

"I'm pleased," Kim said. "In fact I'm thrilled it wasn't destroyed. But you qualified your answer to my question whether you'd found it. What did you mean by 'yes and no'?"

"I meant simply that although I hadn't found the book

itself, I did find reference to the fact that the work did indeed come here to the Law School for the Law Library. I also learned there'd been some confusion and difficulty of how or where to file the work, although it had something to do with Ecclesiastic Law as your letter from Increase Mather suggested. By the way, I thought the letter was a fabulous find, and I understand you have offered to give it to Harvard. That's very generous of you."

"It's the least I could do for all this trouble I've caused," Kim said. "But what about the Rachel Bingham work? Does anybody know where it might be?"

"There is someone," Helen said. "After a bit more digging around, I discovered the work had been transferred from the Law Library to the Divinity School in 1825, right after the construction of Divinity Hall. I don't know why it was transferred; perhaps it had something to do with the filing difficulties here at the Law Library."

"My Lord!" Kim exclaimed. "What a journey this book has had."

"I took the liberty of calling my counterpart over at the Divinity School Library just before noon," Helen said. "I hope you don't mind."

"Of course I don't mind," Kim said. She was pleased Helen had taken the initiative.

"Her name is Gertrude Havermeyer," Helen said. "She's something of a battleax, but she's got a good heart. She promised she'd look right into it." Helen took a piece of note paper and wrote down Gertrude's name and phone number. She then took out a single-sheet map of the Harvard campus and circled the Divinity School.

A few minutes later Kim was on her way across the campus. She passed the Physics Lab and skirted the Museum Building to reach Divinity Avenue. From there it was just a few steps to Gertrude Havermeyer's office.

"So you're the reason my entire afternoon has been wasted," Gertrude said when Kim introduced herself. Gertrude Havermeyer was standing in front of her desk with her hands aggressively settled on her hips. As Helen Arnold had suggested, Gertrude projected a severe, uncompromising temperament. Otherwise her bravado belied her appearance. She was a petite, white-haired woman who squinted at Kim through wire-rimmed trifocals.

"I'm sorry if I've inconvenienced you," Kim said guiltily.

"Since I took the call from Helen Arnold I've not had a second to do my own work," Gertrude complained. "It's taken me literally hours."

"I hope at least your efforts weren't in vain," Kim said.

"I did find a receipt in a ledger from that period," Gertrude said. "So Helen was right. The Rachel Bingham work was sent from the Law School, and it did arrive here at the Divinity School. But as luck would have it, I could not find any reference to the book in the computer or in the old card catalogue or even in the very old catalogue which we've saved in the basement."

Kim's heart fell. "I'm so sorry to have put you through all this for nothing," she said.

"Well, I didn't give up there," Gertrude said. "Not on your life. When I get committed to something, I don't let it rest. So I went back through all the old handwritten cards from when the library was first organized. It was frustrating, but I did find another reference more by luck than anything else except perseverance. For the life of me I cannot figure out why it wasn't included in the main library index."

Kim's hopes brightened. Following the trail of Elizabeth's evidence was like riding an emotional roller coaster. "Is the work still here?" she asked.

"Heavens, no," Gertrude said indignantly. "If it were, it would have been in the computer. We run a tight ship here. No, the final reference I found indicated that it had been sent to the Medical School in 1826 after being here for less than a year. Apparently no one knew where to put the material. It's all very mysterious because there wasn't even an indication of what category it belonged to."

"Oh, for goodness' sake," Kim said with frustration. "Searching for this book or whatever it might be is getting too much. It's becoming a bad joke."

"Buck up!" Gertrude ordered. "I went through a lot of effort on your behalf. I even called over to the Countway

Medical Library and spoke to John Moldavian, who's in charge of rare books and manuscripts. I told him the story, and he assured me he'd look right into it.''

After thanking Gertrude, Kim went back to Harvard Square and reboarded the Red Line for Boston.

It was now rush hour, and Kim had to squeeze onto the train. There were no seats so she had to stand. As the train thundered over the Longfellow Bridge, Kim began to think seriously about giving up the whole Elizabeth quest. It had been like chasing a mirage. Every time she thought she was getting close, it turned out to be a false lead.

Climbing into her car in the MGH garage, Kim started the engine and then thought about the heavy traffic she'd be facing on her way out to Salem. At that hour just getting through the Leverett Circle interchange would probably take close to a half hour.

With a change of heart, Kim turned her car in the opposite direction and headed for the Countway Medical Library. She'd decided she might as well follow up on Gertrude's lead rather than sit in traffic.

John Moldavian seemed perfectly suited for work in a library. He was a soft-spoken, gentle man whose love for books was immediately apparent by the affectionate and caring manner he handled them.

Kim introduced herself and mentioned Gertrude's name. John responded immediately by searching for something among the clutter on his desk.

"I've got something here for you," he said. "Where in the devil did I put it?"

Kim watched him as he shuffled through his papers. He had a thin face dominated by heavy black-framed glasses. His thin mustache looked almost too perfect, as if it had been drawn with an eyebrow pencil.

"Is the Rachel Bingham work here at the library?" Kim hazarded to ask.

"No, it's no longer here," John said. Then his face brightened. "Ah, here's what I wanted." He lifted a single sheet of copy paper.

Kim silently sighed. So much for the Gertrude lead, she thought.

"I looked through the Medical School Library records for 1826," John said. "And I found this reference to the work you're seeking."

"Let me guess," Kim said. "It was sent somewhere else."

John regarded Kim over the top of the paper he was holding. "How did you guess?" he asked.

Kim gave a short laugh. "It's been a pattern," she said. "Where did it go from here?"

"It went to the Department of Anatomy," John said. "Of course today it is called the Department of Cell Biology."

Kim shook her head in disbelief. "Why on earth would it have been sent there?" she asked rhetorically.

"I've no idea," John said. "The entry I found was rather strange. It was in the form of a hastily handwritten card that had apparently been attached to the book or manuscript or drawing. I made you a copy." John handed the paper to Kim.

Kim took it. It was hard to read, forcing her to turn herself in order to take advantage of the light coming through the window. It seemed to say: *Curiosity by Rachel Bingham contrived in 1691.* Looking at the word "curiosity" reminded Kim of Mary Custland telling her that a "repository of curiosities" had been lost in the 1764 fire, suggesting that the Rachel Bingham work had been a part of that collection. Thinking back to Jonathan's letter to his father, Kim surmised that the handwriting she was now looking at was Jonathan's. In her mind's eye she could see a nervous Jonathan Stewart rapidly scribbling the card in a panic to get out of the tutor's chamber where he'd surreptitiously entered to change the name to Rachel Bingham. Had he been discovered he probably would have been asked to leave the college.

"I called over to the department chairman," John said, interrupting Kim's ruminations. "He referred me to another gentleman by the name of Carl Nebolsine, who's the curator in charge of the Warren Anatomical Museum. So I called him. He told me that if I wanted to see the exhibit to come over to the administration building."

"You mean he has it?" Kim asked with disbelief.

"Apparently so," John said. "The Warren Anatomical Museum is on the fifth floor of building A, catty-corner from the front of the library. Are you interested in going over there?"

"By all means," Kim said. She could feel her pulse quicken at the thought that she might finally have found Elizabeth's evidence.

John reached for his phone. "Let's see if Mr. Nebolsine is still over there. He was a little while ago, but I believe he has several offices. Apparently he takes care of a number of the smaller museums and collections sprinkled around the Harvard community."

John had a quick conversation in the middle of which he gave Kim a thumbs-up sign. Hanging up, he said, "You're in luck. He's still there, and he'll meet you in the museum if you head over there immediately."

"I'm on my way," Kim said. She thanked John and quickly crossed to building A, a Greek Revival structure faced with a massive pediment supported by Doric columns. A guard stopped her just inside the door but then waved her on when he spotted her MGH identity card.

Kim got off on the fifth floor. The museum, such as it was, was tucked along the wall to the left and consisted of a series of glass-fronted display cases. They contained the usual collection of primitive surgical instruments capable of making a stoic wince, old photos, and pathological specimens. There were lots of skulls, including one with a hole through the left eye socket and the top of the forehead.

"That's quite an interesting case," a voice said. Kim looked up to see a much younger man than she'd expected for a museum curator. "You must be Kimberly Stewart. I'm Carl Nebolsine." They shook hands.

"See that rod in there?" Carl said, pointing at a five-foot-long steel rod. "That's called a tamping rod. It was used to pack powder and clay into a hole drilled for the purpose of blasting. One day a hundred or so years ago that rod went through that man's head." Carl pointed to the skull. "The amazing thing is that the man lived through it."

"Was he all right?" Kim asked.

"It says his personality wasn't as agreeable after he'd recovered from the trauma, but whose would be?" Carl said.

Kim scanned some of the other exhibits. In the far corner she spotted some books on display.

"I understand you're interested in the Rachel Bingham exhibit," Carl said.

"Is it here?" Kim asked.

"No," Carl said.

Kim looked at the man as if she hadn't heard him correctly.

"It's downstairs in the storeroom," Carl said. "We don't get a lot of requests to see it, and we don't have nearly enough space to display everything we have. Would you like to see it?"

"Very much," Kim said with relief.

They took the elevator down to the basement and followed a labyrinthine route that Kim would not have liked to retrace on her own. Carl unlocked a heavy steel door. Reaching in, he turned on the lights, such as they were: several bare light bulbs.

The room was full of dusty old-style glass display cases.

"Sorry about the mess down here," Carl said. "It's very dirty. No one comes in here very often."

Kim followed Carl as he weaved his way among the cabinets. Passing each one, Kim spied assortments of bones, books, instruments, and jars of preserved organs. Carl stopped. Kim came up behind him. He stepped aside and gestured within the cabinet in front of him.

Kim recoiled with a mixture of horror and disgust. She was totally unprepared for what she was seeing. Crammed into a large glass jar filled with brown-stained preservative was a four-to-five-month-old fetus that looked like a monster.

Oblivious to Kim's reaction, Carl opened the cabinet. He reached in and dragged the heavy canister forward, jiggling the contents so that it danced grotesquely, causing bits of tissue to rain down like a glass bubble snow-scene paperweight.

Kim clasped a hand to her mouth as she stared at the anencephalic fetus, which had no brain and a flat cranium. It had a cleft palate that made it appear as if the mouth were drawn up into the nose. Its features were further distorted by being pressed up against the glass of the container. From just behind its relatively huge froglike eyes, the head was flat and covered with a shock of coal-black hair. The massive jaw was totally out of proportion to the face. The fetus's stubby upper limbs ended in spadelike hands with short fingers, some of which were fused together. The effect was almost like cloven hooves. From the rump extended a long fishlike tail.

"Would you like me to lift it down so we can carry it out to better light?" Carl asked.

"No!" Kim said, a little too harshly. In a calmer voice she told Carl she could see the exhibit just fine where it was.

Kim understood completely how the seventeenth-century mind would have viewed such a beastly malformation. This poor creature could easily have been taken for the devil incarnate. Indeed, copies of woodcut prints of the devil that Kim had seen from that era looked identical.

"Would you like me at least to turn it around so you can see the other side?" Carl asked.

"Thank you, no," Kim said, unconsciously stepping back from the specimen. Now she knew why the Law School and the Divinity School had not known what to do with it. She also recalled the note John Moldavian had shown her in the Medical Library. It didn't say, *Curiosity by Rachel Bingham contrived in 1691.* The word was *conceived,* not *contrived!*

And Kim remembered the entry in Elizabeth's diary where Elizabeth expressed concern over innocent Job. Job hadn't been a biblical reference. Elizabeth had known she was pregnant and had already named the baby Job. How tragically apropos, Kim thought.

Kim thanked Carl and stumbled back toward her car. As she walked she thought about the double tragedy of Elizabeth being pregnant while she was being unwittingly poisoned by a fungus growing in her store of rye. In that day, everyone would have been certain Elizabeth had had relations with the devil to produce such a monster, certainly a manifestation of a covenant, especially since the "fits" had originated in Elizabeth's house and then spread to the other houses where the children had taken Elizabeth's bread. Elizabeth's assertiveness, her ill-timed struggle with the Putnam family, and her change in social status wouldn't have helped her situation.

Arriving at her car, Kim climbed inside and started the motor. For her it was now totally clear why Elizabeth had been accused of being a witch and how she'd been convicted.

Kim drove as if she were in a trance. She began to understand why Elizabeth would not confess to save her life as Ronald had undoubtedly urged. Elizabeth knew she was no witch, but her confidence in her innocence would have been undermined, especially with everyone against her: friends, magistrates, and even the clergy. With her husband away, Elizabeth would have had no support whatsoever. Utterly alone, she would have thought she was guilty of some horrid transgression against God. How else to explain giving birth to such a demonic creature? Maybe she even thought her fate was just.

Kim got bogged down in traffic on Storrow Drive and was reduced to inching forward. The weather had not improved. In fact it had gotten hotter. Kim felt progressively anxious about being cooped up in the car.

Finally she managed to get through the bottleneck at the Leverett Circle traffic light. Bursting free from the bounds of the city, she headed north on Interstate 93. With the literal freedom came a new revelation and the suggestion of figurative freedom. Kim began to believe that the shock of her visual confrontation with Elizabeth's monster had caused her to stumble onto the message that she believed Elizabeth had been trying to communicate: namely that Kim should believe in herself. She shouldn't lose confidence because of other people's beliefs, as poor Elizabeth had. She shouldn't allow authority figures to take over her life. Elizabeth hadn't had a choice about that, but Kim did.

Kim's mind was racing. She recalled all the tedious hours

she'd spent with Alice McMurray discussing her low self-esteem. She remembered the theories Alice had presented to explain its source: a combination of her father's emotional detachment, her vain attempts to please him, and her mother's passivity in the face of her father's womanizing. Suddenly all the talk seemed trivial. It was as if it involved someone else. Those discussions had never punched her in the gut as the final shock of Elizabeth's ordeal had.

Everything seemed clear to Kim now. Whether her low self-esteem came from her particular family dynamics, or from a shy temperament, or a combination of the two, it didn't matter. The reality was that Kim had not allowed her own interests and aptitudes to chart her course through life. Her career choice was a good example. So was her current living situation.

Kim had to brake suddenly. To her surprise and chagrin the traffic was bogged down on the usually freely moving interstate. Once again she was reduced to moving ahead in fits and starts, bringing the summerlike heat swirling in through the open window. To the west she could see huge thunderhead clouds massing on the horizon.

As she inched forward Kim experienced a sudden resolve. She had to change her life. First she'd allowed her father to rule her despite the fact that they had no relationship to speak of. And now she'd been allowing Edward to do the same. Edward was living with her but in name only. In actuality, he was only taking advantage of her and giving nothing in return. The Omni lab should not be on her property, and the researchers should not be living in the Stewart family house.

As the traffic began to free up again, and Kim was able to accelerate, she promised herself that she would not allow the status quo to continue. She told herself that she was going to talk with Edward the moment she got back to the compound.

Knowing her weakness regarding emotional confrontations and her inclination to procrastinate, Kim also emphasized to herself the importance of talking to Edward as soon as possible now that there was reason to believe Ultra was teratogenic, or damaging to a developing fetus. Kim knew such information was crucial for studying an experimental drug not only to protect pregnant women but because many teratogenic drugs were also capable of causing cancer.

By the time Kim drove onto the compound it was close to seven o'clock. With the thunderclouds still building to the west, it was darker than normal for that time of evening. As Kim approached the lab she saw that the lights had already been turned on.

Kim parked but didn't get out of the car immediately. Despite her resolve she found herself debating whether to go inside or not. Suddenly she could think of a lot of excuses to put off the visit. But she didn't give in. She opened the car door and got out. "You're going to do this if it kills you," she said. After smoothing out the wrinkles in her uniform and brushing back her hair, she entered the lab.

As soon as the inner door closed behind her, Kim was aware the lab had had yet another change of atmosphere. She was certain that David and Gloria and maybe even Eleanor had seen her arrive, but they didn't acknowledge her. In fact, they turned away and purposefully ignored her. There was no laughter; there wasn't even any conversation. The mood was palpably tense.

The strained ambience added to Kim's anxiety, yet she forced herself to seek out Edward. She found him in a darkened corner at his computer. The pale green fluorescence from his monitor cast an eerie light on his face.

Kim approached him and stood for a moment at his side. She was reluctant to interrupt him. As she watched his hands play across the keyboard, she detected a trembling of his fingers between individual key strokes. She could also hear he was breathing more quickly than she.

Several minutes dragged by. Edward ignored her.

"Please, Edward," Kim said finally. Her voice wavered. "I have to talk with you."

"Later," Edward said. He still did not look at her.

"It's important that I talk to you now," Kim said hesitantly.

Edward shocked Kim by leaping to his feet. The sudden motion sent his ergonomic chair skidding across the floor on its casters until it slammed into a cabinet. He stuck his face close to Kim's so that she could see red spiderwebs on the whites of his bulging eyes.

"I said later!" he repeated through clenched teeth. He glared at Kim as if daring her to contradict him.

Kim stepped back and collided with the lab bench. Awkwardly her hand thrust out to support herself, and she knocked a beaker onto the floor. It shattered, jarring Kim's already frayed nerves.

Kim didn't move. She watched Edward apprehensively. Once again he was acting like he was on the brink of losing control, just as he'd done when he'd thrown the wineglass back in his apartment in Cambridge. It occurred to her that something momentous had happened in the lab that had sparked a major disagreement. Whatever it had been, it had everybody on edge, particularly Edward.

Kim's first reaction was empathy for Edward, knowing how hard he'd been working. But then she caught herself. With the benefit of her newly acquired self-knowledge, she understood such thoughts represented a falling back on old habits. Kim was committed to heeding Elizabeth's message. For once in her life she had to stand up for herself and think of her own needs.

At the same time Kim was capable of being realistic. She knew there would be no benefit from inappropriately provoking Edward. From his behavior at the moment it was abundantly clear he was in no mood for a discussion about their relationship.

"I'm sorry to interrupt you," Kim said when she could tell Edward had regained some semblance of control. "It's obvious this isn't a good time for you. I'll be at the cottage. I do want to talk, so you come over when you are ready."

Kim turned away from his glower and started to leave. She'd only gone a few steps when she stopped and turned back.

"I did learn something today that you should know," Kim said. "I have reason to believe Ultra might be teratogenic."

"We'll be testing the drug in pregnant mice and rats," Edward said sullenly. "But at the moment we have a more pressing problem."

Kim noticed that Edward had an abrasion on the left side of his head. Then she saw he had cuts on his hands just like those she'd seen on Curt's.

Instinctively Kim stepped back. "You've hurt yourself," she said. She reached for his head to examine the wound.

"It's nothing," Edward said, roughly parrying her hand. He turned from her, and after retrieving his chair, sat down at his computer and went back to work.

Kim left the lab, rattled from her visit; she could never predict Edward's mood or behavior. Outside she noticed it had darkened significantly. There was not a breath of air. The leaves on the trees hung limply. A few birds skittered across the threatening sky, searching for shelter.

Kim hurried to her car. Glancing up into the ominous clouds that had moved ever more closely, she saw short flashes of weblike lightning that stayed aloft. She heard no thunder. On the short drive to the cottage, she used her headlights.

The first thing Kim did when she got home was head for the parlor. She looked up at Elizabeth's portrait and regarded the woman with renewed sympathy, admiration, and gratitude. After a few moments of staring at the strong, feminine face with its bright green eyes, Kim began to calm down. The image was empowering, and despite the setback at the lab, Kim knew she would not turn back. She would wait for Edward, but she would definitely talk with him.

Taking her eyes off the painting, Kim wandered around the cottage that she and Elizabeth had shared. Her recent loneliness notwithstanding, it was a cozy, romantic house, and she couldn't help but wonder how different it would have been with Kinnard around instead of Edward.

Standing in the dining room, which in Elizabeth's time had been the kitchen, Kim lamented how few times the table had even been used. There was no doubt that September had been a bust, and Kim berated herself for allowing Edward to drag her along on his drug-development crusade.

With a sudden flash of anger Kim allowed herself to go a step further, and for the first time she admitted that she was repulsed by Edward's incipient greed as well as by his new persona as defined by Ultra. In her mind there was no place for drug-induced self-understanding, or drug-induced assertiveness, or a drug-induced happy mood. It was all fake. The concept of cosmetic psychopharmacology disgusted her.

Having finally faced her true feelings about Edward, Kim turned again to thoughts of Kinnard. With her new understanding, she saw that she shared a significant portion of blame for their most recent difficulties. With harshness equal to that she'd expressed toward Edward's new greed, she chided herself for allowing her fear of rejection to misinterpret Kinnard's boyish interests.

Kim sighed. She was exhausted physically and mentally. At the same time, she was inwardly calm. For the first time in months she didn't have that vague, nagging anxiety that had been plaguing her. Although she knew her life was in disarray, she was committed to change, and she felt she knew what it was she had to change.

Disappearing into the bathroom, Kim took a long, luxurious bath, something she hadn't done for as long as she could remember. After bathing, she slipped into a loose-fitting jogging suit and made herself dinner.

After dinner Kim went to the parlor window and glanced over toward the lab. She wondered what Edward was thinking and when she would see him.

Kim moved her eyes away from the lab and looked at the black silhouettes of the trees. They were totally motionless, as if imbedded in glass; there still was no wind. The storm which had seemed imminent when she'd first arrived home had stalled to the west. But then Kim saw a bolt of lightning. This time it arced to the ground, followed by a distant rumble of thunder.

Turning back into the room, Kim glanced again at Elizabeth's portrait over the mantel and thought of Elizabeth's gruesome, malformed fetus swimming in its jar of preservative. Kim shuddered anew. No wonder people in Elizabeth's time believed in sorcery, magic, and witchcraft. Back then there was no other explanation for such disturbing events.

Advancing closer to the painting, Kim studied Elizabeth's features. The woman's assertiveness was apparent in the line of her jaw, the set of her lips, and the forthright stare of her eyes. Kim wondered if the trait had been temperament or character, inborn or learned, nature or nurture.

Kim pondered her own newly cultivated assertiveness for which she credited Elizabeth and wondered if she could maintain it. She felt she'd made a start by going to the lab that afternoon. She was certain she wouldn't have been able to do that in the past.

As the evening progressed, Kim began to think about the possibility of changing careers and to question whether she had the courage to take the risk. With her inheritance she knew she could not use economics as an excuse. Such a life-style change was a daunting possibility, especially the idea of doing something artistic. Yet it was also alluring.

One of the unexpected consequences of Kim's efforts at sorting the three hundred years of business documents in the castle was the realization of how little her family had contributed to the community. The hoard of papers and the tasteless castle housing them were the two major legacies. There'd not been one artist, musician, or author among them. For all their money, they'd developed no art collections, philharmonic endowments, or libraries. In fact, they'd made no contribution to culture unless entrepreneurialism was a culture in and of itself.

By nine P.M. Kim was beyond exhaustion. For a brief moment she entertained the notion of going back to the lab, but she quickly discarded it. If Edward had wanted to talk he would have come to the house. Instead she wrote him a note on a Post-It and stuck it on the mirror in the half-bath. It said simply: *I'll be up at five and we can talk then.*

After taking the cat out for a brief sojourn, Kim climbed into bed. She didn't even try to read nor did she even consider the need for a sleep aid. In a matter of minutes she was fast asleep.

# 20

**Tuesday,
October 4, 1994**

A STARTLINGLY LOUD CLAP OF THUNDER YANKED KIM from the depths of a dream in the blink of an eye. The house was still vibrating from the horrendous noise as she realized she was sitting bolt upright. Sheba had responded to the cataclysm by leaping from the bed and diving beneath it.

Within minutes of the thunder came rain and gusty wind. Having held back for so long, the storm hit with unbridled ferocity. Droplets large enough to sound like hailstones battered the slate roof above Kim's head. She also heard the rain beat against the screen of the westerly-facing open casement window.

Kim dashed from her bed to the window and began cranking it shut. She could feel the wind carry rainwater into her room. Just as she was about to lock the window in place, a flash of lightning struck the lightning rod on one of the castle's turrets and filled the entire compound with a blue light.

In the instant the field between the cottage and the castle was illuminated, Kim saw a startling image. It was a ghost-like, scantily clad figure running across the grass. Although Kim couldn't be certain, since she'd had only the briefest glimpse, she thought it might have been Eleanor.

Kim winced as another clap of thunder came close on the heels of the lightning flash. Ignoring the ringing in her ears, she strained to see out in the darkness. With the driving rain, it was impossible. She waited briefly for another flash of lightning, but none occurred.

Leaving the window, Kim ran through the connecting hall to Edward's bedroom. She was convinced she'd not been hallucinating; someone was out there. Whether it was Eleanor or not was immaterial. No one should be out in that storm, especially when there was the added danger of the wild animal that had been plaguing the neighborhood.

Edward had to be told. Kim was surprised to find his door closed. He always had it open. Kim knocked. When there was no answer, she knocked louder. When there was still no answer, she looked down at the lock on the old door. A skeleton key protruded from the keyhole, meaning the door couldn't be locked. Kim opened the door.

From where she was standing Kim could hear Edward's stertorous breathing. Kim called out to him several times in a progressively louder voice, but he didn't stir.

Another flash of lightning filled the room with light. Kim got a brief glimpse of Edward sprawled on his back with his arms and legs outstretched. He was clothed in his underwear. One pant leg had not been totally removed; his trousers were draped inside-out over the side of the bed.

Kim again winced in preparation of the thunder, and it didn't disappoint her. It was as if the storm were centered on the compound.

Turning on the hall light, which spilled into Edward's room, Kim hurried over to his bedside. She tried calling to him again. When that didn't work she shook him gently. Not only didn't he wake up, his breathing didn't even alter. Kim shook him vigorously, and when that had no effect she began to be concerned. It was as if he were in a coma.

Kim turned on the bedside light to its brightest level. Edward was the picture of tranquillity. His face had a slack appearance, with his mouth open. Kim put a hand on each shoulder and shook him insistently, loudly calling his name.

Only then did his breathing change. Then his eyes blinked open.

"Edward, are you awake?" Kim asked. She shook him again and his head flopped from side to side like a rag doll.

Edward appeared confused and disoriented until he noticed Kim. She was still holding his shoulders.

Kim watched Edward's pupils suddenly dilate similar to

those of a cat about to spring. Then his eyes narrowed to mere slits while his upper lip curled back like a snarling beast's. Edward's previously flaccid face contorted into an expression of sheer rage.

Shocked by this horrid, unexpected metamorphosis, Kim released his shoulders and backed up. She was stunned he could be so angry at being awakened. Edward let out a throaty sound akin to a growl and sat up. He was staring at her unblinkingly.

Kim bolted for the door, aware that Edward had sprung after her. She heard him fall to the floor, presumably tangled in his partially removed trousers. Kim slammed Edward's bedroom door behind her, and, using the skeleton key, locked it.

After dashing headlong down the stairs, Kim ran to the phone in the kitchen. She knew that something was terribly wrong with Edward. He wasn't just angry about being awakened. Something had snapped in his mind.

Kim dialed 911, but as the connection went through she heard the door to Edward's bedroom splinter and then bang open against the wall. An instant later she could hear Edward snarling at the top of the stairs, followed by the sound of his coming down.

Frightened out of her mind, Kim dropped the phone and headed for the back door. As she reached it she glanced over her shoulder. She caught a glimpse of Edward crashing into the dining room table and throwing it out of his way in his haste. He was totally berserk.

Kim yanked open the door and dashed out into the rain, which was coming down in sheets. Her only thought was to get help, and the closest source was the castle. She rounded the house and struck off across the field, running as fast as she could in the soggy darkness.

A fearful bolt of lightning crackled out of the sky and illuminated the drenched landscape, briefly silhouetting the castle. The thunder followed immediately, reverberating off its looming façade. Kim did not break stride. She was thankful to see lights in some of the windows of the servants' wing.

Reaching the graveled area in front of the castle, Kim

was forced to slow down. Although her panic had shielded her from most of the discomfort of running barefoot, the stones were too painful to disregard. Moving at a pace akin to a fast walk, she headed toward the side of the building, but as she neared the faux drawbridge she noticed that the main entrance was conveniently ajar.

Breathing heavily, Kim rushed inside. She ran straight through the dark front hall into the great room, where dim illumination spilled in from the huge two-story windows facing south. It was light from the surrounding towns reflected off the low cloud cover.

Kim had planned to head through the dining room to the kitchen and the servants' quarters beyond, but she hadn't gotten far when she all but collided with Eleanor. A wet, white lace nightgown clung to the woman like a second skin.

Kim stopped short, momentarily paralyzed. She now knew she'd been correct: it had been Eleanor she'd seen running in the field. Kim started to warn her about Edward, but her words died in her throat when she saw Eleanor's face in the meager light. It had the same unspeakable feral quality that she'd seen in Edward's when he awoke. To make things worse, Eleanor's mouth was smeared with blood as if she'd been feeding on raw meat.

Running into Eleanor cost Kim her lead on Edward. Gasping for breath, he staggered into the room and hesitated, savagely eyeing Kim in the half-light. His hair was plastered against his wet head. He was dressed only in his T-shirt and boxer shorts, both of which were covered with mud.

Kim turned to face him. Once again she had to catch her breath at his changed appearance. It was not that his features had altered; it was just that his face reflected a beastly rage.

Edward started toward Kim but then stopped again when he caught sight of his research partner. Ignoring Kim temporarily, he lurched toward Eleanor. When he was within arm's length, he warily put his head back as if sniffing the air. Eleanor did the same, and they slowly circled each other.

Kim shuddered. It was as if she were caught in a nightmare, watching two wild animals meet in the jungle to check each other to be sure one wasn't a predator and the other the prey.

Kim slowly backed up while Edward and Eleanor were preoccupied. As soon as she could see a clear route into the dining room, she bolted. Her sudden movement startled the other two. As if by some primeval carnivorous reflex they gave chase.

As Kim rushed through the dining room she yanked a number of the chairs away from the table and threw them behind her in hopes of slowing her pursuers. It worked better than she imagined. As if confused by the unexpected chairs and unable to adjust, Edward and Eleanor collided with them. Amid hideous, inhuman screams they fell. But the ruse did not delay them for long. As Kim passed through the door into the kitchen and cast a fleeting glance over her shoulder, she saw that they were already on their feet, throwing the chairs from their path, mindless of their bruises.

Kim started yelling for help as soon as she entered the servants' wing, but she didn't stop running. She reached the stairs and, still screaming, rushed up to the second floor. Without hesitation she burst into the room she knew was occupied by François. He was in his bed, sleeping with the light on.

Kim rushed over to him, calling his name. She shook him frantically, but he didn't wake up. Kim screamed at him and started to shake him again, but then she froze. Even with her panic she remembered that Edward had been equally hard to arouse.

Kim took a step back. François's eyes slowly opened. Just as it had with Edward, François's face underwent a savage transformation. His eyes narrowed and his upper lip curled back from his teeth. From his mouth came an inhuman growl. In an instant he'd become a demented, raging animal.

Kim spun around to flee, but Edward and Eleanor had reached the doorway, blocking her exit. Without a second's hesitation she hurled herself through the connecting door to the suite's sitting room and then exited to the hall from there. Back in the stairwell, she rushed up to the next level and entered another room she knew was occupied.

Kim stopped at the threshold, her hand still holding the open door. Curt and David were on the floor, scantily dressed and covered with mud. Water dripped from their heads, indicating they had recently been out. In front of them was a partially dismembered cat. Like Eleanor, their faces were smeared with blood.

Kim slammed the door. She could hear the others coming up the stairs. Turning around, she opened the connecting door to the main part of the house. At least she knew her way around.

Kim sprinted the length of the master suite hall. With its southern exposure it was enveloped in similar light as the great room. Kim was able to avoid the console tables, the straight-backed chairs, and the settees. But in her headlong flight she skidded on a throw rug and practically slammed into the door leading into the guest wing. After a moment's struggle with the knob, she threw open the door. The hall beyond was dark, but knowing there was no furniture, Kim ran blindly.

The next thing she knew she had collided with an unanticipated table that dug into her stomach, knocking her off balance. She fell with a tremendous clatter. For a second she didn't move, wondering if she had badly injured herself. Her stomach throbbed and her right knee was numb. She could feel something trickle down her arm, and she guessed it was blood.

Kim felt around her in the darkness. Then she realized what she had tripped over. It was the plumbers' tools and workbench. They had moved their equipment to the guest wing to check and repair the waste pipes there.

Kim listened. She could hear the distant noise of doors opening and slamming shut in the servants' wing. The sounds suggested to her that the creatures—she was loath to call them people in their current state—were searching for her randomly. They had not followed the only route possible, suggesting that they were not acting intelligently.

Kim reasoned they had only limited use of their brains and were operating mostly on instinct and reflex.

Kim stood up. The numbness of her knee was changing to sharp pain. She touched it and could feel it was already beginning to swell.

With her eyes having adjusted to the dark, Kim was able to make out the workbench and some of the other tools. She saw a length of pipe and picked it up as a weapon, but discarded it when she realized it was plastic PVC pipe. Instead she picked up a hammer. But then she discarded that for an acetylene blowtorch and friction lighter. If these creatures chasing her were acting on animal instinct, they'd be terrified of fire.

With the blowtorch in hand, Kim walked as best she could to the guest-wing stairs. She bent over the balustrade and looked down. On the floor below, the hall lights were on. Kim listened again. What noises she heard still seemed to be coming from the opposite end of the house.

Kim started down the stairs but did not get far. After only a few steps she spotted Gloria two floors down on the main level. She was pacing back and forth at the base of the stairs like a cat in front of a lair. Unfortunately Gloria saw Kim and let out a screech, then started up the stairs.

Reversing her direction, Kim fled as fast as she could back down the hall. This time she avoided the plumbers' equipment. She reentered the main house and hobbled to the top of the main stairs. Behind her she heard a crash and a howl which she presumed was Gloria running into the plumbers' tools.

Kim descended the main stair, hugging the wall to keep out of view from below. After reaching the landing, she moved slowly to bring progressively more and more of the great room into view. She was relieved when she saw no one.

Taking a deep breath, Kim descended the final flight. Reaching the bottom, she hobbled as rapidly as she could toward the front hall. About ten feet from her goal she stopped. To her utter dismay Eleanor was slinking back and forth at the end of the hall, directly in front of the main entrance. She was pacing just like Gloria had been at the base of the guest-wing stairs. Unlike Gloria, she didn't see Kim.

Kim quickly stepped to the side so she'd be out of Eleanor's line of sight. As soon as she did so she realized someone was coming down the main stairs and would soon be on the landing.

With little time to debate the merits, Kim limped frantically back across the room and slipped into the powder room tucked beneath the grand staircase. As silently as possible she closed the door behind her and locked it. Simultaneously she heard footfalls on the stairs directly above her.

Kim tried to control the sound of her labored breathing as she listened to the footsteps continue their descent and then disappear into one of the thick-pile oriental rugs on the marbled great-room floor.

Kim was frightened. In fact, now that she had a moment to grasp the gravity of her situation, she was terrified. She also worried about her knee. And to add to her misery she was wet and cold and violently shivering.

Thinking over the events of the last several days, Kim wondered if the primitive state Edward and the researchers were currently suffering had been occurring on a nightly basis. If it had, and if they had had a suspicion about it, it would explain the marked change in the atmosphere of the lab. With horror Kim realized that there was a good chance the researchers were responsible for the recent troubles in the neighborhood blamed on a rabid animal and teenage vandals.

Kim shuddered in revulsion. It was plainly obvious to her that the ultimate cause was Ultra. By taking the drug, the researchers had become "possessed" in a fashion ironically similar to some of the "afflicted" people in 1692.

These musings gave Kim some hope. If what she was thinking were true, then they must revert back to their normal selves come morning, just like in an old gothic horror movie. All Kim had to do was stay hidden until then.

Kim bent down and put the acetylene torch and lighter on the floor. Groping in the darkness, she found the towel bar and used the towel to dry as much of herself as she could. Her nightgown was soaking wet. Then she draped the towel over her shoulders for a bit of warmth and clasped her arms around herself to try to control her shivering. She sat down on the toilet seat to ease the pressure on her swollen knee.

A period of time passed. Kim had no way of judging how much. The house had become quiet. But then there was a sudden loud crash of breaking glass that made Kim jump. She'd hoped they had given up searching for her, but that apparently wasn't the case. Immediately following the loud noise, she heard the sounds of doors and cabinets being opened again.

A few minutes later Kim tensed when she again heard one of them coming down the stairs above her. Whoever it was was descending slowly and stopping frequently. Kim stood up. Occasional violent spasms of shivering had made the toilet seat clank against the porcelain reservoir, and she did not want it to happen when one of them was so near.

Kim became progressively aware of another persistent sound that she could not place immediately. Finally she did, and it made her tremble more. Someone was sniffing, much the way Edward had two nights previously by the shed. She remembered Edward telling her that one of the effects they'd noticed taking the drug was how it improved the keenness of the senses. Kim's mouth went dry. If Edward had been able to smell her lingering cologne the other night, maybe he could smell her now.

As Kim struggled to control her shivering, the person above descended the rest of the way down the stairs. At that point the individual paused again before coming around to stand outside the powder room door.

Kim heard more intense sniffing. Then the doorknob was rattled as someone tried to open the door. Kim held her breath.

Minutes dragged by. It sounded to Kim as if the others were arriving. From their collective sounds Kim could soon tell that a group of them had assembled.

Kim winced as one of them pounded a fist on the door several times. The door held but just barely. It was a paneled door with thin veneers in each panel. Kim knew it would not withstand a concerted assault.

With her panic returning in a rush, Kim quickly squatted down in the darkness and felt for the blowtorch. When her hand did not immediately hit it, her pulse soared. Frantically she felt around in a larger arc. She was relieved when her fingers touched it. Next to it was the lighter.

As Kim straightened up with the blowtorch and the lighter in her hands, the pounding on the door resumed. By the rapidity of the blows she could tell that more than one of the creatures was involved.

With trembling fingers Kim tried the lighter. When she compressed it a spark leaped off into the blackness. Changing hands to hold the torch in her right, Kim twisted the thumbscrew on its side and heard a sustained hiss. Holding the torch and the lighter at arm's length as she'd seen the plumber do, she compressed the lighter. With a whooshing sound the blowtorch ignited.

No sooner had Kim succeeded in lighting the torch than the door began to crack under the repeated blows. Once it began to break, it rapidly splintered, and bloodied hands appeared through fractures in the panels. To Kim's horror, the door quickly fell to pieces as the boards were torn away.

With the door gone, the researchers were like frenzied wild animals about to be fed. They all tried to rush into the powder room at the same time. In a confusion of arms and legs, they only succeeded in blocking each other.

Kim pointed the blowtorch at them, holding it at arm's length. It was making a throaty hissing sound. Its light illuminated their enraged faces. Edward and Curt were closest to Kim. She aimed the torch at them and saw their expressions change from rage to fear.

The researchers shrank back in terror, evincing their atavistic fear of fire. Their beady eyes never left the blue flame issuing from the tip of the blowtorch.

Encouraged by their reaction, Kim stepped from the powder room, keeping the blowtorch out in front of her. The researchers responded by backing away. Kim moved tentatively forward as they retreated. As a group they moved out into the great room, passing beneath one of the massive chandeliers.

After backing for a few more steps, the researchers began to fan out. Kim would have much preferred they stay in a compact group or flee altogether, but she had no way of making them. She could only ward them off. As she moved slowly but relentlessly toward the front hall, they enveloped her. She had to swing the blowtorch around in a circle to keep all of them at bay.

The abject fear that the creatures had initially shown to the flame began to diminish as they became accustomed to it, especially when it wasn't pointed in their direction. By the time Kim made it past the middle of the room, some of them became bolder, particularly Edward.

At a moment when Kim was pointing the torch in someone else's direction, Edward rushed forward and grabbed Kim's nightgown. Kim immediately swung the torch toward him, scorching the back of his hand. He screamed hideously and let go.

Next Curt leaped forward. Kim blistered a swath across his forehead, igniting some of his hair. He yelped in pain and clasped his hands to his head.

On one of her turns Kim saw that she only had another twenty feet to go before she'd reach the hallway, but the constant pirouetting was having an effect on her balance. She was becoming dizzy. She tried to compensate by alternating the direction she spun after each revolution, but the maneuver wasn't as effective in keeping the researchers away from her.

Gloria managed to step in as Kim was changing directions and grabbed one of Kim's arms.

Kim yanked herself free of Gloria's grip, but with her balance already compromised, the sudden motion caused her to twirl out of control, and she fell. In the process of falling, her arm holding the blowtorch hit the edge of a side table with numbing force, causing her to lose her grasp on the blowtorch. The blowtorch bounced off the top of the table and hit the marble floor at a sharp angle, sending it careening across its highly polished surface. It ended up thumping against the far wall at a point where one of the immense damask silk drapes was pooled.

Cradling her injured arm with her good hand, Kim managed to sit up. Looming around and over her were the creatures, closing in for the kill. With a collective screech they fell on her in unison like animals of prey attacking an injured, doomed deer.

Kim screamed and struggled as she was scratched and bitten. Luckily the attack lasted only a few seconds. When a loud, reverberating whooshing sound, accompanied by a sudden bright, hot light interrupted the frenzy, Kim was able to scramble away. With her back against a couch, she looked up at her attackers. They were all staring dumbfounded over her shoulder with their faces reflecting a golden light.

Turning to look behind her, Kim saw a wall of flames expanding with explosive force. The blowtorch had ignited the drapes, and they were burning as if they'd been doused with gasoline.

The creatures voiced a collective wail at the developing inferno. Kim looked back at them and saw terror in their wide eyes. Edward was the first to run, followed instantly by the others. But they didn't run out the front door. Instead they ran in a panic up the main stairs.

"No, no," Kim shouted to the fleeing figures. But it was to no avail. Not only did they not understand her, they did not even hear. The roar of the wall of flames sucked sound into its fury like a black hole swallowed matter.

Kim lifted her good arm to protect herself from the searing heat. Getting to her feet she hobbled toward the front door. It was becoming difficult to breathe as the fire consumed the room's oxygen.

An explosion behind her sent Kim again sprawling onto the floor. She cried out with pain from her injured arm. She guessed the blast had been the blowtorch container detonating. With renewed urgency to get out of the building, she struggled to her feet and staggered forward.

Kim lurched through the door and hobbled out into the gusty wind and driving rain. She limped all the way to the far edge of the graveled area in front of the castle, gritting her teeth against the pain in her arm and knee with every step. Turning around and shielding her face from the heat with her good arm, she looked back at the castle. The old structure was burning like tinder. Flames were already visible in the dormered windows of the attic.

A flash of lightning briefly illuminated the area. For Kim, the scene was like an image of hell. She shook her head in disgust and dismay. Truly the devil had returned to Salem!

# EPILOGUE

## Saturday,
## November 5, 1994

WHERE DO YOU WANT TO GO FIRST?" KINNARD ASKED as he and Kim drove through the gate onto the Stewart compound.

"I'm not sure," Kim said. She was in the passenger seat, supporting the cast on her left arm.

"You'll have to decide pretty soon," Kinnard said. "We'll be coming to the fork as soon as we clear the trees."

Kim knew Kinnard was right. She could already see the field through the leafless trees. She turned her head and looked at Kinnard. The pale, late fall sunshine slanting through the trees was flickering on his face and lighting up his dark eyes. He'd been extraordinarily supportive, and she was thankful he'd agreed to make this drive with her. It had been a month since the fateful night, and this was Kim's first return.

"Well?" Kinnard questioned. He began to slow down.

"Let's go to the castle," Kim said. "Or at least what's left of it."

Kinnard made the appropriate turn. Ahead, the charred ruins loomed. All that was standing were the stone walls and chimneys.

Kinnard pulled up to the drawbridge that now led to a blackened, empty doorway. Kinnard turned off the ignition.

"It's worse than I expected," Kinnard said, surveying the scene through the windshield. He looked at Kim. He could sense she was nervous. "You know, you don't have to go through this visit if you don't want to."

"I want to," Kim said. "I've got to face it sometime."

She opened her door and got out. Kinnard got out his side. Together they strolled around the ruins. They did not try to go inside. Within the walls everything was ashes save for a few charred beams that had not completely burned.

"It's hard to believe anyone got out alive as fast as it all burned," Kim said.

"Two out of six is not a great record," Kinnard said. "Besides, the two who survived aren't out of the woods yet."

"It's a tragedy in a tragedy," Kim said. "Like poor Elizabeth with her malformed, miscarried fetus."

They reached a hillock where they had a view of the entire incinerated site. Kinnard shook his head in disgust. "What a fitting end to a horrid episode," he said. "The authorities had a hard time believing it until the dentition of one of the victims matched the toothmarks on the bone of the dead vagrant. At least you must feel vindicated. They didn't believe a word you said in the beginning."

"I'm not sure they really believed it until both Edward and Gloria had another transformation in the burn unit of the hospital," Kim said. "That was the clincher, not the teethmarks. The people who witnessed it attested that it had been brought on by sleep and that neither Edward nor Gloria had any recollection of it occurring. Those were the two key points that were critical for people to believe what I told them."

"I believed you right away," Kinnard said, turning to Kim.

"You did," Kim said. "I have to give you credit for that and for a lot of other things."

"Of course I already knew that they were taking their untested drug," Kinnard said.

"I told that to the District Attorney right from the beginning," Kim said. "It didn't influence him that much."

Kinnard looked back at the impressive ruins. "This old building must have burned awfully quickly," he said.

"The fire spread so fast it was almost explosive," Kim said.

Kinnard shook his head again, this time in gratitude and

awe. "It's a marvel that you got out yourself," he said. "It must have been terrifying."

"The fire was practically anticlimactic," Kim said. "It was the other stuff that was so horrifying, and it was a hundred times worse than one could ever imagine. You can't believe what it's like to see people you know in such an animal state. But the one thing it did for me was underline that all drug taking, whether steroids for athletes or psychotropic drugs for character enhancement, is a Faustian contract."

"Medicine has known that for years," Kinnard said. "There's always risk, even with antibiotics."

"I hope people will remember it when they are tempted to take drugs for what they believe are personality flaws, like shyness," Kim said. "Such drugs are coming; there's no stopping the research that's going to develop them. And if someone doubts they will be used for such purposes, all they have to do is look at the expanded use of some of the current antidepressants in such questionable ways since they've been on the market."

"The problem is we're developing a culture which thinks there is a pill for everything," Kinnard said.

"That's exactly the reason that there is bound to be another episode like the one I just lived through," Kim said. "It's inevitable with the potential demand for psychotropic drugs."

"If there is another such episode, I'm sure the witch industry in Salem hopes that it will occur here," Kinnard said with a laugh. "Your experience has been a boon for business."

Kim picked up a stick and poked into the rubble of the castle. Metal objects had been distorted out of shape because of the intense heat.

"This house contained all the material legacy of twelve generations of Stewarts," Kim said. "Everything is lost."

"I'm sorry," Kinnard said. "It must be very upsetting."

"Not really," Kim said. "Most of it was junk except for a few pieces of furniture. There wasn't even one decent painting except for the portrait of Elizabeth, which sur· vived. The only thing that I truly regret losing are the letters and papers I'd found about her. I've lost them all and only have copies of two that were made at Harvard. Now the copies are the only corroboration that exists concerning Elizabeth's involvement in the Salem witchcraft upheaval, and that's not going to be enough to convince most historians.''

They stood for a time gazing at the ashes. Finally Kinnard suggested they move on. Elizabeth nodded. They walked back to the car and drove over to the lab.

Kim unlocked the door. They passed through the reception area and Kim opened the inner door. Kinnard was amazed. It was just empty space.

''Where is everything?'' he asked. ''I thought this was a lab.''

''It was,'' Kim said. ''I told Stanton everything had to be out immediately. I told him if it weren't, I'd donate it all to a charity.''

Kinnard made a motion of dribbling a basketball and shooting it. The sound of his heels echoed in the room. ''You could always convert it to a gym,'' he said.

''I think I'd prefer a studio,'' Kim said.

''Are you serious?'' Kinnard asked.

''I think I am,'' Kim said.

Leaving the lab, they drove on to the cottage. Kinnard was relieved to see it hadn't been stripped like the lab. ''It would be a shame to destroy this,'' he said. ''You've made it into a delightful house.''

''It is cute,'' Kim admitted.

They walked into the parlor. Kinnard walked around the room and examined everything carefully.

''Do you think you'd ever want to live here again?'' Kinnard asked.

''I think so,'' she said. ''Someday. What about you? Do you think you could ever live in a place like this?''

''Sure,'' Kinnard said. ''After taking the rotation out here I've been offered a position with a group at Salem Hospital that I'm seriously considering. Living here would be ideal. The only trouble is, I think it might be a bit lonely.''

Kim looked up into Kinnard's face. He raised his eyebrows provocatively.

"Is that a proposition?" Kim asked.

"It could be," Kinnard said evasively.

Kim thought for a moment. "Maybe we should see how we feel about each other after a ski season."

Kinnard chuckled. "I like your new sense of humor," he said. "You can now joke about things that I know are important to you. You've really changed."

"I hope so," she said. "It was long overdue." She gestured up at Elizabeth's portrait. "I have my ancestor to thank for making me see the need and giving me the courage. It's not easy breaking old patterns. I only hope I can maintain this new me, and I hope you can live with it."

"I'm loving it so far," he said. "I feel less like I'm walking on eggshells when we're together. I mean, I don't have to guess continually how you are feeling."

"I'm amazed but thankful that something good has come out of such an awful episode," she said. "The real irony for me is that I finally had the courage to tell my father what I think of him."

"Why is that ironic?" he asked. "I'd say it's perfectly in keeping with your new ability to communicate what's on your mind."

"The irony is not that I did it," she said. "It's because of the result. A week after the conversation that turned very nasty on his part he phoned me, and now we seem to be enjoying the beginnings of a meaningful relationship."

"That's wonderful," Kinnard said. "Just like with us."

"Yup," Kim said. "Just like with us."

She reached up and put her good arm around his neck and hugged him. He reciprocated with equal ardor.

## Friday, May 19, 1995

Kim paused and looked up at the façade of the newly constructed brick building she was about to enter. Above the door set into the brick was a long white marble plaque on which was carved in low relief: OMNI PHARMACEUTICALS. She was not sure how she felt about the fact the company was still in business in light of all that had happened. Yet she understood that with all his money tied up in the venture, Stanton was not about to let it simply die.

Kim opened the door and entered. At a reception desk she left her name. After waiting for a few minutes a pleasant, conservatively dressed woman appeared, to escort her up to the door of one of the company's labs.

"When you've finished your visit do you think you will be able to find your way out without difficulty?" the woman asked.

Kim assured her she could and thanked her. After the woman left, Kim turned to the lab door and entered.

From Stanton's description, Kim knew what to expect. The door that she'd just passed through did not take her into the lab. It took her into an anteroom. The common wall with the lab itself was glass from desk height to the ceiling. In front of the glass were several chairs. On the wall below the glass were a communications unit and a brass-handled door that resembled an after-hours bank drop.

Beyond the glass was a modern, state-of-the-art biomedical laboratory that bore an uncanny resemblance to the lab in the stables building in the compound.

Following Stanton's instructions, Kim sat in the chair and pressed the red "call" button on the communications console. Inside the lab she saw two figures stand up from behind a lab bench where they had been busy working. Seeing Kim, they started over.

Kim immediately felt a wave of sympathy for the pair. She never would have recognized them. It was Edward and Gloria. Both were tremendously disfigured from their burns. They were essentially hairless. Both were also facing more cosmetic surgery. They walked stiffly and pushed "keep open" IVs in front of them with hands that had lost fingers.

When they spoke their voices were hoarse whispers. They thanked Kim for coming and expressed their disappointment that they were unable to show her around the lab that had been specifically designed with their handicaps in mind.

After a pause in the conversation, Kim asked them how they were getting along healthwise.

"Pretty good considering what we have to deal with," Edward said. "Our biggest problem is that we're still experiencing 'fits' even though the Ultra has completely been cleared from our brains."

"Are they still brought on by sleep?" Kim asked.

"Not by sleep," Edward said. "They now come on spontaneously like an epileptic seizure, without any warning. The good part is that they only last for a half hour or less, even when untreated."

"I'm so sorry," Kim said. She struggled against a sadness that threatened to well up inside of her. She was facing people whose lives had been all but destroyed.

"We're the sorry ones," Edward said.

"It's our own fault," Gloria said. "We should have known better than to start taking the drug until all the toxicity studies were completed."

"I don't see that would have made any difference," Edward said. "To this day, no animal studies have shown this human side effect. In fact, by our taking the drug when we did, we probably saved a large number of human volunteers from experiencing what we've suffered."

"But there were other side effects," Kim said.

"True," Edward admitted. "I should have picked up on the short-term-memory loss as being significant. The drug was obviously showing its capability to block network-level nerve function."

"Has your subsequent research led to any understanding of your condition?" Kim asked.

"By studying each other in the throes of an attack we've been able to document what we had originally proposed as the mechanism of action," Gloria said. "Ultra builds up to a point where it blocks cerebral control of the limbic system and lower brain centers."

"But why are you getting attacks now that the drug is gone?" Kim asked.

"That's the question!" Edward said. "That's what we are trying to learn. We believe it is through the same mechanism as 'bad trip' flashbacks which some people suffer after hallucinogenic drug use. We're trying to investigate the problem so that we might be able to figure out a way to reverse it.''

"Dilantin worked for a short time to control the fits,'' Gloria said. "But then we began to become tolerant, so now it no longer works. The fact that it influenced the process for a short term has us encouraged we might find another agent.''

"I'm surprised Omni is still in business,'' Kim said to change the subject.

"We are too,'' Edward said. "Surprised and pleased. Otherwise we wouldn't have this lab. Stanton just has not given up, and his persistence has paid off. One of the other alkaloids from the new fungus has shown significant promise as a new antidepressant, so he's been able to raise adequate capital.''

"I hope at least Omni has abandoned Ultra,'' Kim said.

"No, indeed!'' Edward said. "That's the other major thrust of our research: trying to determine what part of the Ultra molecule is responsible for the meso-limbic-cerebral blockage that we've labeled 'the Mr. Hyde Effect.' ''

"I see,'' Kim said. She started to wish them luck but couldn't get herself to do it. Not after all the trouble Ultra had already caused.

Kim was about to say goodbye and promise she'd be back to visit when she noticed Edward's eyes glaze over. Then his entire face was transformed just as it had been on the fateful night when she'd awakened him. In an instant he was in an uncontrollable rage.

Without any warning or provocation he launched himself at Kim and collided with a thump against the thick glass shield.

Kim leaped back in fright. Gloria responded by swiftly opening Edward's IV.

For a brief moment Edward clawed vainly at the glass. Then his face went slack and his eyes rolled up into his head. In slow motion he sagged like a balloon with its air slowly let out. Gloria skillfully guided him to the floor.

"I'm sorry about this,'' Gloria said as she tenderly adjusted Edward's head. "I hope Edward didn't frighten you too much.''

"I'm fine," Kim managed, but her heart was pounding in her chest and she was trembling. Warily she stepped close to the window and looked down at Edward lying on the floor. "Will he be all right?"

"Don't worry," Gloria said. "We're rather used to this sort of thing. Now you can see why we have these IVs. We've been experimenting with various tranquilizers. I'm pleased with how quickly this one worked."

"What would happen if both of you had an attack simultaneously?" Kim asked to try to focus her mind.

"We've thought about that," Gloria said. "Unfortunately, we've not been able to come up with any fail-safe ideas. So far it hasn't happened. I guess all we can do is the best we can."

"I admire your fortitude," Kim said.

"I don't think we have much choice," Gloria said.

After saying goodbye, Kim left. She was unnerved. As she descended in the elevator her legs felt weak. She was afraid her little visit would bring back the recurrent nightmares she'd had immediately after the terrible night.

Emerging into the warm midspring sunshine, Kim felt better. Just being outside helped, but she could not keep from replaying the image of Edward furiously slamming into the glass of his self-imposed prison.

When Kim reached her car, she stopped and turned to face Omni. She wondered what kind of drugs the company would be loosing on the world in the future. She shuddered. The thought made her vow to be even more conservative than she'd been in the past about taking drugs, any drugs!

Kim keyed open her door and got into the car. She didn't start the engine immediately. In her mind's eye, she could still see Edward's face as it underwent its ghastly transformation. It was something she never would forget.

Starting out of the parking lot, Kim did something that surprised her. Instead of returning back to Boston as she'd planned, she impulsively headed north. After the unnerving experience at Omni she felt an irresistible urge to return to the compound, where she had not gone since the visit with Kinnard.

With little traffic the trip passed quickly, and within a

half hour Kim was unlocking the padlock on the gates. She drove directly to the cottage and got out. Immediately she felt an odd sensation of relief as if she were coming home after an arduous journey.

Fumbling with the keys, Kim opened the lock and entered. Stepping into the half-light of the parlor, she looked up at Elizabeth's portrait. The intense green of the eyes and the determined line of the jaw were as Kim remembered, but there was something else, something she'd not seen. It appeared as if Elizabeth were smiling!

Kim blinked and looked again. The smile was still there. It was as if Elizabeth were reacting to the fact that after so many years some good had come from her terrible ordeal; she had been ultimately vindicated.

Amazed at this effect, Kim stepped closer to the painting only to appreciate the sfumato that the artist had used at the corners of Elizabeth's mouth. Kim smiled herself, realizing it was her own perceptions that were being reflected in Elizabeth's visage.

Turning around, Kim gazed out at the view Elizabeth saw from her position over the mantel. At that moment Kim decided to move back to the cottage. The emotional trauma engendered by that last terrible night had already significantly lessened, and Kim wanted to come home to live within the penumbra of Elizabeth's memory. Remembering she was the same age as Elizabeth had been when Elizabeth had been so unjustly killed, Kim vowed to live the rest of her life for both of them. It was the only way she could imagine to repay Elizabeth for the self-understanding she'd provided.

# SELECTED
# BIBLIOGRAPHY

1. Boyer and Nissenbaum, *Salem Possessed.* Cambridge, MA. Harvard University Press, 1974.

   For those people who might be tempted to read more about the Salem witchcraft episode, this book is one of two I'd recommend. I'm sure Kim and Edward would heartily agree. It is fascinating reading and shows how history can come to life by using primary sources dealing with ordinary citizens. It gives an entertaining look into life in New England during the last half of the seventeenth century.

2. Hansen, Chadwick, *Witchcraft at Salem.* New York. George Braziller, 1969.

   This is the second book I'd recommend about the Salem witchcraft affair. It takes the viewpoint that not everyone involved was innocent! Such an attitude surprised me at first but then turned out to be provocative.

3. Kramer, Peter, *Listening to Prozac.* New York. Viking, 1993.

   Although this book is more positive than I am about the use of psychotropic agents for personality alteration, there is a discussion of both sides of the issue. It is enlightening, enjoyable, and provocative.

4. Matossian, Mary, *Poisons of the Past: Molds, Epidemics, and History.* New Haven, CT. Yale University Press, 1989.

This book certainly gives one an added respect for the lowly mold. For me it was particularly stimulating in regards to the storyline of *Acceptable Risk.*

5. Morgan, Edmund, *The Puritan Family.* New York. Harper & Row, 1944.

My high school American history course didn't provide me with adequate backround in relation to Puritan culture. This book helped fill the void.

6. Restak, Richard, *Receptors.* New York. Bantam, 1994.

This book is for those readers who would like a readable, stimulating, up-to-date explanation of current knowledge of brain function and the direction of research.

7. Werth, Barry, *The Billion-Dollar Molecule.* New York. Simon & Schuster, 1994.

If anyone doubts the deleterious effect of entrepreneurialism in today's scientific world, this book is a must.